A LIGHT IN THE SKY

A LIGHT IN THE SKY

SHINA REYNOLDS

WINK ROAD PRESS

WINK ROAD PRESS

Paperback ISBN: 978-1-7334511-1-6
Hardcover ISBN: 978-1-7334511-0-9
Ebook: 978-1-7334511-2-3

A Light in the Sky

This first edition published by Wink Road Press.

For more information, or questions or comments about the quality of this book, please contact us at winkroadpress@gmail.com.

Cover Design and Map Illustration by Micaela Alcaino
Edited by Erin Young and Lauren Smulski
Proofread by Kara Aisenbrey
Interior Layout by Damonza
Cover Images © Shutterstock.com

www.winkroadpress.com

For Ben:
my best friend, my confidant, my love.

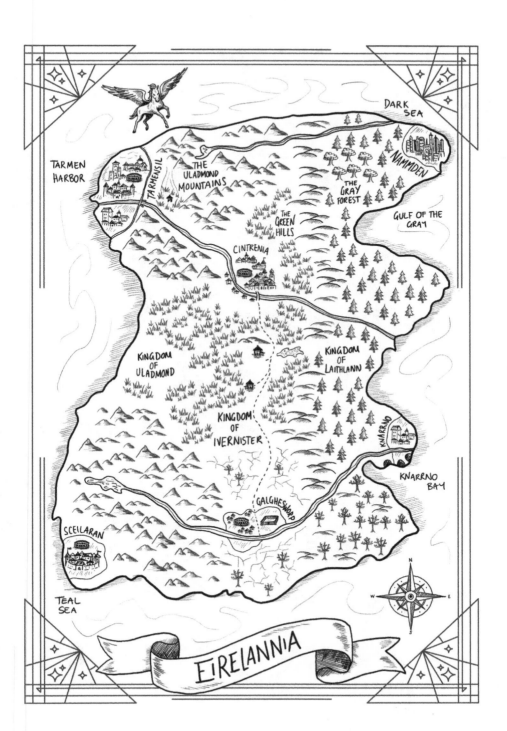

No bird soars too high, if he soars with his own wings.

—William Blake

 ONE

In the sky, I am free.

Wrapped in the cold, dark blanket of night, I'm free from all of the constraints and watchful eyes that follow me down below. In the sky, my choices are my own.

I'm alive as we glide through the darkness. My hands entwine through Darwith's thick black mane, and his wings push the air away, propelling us higher into the starry sky.

In less than an hour, when the sun rises over the brow of the Green Hills, I'll be back in my bed. There'll be no trace of my having flown. I'll be back in reality—mucking stalls and preparing breakfast for my father and my younger brother, while a select group of other seventeen-year-olds compete to become Empyrean Riders. Because the reality of my life is that my choices are not my own.

I'm not free.

While most girls from the wealthy neighboring kingdom of Uladmond—the Otherside, as we like to call it—are gossiping about who they will marry, I'm dreaming about soaring through the sky on an Empyrean steed. Or riding around an open arena on a wingless horse before it's given wings, preparing it for the sky. That's where I belong.

There are old stories of riders on their steeds flying free in numbers—before flying became a privilege granted to the king and his chosen warriors alone, to keep the people of the enemy kingdom of Laithlann on their side of the border. I prefer to imagine what it was like to live back then. If freedom existed in those days, it can exist again.

Living in one of the two joint kingdoms on the island of Eirelannia means that I have to abide by the rules of the king of Uladmond. Generations ago, during the Dark Wars, his ancestors conquered our once-sovereign central kingdom of Ivernister, combining the two lands under one rule. The current king would love to add the third, fallen kingdom of Laithlann to his empire as well, but he has yet to succeed. Bringing the rebel Laithlanners to their knees is the only thing that seems to matter to him anymore, leading many Ivernisterians to starvation and death as he bleeds our lands dry to support his never-ending war.

I shake these grim thoughts from my mind and lean closer to Darwith's neck as we speed through the clouds. My face is frozen, and the air is thin, but I don't mind the chill or the slight lack of oxygen—it goes with the territory. Flying on the back of an Empyrean steed is in my blood. Like father, like daughter.

The Empyrean Cavalry and their steeds are a big deal here in Eirelannia. My father, a former Empyrean Rider, is a legend of sorts. Decorated and now retired, he continues to train the winged horses, giving me ample time to watch and learn.

It's not all it's hyped up to be, my father has told me, more times than I can count. *Training on the ground is dangerous enough, but flying into battle is a whole other story. If something happened to you, I'd never forgive myself. You're safer on the ground.*

If my father saw how daring I am on an Empyrean steed—*his* steed—maybe he'd rethink his stance. He'd see that, like him, my heart belongs in the sky; I can't resist the freedom I find here.

Only the Riders in the Cavalry are permitted to fly an Empyrean steed. And the Riders are warriors. That's what Father says. Most of the Riders *are* eager young warriors, or worn-out warriors who were once like them. And my father won't give in to his only daughter becoming a warrior.

Maybe he shouldn't have taught me how to throw a punch, wield a sword, or shoot an arrow, then.

When we break through the cloud tops, I direct Darwith to the east. His ears turn backward. He knows where we're heading—the Gray Forest. His long, feathered wings branch out stiffly on either side as we coast, allowing us to surf the air like invisible waves in the sky.

A blur of gray and brown wings rips through the white veil of clouds.

My heart jumps, then settles as my eyes adjust to the blur—a flock of mud-colored coastal birds emerging from the moonlit cloud cover. They fly straight at us like a storm. Thank the stars it's not the Empyrean Cavalry coming to drag me back to the ground and the inevitable punishment that would follow. I'm well aware of the consequences I'd face if anyone caught me riding, or *flying*, an Empyrean steed: imprisonment, my family's well-being, my *life*—and, worst yet, my father's disappointment in me for stealing his steed and flying behind his back.

The ugly birds pass, their wings brushing against Darwith's, their pointy orange beaks clacking in the dark light.

I'd take a hoof to the gut over causing my father any more disappointment. He's had enough of that, what with my mother disappearing when I was nine, and me too young to realize she wasn't coming home to us. I kept insisting she would, but of course she never did. And my years of daily optimism on the matter had reminded my father of that far too often.

I know I'm risking too much. The king makes the laws, and most people follow them. But we're close to starving back home—we need more food. I don't want my family to starve, so here I am.

The temperature drops as the Gray Forest sprawls out beneath us. Scraggly gray trees trickle out like skeletons in the night, overtaking the smooth, rolling hills of the Green until there's only a dense thicket below. Darwith tenses as he resumes flapping his wings.

No more coasting. We're in Laithlanner territory now.

The Gray Forest borders our central kingdom of Ivernister and the Old World, the fallen kingdom of Laithlann. Crossing the border into Laithlann is now forbidden to everyone in the king's two joint kingdoms—everyone except for the king's elite Empyrean Cavalry. They're the ones fighting the war against the Laithlanners. The combined ground army patrols the border, but they never cross it. We're told it's too dangerous.

Then again, we've also been told that we're at war with the Laithlanners because they're encroaching on our land, trying to steal or destroy our already dwindling resources. But I've never met a Laithlanner. The only people who *do* steal our resources are the king's soldiers, taking what little we have, and driving me to fly out here to enemy territory in secret.

The wind picks up. I crouch low over Darwith's neck, and his long mane blows across my face as we rush past the tops of the bony trees. Perhaps I'll spot one of the beasts I've been told so many stories about—terrible fanged creatures rummaging through the forest, searching for fallen prey. *If* they exist. Or perhaps I'll see a Laithlanner. There are many rumors about the people who dwell in the fallen city beyond the forest—*Scalers*, as most call them, the only people who still live in the Old World. I've never been past the Gray Forest, but I've heard tales of the Scalers' grotesque features, the result of generations of malnutrition and near-constant cloud cover. Some say they don't even look like the rest of us in Eirelannia, but rather like the very beasts that scavenge the forest. They say they're just as ruthless as the beasts, too, attacking anything or anyone who crosses into their territory.

My right hand reaches for the hilt of my sword at my left hip, my palm and fingers falling into the familiar grooves of its grip. I've trained in swordplay for years, but that training has never been tested in combat, when my life would truly depend on those skills.

A familiar copse of trees—the reason for my forbidden journey into Laithlanner territory—stands out among the rest. They're shorter and bushier than the skeletal gray trees that comprise the rest of the forest. From up here, the tiny grove looks like an island of green in a sea of bones.

I give Darwith a squeeze with my legs, and we descend into the forest.

When his hooves hit the ground, I slow him to a canter. He tucks in his wings as we move through the small clearing. Even from this distance, I can see the squatty trees are chock-full of what I've come to collect—*pompidorris*. The moonlight illuminates the glossy magenta fruits dangling above, ripe for the picking, like little beacons of hope.

"Would you look at that?" I whisper to Darwith.

We stop in front of one of the smaller pompidorri trees in the middle of the grove. It may be small, but this tree always has the best fruit, loaded with nutrients. It's the kind of fruit that's worth risking everything for. If I can pick enough now, we'll have pompidorri jam all winter and the energy to work. We may not starve to death. And if we do starve, at least it'll be sweet.

I leave my sword in its scabbard, attaching it to Darwith's saddle. I've learned the hard way that it's difficult to climb a tree with a sword on my hip. I dismount, scurrying to the wide base of the pompidorri tree, where I latch on to a chunk of bark and swing my right leg into the crease of the tree base, locking my heel into place. In a solid position, I drag my knapsack around and pluck the ripest palm-sized pompidorris. One by one, I place them in the bag, their smooth skin like cool stones against my hands, heavy with sustenance.

A rustling of fallen leaves stirs deeper within the forest, accompanied by a low growl. My mind races to the descriptions of the wild beasts in the stories I've heard: sharp teeth, red eyes, big like a bear, hungry like a wolf. A chill runs through my body, each tiny hair on my arms prickling toward the sky.

I drop, stumbling onto the damp ground. My knapsack falls after me, the top bursting open, the fruits rolling out into the darkness, just beyond my reach. My eyes dart around—nothing but trees.

Another growl. Closer this time.

I squint into the shadows where the growling came from—and where the fruit rolled.

The fruit. I grit my teeth.

Darwith stomps in place, jerking his head, as if he's urging me to hurry.

I pull in a ragged breath and crawl as fast as I can toward my knapsack, reaching out and rolling an armload of fruits into the opening. Springing to my feet, I pull the knapsack over my back and sprint to Darwith. I grab his mane at his withers and swing myself into the saddle behind his wings, pressing my legs to his sides. He immediately breaks into a gallop.

I wait until we make it to the clearing before I glance over my shoulder. An eerie fog rolls through the trees, and I gulp down the wild ideas my imagination attempts to create—like the horrid *creature*, lurking just out of sight.

As we clear the pompidorri trees, I give Darwith another squeeze. His wings stretch out to his sides, lifting us into the dark sky. My grip loosens as my heart rate returns to a normal pace. We fly west, away from the murky forest, back toward the border. My knapsack feels heavy—it was a good run, even despite the ominous growling I heard.

We will have jam.

Darwith slows as our city of Cintrenia comes into view, serene in the pre-dawn light. Cintrenia is the heart of the island of Eirelannia—a beautiful green heart, pumping life into the surrounding areas. This northern part of Ivernister—the Green—is the most fertile area in both kingdoms, with lush fields stretching out for miles.

As we descend, the Empyrean arena stands out from the rest of the city, a boulder amongst pebbles. The colossal stone structure sits in the center of Cintrenia, its green and yellow lights sparkling against the black canvas of the sky. In a few hours, when the sun rises and the Autumn Tournament begins, the arena will come alive. Empyrean Rider hopefuls, horses, and spectators will flood through the gates and fill the seats and field. But for now, it's a silent, twinkling monolith, standing loftily in our otherwise modest city.

A white spotlight flashes at me from beyond the arena. My heart skips a beat, panic racing through me.

I'm caught.

 TWO

The light flashes again, and I relax, recognizing the sequence. I *know* that signal.

"Time to go back," I whisper. Darwith's ear twitches in recognition, and we turn in midair toward the Empyrean stables.

I wind my gloved fingers through Darwith's mane, further shielding them from the frosty air as we make our descent. It's as bitter as the three other times I've snuck out this month. Autumn is in full swing, and I underestimated the chill once again. I never dress warm enough—my riding tights and my father's tattered gray sweater aren't cutting it anymore. At least my toes move when I wiggle them in my brown riding boots—the most useful pieces of clothing I have. Thanks to my mother, wherever she is, for leaving these gems behind.

Darwith pulls in his long wings when we land. The door to the main stable is still open, so I ride him straight in, despite everything I've been taught against riding indoors. I swing my legs around to one side of his body, ready to dismount.

"Aluma," a voice calls from behind me.

My body fails me as I slide—nearly fall—off of Darwith.

A familiar face emerges from a stall near the end of the aisle—

Thayer Pridfirth, the one person my secret is safe with. Even when I split my right arm open flying for the first time, he didn't tell a soul, *and* he patched me up. He's been my confidant ever since.

Thayer grins. "Glad to see you're not in shackles."

"You've got to stop doing that," I say, catching my breath.

"You should stop being so jumpy. Although, at this rate, you might as well turn yourself in." His tone shifts. "I can't always be your lookout."

I look away. It's true—after today, he may never be my lookout again. If he becomes an Empyrean Rider, he'll be shipped down south to Galghesworp for training. He'll be gone for weeks, even months at a time. I won't have him to alert me about whether I'm safe to land without being seen. That, and I might miss him—a little.

Thayer's eyes glisten under the stable lights, the same way dew-drops sparkle on russet leaves in the autumn morning sun. He glances at my knapsack. "Well?"

I swing it around and open the top for him to peek in.

He tilts his head. "Not bad."

I hang my knapsack on an empty hook on the wall. I'll give him a fair share of the fruits later. His family isn't doing much better than mine when it comes to starving—or being dirt-poor. I wish I had more to give him than fruit. But our arrangement works out well enough: him watching out for me when I fly, and me collecting winter sustenance for both of our families.

When I turn back, Thayer is staring at me curiously.

"See anything in the forest—or the arena?" he asks as I unsaddle Darwith.

I decide not to mention the growling I heard in the Gray Forest. I don't want him telling me I shouldn't fly anymore. "Lots of test jumps set up in the arena."

"Do tell." He rubs his calloused hands together, perhaps out of excitement, but also to keep warm.

"They look *difficult*," I tell him. And I'm not lying, they did look challenging.

His shoulders slump, his tousled brown hair falling across his forehead as he pushes his rust-colored boot through the dirt.

"Come on, it always looks difficult."

He shakes his head, the playfulness in his eyes diminishing. "I don't know if I can do this. I'm not ready."

"You've been training nonstop for over a year now. You can do this."

"*You* could do it," he mutters, staring at the ground.

He's right. I *could* do it. I could be an Empyrean Rider. I can ride, I can fight, I can *fly*. And I just know if I were allowed to compete, I'd have a shot at joining the Cavalry. But when I begged my father to let me attend tryouts back in the spring, after I turned seventeen, he forbade it, fearing what might befall me in battle. Without his approval—or a nomination from another former Empyrean Rider—I'm destined to remain on the ground forever.

"Well, then use me as motivation," I tell him, my fingers smoothing over the curved front edge of Darwith's tucked black feathered wing. "It's not like the Autumn Tournament is my yearly reminder that there's no place for me in the sky, or anything." I roll my eyes as I grab a curry comb and groom Darwith near his withers. "I'd love to be in your shoes."

"Sorry." He grabs a brush and works on Darwith's neck. "I didn't mean…"

An awkward silence falls between us.

I toss some of Darwith's long mane at Thayer's face. It lands on top of his head, giving him a wavy black hairdo that hangs haphazardly over his light beige skin.

Thayer strikes a dramatic pose. "How do I look?" He lifts his chin.

"Dashing," I say, giggling as Darwith shakes out his mane, ruining my masterpiece.

Thayer glances at the clock on the wall. "We need to get going." He looks me over and makes a face. "And you might want to fix your hair."

I run my hand over my head. "What's wrong with my hair?"

"Looks like you stuck your head in a windstorm." His eyes are laughing at me.

"More like a *bird* storm," I mutter, knowing he won't understand the reference.

A wall of gleaming plaques awarded to past Empyrean Riders is the closest thing to a mirror here in the main stable. I scowl at my reflection—my pale white complexion has turned a pinkish hue, as have the spaces around my teal eyes, cold and bloodshot from the wind. And Thayer wasn't exaggerating about my hair; the normally straight blonde locks are a knotted, windblown mess.

You're my shiny girl, my father would say when I was little, looking at my then whitish-blonde hair, *full of light*. It was lighter when I was young—now it's some straw shade of yellow. I twist the tangled disaster until it curls in on itself, securing it into a knot high on the back of my head. I can't stand it in my face. "There," I say, glancing at Thayer. "Satisfied?"

Thayer purses his full lips together and his eyes crinkle in the corners, curling up to his temples. He's the only person I know who smiles with his eyes and his lips at the same time. I find it irritatingly adorable.

"Ready?" He turns away, and I'm grateful for it. Suddenly my face feels impossibly hot. Not my best look, I'm sure.

"Coming." I hurry over to Darwith and kiss his soft muzzle before I close his stall.

Outside, Thayer pulls me onto the back of his wingless bay mare, Yulla. I wrap my arms around Thayer's waist as we take off into a canter. My hands rest against his taut abdomen, and his strong back tightens against my chest. We've ridden together a hundred times, and yet this stirs something inside of me. I adjust my hands so they're no longer lying across his muscles, looping my arms underneath his and cupping his shoulders instead. But there's still a strange flutter in my stomach. Is it just because he might be leaving me today?

Yulla's hooves beat the ground in a soothing rhythm as we near my family farm, sending me into such a calm state that everything feels like a dream. A sliver of sunlight peeks over the Green Hills, illuminating our little house, making the fields glisten with morning dew. Coming home never gets old.

As we approach the turnoff to our farm, we ride near the big hill that we dubbed *Turtle Hill* when we were kids. From a distance, it looks like a giant version of one of the turtles we used to watch at the nearby pond—a turtle who meandered away from the rest of the turtles that make up the Green Hills. But big Turtle Hill isn't lonely; it's just a solitary turtle with lots to see. I glance out at it, remembering each time Thayer and I would sit at the top, looking out over our city, imagining who we'd be when we grew up. In the summer we'd lay out on the grass at night, counting stars until we fell asleep. And in the winter, when it snowed, we'd sled down, trying to push each other off into the drifts.

I smile to myself. Even if he makes it into the Cavalry, at least I'll have those memories of him—of *us*.

Thayer directs Yulla to the right, straight at the big hill. "One last stop," he says, and I realize he means to run Yulla to the top of Turtle Hill, instead of riding around it like we have since last year, when he backed out of the tryouts for the Tournament and tried to settle into the life of a farmer, as his parents wanted. Unsurprisingly, that effort didn't last very long—Thayer's always been meant for adventure.

"You might want to save her energy for the competitions," I suggest, but Thayer has already given Yulla all the rein she could want, and she's running straight for the grassy slope.

"It's a good warm-up," he teases. I pull myself closer to him and hold on tight as Yulla bounds up the long hill.

Once at the top, Thayer pats Yulla's neck. I slide off her back, and Thayer follows.

"Think she's warmed up?" I snort as Yulla prances in place, proud of her quick ascent.

"A snippet of what's coming—just you watch." Thayer raises his eyebrows. "She's come a long way since last year."

"So have you," I say, then realize I'm staring at him. *He's* come a long way in terms of riding since last year. But that's not really what I mean. Lately, I can't help noticing how much he's changed physically—or how much I'm noticing him. I've known him for so long, but it's as if I'm only truly seeing him now, for the first time. It must be because he's leaving soon, but he's like a growing tree, shedding his bark, standing tall and strong, with all his features laid out for me to admire.

In the dim light, I think I see his cheeks flush before he plops down onto the grass. A tingle trickles throughout my body. At first I think I'm cold, but then I realize it's a warm tingle: the kind you get when you bask in the sun with your eyes closed and all you see are oranges and reds behind your eyelids, and the warmth from the rays of the sun ripples through your body, like the moment could last forever. As the warm tingle escapes down my arms and out through my hands, I want to pull it back, so I can replay the sight of Thayer's cheeks flushing in the early morning light.

I wait a moment before sitting next to him, gazing out at the glistening city lights to the north. From here, you can see the whole city and beyond. And if you turn in a circle, you can see the Green Hills to the east, and the Gray Forest in the far distance behind them; to the south, our farm and the road to Galghesworp; and to the west, the kingdom of Uladmond. And if you could see farther, you might glimpse the Uladmond Mountains, and beyond them, Tarmensil, the capital city where the king lives.

"Do you remember a few summers ago, when we were both carting a load of crops into town at the same time?" Thayer says, still looking out at Cintrenia, a faint smile crossing his lips.

"You mean when we *raced* into town with two carts full of crops? Yeah, I remember." I shake my head at the old memory. "I also seem to recall one of your wheels breaking and half of your cartload ending up at the bottom of the Tarmen Canal. Do you remember *that*?" I chuckle.

"To be fair, I crossed the bridge first. So, I still won the race," he says, turning to face me with a smirk.

"If you count almost losing a hand as *winning*, then sure, you won." I remember how the king's soldiers questioned me and Thayer about his crop loss. If I hadn't lied for him about the freak nature of his wheel busting off and half the contents of his cart falling into the canal—and pointed out that the soldiers shouldn't have been spending the funds for road maintenance on ale at the tavern—they might have taken Thayer's hand for stealing, or figured out we were racing like irresponsible children. And with the ongoing war and the gluttonous people of the Otherside draining our already dwindling food supply, reckless behavior is just as bad as stealing.

"Thanks for having my back that day," he says, his voice lowering. "You've always had my back."

I elbow his arm. "Stop that—stop being all serious and sentimental right before you might leave forever."

"Forever?" he echoes, tilting his head to the side. "This is my home." He pauses, then whispers, "And you're here…"

I can't help smiling, but I'm trying my best not to let a silly, full-on grin take over.

"I'm coming back, you know? You'll be bored out of your mind without me. But then again, you'll probably be a married woman by the time I return, and far too busy for cart racing," he says, but it feels like a question, with hope and fear mixed in.

A tinge of frustration wrinkles my brow. "What other choice do I have?"

He nudges me. "I'm not serious," he says. But he and I both know that if I can't become an Empyrean Rider, my future is clear: marry, move to my husband's farm, and have children who will someday be forced into serving the king—just like the rest of us.

"Maybe I will be married, and then you can win a cart race against someone less skilled than me," I say lightly. I don't want to spend the little time we have left together fretting over the inevitable. I want to pretend moments like this, sitting at the top of Turtle Hill next to him, can last forever.

"Maybe," he says, a touch of sadness hovering around his voice. "But we're here now, aren't we?"

I lean against his arm, laying my head on his shoulder. Thayer's hand stretches across my lower back and clasps my waist. His touch is familiar, but also new. It makes my breath catch. It's not like him to reach out to hold me like this, in such a non-playful manner. I'm nervous, but excited, too, the same way I felt moments before I first flew on Darwith: fearful of the unknown ahead of us, but eager to experience it all the same.

Thayer rests his lips on the top of my head and breathes in. He's become much more prone to these affectionate gestures lately, and my mind drifts to what it would feel like for his full lips to touch my own. We sit in silence as the warmth of a few golden rays of the rising sun touches our faces like outstretched fingers. I close my eyes to see all oranges and reds as a warm glow glides throughout my body. I want to memorize everything about this moment, imprint it into my mind for safekeeping.

"We should get going," Thayer says finally, his voice soft, remorseful. I don't want to leave—not now. Not yet. But he's right—the sun is threatening to expose our secret with every new sliver of light, beaming on us like little spotlights.

Thayer stands, and I'm left sitting on the damp grass. He glances down at me, his eyes meeting mine, as if he's speaking invisible words through them. Words I can't read—a foreign language.

I smile awkwardly and scramble to my feet. Thayer watches me, pressing his lips together and scrunching his brow. My eyes narrow as I attempt to decipher what he's thinking. Are his lips chapped? Is he tired? Does he want to *kiss* me?

"You're right," I say, nodding swiftly. "Let's get going."

He exhales, as if a weight has been taken off his chest and added at the same time. I hurry over to Yulla and wait for him to mount. When he pulls me up, I wrap my arms around him, this time allowing my hands to rest across his abdomen.

When Thayer drops me off at home, the sun is already higher than I feel comfortable with. I'm usually home before the light leaves the crevices over the Green Hills.

"Thanks for the ride," I whisper, sliding off of Yulla.

"See you soon," Thayer says, smiling down at me before riding away. And I realize right then, that even if I get caught, it was all worth it. In a moment, Thayer and Yulla are specks in the distance as they move toward the Pridfirth farm.

The window to my room is still cracked, just how I left it. From the silence inside the house, I hope my father and younger brother are still asleep. I grab one of the pompidorris from my knapsack and stuff the rest under my loose floorboard. I can't let my father spot me with this many of the rare fruits. Obtaining one or two at a time is one thing, but if I plopped half a knapsack worth of them on the table, he'd get suspicious.

When I creep out into the hallway, the heat from the fireplace wafts out, along with the scent of one of Father's teas brewing.

Too late. He's awake.

 THREE

When I enter the kitchen, my father is sitting at the table with his back to me. I discreetly place the pompidorri on the counter, straighten my sweater, and smooth the top of my twisted hair.

"Good morning," my father says, turning to face me. I place my hand on his shoulder and lean over for him to kiss my forehead. I hope he doesn't notice the cold on my face.

"Morning." I smile at him.

"You look tired," he remarks, his crystal-blue eyes surveying me. I stifle a yawn. "I didn't sleep much last night." That's half true.

"Trading for that pompidorri?" He eyes the fruit on the counter. I nod, hoping he doesn't press me for more details.

"Is everything else okay?" he asks. He's too perceptive for his own good.

"Of course. Just excited for today." I move to the cabinet and take out our plates for breakfast, aiming to avoid more questions. He rarely asks how I get the pompidorris. I've had to lie about it, saying I trade for them in town by cleaning horse stalls. I'm not proud of lying to him, but many of the nobles have access to the fruits, so it's not too unbelievable that I'd muck stalls in exchange.

Maybe I shouldn't be risking so much. Lying isn't my thing. But every crop we grow has to be accounted for, and nearly all of it is shipped away to the king and the plump folks of Tarmensil before we can even spark up the stove. It's all under the guise of it going straight to the soldiers on the front lines, but most of us are keenly aware that the Uladmondians being so well-fed isn't an accident. Still, we have no choice. The king and his army will seize our farm if we resist, and then we'll die like all the other families who were starved or killed, thinking they could break free from his tyranny. Father likes to pretend that we'll be all right, that somehow we'll scrape by. But I know better.

His forehead furrows as he lowers his teacup. "Big day, I suppose."

"Judging the competitions, a demonstration with Darwith, *and* receiving a lifetime achievement award? Yeah, I'd say." My eyebrows raise. "It's a big deal. These awards aren't just handed out to anyone. You're a legend."

"It's a useless award. It doesn't put more food on the table. I'd sell it if I could." There's a bitterness in his voice, an edge I've heard before. These awards, being a judge—it's all a joke when you can't feed your family.

Even though my father is widely known and respected for his days as an Empyrean Rider and now as a trainer, he's still never been invited to move us to the Otherside to improve our situation. We've never been allowed to keep more of what we grow and fill our stomachs like the overfed elite. The king has my father right where he wants him—a loyal military hero and a success, who still lives like any other commoner, humble and poor, and content to be so. He's a great example of a well-placed citizen; a figurehead to appease the masses.

I know there's more to it, of course. From the way my father talks about the Otherside, I'm surprised he accepted the judging position this year. Father wouldn't take the award or judge the competition if the king didn't demand it—and unfortunately, these aren't the types of things you can turn down. Not if you want to keep your life.

"Well, you're a legend to me," I tell him, "award or not."

He shrugs as his pale cheeks turn pink. Humble as ever.

I hurry outside to our chicken coop with a wicker basket on my arm. A sea of fog rolls out over the Green Hills, and in the distance, the scattered trees rise up like whitish-gray clouds, blending between fog and sky.

The hens are fast asleep when I enter the coop. The smell of dust and straw tickles my nose as I rustle through the hay, collecting fresh eggs. Slowly, the ladies begin to wake, their wings ruffling. I bet they were dreaming little chicken dreams about being allowed to fly, just like me. A dream that's so close, yet so far.

Back inside, my younger brother Kase has made his way out of his bedroom. He sits with perfect posture across the table from Father. He's a year younger than me, but he looks like a sixteen-year-old going on twenty with his mustache stubble having grown in. His face stays obscured behind today's newspaper, his meticulously combed dark blond hair peeking over the tops of the pages.

I spark the stove. "Scrambled eggs, coming right up."

"Sounds delicious." My father winks.

It's always scrambled eggs. Scrambling them makes it seem like we're eating more than we have—a trick I've figured out over the years of food shortages, since we often have nothing but eggs for breakfast. I shouldn't complain—at least we *have* eggs. Many Cintrenians don't have any hens, and that often means no breakfast. And I like breakfast.

"Any news on the position in Tarmensil?" my father asks Kase while I dish up a plate of eggs for each of them.

"Nothing yet," Kase mutters, barely glancing up. His blue eyes are bright like my father's, one of the few things they have left in common. Kase has been vying for an internship in the capital for more than a year. Each time Father has expressed his frustrations with the king and the politicians of the Otherside, Kase has made an even greater effort to fit in with them. It reminds me of why we Ivernisterians nicknamed Uladmond *the Otherside*: first, because it's on the other side of the Uladmond Mountains, but even more importantly, because it's the other side of what's possible for us. It's the opposite of the way we live here.

In the Green, we don't get to enjoy the same types of luxuries as the elites in the kingdom of Uladmond.

"Thanks, Lumi." My father smiles as I place his plate in front of him. "Say, do you have time to ride into town this morning? My suit is at the tailor shop, and I need it for the Tournament later. I've got more work to do here, otherwise I'd go myself."

"Sure." I dig into my plate of eggs. Flying always makes me hungry. When my father raises an eyebrow at me, I slow my pace.

"Are you going to attend the Tournament?" Father asks as his gaze returns to Kase, giving me a moment to dig back into my eggs.

"For the king's opening address, yes," Kase says from behind the paper. "Speaking of which, did you see the news?" He points to a photo on the cover page of the king of Uladmond in front of the palace in Tarmensil. The king's younger and much more tyrannical brother, Sutagus, stands beside him with his ridiculous mustache. It's well known that Prince Sutagus is the voice behind most of the king's decisions—and always the worst of them.

Father squints at the headline, and I follow his lead.

The Cost of War—New Property Law Declared.

"'A new law has passed,'" Kase reads aloud. "'Because of the ongoing war with the kingdom of Laithlann and the food shortages in both Uladmond and Ivernister, King Breasal has declared property rights in Ivernister shall be limited to those who have a household member serving as an enlisted soldier in the king's ground army, or as an active Empyrean Rider. It requires all other farmers and property owners to register under the king.'" Kase sets the paper on the table and takes a bite of his eggs.

My father lowers his fork to his plate with a *clink*.

"What will they do?" I ask.

"It's clear," Kase says. "If we don't obey the new law by registering our farm or by one of us joining the ranks, the farm will become property of the king."

He's far too nonchalant about this.

"So, either we starve, fight a pointless war, *one of us* becomes an

Empyrean Rider, or they'll take our farm—our *home*?" I ask, pushing my plate away. I've lost my appetite.

"Aluma…" My father searches my eyes.

"If we register our farm with the palace, they'll take even more of our crops, leaving us with nothing," I snap. "We'll starve, just like the rest of the registered farmers in Cintrenia. We're barely getting by as is."

Father stares down at his plate. "I'll come out of retirement."

I shake my head. "Father, no—you can't." I dart a look at Kase, hoping he'll agree with me for once.

Kase shrugs. "This is a necessary law. We *all* must sacrifice for our king and for the good of the two kingdoms."

"Father paid his dues. What have you done to help?" I glare at Kase and turn back to my father. "They can't do this. You can't go back. I'll do it. I'll become an Empyrean Rider, or I'll enlist in the ground army." I say the words, but I know Father won't allow it.

Kase nods. "Now, there's a solution."

"No," my father insists. "I won't let either of my children go to war." He tries to smile reassuringly, but he knows as well as I do that coming out of retirement won't last long. *Flying is for Empyrean Riders, and Empyrean Riders are warriors.* And we are at war. It's a miracle my father even made it to retirement.

I stand, taking another moment to glare at Kase. He says nothing. He does nothing. He's no better than the king or the people from the Otherside, ruling everyone into submission.

I flee the kitchen and race outside, the cool air filling my lungs. Cintrenia and the Empyrean arena loom on the horizon—a terrible reminder of the truth I'm facing. If my father rejoins the Empyrean Cavalry, it's unlikely he'll ever come home. If he doesn't rejoin, we'll have to register our farm, and we'll starve. And if we don't register, Kase or I will have to join the ground army or the Empyrean Cavalry.

But Father won't allow it. And if we do nothing, we'll lose our farm.

Undigested bits of eggs work their way back up to my throat. *We'll lose everything.*

 FOUR

If I make it to the city soon, I may miss the bulk of the crowds on my way to the arena. The Autumn Tournament doesn't begin until the afternoon, but the streets will be congested well before that. Spectators from the Otherside, the kingdom's wealthy elite, prefer to arrive a few hours ahead of the competitions, by luxury water or land heliakarriers—or, as we call them, karriers.

Karriers are a mystery to me. Land karriers consist of four wheels with an enclosed rectangular metal box on top. Most are the size of about three big horses standing shoulder to shoulder and have four doors with windows and seats inside. I peeked around an open door once; there's even a wheel in front that the driver controls. The water karriers, on the other hand, are much larger—close to the size of a barn.

Father told me the karriers collect their power from the sun, absorbing the light through the black panels on their roofs, and that's what propels them forward. The technology existed before the destruction of the Old World. Some karriers remained safe in the Otherside, away from the shockwaves—the Uladmond Mountains created a protective barrier separating the Uladmondian elite in the

Otherside from us here in Ivernister and the Laithlanners in the Old World—but none of the other karriers were salvageable. The Ulad-mondians get to use the karriers that survived, but that's it. And no one has yet figured out how to create more.

The sun is out in full force, but the air is still cool. I saddle Kase's wingless black-and-white paint mare, Blossom. She was once my mother's horse, a gift from my father. But a few weeks before she disappeared, she gave Blossom to Kase.

He was always her favorite.

So far he hasn't complained too much about my riding Blossom into town, which is a relief. I'd love to keep Darwith at our barn at home and ride *him*, but since he's an Empyrean steed, we're required to keep him at the Empyrean stables. That, and I'm not an Empyrean Rider, so I can't be caught riding an Empyrean steed. He's my father's mount, yet he's also the king's property, given his wings.

I hoist myself onto Blossom, sink my heels into the stirrups, then press my calves to her sides. She takes off into a bouncy trot; she's awfully chipper today. I give her some rein, and she leaps into a gallop. Mother enjoyed riding fast, and Blossom moves like a gust of wind, blowing past the landscape as if nothing can stop her.

I replay the conversation from breakfast in my mind, frustration gnawing at me. My father built our farm with his own two hands. My father, who was an Empyrean Rider for years. He risked his life more than once for the king. Why should he have to fight *again* to keep our farm?

The city limits are marked by an old dry stone wall, covered in green peat moss. As we pass through the opening in the wall, Blossom's hooves clack against the stone bridge over the Tarmen Canal. At the top of the bridge, a glare hits my eyes as the Empyrean arena comes into view, its pale facade glistening in the sun, reflecting the sunlight across the city.

When Ivernister had its own king, Cintrenia was a small town with rolling pastures, farms full of livestock, and fields of crops surrounding it. But after the king of Uladmond seized the throne in Ivernister during the Dark Wars, he ordered the construction of four new Empyrean arenas, one in the center of each city throughout his two separate, but newly joined kingdoms.

Each year, a select few people from each city compete to join the king's elite Empyrean Cavalry in the Autumn Tournament. Only the most skilled warriors and their equally remarkable horses are given a chance to participate. After, horses belonging to the new Empyrean Riders are granted their wings, going from a wingless horse to an Empyrean steed overnight. Positions in the Cavalry are extremely limited because of the power it takes to give the horses their wings, so the competition is fierce. But anyone who has to fight for the king would rather battle in the sky on the back of an Empyrean steed.

The arenas were meant to bring people together in the most central locations throughout the kingdoms. And they did, along with creating many year-round jobs for the locals. When not in use for the Autumn Tournament, the arenas are used for training, small-scale local competitions, and public meetings—and far too often to demonstrate what happens to people who attempt to live a life different from the one laid out for us by the king. The creativity of the public executions, most often designed by Prince Sutagus, never ceases to draw a crowd.

I slow Blossom to a walk as we make our way onto the main street that leads straight to the arena. The tailor shop is located a few blocks before. I remember the sign from when I was younger—an outstretched silver wing, framing one side of the word *Tailor*.

The scent of Autumn Tournament baked goods fills the air—sweet and savory treats I have rarely had the pleasure of tasting. Last year my father spoiled me with half of a frunkin loaf he was given. The frunkin is a hardy vegetable, but mashed down, baked, and sprinkled with sugar, it becomes quite the treat. My stomach growls at the memory.

My plan to beat the crowds has failed. The city is already in full swing. Ivernisterians on their horses and Uladmondians in their fancy black karriers swarm the roads, trying not to collide with one another. Blossom snorts as she sidesteps a silent land karrier. It coasts past, nearly running into us.

"Hey, thanks!" I yell out. I know they won't hear me, and they wouldn't care if they did. These roads weren't designed for horses and karriers to pass through at the same time. Accidents happen, with horses and their riders mangled far too often. It's never the other way around.

"Aluma!" a high-pitched voice yells from behind me.

I glance over my shoulder at a young woman pushing her way through the crowd. Farann Ross. I rein Blossom to the side of the street and wait, mustering a smile. She isn't normally this intent on getting my attention, not unless she wants something.

"I thought that was you!" She pauses to catch her breath, pushing her wavy, copper-colored hair away from her round face. Her fair white skin is flushed pink across the bridge of her freckled nose and onto her cheeks. Farann is sixteen, but already has the delicate feminine features of a lady, with curves in all the right places. There's a long line of suitors pursuing her hand in marriage. She's everything my mother once wished I would grow up to be, and everything I'm not.

Farann digs through her satchel. "Would you give Kase something for me?" She doesn't wait for my answer before handing me a white envelope.

"What is it?" I flip the envelope over.

"I'm not sure. My father gave it to me." She shrugs. "I was supposed to give it to Kase last night when we arrived in town, but I got caught up with some old friends and completely forgot about it."

Of course it's for Kase. Why would she be talking to me otherwise? Kase has always liked Farann. I bet he wishes he could be her suitor someday. Her father, Jarek Ross, was an Empyrean Rider like my father before he weaseled his way into Prince Sutagus's inner circle. Now they live in the Otherside, in Tarmensil. My brother's dream.

Farann's hazel eyes widen. "It's no trouble, is it?"

"I'll give it to him as soon as I get home." I place the envelope in my saddlebag and give Blossom a squeeze. "I have to get going. It was nice seeing you."

Farann nearly knocks a basket out of a woman's hands as she tries to keep up beside Blossom. "I hope I see you later at the Tournament. Did you get an invitation to the party at the Green Barn afterward?" She raises her manicured eyebrows.

She can't be serious. I've never been invited to that gathering. And Farann hasn't bothered including me in anything for years—since before she moved and became too popular to be my best friend.

"I'm sure I'll see you later. I have to go!" I force a smile and give Blossom a firmer nudge, sending her into a quick trot.

"See you!" Her voice fades away behind me.

I wave without turning, thanking the stars that I'm on horseback and can ride away faster than she can keep up.

The silver-winged sign for the tailor shop comes into view. There's one tie-up spot left out front. I leave Blossom there and hurry inside.

The shop is empty and much quieter than the street outside. There's a counter at the back, and a door leading into another room. A square wooden platform is situated along the left wall with mirrors surrounding half. A few green-and-yellow tapestries, Cintrenian colors, adorn the walls on either side. Another tapestry hangs beside them, with one outstretched silver wing, like the one on the sign outside. A machine hums somewhere in the back room.

"Hello?" I call out.

"Be right there!" a voice answers from behind the counter, making me jump. An old man with a bald head and rosy white cheeks pops up and smiles. "What can I do for you?"

"I'm here to pick up my father's suit. The order should be under 'Banks.'"

"Aluma—is that you?" His eyes widen as his jaw drops.

I nod hesitantly as the man shuffles around the counter, adjusting his oversized spectacles.

"I hardly recognized you! I haven't seen you since you were about this high." He holds out his hand about two feet off the ground. I'm not sure I've ever been *that* short.

"I'm sorry..." I'm embarrassed to admit I'm still not sure who he is.

"Oh, forgive me!" He shakes his shiny head. "You don't remember. I'm Lermyn Githah. Your father once worked on my farm, long ago."

His name sounds familiar.

"I was an Empyrean steed trainer..." He tilts his head and waits.

A rush of excitement passes through me. "You're *the* Lermyn?" The same man who helped my father get into Empyrean steed training? The only retired Empyrean Rider and trainer even more talented than my father?

"One and the same." Lermyn chuckles at my sudden enthusiasm.

"Why are you working as a—" I catch my tongue. I shouldn't pry.

"As a tailor?" He finishes my thought with a knowing smile. "I'm retired from all things Empyrean. An old man like me can only work for so long with such powerful creatures. The years go by, and you're old before you know it. Your bones get brittle and your skin gets thin." He opens and closes his callused hands, a small grimace tracing across his pale, weathered face. "Working as a tailor allows me to put my body out to pasture, so to speak." He chuckles.

The stories he must have to tell. I feel myself smiling, but then I imagine my father turning old and weak—while still being forced into more dangerous work in the sky—and my smile disappears.

Lermyn slaps his crooked fingers on the counter. "Here I am, jabbering away. Let me go get your father's suit." He hobbles off to the back room.

I glance down at my unwrinkled hands, opening and closing my fingers, waiting for pain to follow and thankful when none does. Maybe one day, I'll be like Lermyn, old and withered from all the training and riding. My fingertips trace the scar next to my right elbow, remembering the night Thayer had to patch me up. Falling off an Empyrean steed wasn't great; still, there are worse ways to spend my life.

Lermyn returns, carrying a garment bag. He hangs it on a hook. "Here we are."

"Thank you," I say. "It was nice to see you." I pick up the bag.

"Oh, before you go, please do me a favor?" Lermyn scans the room and lowers his voice. "Would you relay a message to your father?"

"Sure. What is it?"

Lermyn glances at the front door and moves closer to me. His cheeks have lost all color. "Tell your father…" His voice quivers. "…*the old will soon be made anew.*"

A chill runs through my body as each word etches itself into my mind.

"Please tell him for me." He places his wrinkled hand on top of mine. "It's important that you do, and *soon*, before the Tournament."

An uneasiness falls over me. "I'll tell him."

"Thank you." He pats my hand, and the pink returns to his cheeks.

"Are you not attending the Tournament or my father's demonstration?" I ask, realizing he would surely pass along the message himself if he were.

"I fear I will have to miss it this time. I will be here, working. It was lovely to see you, Aluma. Please do tell your father what I said," he says, imploring me with big eyes.

As I leave, I glance at the silver wing emblem on the tapestry hanging on the wall—it's the same as the one on the front of the shop. I've seen that symbol before.

Lermyn's message replays in my head the whole ride back to our farm.

The old will soon be made anew.

Something about how he spoke those words makes me hesitant to share them with my father. Lermyn has been in the city working as a tailor all these years, and my father never told me he was there—not once. I'd just assumed Lermyn had retired to the countryside, far away, and that's why I hadn't had the chance to meet him at an age when I'd actually remember.

When I return to our farm, I unsaddle Blossom and fetch her some fresh water before seeking out my father. He's not in the barn, and I don't see him in the house when I hang his suit in the closet. The message from Lermyn will have to wait.

I knock on Kase's door, holding the sealed envelope Farann gave me earlier. I'm impressed with myself for not opening it—my curiosity often gets the better of me.

"Yes?" Kase responds from inside his room.

I turn the handle. It's locked. "Can you open the door?"

"What do you want?" His voice is gruff.

I tap my boot against the wood floor. "Come on, open up. I have an envelope for you."

Silence.

"From Farann."

The door clicks open. Kase glares at me before glancing at the envelope in my hands.

I raise my eyebrows. "It's about time."

He snatches the envelope and tries to slam the door again. I stop it with my boot, placing my hands on my hips. "What's in the envelope?"

Kase sticks his head out, peering into the hallway. There's still no one else but us. He lets out a puff of air, crossing his arms. "I am assuming—*hoping*—it's my acceptance letter for the internship in Tarmensil."

"No reason to be so secretive. Father knows you want to go. It's not like it's a surprise or something." I roll my eyes. His attitude is getting old.

"I'm not being secretive. I just don't want to rub it in his face." He frowns. "He's already disappointed with me."

"That's not true. I'm sure he's proud of you. He even asked you about it this morning."

Kase snorts. "Not because he wants me to get the position. He doesn't respect me or my dreams. You know I'm right." His lips pull to one side, and his icy blue eyes gleam with unshed tears.

So, he *does* care what our father thinks. He wants to impress him. This is news to me.

"I don't *know* that," I say. "And neither do you." A part of me wants to reach out and hug my little brother, but I don't. He wouldn't react well if I did.

"Actually, I do. Now, can I get some privacy, please?" He tries to close the door.

I stop it with my foot again. "What's going on with you?"

His nostrils flare at my question.

"What is it?" I can tell he's still mad about something.

Kase exhales. "It's clear Father doesn't respect the king, or his new law."

My empathy for him immediately goes up in flames. "What are you on about?"

"He's not being loyal to the king. He needs to show some respect."

"*Respect?*" I scoff. "He's served one king or another his whole life. Now he'll be forced to come out of retirement. How is he not loyal?"

"He's carrying out his duties, sure, but nothing more. He doesn't support the king's choices."

"Why isn't that enough? What else do you expect from him?"

He drags in a frustrated breath. "Father needs to understand that this war is necessary for the future of our kingdom. And with war comes the need for sacrifice, and for someone to lead the way." He pauses before adding, "Anyone who doesn't support the king is a traitor."

"*Traitor?*" I echo, stepping back from him in surprise. Father is *not* a traitor. My fists clench at the very idea of Kase thinking this way.

His door closes between us.

The air is caught tight in my chest. I push it all out and trudge down the hallway. I can no longer relate to the angry young man hiding out in my brother's room.

Not even a little.

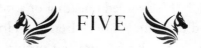 FIVE

The sun is warming the air as I head back to the barn. My father should be around by now. He has to collect his suit before the Tournament. But given Kase's negative attitude after I handed over the envelope from Farann, I'm even more reluctant to tell my father Lermyn's message. I don't want to burden him with one more thing on his big day.

As I approach the barn doors, I notice my father in the round pen on the side of the barn. He's lunging a stunning wingless horse in a wide circle. The horse is a dark dapple gray with a long charcoal mane, its markings like a storm and movements like a smooth breeze.

My mouth falls open as I climb onto the wooden railing of the pen. "Who is *that*?"

My father turns and smiles. "This is Cashel. Care to meet him?"

He doesn't have to ask me twice. I hop over the fence, landing on the soft dirt in the round pen.

Cashel stretches his strong neck out to me. I raise the back of my hand underneath his black nostrils for him to sniff. A dark blaze runs jagged between midnight eyes on his otherwise pale gray face. His hair is smooth beneath my fingers as I pet his forehead.

"Is he yours?" I ask. *Please, please, please say yes.* Cashel is the most beautiful horse I've ever seen.

"Unfortunately not." Father's smile creeps down into a slight frown.

"Oh." I try to hide my disappointment. "Who does he belong to?"

"You," my father says, smirking.

"Lucky," I say automatically, still processing. "Wait, what?" I bounce in little bunny hops before hugging my father. "He's *mine?*"

"Yes!" My father chuckles. "I was going to wait until after the Tournament, but I decided now is as good a time as any."

"Father—I mean, *wow.*" I hug him again. "Thank you!"

"You're welcome, Lumi." He smiles. "Most riders get their first wingless horse at seventeen, haven't you heard?" He wraps an arm around my shoulder and adds, "I know I'm more than a few months late, but I hope he was worth the wait."

"Thank you—he's amazing!" My jaw hurts from smiling so much.

I have my own horse. Not everyone does. A wingless horse isn't a rarity in Eirelannia by any means, but to have your own horse with no plans of joining the king's military or hauling crops *is* rare. Owning a horse for the sheer appreciation of its nature, movement, and beauty isn't the norm—but it should be.

"Why don't you see how he rides? I'll set up a few jumps."

He doesn't wait for me to agree as he hurries into the training arena.

I lead Cashel into the barn to saddle him. I rub his arched neck. He's stunning. The smudged gray markings on his sides are like dark rainclouds painted over a light gray sky. His legs are covered in all-black stockings, blending into the gray markings covering the rest of his athletic frame. His mane is charcoal-gray, as is his tail, save for one long, whitish streak.

Breathtaking.

There's new tack laid out next to the grooming area, presumably for Cashel. I run my hands over the saddle, admiring its craftsmanship. As I lay the green saddle pad over Cashel, I notice the same outstretched silver wing emblem I saw embroidered on the tapestry in the tailor shop and on the front sign.

Strange.

Outside, in the large arena, I boost myself onto Cashel for the first time and find my seat. My father watches from the other side of the arena. I bask in the moment, appreciating my new horse.

"Try him out." My father waves at the jumps.

I give Cashel a tiny squeeze, and he begins to walk. After we turn the first corner, I give him another, and he trots. My father smiles proudly as I pass him. With another command, Cashel breaks into a smooth canter. I keep him going, staying close to the edges, getting a feel for his stride.

"When you're ready," my father says, his eyes smiling the same way they did when he first taught me to jump. It was a perfect autumn day, not much different from today, when my father and I had gone riding near the canal. Thanks to a fallen tree and some small streams, I had my first jumping lessons, and I've been hooked ever since. I love the freedom of jumping, flying through the air for those brief few moments.

I'm sure my father would be thrilled to learn that his teaching me how to jump led me to fly Darwith—behind his back.

I set my sights on the first jump. I slow Cashel into a gentle canter and direct him toward it. His ears twitch in recognition when I click my tongue, and his pace quickens as he times his ascent. I balance in my seat, holding my legs to his sides, my hands near his withers and my elbows at my waist. I gaze straight ahead, and in another moment he pushes off. He jumps higher than necessary, springing over with ease.

I grin as we land on the other side. I give him a pat on his neck and we continue to the second jump. Over the next two hurdles we go, together as horse and rider.

"You've sure got something there," my father says as Cashel and I trot over to him.

"Thanks to you—he's incredible!"

"I was talking about you." He raises an eyebrow. "You're a great jumper. A great rider."

I sit straighter in my saddle as my eyes dampen at the compliment. "Thank you, Father."

A warmth fills me as I hop off Cashel and give him a kiss on his neck, breathing in his wonderful horse scent. It smells like hardy soil being warmed by the sweetest rays of sunshine.

My father and I walk side by side as we lead Cashel into the barn. His pride in my ability radiates through me, and for a moment, I feel like I could fly—without sneaking out on his Empyrean steed to do so.

"I'd best be getting ready for the Tournament," my father says, breaking my momentary glow.

The warmth inside me quickly dissipates into a cool frustration at the reminder that I'm not allowed to expand on my skills as a serious rider—not to the point of being able to join the Empyrean Cavalry, anyway. The Autumn Tournament is in less than two hours, but still out of reach for me. No matter how great of a jumper or rider I am, or ever will be, no matter how proud my father is of me—becoming an Empyrean Rider is out of the question, unless Father suddenly changes his mind about letting me compete.

Lermyn's message runs through my head as Cashel takes a long drink from the water trough.

"Father…" I scratch my neck.

He glances over at me, a smile still on his face.

"I saw your old friend, Lermyn Githah, this morning."

His smile fades as he shakes his head. "Right, I should have mentioned he runs the place."

"Well, he told me to tell you something. He said it was important to tell you right away."

Father's brows scrunch together as he scans the barn, like Lermyn did in the shop, before directing his gaze back at me. His voice is hushed when he asks, "What did he say?"

I wait for a moment, biting the inside of my cheek. "He said, 'the old will soon be made anew.'"

His jaw clenches.

"What does it mean?" I ask.

My father stands motionless, staring off as his eyes narrow.

"Father?"

"I'm sorry." He forces a smile. "It's nothing, just an old expression between friends."

My lips press together. I won't push it any further, but I know he's hiding something.

"Thanks for the message," he says. He's looking right at me, but his mind is clearly somewhere else. "Aren't you supposed to meet Thayer?"

I grit my teeth. Judging by the amount of sun filtering in through the barn door, I'm running late. Too distracted by Cashel to be on time. "Yes, I am."

"I'm sure he could use a good pep talk. And I need to prepare." Father kisses my forehead and makes his way back to the barn door.

"Father," I call after him.

He turns. "Yes?"

I pause, my many questions swirling in my head like a blizzard. But it's not the right time to pry, after he's just given me the best gift ever. And I'm not so sure I'd get any answers anyway. Whatever it is he's not sharing with me, he doesn't want to say.

"Thank you," I say. "Cashel is perfect."

He smiles, his eyes bright from across the barn. "You're welcome, Lumi."

Despite my father's reassurances and my new horse, the churning in my stomach now is even worse than when Lermyn first gave me the message.

Something isn't right.

 SIX

By the time I ride Cashel over the stone bridge into Cintrenia and make it to the Empyrean Rider stables, it's half-past eleven—only an hour and a half before the Autumn Tournament's opening events and fifteen minutes later than I told Thayer I'd meet him. I knew the city would be nearly impenetrable by now with the crowds, but this year seems worse than ever before. There's a veritable horde of spectators on horseback, on foot, and the elites in their karriers, packing the streets like a herd of sheep, all bunching together, moving in the same direction, none questioning why they're going where they're going. Plus, the sweet scent of frunkin loafs and other treats has been replaced with the stench of manure.

Delightful.

The day has been going too fast. Before I left the farm, I took a few extra minutes to get changed into my nice clothes: a brown jacket, dark jeans, and a green blouse, paired with my same old trusty boots. Not a fancy outfit by any means, but it's the best one I've got. I'm lucky—many young Ivernisterians don't have a solid pair of shoes.

I take off Cashel's tack and turn him out to graze in the small pen behind the stables. I step back, inspecting him. It still has yet to sink in. *I have my own horse.*

When I walk through the back door of the main stable, Thayer is pacing. My mind races with all the things I want to tell him, but from the looks of him, he's in full-on panic mode.

Thayer spots me and clears his throat. "You made it."

"Sorry I'm late."

He rubs his neck.

"Wow. Look at you." I smirk as I pull on his tucked-in shirt. He looks good.

He looks *handsome.*

Thayer blushes. "Thanks." He glances at his shirt, smoothing it back into place with quick hands.

"How are you feeling?" I ask him, despite the obvious.

"Ah, you know, like I might vomit." He chuckles as he runs his hands through his unkempt hair. "Otherwise, fantastic."

"You've got this. You'll do great."

Thayer lets out a long breath, his full lips parting to let the air escape. "Thanks."

I raise my hands to shoulder level. "Plus, I'll be there to cheer you on." I twinkle my fingers.

He half smiles, shifting his weight. He's a ball of nerves, and my pep talk isn't working.

"Hey, I have someone I want you to meet," I tell him. I attempt to hide my excitement, but I'm still giddy, with a bounce in my step.

Thayer catches a glimpse of my new horse grazing when we exit the stable. His eyes widen, and he darts off to the pen where I left Cashel. "Whoa, did you—is he *yours?*" He opens the gate and hurries inside.

"Yes." I grin. "My father gave him to me. His name is Cashel."

"He's amazing! I'm so happy for you." His lips turn up and the corners of his eyes crease into happy little folds. Finally, a *real* Thayer smile. My distraction is working.

"Already took him for a test ride. He can jump."

"He *looks* like a jumper."

"Cleared them like it was nothing." I rub Cashel's neck underneath his mane.

"I bet he'd be brilliant with win—" Thayer cuts himself off.

My shoulders tense a little. Cashel *would* be unstoppable with wings. Wings he'll never get, because he's mine.

"But I bet he'd be good at just about anything," Thayer says. "Look at him—he sure is something."

"He would be a great Empyrean steed," I say, falling back into a pit of disappointment.

Thayer's mouth turns downward.

I take a sharp inhale and force myself to smile. Today is Thayer's big day, not mine. He has a shot at flying, and I'm happy for him.

"Just think," I say, forcing excitement into my voice. "Yulla could be one step closer to becoming an Empyrean steed after today. She could get her wings soon. And then you'll be flying before you know it."

Thayer glances back at the main barn. "Speaking of which, I need to get going."

Inside, Yulla waits patiently as we gather her tack. Thayer hands me a green saddle blanket, and I place it on her. The same emblem of one outstretched silver wing is stitched in on the corner.

"Where did you get this?" I ask Thayer.

"My father gave it to me this morning. Nice, right?"

I nod as Lermyn's message runs through my head. I want to tell Thayer, but I can't hold him up any more than I already have.

When Thayer finishes saddling Yulla, he strokes her face. "You ready, girl?"

"She's ready. And so are you," I tell him.

Thayer sighs, but his face is not nearly as pale as it was when I arrived. At least I managed to distract him a little. If someone doesn't intervene now and then, Thayer gets trapped in his own mind, fighting his doubts like he's stuck in a dark cave, swatting at an endless colony of bats. I'm glad I could shed some light.

He leads Yulla to the front of the stables, his head held high as he walks beside her. "I need to pick up my registration number at noon and get ready with the other riders."

My shoulders tense. I wish I were going to compete, but that's not in my future. "I'll stay here until the opening ceremony gets a little closer," I tell him. I want to absorb the silence before the crowds. I want to be alone. I'm trying my hardest not to sulk, not to worry about Lermyn's message, but I'm failing miserably.

Thayer stops with Yulla next to him. He stands tall, lifting his chest high. His hair falls around his face like it has a mind of its own, framing every angle. The reddish-golden specks in his brown eyes shimmer as the sunlight dances across them.

"Well, this is it." He shrugs, and I wonder if he's caught me staring.

"Good luck, Thay." I reach out, instinctively wrapping my arms around him.

Thayer's hands land softly on my lower back as he pulls me to him, the warmth of his body radiating against mine. The scent of him is calming and invigorating, like the forest after a spring rain. And for a moment, I forget about everything else.

When we finally pull away from each other, his eyes lock with mine, and the heat lingers between us.

"I better go," he says. He smiles his Thayer smile and hoists himself into the saddle. He clicks his tongue, and he and Yulla take off toward the glimmering stone Empyrean arena in the distance. The next time I see Thayer, he'll be in that arena. Thousands of spectators will have their eyes transfixed on him and Yulla.

And I'll be just another body in the crowd.

I'm standing in Darwith's stall when the main door to the stable screeches open, jerking me away from my racing thoughts. Maybe Thayer forgot something. I poke my head out of the open top of the stall door, noticing the clock on the wall. It's past noon already. I've wasted over half an hour sitting here sulking.

Someone walks in—someone who is clearly not Thayer. It's another familiar face, but one I didn't expect to see here: Prince Sutagus Molacus, with his silly pointed mustache and all. He's much taller than he appears in the newspaper. His beige skin is pale and smooth, as if he hasn't worked in the sun a day of his life. His body is slender, his clothing pristine.

He slides the door closed behind him, failing to notice me near the end of the aisle of stalls, sticking my head out like a horse. I instinctively duck back down behind Darwith's stall wall, sliding over to the inner corner. Why is the prince of Uladmond *here*?

From my hiding place, I can hear Prince Sutagus at the other end of the stable, opening the tack room door, then closing it—he's checking to see if he's alone. My eyes dart around the stall: wooden walls, the stall door opening up at chest level for the horses to peek out, a water bucket, Darwith in the other corner munching on hay— *the hay*. I crawl to the yellow heap and cover myself with it until I can barely see Darwith, who looks confused about why I've hidden myself in his lunch.

I freeze, hoping Sutagus doesn't find me. I'm not allowed to be in here unless I'm with my father or mucking stalls for work. And I *should* be at the arena by now.

The horses stir, giving me an idea of where Prince Sutagus is as he makes his way down the aisle between the two rows of stalls. From the sound of it, he must be leaning his head into each stall, checking them one by one. Darwith moves to his own stall door and arches his neck out, his big head and long mane creating a visual barrier between me and the outside of the stall.

I hear Sutagus at the stall next to Darwith's, bumping against the door. I inhale and hold my breath. Darwith kicks a hoof into his stall door, and I know Sutagus is standing just a horse-length away from me. Through the blades of hay I can just make out Sutagus's long hand, shoving against Darwith's neck.

"Move," Sutagus growls at Darwith, and I'm afraid I've jumped at the sound of his voice. Darwith steps back, whipping his head, his mane dropping like a thick black curtain over his neck. I can see Sutagus leaning his head into the opening of the stall door, turning to the right—toward the same corner I was just sitting in. Darwith steps between me and Sutagus, blocking my view. I can only imagine

Sutagus surveying the rest of the stall, his eyes trailing over the parts of the hay pile that Darwith isn't blocking. I just hope that no part of my clothing is sticking out, uncovered.

I don't breathe. I don't move.

Sutagus bumps against the next stall, and I know I'm almost in the clear. When he reaches the end of the aisle and turns back, I hear him pass Darwith's stall again, his boots crunching against the tiny pebbles on the ground.

My lungs feel like they'll burst, but I wait for the sounds of Sutagus's step to be further away before I exhale as quietly as possible.

The main stable door squeaks open again. I stay silent and still.

"Are you alone?" Sutagus asks someone, his voice low and gravelly.

"Yes," a familiar voice replies.

My stomach clenches. *Kase.* What is my brother doing here?

"Hearn and Aluma?" Sutagus asks.

Why is he asking about my father…and *me*?

"He's still at home, and Aluma went to the Tournament with her friend," Kase answers.

The main stable door bangs shut, making me jump where I sit, hay falling from my head. Darwith moves over to the stall door, sticking his head out through the top again. I don't move—I *can't* move.

"Did you bring what I asked?" Sutagus's tone is stern.

"It was easy to get. Hidden in our barn. Right where you thought it might be."

"Well, where is it?"

"I'll give it to you soon, but first, do you have the papers?" Kase is confident, almost cocky. He never talks that way around me or Father—and when did he get so comfortable speaking with royalty?

"Where is it?" Sutagus growls. There's a rustle, a thud, and then Kase lets out a groan. "I don't have time for your games. Give me the box, now."

I should help. The prince could be hurting Kase. But instead I pull my knees to my chest, hiding under the hay like a scared mouse.

"Okay, okay," Kase says. "I left it in my saddlebag."

"Go!" Sutagus orders.

I hug my knees closer as the main door slides open. Moments later, it closes again.

"Here it is," Kase says.

"Good job, boy."

"What's so special about this box, anyway?" Kase pries.

"Here are your papers," Sutagus says. "No more questions, and not a word about this to anyone. If I so much as think you've opened your mouth, you won't have a position waiting for you—let alone the health to carry on. Am I making myself clear?"

"Ye-yes, sir." Kase's voice cracks.

The door slides open again.

I wait, frozen. There's no more talking, but someone is still in the main area of the stable, pacing.

A few moments pass.

Papers ruffle.

Kase, I'm sure, with whatever papers Sutagus gave him. I should stand and confront him. But my legs feel weak, and suddenly I'm afraid of Kase—afraid of my own brother. He's more secretive than I've given him credit for.

More secretive than me.

I try not to breathe too loudly, but I can't catch my breath. He's still hiding something from me, and now he's stolen something—*a box*—from our father and given it to the prince of Uladmond. Kase may not respect Father, but stealing from him is a new low. This isn't like my little brother at all.

When the main door finally slides closed again, I stay in Darwith's stall for several more minutes. I hear nothing other than the sounds of the other horses chomping away at their lunches. I stand slowly, hay falling off of me, and peek through the top part of Darwith's stall to confirm.

I'm alone again.

My mind races. Father needs to know about this. Kase and Prince Sutagus are working together on something. I search my memories, trying to think of any boxes my father has lying around that might be of significance to *anyone*—let alone Sutagus—but I can't figure it out.

Twelve forty-five—the time on the wall stands out like a sore thumb. Fifteen minutes to get to the arena. I promised Thayer I'd be there, and my father should be there by now. He'll send someone for Darwith soon, if he hasn't already.

I brush the hay off my clothing and pick the little pieces from my hair. I have to tell my father about the exchange between Sutagus and Kase. Whatever they're up to, it has bad news written all over it.

SEVEN

If I can make it to the judges' circle before the Tournament begins, I can tell my father what I overheard. There are just two things standing in my way: I don't know how to get in, and I don't technically have access to that section of the arena. I'll have to find a spot close enough to get his attention.

The crowds have diminished as I rush down the main street through Cintrenia. I'm later than I thought—only a few people are still filtering in through the giant arena arches. I break into a run when I hear the inaugural opening trumpets sound from inside, a brazen reminder of my constant tardiness.

A uniformed doorman scans my identification card before I pass through the entrance. I ascend the main set of stairs, and the sight of the arena immediately overwhelms me: open above, a long and wide dirt field at the base, surrounded by looming walls with rows upon rows of seats, stacked four stories high. The afternoon sun is too bright, glaring down on me from the cloudless blue sky. This place seems even larger than it did from above on Darwith's back. I swear it gets bigger every year.

The crowds hum a familiar melody as Cintrenia's anthem plays over the speakers—the only soothing sound echoing out over the thousands of spectators. A violinist stands in the middle of the field, the solo performer. Above the rows of seats, a few giant screens feature the woman and her instrument, her hand guiding the bow back and forth across the strings, like a smooth dance.

The remnants of technology from the past never cease to amaze me, and the bittersweet cry of the violin reminds me of the time before the most recent war broke out. And for a moment, I am comforted, but the moment quickly passes as I'm bumped by several people with drinks and snacks in hand, trickling back in to find their seats.

My body feels hot. The cool air should flow in through the top of the open arena, but the thousands of bodies packed together in here make this autumn day far too warm. I yank off my jacket, carrying it underneath my arm as I descend a short set of stairs, entering a new section. Every few steps down is a new row, and each row holds twenty-plus seats, all of them occupied. I glance out at the other sections, rows, and seats—out at the sea of people with heads bobbing, shoulders bumping, feet stomping.

I thank the stars I don't have to find a place to sit amongst them.

Another doorman scans my identification card when I enter the lobby area of the reserved section. It's on the mid-level, one story up from the exact center of the arena field, and admits only retired Empyrean Riders and their families. One section is all that's needed for local retired Empyrean Riders—there aren't many left alive. And since Father is one of the judges, he'll be sitting in the judges' circle: the even fancier royal section directly across the field, luxurious and guarded, with a perfect view of the events. But my father saves seats for me and Kase in this reserved section every year.

Kase. I doubt he'll come to his seat just to watch the king's opening address. He'll probably watch it from the lobby, then leave soon after. He hasn't sat with me in years. And after hearing him speak with Prince Sutagus, I'm not so sure I want him to show. I have too many questions and a few choice things to say to him—none of it nice.

A suited man offers me a fizzy golden drink in a glass flute. I accept it. I'm as thirsty as Darwith after a late-night flight, and we

Cintrenians rarely see such opulence. I hold the flute to my nose; the liquid smells of pears. I take a deep gulp, and the flavor hits my taste buds all at once. It's bitter and strong. I resist the urge to cough, the cool liquid tickling my throat on its way into my nervous stomach.

Before I leave the lobby to find my seat, I peer across the field, attempting to locate my father on the judges' balcony. I spot him. He's in his dark blue suit, sitting a few seats from the king's smaller balcony, which is raised higher than the rest. It's strange seeing my father so close to King Breasal—the same king who created the law that will force my father out of retirement.

Our seats are at an angle from the judges', across the width of the arena, in the first row at the edge of the balcony. I have to focus so I don't fall over the waist-level wall, or knock knees with every seated person. When I raise my eyes, I stop in my tracks. Farann is sitting in the seat next to the only other two empty seats in our row—Kase's seat, and mine. My lips press together, and I seriously consider returning to the lobby.

Too late. Farann turns and spots me, her hazel eyes widening. "You made it!" She stands with a plastered smile. By the looks of her, she's spent more time getting ready than I ever have. Her long, wavy hair has been curled into perfect copper ringlets; her lips are a deep shade of red, matching her dress; her big eyes are outlined in black; her dress is tight at the top and loose at her legs, separated by a wide golden ribbon at her waist. She fits in well with the other Uladmondians here, in their lavish outfits. It's me who is out of place.

It always is.

"I wouldn't miss it," I say, forcing a smile. I consider leaving Kase's vacant seat between us, but decide against it and sit next to her.

I gaze out at the empty dirt field. *No small talk, no small talk.* I am uncomfortable enough as it is. My hands are clammy and the sounds of the crowd are reverberating in my ears. Perspiration clings to my skin after my sprint from the stables, burying me under layers of noise and waves of heat, reminding me of why I hate crowds. I swear it's more crowded today than any other year. The Tournament hasn't even started yet, and I'm ready for it to end.

"Did you give Kase the envelope?" Farann asks, leaning closer. My nose tingles as I catch a whiff of her peachy perfume.

"Yes, I did." My eyes stay on the arena, but my mind darts back to Kase. Where is he, anyway? I guess he's too busy making trades with Prince Sutagus.

I clench my jaw and turn to Farann. "What was in it—the envelope?" The words escape my mouth much more boldly, more accusatory, than planned.

Farann sits straight, acknowledging my sudden shift in tone. "I'm not sure. My father instructed me to give it to him last night. I believe it's from the prince." She watches me, her face mirroring my own puzzled look.

I stare at her, remembering her the way she was when we were kids—when she was my friend. She looks at me with concern, the same look she used to give me when I was in trouble with my mother. And right then, I know it: she's telling the truth.

I return my gaze to the arena. An unfamiliar song is playing over the speakers. It's not soothing like Cintrenia's song, and my ears pulse as the beat thumps. What is my brother hiding? Even Farann doesn't know what was in the envelope.

"Aluma…" Farann's voice is a whisper beside me.

I face her, half expecting her to call me out for my intensity. Farann's lips twist to one side, and she lets out a sigh through her nose. "It's been a long time since we've spent time together. Remember when we used to come to these?"

Of course I remember. She was once my best friend.

"When my father moved us to the capital, I had no friends," she says. "I was alone, and I missed you. I think I cut you out of my life because it was easier to pretend I didn't have any friends than having one best friend that I'd never see."

Her eyes are glossy. The old me would put a hand on her arm, tell her everything is all right. But I'm still hurt by what she did.

"I've been wanting to say…" She shakes her head and sighs again. "I'm sorry."

I'm sorry. I never realized the weight I'd been carrying around until this moment. It's nice to hear her explain, but it's still strange, after all these years. I'd long since ceased to expect a sincere apology after such a hurtful rejection.

"I had my father get our seats close together, so I could tell you that. I'm sorry, okay?" She smiles, in a desperate sort of way—a way I haven't seen her smile since we were kids.

Gratitude washes over me. "Thank you," I tell her.

The horn announcing the king's arrival blares from the speakers, jolting me. Large monitors on either side of the king's balcony display his pallid, round face as he ascends the few stairs to his raised dais. He looks much older than my father. His hair is gray, at least what's left of it. Ornate shapes cover his golden throne, reflecting the sunlight, causing a glow to fill the small stage. The king seems to be shining, too—especially his balding head.

Thousands of people stand at once. Not because most of them want to stand, but because they are cued to do so. Uladmondians love their king, and all the accompanying lifestyle perks of living in the Otherside. Cintrenians, on the other hand, aren't as keen on the king, or any of his laws. Some may even remember what Ivernister was like before Uladmondian rule. When we had our independence. Our own king.

Our freedom.

But they stand all the same.

I stay in my seat.

"People of Eirelannia," a high-pitched voice screeches over the speakers. A tall, slender man with light brown skin and close-cropped black hair, wearing a lavender suit, holds a microphone as he emerges onto the dirt arena below the king's stage. "I, Egan Frye, give you your protector, your merciful leader, your gracious royal highness…King Breasal Molacus the Third!"

Egan Frye lifts his free hand and flips his wrist so his palm is facing the sky, as if he's letting a dove fly free. The crowd erupts, stomping their feet in unison, awaiting the king's opening address.

I squint to where my father is sitting, beneath the king's balcony to the right, just as Prince Sutagus walks in through the door to the stage, carrying a small black object. I can't make out what it is, and the cameras are still fixed on the king. As Sutagus moves to his chair, my father catches sight of the box-like shape in Sutagus's hands and stands immediately. A guard steps forward, and my father slowly takes his seat again. But even from this distance, I can see his eyes are still trained on the rectangular black box.

The stomping increases, making the ground shake. I wipe my damp hands on my pants. The cameras pull out from their focus on the king for a wide view. My father and Sutagus are in the foreground on the screen. My eyes dart to the object in Sutagus's hands—a shiny black box with three silver lines standing upright on the side.

It catches the light as Sutagus places it between his shoes. The light flashes into my eyes, all the way from across the arena. My vision blurs as I catch another glimpse of my father. A hardness covers his face. I want to run to him and explain how the box came to be here. Judging by his expression, there must be something important inside of it.

"Are you okay?" Farann's hand lands on my shaking fingers.

I blink at her, unable to find the right words. "I…"

The king's voice booms from the speakers. "My dear Eirelannians!"

My eyes refocus on his plump face as it fills the monitors.

"Welcome to yet another year—another Autumn Tournament!" His lips curve on either side into a tight smile. The roar of the crowd rises and falls like a wave, cresting and breaking.

"On this day, we shall test the new, reward the old, and select the next generation of Empyrean Riders." He gestures at the audience. "Empyrean Riders who will work tirelessly around the clock to keep you and your fellow Uladmondians and Ivernisterians protected from the darkness that continues to seep in from the Old World."

The king pauses, turning to face the balcony where my father is sitting.

"Thanks to the Empyrean Cavalry that my grandfather, the great King Murchad, created to protect us, we can rest assured we will all remain safe here in our joint kingdoms."

On the monitor, I see my father shifting uncomfortably in his seat.

For a quick moment, the king's eyes meet my father's steely gaze. The moment passes, and the king turns back to face the people. The crowd is none the wiser.

But *I* saw the way the king looked at my father—as if he were warning him.

"Today, I hope to give you a preview of what's to come. Our two kingdoms, Uladmond and Ivernister, *united*, stronger than ever, with the common goal of shutting out the evil attempting to infiltrate and destroy our righteous kingdoms."

The crowd stomps, and my body tenses as the vibrations of thousands of pounding feet rattle my whole body from the inside.

"We shall destroy those who fight against us. Once and for all!" The king's voice echoes. "We shall free Eirelannia from all the darkness, bringing in a new age—a time when people will work together for the greater good of their fellow man. For our kingdoms!"

I can't take it anymore. I have to figure out a way to my father. Right now.

I jump to my feet and thrust myself down the narrow row of stomping spectators. When I reach the end of the seats, I flee into the lobby. My heart is pounding and I can't catch my breath. There are too many people, and they're all staring at the large monitors displaying the king's face. The cameras zoom out and display the dirt field in its entirety, the king's balcony precisely at the midpoint, jutting out like a petulant bottom lip.

"Let the Autumn Tournament begin!" The king raises his hands and the crowd cries out once more.

I hurry to the lobby balcony and grip the railing, the wide-open field in front of me. A dozen wingless horses with their riders gallop out from the main arena doors at the left curve of the arena. Half the riders direct their horses in one direction, staying on the border, while the other half speed the opposite way, launching into the pre-competition spectacle.

As the riders reach the other end of the arena, they look as if they'll crash into one another. Instead, they maneuver their horses, crisscrossing between each other. The first horse running from one direction edges between the two in a row speeding toward him. Back and forth they go, running at full speed, braiding their way through the line of horses. A grand, but frightening display of agility and skill.

The monitors on the sides of the judges' circle zoom in for close-ups of the riders. The cameras pan over each rider, all dressed in their competition jerseys. Their faces stony and alert. Thayer's face fills the big screens for a moment. His eyes are focused past Yulla's head as he weaves his way through the other horses blazing straight at him. He seems confident and calm. And despite the uneasiness spilling over my body, a moment of happiness—a moment of pride—passes through me. Thayer is finally in the Empyrean arena.

Someone touches my arm, and I whip around.

"Aluma? What's going on? Are you ill?" Farann's eyes are wide.

"No, I—I need to talk to my father."

"You just took off, and you look like you've seen a ghost." She cocks her head, studying my face. "What's going on? You can talk to me."

I suck in a breath. I *can* talk to Farann. She was my best friend once, and I don't really have any other options—Thayer is racing around the field, and my father is on the other side of the arena. I swallow my pride, pushing aside the years of rejection I felt because of her. At least she never betrayed me, told none of my secrets. And somehow, I know I can still trust her.

"My father—something's wrong," I say finally. "I don't know what it is, but something strange is going on."

"What do you mean?" Farann twists me around to face the monitors. "Look—you can see him."

It's true. My father is still sitting in his seat on the balcony near the king.

"He's right there, doing his job," she says.

The camera pulls out into a wide angle to show the king's stage, the judges' circle, and the dirt field below. The riders and their horses blaze past the cameras. I squint at Sutagus still sitting in his chair, the little black box resting between his feet.

"Farann, do you know what that is? There?" I point to the screen. "Between Prince Sutagus's feet. What is that?"

She blinks. "It looks like a box?"

"That's what I thought. Any idea what the prince might want with it?"

Farann wrinkles her brow. "Actually, I might…I remember hearing something about a box, yesterday."

"And?"

"Before we left Tarmensil. I overheard my parents talking."

"What did they say?"

She frowns. "Something about the final boxes being collected." She pauses. "Oh, and that a message would be sent, *loud and clear*."

I stare at the ground. A message. What message?

She crosses her arms. "What's going on?"

"That's what I'm trying to figure out." I run my hand through my hair. "I need to find out what's in the box. I think it belongs to my father."

"Belongs to your father?" Her eyes narrow.

"Before I came to the Tournament, I saw Prince Sutagus with Kase." I lower my voice, but no one is listening. They all seem too entranced by the opening performance. "I think Kase stole it from my father and gave it to the prince. An exchange or something…"

Farann stares at me blank-faced. "You're right, something weird is going on." She bites her lower lip and grabs my hand. "Come on, we're going to find out." She uses her hips to bump her way through the crowd to a door in the corner of the lobby area, pulling me along.

"Where are we going?"

"The back way to the judges' circle," she says.

"A back way?" I stop behind her at the door. "You know a back way to the judges' circle?"

Farann turns around, holding her pointer finger to her mouth, surveying the nearby area. No one is watching. She pulls her identification card out from the ribbon at her waist. "One of the perks of your father getting in with the king's circle—special privileges and shortcuts." She shrugs. For a moment, I want to hug her.

She inserts her card into a thin slot by the door handle. The lock clicks. Farann pushes the door open, and I follow her in.

 EIGHT

A blast of cool air hits my skin, and I'm grateful for it. Farann pushes the door closed behind me, and I hear the lock engage once more. Aside from the muffled applause and my heart pounding, the hallway is nearly silent. Long and dimly lit, I can see that it runs in both directions. Farann leads us at a quick pace to our right where the hallway appears to curve off in the distance, presumably around one of the narrow ends of the arena.

The image of my father's face when he saw Sutagus with the box circulates through my mind. I realize I might miss the rest of Thayer's performance, but the sinking feeling in my stomach is deepening, and it's too strong to ignore.

We walk for what seems like forever before arriving at another door. Farann uses the same keycard to open it. The light from outside glares into the dim hallway. I lift my hand, shielding my eyes as they readjust.

The crowds are quieter when we scamper out. Finely clothed Uladmondians saunter across the fountain-laden deck, sipping on sparkling drinks to the soft sounds of a harpist. It's even more luxurious in person. I've never been given the chance to see this area before, given that it's strictly reserved for the king's inner circle and the upper elite. Even Farann has to sit in the section for retired Empyrean Riders with me; only her father gets inner circle privileges.

"This way," Farann says, tilting her head toward a grand staircase made of white stone.

The glistening steps curve around, up another level. It's fancier than anything I could imagine. But I'm not too surprised—everything Uladmondian is opulent.

The field comes into view as we ascend the stairs. It's cleared, no horses or riders in sight. A wave of disappointment washes over me—I missed the rest of Thayer's performance. Hopefully I'll be able to see more of him during the competition phase.

Egan Frye struts back out onto the field with a microphone in hand. He's changed out of his purple suit and into an even more lavish outfit—a white suit with golden sequins, stitched in the shape of the sun, rays and all, sparkling in the light of the real sun.

"Wow, wow, wow!" Egan's shrill voice echoes through the speakers as we reach the top of the stairs. "What do you think of this year's Empyrean Cavalry hopefuls, hm?"

The audience shouts its approval.

Farann and I pause at the top of the stairs, watching as Egan speaks. He moves closer to the center of the field. His gray eyes and long face fill the big screens, and suddenly I feel like the king's announcer is staring directly at me. As if he's watching my every move.

I glance around, but somehow, no one seems to have noticed us. Farann fits in well, but in my plain clothing, I must look like a yellow duckling in a pen of peacocks.

"There is an abundance of talent this year, wouldn't you say?" Egan purses his pouty lips to a chorus of approving whistles and shouts. "And plenty more to come when the competitions begin!"

Farann and I surge forward, bumping into the guard standing at the entrance to the judges' circle. I peek around him and notice with alarm that the judges' seats are empty, including my father's.

"But first—people of Eirelannia, are you ready to watch one of the most talented Empyrean Riders of all time, as he demonstrates what an Empyrean steed can *really* do?" Egan tempts.

The crowd stomps just as much as they did earlier for the king. The vibrations shake inside my ears. Only one other person gets this much attention, this much actual praise and respect in Eirelannia.

My father.

"I give you…Hearn Banks!" Egan lifts his hand to the sky, and the crowds erupts with cheers.

My eyes stay on the wide-open field as Egan quickly strides off. Above the stands, on the far side, something catches my eye. Darwith flies over the top of the open arena, my father on his back. They dive above the stands, barely out of reach from the crowd's outstretched hands. My father directs Darwith to the middle of the field, right where Egan was standing moments before.

Farann grabs my arm. "There's the prince!" she says in a loud whisper, pointing at Sutagus as he ascends the stairs to the king's balcony, the small black box in his hands. The king approaches him with a smug look on his face. Farann tries to move past the guard in front of us, but he doesn't budge.

"This is a restricted area," the guard says.

"We're not getting through this way," I tell Farann.

And I need to get closer.

I rush back down the grand staircase, darting across the deck, bumping into Uladmondians left and right.

The crowd *oohs* and *ahhs*, shielding their eyes as my father and Darwith fly straight up over the center of the field, like an arrow blazing at the sun. The crowd lowers their hands and seems to hold their collective breath as Darwith and my father come back into clear view in their trademark tailspin, spiraling straight toward the ground.

A dark shadow falls over my father and Darwith. I glance toward the sun, expecting to see a cloud overtaking it—but there isn't one. A chill runs through me as I look back at the field. This is the moment when my father should pull Darwith out of their spin.

But he doesn't.

Time seems to slow as they continue to spin. Suddenly, Darwith's left wing breaks from its outstretched position, fluttering wildly at his side. My father leans over to look. They're still at least a hundred feet from the ground when Darwith drops hard to his left, *falling*—not flying. My father loses his grip at the unexpected movement, tumbling out of the saddle and plummeting straight toward the ground.

"No!" My voice leaps from my throat, my hands reaching out in a futile effort.

A bright light erupts from near the king's balcony. A feeling of warmth fills my body as I squint past the beam of light. Darwith's broken left wing is flapping vigorously again.

Then the light and the warmth vanishes.

Darwith dives to reach my father.

But it's too late.

My heart stops as my father crashes to the ground—legs breaking beneath him, back bending, and head thumping against the dirt. Darwith lands on all four hooves beside him, with only a minor stumble.

The crowd falls silent.

"Father!" I dart around a distracted Uladmondian guard standing in front of the smaller set of stairs leading to the ground level. As I nearly stumble past Egan Frye in his bright outfit, I know I'm heading straight to the field.

When my feet hit the dirt, I sprint to my father. Darwith is nudging his motionless form with his muzzle. I collapse to my knees beside them, cradling my father's head with one hand and reaching for one of his hands with my other.

My vision blurs. "Father…"

His eyes barely open as he tries to speak. He lets out a painful groan.

"You're going to be okay," I assure him. He *has* to be okay.

The large doors at the end of the field burst open and a group of medics rush out with a stretcher.

"Hurry!" I yell to them.

"Aluma…" My father attempts to squeeze my hand.

"I'm here." I lean closer to him.

He locks eyes with me. "You must join the Empyrean Cavalry. Now." His voice is a faint whisper.

"But Father—"

He grimaces. "Lermyn...get Lermyn to nominate you..."

"But you told me—"

"I know, little Lumi," Father says. "But you must do this. You were made to fly. And you have an advantage with all your practice." He tries to smile, but his face tenses with pain.

He *knows* I've been flying. I have no idea how, but it doesn't matter now. His legs are mangled, and even if he survives, he'll never fly again. I choke back the bile that rises in my throat and look into his pained eyes.

"I wanted to protect you from the darkness, but now you're the only light—" He coughs, and blood covers his lips, dripping down his face.

I wipe the blood away from his chin, my eyes filling with tears.

"Find Rinehart Quin." More blood trickles from his nose and mouth.

"Hold on!" I plead.

"Be strong, and don't trust anyone..." His eyelids flicker, and he starts to lose consciousness.

"Father!"

He pushes his eyes open once more. "Keep the light. Keep the light..." Then his eyes close, and he goes limp in my arms.

Tears stream down my face and onto his. The medics rush over, prying me away as they check his pulse.

"He's still alive," a medic declares as they hoist my father onto the stretcher.

I am lost. I am frozen. *I am broken.*

They carry him to the arena doors. I run next to them, taking my father's limp hand into mine, squeezing it tight. The crowd has risen from their seats, but they remain eerily silent.

"He's in bad shape," one medic says. "Bring him straight to Tar-mensil—it's his only chance."

Everything inside of me wants to stay by my father's side. I can't let him go to Tarmensil without me. He needs me.

Then his hand twitches in mine. I squeeze it as his voice replays in my mind—*you must join the Empyrean Cavalry.*

And I know—I have to stay here. I have to trust my father. *Darkness—the only light?* He's not making sense; the damage to his body must not only be external. But still, he shouldn't have fallen at all. It's almost as if something *caused* him to fall—and I need to find out what it was.

I lift his hand to my face, touching it to my cheek before placing it gently to his side. "I love you," I whisper to him as they lift his stretcher into the emergency karrier. They close the doors, and in another moment they take off through the tunnel and out of sight.

I'm left shattered, like the bones in his body.

I turn back to the arena. Darwith walks toward me, his head low. I hurry over to him, wrapping my arms around his thick neck. Bursts of sobs escape me as Darwith rubs my shoulder with his warm muzzle.

"Please, everyone, remain in your seats," Egan Frye's chipper voice says over the main speakers. "The situation is under control."

But it's not. *It's really not.*

A few arena workers rush onto the field, using shovels to scoop my father's blood from the ground, kicking new dirt over top of it, making it look as if nothing happened. As if they could ever erase the image of my father, one of the greatest Empyrean Riders of all time, falling from the sky.

 NINE

My body won't stop shaking as I lead Darwith away from the large doors, farther into the tunnel, away from the murmuring crowd.

Someone grabs my free hand and squeezes. I turn to face Thayer; his face is devoid of color and his eyes are full of tears. I know in a heartbeat he saw my father's fall.

He draws me to his chest. "I'm so sorry."

Thayer's warmth surrounds me as I dissolve in his arms. "I don't know what to do," I blubber into his shirt. "I need to find Kase. I need to tell him…" I pull away, my eyes darting around, searching for my brother.

Farann scurries over to us. "What happened—is he okay?" She throws her arms around me. I haven't hugged her like this since we were kids, but I need all the comfort I can get right now, so I give in and embrace her in return.

"They took him to Tarmensil," I tell her, my body trembling from head to toe.

Pull it together. Pull it together.

"He's still alive?" She draws back and rests her hands on my shoulders, steadying me.

"He's still alive," I echo, my own words sinking in.

My father is still alive. A bit of hope remains.

Farann exhales. "Thank the stars!"

I suck in a breath and turn back to Thayer. "Will you help me find Kase? He needs to know what happened."

"Of course. Anything you need," he says.

"I'll help, too," Farann tells me.

"Thank you. If you find him, tell him to come back here. And then find me," I direct her.

She touches my shoulder, giving me a sympathetic smile, before hiking her dress up off the ground and dashing away.

"I have to go. There's something else I have to do," I tell Thayer, my father's instructions repeating in my mind.

His eyebrows pull together in confusion.

"I have to find someone—I have to compete today," I sputter.

Thayer looks startled. "What are you talking about?"

"My father, he told me to find—" I stop myself, remembering my father telling me not to trust anyone. But I can trust Thayer. "He said I need to join the Empyrean Cavalry—*today.*"

Thayer tilts his head, studying me. "Your father told you that?"

"Before he lost consciousness, he told me I need to join the Empyrean Cavalry. I have to follow his wishes. I have to find Lermyn Githah—Father said he'll nominate me, so I can compete."

"Who? You're going to *compete*?" He stands frozen, pale-faced. "But it's—it's *dangerous*, Aluma." He rests a hand on his forehead, like he's shielding himself from what I'm telling him.

I turn to Darwith, checking him over for injuries. His wings are pulled to his sides and his head is low, much lower than I've ever seen such a proud steed carry it. He doesn't appear to have any external trauma, but from the way he's standing and the emptiness in his eyes, I can feel it: he's hurting inside—just like me.

Thayer's gaze remains on the ground when I mount Darwith.

"Thay." I wait for his eyes to meet mine. "Please. I have to go. If you find my brother, make sure you keep an eye on him." My teeth clench together before I let my next words out. "I don't trust him."

Thayer frowns, reaching his hand up to squeeze mine. "Be careful."

Darwith and I take off. We canter past a group of Empyrean Cavalry hopefuls on the way out of the arena. Their jaws drop at the sight of me.

I grip the reins more tightly as I realize: I'm on Darwith—an *Empyrean steed*—for the first time in public. No longer masked by the night. I'm riding an Empyrean steed, and I'm not an Empyrean Rider.

I'm going to be in so much trouble.

The sun blazes down on us when we exit the arena doors. I direct Darwith toward the tailor shop and give him a squeeze. Lermyn should still be there—he said he had work to do today. I attempt to keep my head low as we speed along. We don't need an audience. Darwith's large black wings are tucked in at his sides, but they're still conspicuous, and he's more recognizable than most other Empyrean steeds.

A stunning dapple-gray horse canters over to us on the deserted road to the tailor shop, a rider on its back. My eyes widen when I realize it's *my* horse, Cashel, with Lermyn riding him.

"Mr. Githah?" I call out as they approach.

"Aluma," he says, blank-faced. It only takes a moment for me to register that he's not surprised to see me.

"My father—did you see?" I move Darwith next to them. "Why are you riding Cashel?" My eyes dart between Cashel and Lermyn.

"I was there, Aluma. I'm so sorry," he says, pain in his voice.

"He told me to find you. He told me to have you nominate me to compete in the Tournament today."

He lets out a ragged breath. "And did you give your father my message?"

My body trembles. "Yes."

"Then it makes sense. *They know.*" His grip tightens on Cashel's reins.

"*Who* knows—*what* do they know?"

He shakes his head. "I had hoped it wouldn't come to this. When your father fell, I went straight to the stables to retrieve Cashel for you. You'll need him to compete."

"How did you even know about Cashel? Father only gave him to me this morning, after I visited your shop."

Lermyn wipes his forehead. "There's no time to explain, but you must compete. You *must* join the Empyrean Cavalry. It has to be you." His tone is deeper as he says almost the same things as my father. "I will nominate you to compete today."

I open my mouth to speak, but no words come out. I clench my fists, attempting to steady my nerves.

This is really happening. I'm actually going to compete.

"We must hurry. Follow me." Lermyn turns Cashel in a tight circle. Darwith and Cashel carry us back toward the arena—the last place I want to be right now. And I notice, despite my grief, that Lermyn can still ride well, even if he is retired, old, and in pain.

Thousands of spectators cheer in the distance; by the sound of it, they didn't waste any time moving past my father's horrific fall. The knot in my stomach twists tighter as I replay his accident in my head. Darwith's hooves pound the ground beneath us, and I glance at his left wing, the same one that seemed to break in the sky. There's nothing wrong with it now. Why did it stop working for those few critical moments?

We pass the same doors where I exited to find Lermyn earlier—the same doors through which they took my father. I push back against the urge to cry as we ride close to the walls of the arena; they curve around to the narrow end, toward the same section Farann and I must have gone through on the inside.

Ahead on the right, a group of trees sits between the bordering Tarmen Canal and the arena. To the left there's a docked water karrier. It's a stately karrier in a rectangular shape, nearly the size of our barn at home, with black sun panels lining the top and windows in the shape of mountain peaks on the exterior. It's not a basic emergency karrier like the one they must have transported my father on. This one in the canal looks fit for a king—*the* king.

Lermyn slows Cashel into a slow trot as we approach the trees.

SHINA REYNOLDS

We maneuver down a small path. To our left, there's another path leading to the water karrier, but to the right, there's an entrance to a cave that appears to go *under* the arena in the direction of the king's balcony, where I watched my father fall.

Once we're inside, Lermyn stops Cashel. "We can walk from here."

I slide off Darwith and rub his jaw, looking into his dark eyes. I sense his pain, because I feel it, too: a dull ache rolling over my heart like a giant boulder crushing everything in its path. Darwith's not responsible for my father's fall. I know that much. I wish I could take away his pain and guilt.

"It's okay, Dar," I whisper to him, holding his whiskered muzzle in my hands. He putters when I kiss him on his forehead.

Lermyn dismounts Cashel and hobbles over to the side of the cave. "We can leave them here. They'll be safe." He gestures over to a water trough set against the stone walls.

I lead Darwith and Cashel to the water. Darwith takes a long drink, and I watch as he allows his wings to relax. They've been tucked to his sides since the medics carried my father away.

"Let's go," Lermyn says. He's already walking ahead, scanning the cave.

The darkness is a welcome change for my eyes. It's quiet, too, aside from the muffled sounds of the arena, presumably above us now. The cave looks abandoned, or maybe hidden, compared to the large tunnel where the competitors usually wait. There's no one lingering in here, and I'm thankful for it.

"Where are we going?" I ask, catching up with Lermyn in a few quick strides.

He glances at me, picking up his pace. "Did your father ever tell you about the Empyrean Committee?"

I blink, trying to remember. "*Committee?* No."

"To be nominated, one must first be presented to the Committee, especially in this type of last-minute ordeal." He squints into the darkness ahead. "I haven't been on the board for some time, but I was once the head of the Committee. I should still be able to nominate you."

My mind spins. There's so much my father never told me. Why is it all coming out today?

The light diminishes as we trudge deeper into the cave. Water drips somewhere ahead, and the temperature has dropped to the point where I'm now wishing I hadn't left my jacket somewhere earlier in all the confusion.

I follow closely behind Lermyn, trying not to lose him in the darkness. A few lights are situated along the path, barely illuminating more than a few feet out from where they're placed. Hardly useful.

A reddish glow flickers from the right side of the cave. "What's that?" I ask, alarmed.

"Ah—here we are." He turns to the red light. For a moment, it appears he will walk directly into the stony wall of the tunnel, but instead, he passes straight through it. "This way."

I follow him through the false wall into an even smaller cave, and a chill falls over my whole body. By now we must be far beneath the arena. There's no sunlight down here, and the air is damp and frigid, the cold sinking in through my pores.

Lermyn stops under another flickering red light that sits above a wooden door. He leans the side of his head against the wood, pressing his ear flat. He peers over at me. "Are you ready?"

I shrug. "I don't know." *How could I be?*

Lermyn places his hands on my shoulders. "You can do this. Your father wouldn't have asked if he didn't believe in you."

A lump forms in my throat. "Thanks." I gulp down a deep breath and try to force a smile.

Until today, my father made me promise never to join the Empyrean Cavalry. But everything is backward now. Nothing makes sense.

I want to sprint off at full speed back in the direction we came from. But it's too late. There's nowhere to run.

 TEN

L ermyn taps on the door.

    I stand frozen. I should be excited. I'm at the door of possibility. And yet, my father's pained face keeps crossing my mind, over and over.

I'm here for him. I'm here to become an Empyrean Rider.

I'm the only light—

Whatever that means.

Muffled voices echo from the other side of the door. After a few long moments, it unlocks. I catch myself holding my breath and force it out.

Lermyn glances at me with a reassuring smile.

Here we go.

A statuesque woman opens the door. The skintight yellow ensemble she's wearing stands in contrast to her deep brown skin and her buzz-cut black hair. She's maybe a few years older than me and at least several inches taller.

She glares at Lermyn with piercing golden eyes.

"Zarshona?" Lermyn shuffles a step back. His mouth drops as he adjusts his glasses.

She doesn't flinch.

A pained expression falls over Lermyn's face before he clears his throat. "I'm here to speak with the Committee."

Zarshona raises her arched black eyebrows. "In what regard?" Her voice slithers out like a protective hiss.

"I've come to nominate a new Empyrean Cavalry hopeful for the competitions today," he tells her, pulling his shoulders back.

Zarshona's eyes land on me, and her full lips turn into a sneer. *"Her?"* A small laugh escapes from her nose. "You are aware the competitions are about to begin?"

Lermyn's eyes narrow. "Hence the need for me to speak with the Committee *now*."

Zarshona waits a moment, tilting her slender face. Then she pulls the door open further. "This way."

A rush of warm air sweeps across my skin as we pass through the doorway. Bright lights adorn the old stone walls and a large metal door sits on the opposite side of the room. This room and the cave we came from must have been here for generations, long before the arena was built above. Uladmondian men lounge around small tables, staring at us with disapproving eyes as we walk past, whispering to one another.

Zarshona pauses in front of the metal door. She turns to face us, pushing the door open with one hand. She lifts her chin, signaling for us to enter. "Good luck," she says, a smirk forming on her lips.

I glance back over my shoulder after we enter. Zarshona watches me as she closes the door between us. I turn to Lermyn, tempted to ask what her problem is. But I keep my mouth shut.

This room is smaller than the previous. A domed shape made of glass sits in the middle, like a smaller-scale version of the arena above us. A few more Uladmondian men, this time in uniform, sit in swiveling chairs around the dome. They're silent, watching us as we near them. A desk rests at the end of the room with a tall chair behind it, turned away from us, facing a wide map of Eirelannia on the wall.

My gaze moves from side to side. There aren't any more doors other than the one we came through. No more rooms to enter. My heart rate quickens as I realize we're here—wherever *here* is. The seated men turn in their chairs as we cross the room, eyeing us as we approach the large desk.

"When I heard the great Lermyn Githah was making his way through the halls, I couldn't believe my ears," a husky voice says from behind the large chair. "To what do I owe the pleasure?" The chair swivels around on its axis, and Prince Sutagus's icy blue eyes stare directly into mine.

Lermyn stands tall. "I'm here to nominate Aluma Banks as a potential Empyrean Rider, to compete in the competitions today."

Sutagus flashes a wicked smile, his pointy ash-blond mustache curling up on either side of his lips. "Now that's something I didn't see coming." He looks me over from head to toe.

My body tenses as the urge to run and hide overwhelms me, like a small animal trying to protect itself.

"I am so sorry about your father. What a tragedy." The prince opens and closes his spindly hands. "But rest assured, he will receive the *best* care in Tarmensil."

"Where did they take him?" My voice lurches out of me, as if it could attack the prince and his ridiculous mustache. "Is he safe? What happened out—"

Sutagus raises his hand to silence me, taking his time to respond. "He's on his way to Tarmensil, where he will receive the utmost attention. Trust me when I say we will do our very best to keep your father alive."

Keep him alive. Why don't I feel comforted by any of this? Why does every word Sutagus says feel like little pieces of gravel being caught in an open wound?

I should have gone with my father.

Sutagus's eyes linger on me for far too long before he turns back to Lermyn. "All twelve spots are filled," he says, another smile forming on his face. "Are you suggesting we instate the thirteenth rider option?"

"Indeed." Lermyn nods. "She meets the age requirement *and*, as a bonus, she is of Empyrean Rider blood."

Sutagus snorts. "Well, of course she is."

A few chuckles echo from behind us. The uniformed men have risen from their seats and moved to surround us, creating a barrier, blocking our way to the door. My heart speeds up as the urge to escape intensifies. Lermyn peers over at me and shakes his head slightly.

But I am ready to run.

"You know," the prince says, placing his hand on his square chin, his eyes falling back on me, "she bears a striking resemblance to her mother, *Caelina*."

My mother. I haven't heard her name spoken in a long time. What could he possibly know about *my* mother?

"I was referring to her father, *Hearn*," Lermyn says.

Sutagus's smile disappears. "But of course." His eyes finally move away from me.

Lermyn clears his throat. "As the former head of this Committee, and considering the requirements she meets, I give my personal recommendation and support to Aluma Banks."

The room falls silent. I can hear my heart thumping in my chest.

"Committee members," Sutagus says with a teasing laugh, looking past us. "What say you? Should this girl be nominated to compete today?"

"Sutagus, we both know the decision is *yours*," Lermyn interjects, shaking his head. "Let's not waste any more time."

"Be calm, Mr. Githah, there's plenty of time yet." Sutagus rises to his feet, and Lermyn takes a small step back. Sutagus traces the corners of his desk with a long, pointy finger as he circles around it, until he's standing before us. He's even taller than I thought, just like the rest of the Uladmondians.

He steps closer to me, and my muscles twitch to move. But somehow I remain still as his hand lands on my arm, his thin fingers gripping my shoulder, like a spider clutching its prey. I keep my eyes down, so I can only see his mouth.

"Aluma…" Sutagus almost whispers my name, sending a shiver down my spine. "You certainly have grown since I last saw you."

Last time he saw me—we've met? Where have I ever seen him

in person before he met with Kase this morning? My eyes dart up, searching his face for some sort of clue, any explanation.

Sutagus cocks his head. "I'll allow you to compete. But your safety can't be guaranteed. You will be in the same position as any other competitor." He raises his eyebrows, releasing my shoulder.

I exhale. *Finally.* My nails dig into my palms as my fists tighten. "That's fine with me," I tell him, once again surprised by my boldness.

He glances at my fists and smiles. His eyes are wide with appreciation when they meet mine again. I hold his gaze, and the smile on his face becomes a full-on grin. "Just as I thought—much more like your mother."

Lermyn clears his throat. "Is the nomination complete?"

"Yes, you have my permission to proceed." Sutagus gives my arm another uncomfortable squeeze and gestures to the door with his chin, but his gaze stays fixed on me.

I turn to Lermyn. He's staring at Sutagus with the same hostility boiling up inside of me.

"Let's go," Lermyn says, edging his way between the uniformed men.

I exchange another glance with Sutagus before backing away through the parted men, away from him and his unnecessary closeness.

The door opens as we approach. Zarshona is waiting outside.

"Tread carefully, *little Lumi*," Sutagus calls after me as I step over the threshold.

I stop in my tracks. *Lumi*—my father's nickname for me. I whirl back around to face him, but Zarshona shuts the door behind us before I can say a word.

When Zarshona leads us back through the first room, the Uladmondian men are gone. The competitions start soon, and *I* will be in them. It doesn't seem quite real.

Zarshona peers at me with a strange smirk before she leaves Lermyn and me on the other side of the first door to the cave. She seems to have a secret—one she'll never tell, I'm sure. And as much as I'd like to know what it is, I'm thankful when she closes the door, and Lermyn and I are alone again.

We wait a moment, standing under the flickering red light in the cave. I inhale, and the cold air fills my lungs. There's something strange going on. Everything in me is screaming for me to open my eyes and pay attention—and that my father's accident wasn't an *accident*. It makes little sense, and I have to know the truth.

"I'm sorry," Lermyn says, finally. "I should've warned you about Sutagus." He scoffs at the prince's name and trudges off back through the cave.

"I didn't know there was a Committee," I say, scurrying after him. "Or that *he* was the head of it."

"Sutagus was appointed by the king after your father retired."

"And that woman—"

"Zarshona."

"She knows you?" I ask, remembering how they reacted to seeing each other.

He glances over at me. "She was once in a position similar to yours. But it would appear she's since found a new place in this world." Pain—or maybe sadness—flickers in his eyes.

My mother's face, or at least how I remember it, flashes through my mind. "How does Sutagus know my mother?"

Lermyn stops in his tracks, searching my face. "Your father..." He shakes his head. "I can't. That's up to your father to discuss with you." He moves ahead, and I hurry after him.

"But I can't ask him now." There's a bitterness in my voice. "What do you know? Do you know anything about that box Sutagus had right before my father fell?"

Lermyn stops and turns to me.

"You can't really believe what happened to my father was an *accident*?" I say, my muscles clenching as I imagine my father hitting the ground again and again, like a wheel of pain in a never-ending cycle. "Something happened to him. My father—Darwith—that couldn't have been an accident." I shake my head, refusing to believe that what I saw was my father's or Darwith's fault.

Lermyn lifts his palm to his forehead and sighs. "There are many things you don't yet understand, but there isn't time to explain it all now. The time will come when all will be made clear. But for now, you must focus on the task at hand. Trying to explain everything would only distract you from what you must do."

I examine his wrinkled face. "Please. Why can't you just tell me?" My voice squeaks, and I feel like a child again, one who isn't mature enough to be let in on the adults' secrets. He's hiding something. Just like my father did. Just like Kase did. And I hate it.

Lermyn shakes his head and hobbles off. "It isn't my place to tell you. And as I said, there's no time. We need to hurry."

I stop in my tracks. My lips pinch together, and my hands find my hips. "I'm going to find out what's going on. With or without your help."

He turns and waits, glancing at me once more with a trace of remorse. "I'm sorry. But you need to prepare for the competition. They don't think you have a chance at succeeding, but you *must*."

I decide I can't win this battle. He won't budge. I'll figure it out without him later. I remember what my father told me before—join the Empyrean Cavalry. Find Rinehart Quin.

I have to do this. For him.

Darwith and Cashel are waiting just where we left them at the end of the tunnel.

"You should ride alone," Lermyn tells me. "You'll need to register in the main arena tunnel. I'll look after Darwith."

"You're not coming with me?" I ask, any confidence I had a moment before fizzling out in a heartbeat.

"I'll be there to watch you, but you're on your own from this point on." He gestures to the opening of the tunnel. "Now go."

I let out a long sigh. *I'm on my own. Great…just great.*

70

When I reach the main arena tunnel, I'm a ball of nerves. I try to calm myself before entering, but it's useless. My shoulders are as tense as they were when Sutagus laid his hand on me. My mind is jumping from one thing to another, faster than I can process. Still, somehow I made it to where I was told to go.

I'm here.

A few Empyrean Cavalry hopefuls are mounting their horses inside the wide tunnel; they watch me as I ride past. I dismount Cashel and lead him off to the side near the registration sign. A round woman stands behind a half door as I approach.

"May I help you?" she asks, her tone uncertain.

"I'm here for my competition number." My hand trembles as I run it through my hair. "I'm Aluma—Aluma *Banks*."

"Oh, Miss Banks!" Her eyes go wide. "I just received the news." She turns around and grabs something. "Here you are," she says, handing me four pins and a small paper with the number thirteen typed in large black print.

I fumble with the pins, attempting to fasten the number to my shirt.

An encouraging smile spreads across the woman's face. "Be safe, Miss Banks."

"Thank you," I say, standing a little straighter at the sound of my last name. My father is Hearn Banks, and it's up to me to carry on his legacy. That means something. I can't forget that now.

When I turn around, the other twelve Empyrean Cavalry hopefuls are all staring at me—including Thayer, with a number four pinned to his shirt.

"You're really going to do this?" He bites his lower lip and pulls me into a hug.

"I have to."

"Aluma…" He draws back slightly. "Your brother—he's gone. Farann heard he went to Tarmensil, to be with your father. Apparently he got on the same karrier."

"He went *with* my father?" I ask skeptically.

"Riders, please make your way to the arena," Egan Frye's sharp voice echoes over the tunnel speakers, distracting me from the confusion and anger building in my chest.

Worry fills Thayer's eyes. I wrap my arms around him again, my ball of nerves winding up tighter than before.

"We can do this," I whisper before stepping back. But I don't believe it—not all the way.

He smiles awkwardly, as if he can smile his way to making himself feel better. "Yeah. We can."

I force myself to give him a reassuring nod, but inside, I'm falling apart.

 ELEVEN

The sun has dipped behind the tops of the stands, and the arena lights are like a hundred miniature suns, beaming their heat directly at my forehead. It's blinding. I remember how I felt as a spectator in years past, when I could sit on the edge of my seat, excitement coursing through my veins. I'd watch the sun on its descent to the horizon, knowing the most exciting part of the night was about to begin—*the competitions.*

I trot Cashel onto the field, following the other twelve Empyrean Cavalry hopefuls. The roar of the crowd is deafening. A loud song full of heavy bass notes blares out over the arena, making my ears throb with every beat. Cashel stiffens beneath me, his gait uneven. For a moment, nothing seems real—it's as if I've been caught inside one of my dreams, but none of this is as dreamy as I would've hoped.

The thirteen of us line up on our horses, side by side, facing the king's balcony. Prince Sutagus is sitting near the small set of stairs that leads to the dais. He looks down at me, blank-faced, making my grip tighten around Cashel's reins.

My eyes move to my father's now-vacant seat, and my heart aches. I ask the stars to keep him safe. *He has to be safe.* After all these years,

years I spent dreaming of competing, I'm finally getting my chance. But he won't be here to see it.

Thayer sits at the beginning of the pack. He gazes past the rest of the riders until we lock eyes. I smile, hoping to lessen his nerves and my own. But it's not working. A sheen of sweat is building under my clothes, the kind that makes you feel cold and hot all at the same time.

Egan Frye emerges from the stairwell beneath the king's balcony. He prances onto the field until he's positioned in front of the thirteen of us. He's changed his outfit again; this time he's dressed for the night—a jet-black suit with glistening rubies. A thousand blood-red stars prepared to sparkle.

"People of Eirelannia, we have come to the highlight of today's Tournament, which just so happens to be *my* favorite part," Egan says into a shiny golden microphone. "These thirteen hopefuls will compete for the honor of advancing to the final showdown, where we shall see who truly has what it takes to join the elite Empyrean Cavalry!"

My eyes wander from left to right until I pass Prince Sutagus, who continues to stare right at me. It's as if his spindly fingers are still gripping my shoulder.

Stay calm. Focus. I turn away from his penetrating stare, forcing myself to reserve the urge to run from the competitions, where going fast and getting away from the others will work in my favor.

"No one may fly until they've been inducted in as an official Empyrean Rider in the Empyrean Cavalry," Egan continues. "Therefore, we shall test these thirteen hopefuls with a challenging course of seven jumps—our most advanced course yet." He waves his hand at the jumps arranged throughout the rest of the arena.

From where I'm sitting, the jumps look just as intimidating as they did from the sky. But finishing the course has to at least be in the realm of possibility. I have to believe it is.

"We have a fine group of twelve Empyrean Cavalry hopefuls who have been training all year for this year's Autumn Tournament," Egan says. He glances at all of us sitting atop our horses. "But today, we also have a rare last-minute nomination taking the *thirteenth* spot—Miss Aluma Banks! A beacon of hope. A young woman who rides, even after her father's devastating fall, in order to protect what she cherishes most—her beloved kingdom." Egan gestures to me, pointing me out like a wild horse who has just been caught and needs some discipline, and maybe a little compassion, too. If people didn't notice me before, they certainly will now.

My face fills the large screens, and the crowd's focus zooms in on me. Gasps and murmurs swell into a crescendo as people realize the thirteenth spot has been filled by the daughter of Hearn Banks, the same man who just fell before them. Then silence settles over the crowd for an unnerving moment.

I sit frozen, holding my breath.

The crowd claps excitedly when the cameras leave my face and the big screens cut back to Egan's arched eyebrows.

And I can breathe again.

"There will be two rounds. The first round to separate the weak from the strong, in a speed-jumping skills test." Egan grins, waving his free hand at the jumps. "But in the event of a thirteenth rider, like we are facing today, one of the groups of two in the first round will include a third competitor—the thirteenth rider. Only one rider from each group will continue to the second round."

My face fills the screens once again. To my left, the other Empyrean Cavalry hopefuls are eyeing me—and cursing me, I'm sure. *I'm* the thirteenth rider, the rider changing the rules for everyone else. I'm the rider making someone miss their fifty-fifty shot of making it out of round one.

"Let's look at this year's jumps, shall we?" Egan suggests. An aerial view of the jumping course fills the big screens. "Riders will start and finish in nearly the same spot on their respective courses. At the sound of the buzzer, each rider will ride to their left, to jump one."

Jump one fills the screens; it looks simple enough. Just like one I did this morning. I can only hope the rest are similar, but I know they're not.

"The first jump is a double rail with a wall—our most basic jump," Egan continues. "Then riders will swing to the right for a combination jump—two equally sized hedges, back-to-back." The two hedges are bright green and higher than I expected, with only a couple strides of distance between them. But still doable.

"Then riders will turn left, and it's on to the third jump—the infamous water jump. It starts with a log and then a horse-length body of water to clear, in the air, of course." Egan giggles, and the screens cut to the water jump. It's just as intimidating as it looks every year—even more so now that I know *I* have to jump it.

"To the left and back down the center of the course is the fourth jump and second combination obstacle—a double plank, up onto a raised grassy area, then another double plank back to a lower level—all within a few quick strides of each other."

I reach down and rub Cashel's neck. That's not an easy jump, with the alternating levels. We've never practiced that. I'm not sure I'm ready to see what's next.

"Riders curve to the right, and then it's on to the fifth jump—another combination obstacle, and my favorite jump of this Autumn Tournament," Egan says. "Riders must jump *up* and over a moat of water, onto a grassy mound, and over a large stone wall, then back to ground level. It's essentially a more challenging version of the previous jump, with two difficult movements in a row. There's no room for mistakes, my friends." The camera pans over the monstrosity of a jump—that one will be extremely difficult, at best.

What was I thinking, ever wanting to do this before?

"Then it's back to the right for the sixth jump—the mighty fallen tree trunk." And it's exactly what he says, a *mighty* tree trunk. I learned to jump over fallen trees, but I've never seen one this big.

"And this year, for the seventh and final jump before the finish line, riders must jump through the *Ring of the Green*, Cintrenia's specialty jump for this year's Tournament—a circular hedge. You can't jump too low *or* too high on this one, folks."

The screens cut to Egan's wide grin for a moment, and then it's back to a wide view of the whole course. My fears are confirmed: it's worse than I thought it was from the sky.

"There you have it! This year's jumping course," Egan concludes, his face lighting up with glee.

The crowd shouts their approval as every little muscle in my body tightens. I'm not ready for this. Not like I thought I was. I've only jumped Cashel once before, just this morning. And although he did well on that course, this is on an entirely new level. But deep down, I know there's no way my father would've told me to compete on a horse that wasn't ready. If my father has trained Cashel to jump, then we can do this.

We *have* to do this.

"The second round this evening separates the strong from the finest, with a mock battle between pairs." Egan flashes his flawless white teeth. "And then a wildcard shall be selected, by the king himself."

Reality sets in at rapid speed.

"Only four of these Cintrenian hopefuls before you will go on to Galghesworp to join the other twelve winners," Egan tells us. "Namely, the winners from the other three Autumn Tournament competitions across Eirelannia—from Tarmensil, Sceilaran, and Galghesworp. Those winners will train to become Empyrean Riders. Four per year, per city. Nothing but the best of the best."

Doubt crosses the faces of the other hopefuls to my left, all dressed in the same green and yellow-striped jerseys—Cintrenia's colors. Even the boldest, steely-faced boys and girls are showing concern, Thayer among them. Belatedly, I realize I never received a jersey; I must stand out in my all-green blouse. But it's too late now, and that's the least of my worries.

"As a final reminder—if a rider falls or touches the ground during their competition rounds, they will be disqualified," Egan adds.

My gut clenches at the word *falls*.

"Earlier today, the groups were chosen at random. Each rider has been given their corresponding number," Egan says. "Riders, you will compete with the person next to you—rider one versus two, rider three versus four, and so on."

I glance down the line. Only four of us are moving on, and I'm determined to be one of them.

"Without further ado—let the competitions begin!" Egan proclaims, lifting his hand in yet another one of his dramatic flourishes.

My eyes linger on the spot where my father fell from Darwith, staring at the newly smoothed dirt. My vision blurs as I attempt to refocus, but I can't seem to move my eyes.

Even the best can fall.

~

We are divided into our round one groups. As the thirteenth rider, I'm grouped with riders eleven and twelve. Neither of them seems happy about my being added to their group, and I can't blame them. Only one of us will move on to the next round, which means all of our chances are slimmer with me competing.

Rider twelve has fiery red hair, and her horse is as white as snow. She glances over at me for a moment. There's a cold determination in her pale blue eyes. She's not going down without a fight. Rider eleven is much bigger than rider twelve, and way bigger than me—a tall boy riding a towering chestnut. From the looks of it, his horse will be a good jumper.

"Riders one and two, please make your way to your marks," Egan calls out, his piercing voice making me flinch.

I'm not going first. I can breathe—for now, at least.

Five other groups will go before me. Thayer is in the second pair, and he and his opponent have already made their way to the middle of the arena, to the standby area. The remaining nine of us stay put atop our horses near the king's balcony. The first two riders position themselves on the other side of the arena near the jumps. They bring their horses to a stand at their starting marks. The cameras pull out from the two riders—one fair-haired young man and a young woman with dark brown hair—to a wide shot of the arena. There are *three* identical, but mirrored courses laid out.

They've opened up the backup course for me. I can't remember a time when they needed to use the third course—it's been years since there were more than twelve riders competing in the Autumn Tournament.

A thrill courses down my spine. This is really happening.

Egan lifts his hand. "Let the first round begin!"

A split second of silence—then a loud buzzer sounds over the speakers. Riders one and two dart into action on their horses, racing across the starting line to the first jump. The cameras follow each rider, their faces filling either side of the large split screens, before zooming back out to show horse and rider.

The rider on the right, rider two, has a minor stumble when her horse lands after the second set of jumps. The small mishap puts her strides behind rider one.

The water jump is next—a narrow log with a wide body of water directly after it, just as Egan described. But somehow it looks worse with a horse and rider rushing toward it. Rider one doesn't give his horse enough rein, and his mare hesitates at the last moment, missing her mark, refusing to jump. The rider tumbles over his mount's neck, past the log, and into the murky water. Rider two continues to the fourth obstacle, but she's already won the round by default—rider one fell.

If you fall, you're out.

Rider two finishes the course, maybe just to prove she can. Or maybe her family is watching, and she wants to make them proud. Either way, I'm thankful that she does; it gives us time to watch and learn the rest of the jumps.

"Rider two wins the first round—Petra Sardsen!" Egan exclaims as the girl races across the finish line.

I rub Cashel's neck, trying to keep him calm—trying to keep *myself* calm. Thayer is next; I can't make out his face, but I can imagine his expression. From the distance between us, Yulla seems composed. I thank the stars that Thayer is at least riding a sturdy horse.

"Riders three and four to the starting line," Egan says.

Thayer's opponent has a much taller horse. Yulla has her competition cut out for her. Thayer glances over to the rider next to him, sizing him up. I hope he can maintain his composure. So far, so good.

"Group two, round one!" Egan blares into the microphone.

The buzzer sounds. Thayer and Yulla dart off. Thayer stays steady on Yulla as they land on the other side of the first jump. Rider three is ahead, but only by a small amount. At jump five—the across the moat, up to a raised level, and over a stone wall jump—rider three makes a mistake, cutting the corner too soon. His horse takes an awkward approach, not jumping off until halfway through the moat instead of from the firm ground before. Thayer and Yulla hit their mark and are over the stone wall before rider three and his horse are on the raised level.

Thayer can still win.

My fingers squeeze around Cashel's reins when Thayer and Yulla leap through the final jump—the Ring of the Green—and straight to the finish line. Rider three is now only steps behind them. Thayer and Yulla's timer stops on the big screen. My mouth drops open—they've won their round.

"Rider four wins!" Egan blurts out.

I almost clap my hands together, before quickly remembering my place. Rider hopefuls are to remain neutral during the competitions. No cheering for me. I dig my fingernails into my palms instead, trying to contain my excitement.

He's done it.

Thayer trots Yulla to the arena tunnel, first directing her a little closer to where the rest of us are waiting so he can flash me a smile— his Thayer smile. I can feel his pride radiating out from him like the warmth of the now-retired sun. I want to reach out and hug him. He's one step closer to becoming an Empyrean Rider.

He nods at me. It's *my* turn now.

Time speeds by as the fourth group finishes and the fifth group approaches the starting line. Cashel and I move to the waiting area in the center of the arena. The jumps are close now—too close. Too real.

I open and close my clammy hands around Cashel's reins.

A loud whistle rings out. Cashel's head turns toward the high-pitched sound, and I follow his gaze. My eyes scan the first row of seats to my right. A waving hand catches my eye—*Lermyn.*

"You can do this!" Lermyn yells out before the buzzer sounds for the fifth group.

I lift my right hand off the reins, opening my fingers in a small wave.

He's here. *I'm not alone.*

A bittersweet relief surges through me. Lermyn was there for my father, and now he's here for me.

The fifth group finishes. None of the groups have been far apart in their speed times. But little mistakes have caused even the best horses to falter.

Steady. That's what I need to stay focused on. One jump at a time. I keep reminding myself that Father wouldn't ask me to do something he didn't think I could do. Cashel must be trained and ready.

"Riders eleven, twelve, and *thirteen*—to your starting lines," Egan says, with some weight to his voice this time.

My eyes find Lermyn's in the crowd. He nods at me with a reassuring smile, and I feel my nerves calm just slightly. I hope Thayer is also watching from inside the tunnel.

I ride Cashel toward the starting line on the far right side of the arena. Rider twelve is in the middle, her white horse digging a hoof into the dirt. Rider eleven is on the far left.

My body trembles as the starting line comes into view. The line blurs in and out of focus as Cashel stops at our mark. I blink rapidly, trying to clear my vision.

I can do this. *I have to do this.* For my father.

For *me.*

I pull my shoulder blades back and lift my head high, scanning the jumps in front of us. I've waited for this moment for so long. I never believed it would happen, but now it's staring me right in the face.

Now, it's mine for the taking.

 TWELVE

The buzzer sounds, and we speed into motion. My body connects to Cashel's, stride after stride. Then the first jump is in front of us, and everything but the course becomes a blur.

Cashel's hooves leave the ground, and in a quick moment we're landing on the other side of jump one.

The crowd roars.

I stay focused on the present—jump two. We soar over the back-to-back green hedges, taking each one effortlessly. I tune into Cashel's breathing. My heart beats fast, but in rhythm, as we approach jump three—the water jump.

From the corner of my eye, rider twelve's fiery red hair is bouncing on top of her head, her white horse heading to the same mirrored jump as us. My right hand opens as I brush Cashel's neck with my fingers for some last-second reassurance.

We hit our mark.

And we're in the air.

The water passes beneath us, and for a split second, it's like flying without wings. For a moment, I am free.

Then Cashel's hooves hit the ground, jarring me back to reality. He stumbles, but quickly regains his footing. My heart thumps faster.

We sprint back down the middle toward jump four. We're almost halfway through—only a few jumps remain after this. My eyes dart up to the big screen—rider eleven is at the same jump, and so is rider twelve. All three of us are on the same area of our courses.

The win is still for the taking.

I squeeze my calves around Cashel. Time to make my move. I give Cashel his rein, and he kicks it into gear.

We take the first half of jump four, moments after rider twelve and her white horse are leaping into the air. Then we're on the ground again, neck and neck, and over the second part.

I glance at a screen again as we swing to the right, toward jump five. Rider twelve and her white horse are falling behind rider eleven and me.

Then we're at the moat jump—the last combination jump of the course. Before I can overthink how difficult a jump it is, we're over the moat and up onto the raised area, then jumping over the stone wall. It's faster than I can process, but we're over them.

Two jumps left. I steady my breath.

Rider eleven takes the lead. His horse is fast—he could've been a racer, under different circumstances. But the rider is bouncing in his seat as if he'll spring right off his horse's back. My father always taught me that a well-balanced seat is more important than speed. Cashel makes my job a lot easier. As he glides forward at an even tempo, I can tell he's the type of horse who will choose his steps carefully, and he won't rush the jumps. He's meticulous, which is great for an Empyrean steed. He'd be a smooth flyer, I'm sure.

We leap over the giant log, and for a moment, I feel the way I did when I was younger and carefree, first learning to jump with my father, over fallen trees and little streams.

I peek at a screen again. Rider eleven's horse is throwing his head, and they've fallen behind us. Their reckless quest for speed is getting the better of them.

One jump left—the Ring of the Green.

Cashel's muscles pulse beneath me, propelling us to the final jump. One last squeeze of my legs as I give him some rein, and we are in the air once again, soaring between an all-encompassing ring of green.

This is it.

We land and sprint past the finish line. Rider twelve is nowhere in sight, but to my far right, rider eleven is also passing the finish line.

"Number thirteen wins!" Egan screeches into the microphone.

My jaw drops as I rotate Cashel toward Egan.

I won?

My face fills the big screens. It's not a joke. I've won my round.

I spin Cashel in a quick circle. Rider twelve's white horse is muddied. It stands near the young woman, who is lying halfway in the moat on jump five. She doesn't appear to be moving. I urge Cashel in her direction, but the medics are already rushing out to her.

For a second, my body clenches—that could've been me, or Thayer. But it's not. We're going to round two.

Cashel is still full of energy, but his breath is heavy. I turn him back toward the large tunnel and pat his damp neck.

"That's it for round one," Egan announces over the speakers. "The jumps sure have proven to be much more challenging this year—haven't they?"

The large screens display rider twelve limping out of the arena with her muddied white horse in tow.

"Don't go anywhere—the Tournament will resume shortly with round two!" Egan's voice echoes throughout the arena.

When we exit the arena into the large tunnel, I slide off Cashel.

"Thank you," I whisper to him, brushing his dark gray mane back and giving him a kiss on his forehead.

Thayer jogs over and pulls me into his arms, and I'm immediately warm from head to toe. "You did it!"

"*We* did it," I tell him, laughing with delight.

He holds me out at arm's length, his eyes locking with mine. My face heats, even warmer than before, but his eyes soothe me. The part of me still rushing over the jumps. The part of me that knows we aren't done yet.

⁓

While we wait for round two, Cashel enjoys a deep drink from the water trough. My heart settles a little when Thayer brings me a cup of water and nudges me in the side with his elbow.

"Let's see who you'll be going against now," Thayer says, his eyes wandering over the remaining competitors. With fewer riders waiting to compete, I can make out each one of their faces. From their hard looks and rigid stances, they're *all* ready to win.

"Lower-numbered winners against larger-numbered winners," Thayer reminds me. I was so focused on round one before that I hadn't even considered who I might face if I made it to round two. But now I'm here. "Since you're number thirteen, you'll be with the first winner of the day—number two," Thayer says.

"Who is it?" I ask, my eyes darting around.

Thayer's gaze stops on a young woman with the number two—the one with dark brown hair who went first in round one. "Petra. I've trained with her before. She's talented."

"Great," I mumble, hoping my sheer excitement doesn't seep through my teeth.

"And that puts *me* with number nine," Thayer says, scanning the remaining riders, looking at their numbers. I follow his gaze. "Oh." His lips twitch to the side. "That's Xander—*Xander Corellius.*"

We both stare at Xander. I've heard of him—he's one of the young men many Cintrenian girls swoon over. They're always talking about him, and now I see why. He's tall and lean, and his pine-green eyes are noticeable from all the way over here, shining bright against his golden brown skin and cropped black hair.

"He's one of the best," Thayer whispers before forcing out a puff of air.

Thayer doesn't need to tell me. Xander is the son of the famous Empyrean Rider Dom Corellius. The Corellius family moved to

Cintrenia from the sunbathed city of Sceilaran, in the kingdom of Uladmond. They're one of the families who came to Eirelannia from across the sea before the most recent war. I've often wondered what their homeland is like.

Thayer shifts beside me. Even with a horse like Yulla, Thayer doesn't have the upper hand against Xander Corellius. It's in Xander's blood to become an Empyrean Rider, just like his father.

Thayer and I watch as Xander adjusts a stirrup on his saddle. His long-legged bay looks like a perfect jumping horse. Xander glances over, catching two sets of eyes on him. In a blink, he starts toward us, his horse in tow.

Oh, no.

I twist around, pretending I wasn't staring just a second before.

"Hello, Thayer," Xander's smooth voice calls from behind us.

I turn back to face a smiling Xander. He stands taller than Thayer, his shoulders broader, his teeth perfectly white. He looks right at me, and I realize I must look ridiculous, pretending I hadn't been watching him.

"Xander, good run out there." Thayer plays it cool with his *surprised to see you, didn't know you were there* voice.

"Thank you." Xander bows his head slightly. "It appears we will compete against one another." Xander speaks eloquently—formally, sounding more regal than our own king. He must have learned Eirelannish as a second language. He's had years of practice to speak articulately, without all the careless slang we use.

"Yeah," Thayer says. "Looks like it."

Xander glances at me, and our eyes lock for a moment. I try to look away, but I can't. He smiles with full lips this time—his cheeks smooth, but his jaw strong. It's no wonder the other girls swoon.

Thayer clears his throat. "This is Aluma."

"Nice to meet you. I have heard so much about you," Xander says to me, and I feel my eyes widening. "From your father," he clarifies. "I am so sorry." His expression softens.

"Thank you." I try to smile, but my heart breaks a little at the reminder of my father's absence. "You know my father?"

Xander nods. "I have trained under him before. He spoke of you often."

I press my lips together, feeling like I could smile and cry at the same time.

A hand lands gently on my lower back. I glance at Thayer, his eyes questioning my comfort level with his hand placement. My eyebrows raise a little, but Thayer doesn't flinch. A warmth pools through his hand and into my back.

"Well, I will leave you two," Xander says, noticing the exchange between Thayer and me. "I just wanted to say hello to you, Thayer, and to introduce myself to you, Aluma." He nods in my direction with a warm smile and turns back to his horse.

"Nice to meet you," I call out, but Xander is already out of range.

When I turn back to Thayer, his face is pinched together, like he's holding back a sneeze. His eyes are still on Xander as his hand falls away from my back.

"What was that all about?" I ask him, my cheeks warm.

"I'm sorry." Thayer's jaw flexes. "I—I feel protective of you."

I raise my eyebrows. "How so?"

He sighs. "I wanted Xander to see I—" He pauses, looking me in the eyes, like he's attempting to will his next words into my mind, instead of just saying them.

Wanted him to see what?

"I need to go check on Yulla," he says finally, and in a second, he's gone from my side.

I shake my head. There's no time for any of this—whatever *this* is. Not right now. I need to focus.

Round two is next.

THIRTEEN

By the time Egan Frye announces the beginning of the second round, the effects of the long day are wearing on me. My neck muscles are tight, my eyes are hazy from the bright arena lights, and my mind is exhausted. My energy levels are plummeting fast. I shake out the heaviness in my arms and legs before mounting Cashel.

The roar of the crowd amplifies as the remaining six of us make our way to the center of the dirt field. The spectators have been here for hours, still full of an unrivaled enthusiasm. Their cheers blur together, keeping my energy from flatlining.

"People of Eirelannia—it's time for our second and final round!" Egan's voice is as lively as it was in round one, and I wish he could will me some of his vigor. "These final six contestants will duel one another with our special mock weapons. We don't want any of these hopefuls losing a limb—or getting killed—now do we?"

When I glance over at Thayer, he's watching me with a look I can't quite decipher. His jaw flexes, but doesn't release; his eyes dart from left to right. It's like he's fighting back the urge to gallop Yulla over and protect me from an enemy visible only to him.

But I'm ready for this round. All my years of weapons training with my father, Kase, and Thayer will finally pay off. And I'm up against Petra Sardsen. It could be worse. I could be going against Xander instead, like Thayer is. At least if Petra and I both fight with a sword, we'll be somewhat fairly matched. Sure, she's got a few inches on me and she looks built, but I'm quick with a blade. And I learned from one of the best—my father.

"The first contestant to get three hits will advance," Egan says. "And, following the same rules of round one, if a contestant falls from their horse and hits the ground, their opponent wins the round."

I scan the sectioned-off fighting area. The three jumping courses are gone, replaced by an obstacle course of sorts: fallen trees, trenches of water, walls of mock stone. An assortment of wooden swords, bows, and quivers full of dull, paint-tipped arrows are laid out on a rack near the opening to the course. I've practiced with weapons on horseback, but not as extensively as I have on the ground.

"What are you going to use?" I whisper to Thayer.

"A bow," he says. No surprise there. Thayer is a great shot, which means he won't have to get close to his opponent.

My skill with a bow is only fair at best—I should've practiced more, but I've always been better with a sword. I can only hope Petra picks a sword, too, so that I stand a fighting chance against her.

"First, we have Petra Sardsen, of Cintrenia," Egan announces. The crowd claps as Petra's long face fills the screens. She looks right at a camera and grins before pulling her brown ponytail tighter. Her confidence is unparalleled, and more than a little intimidating.

"And her opponent, our last-minute nomination today, our dedicated *thirteenth rider*, who in an unexpected turn of events has made it to the second round to fight for her fallen father—Aluma Banks, of Cintrenia." Egan waves his hand in my direction.

My heart pounds as my face takes its turn filling the big screens. The crowd's applause isn't nearly as loud for me as it was for Petra, and for a moment I consider tightening my ponytail like she did, thinking somehow it might win me some of their support.

"Pick your weapons!" Egan shimmies in place, grinning from ear to ear.

Petra and I ride our horses over to the rack of weapons near the opening of the sectioned-off fighting area and dismount. I select a medium-sized wooden sword—not balanced like live steel, but it's similar enough to the real one I practice with at home and carry when I fly to the Gray Forest. Petra also selects a sword, and I thank the stars under my breath. At least this will be a close contact fight—and hopefully a quick one.

We both remount our horses, weapons in hand. Cashel hooves at the ground. The crowd falls quiet as a silent tension builds in the arena—like a branch bending, right before it snaps. My shoulders tense as we direct our horses into the sectioned-off area. There is a starting point for each of us, marked by a white line in the dirt. Petra rides her horse along the perimeter until she's directly across the length of the field from me.

I sink into my seat. My left hand wraps through Cashel's mane and reins, and my right hand tightens around the grip of the wooden sword. My heart thumps in my chest, a war drum ready to be heard.

"Let the battle begin!" Egan's voice rings out over the speakers. The buzzer rings.

I squeeze Cashel with my calves and we dart toward Petra. I can't afford to wait.

And neither can Petra. Her heels kick against her horse's sides, and it bolts into action. Petra's teeth are bared, and her brown ponytail jerks up behind her like a dark whip ready to crack. Her horse is covering ground quickly, in a straight line to my right.

A moment before we are to pass each other head on, both of us with our swords in our right hands, I rein Cashel hard to the right, cutting in front of Petra. Her horse rears back, forcing Petra to rebalance. I turn Cashel in a tight circle to the left and trail the tip of my sword across the side of Petra's arm.

The crowd gasps. Petra's eyes go wide until they're like two white balls bulging from her face. She readies her sword, but I'm already out of range.

Point one for me.

Cashel snorts as I bring him to a halt near a mock stone wall, and we wait for Petra to make the next move.

Petra's face contorts as she kicks her horse into a faster gait, and I swear I hear her growl. They barrel at us, her horse's nostrils flaring with every breath.

I turn Cashel sharply behind the wall, readying my sword again. When we turn past the end of the wall, Petra is on my left. She's slowed her horse and her sword is in full swing—aimed right at my head. I hinge backwards at my hips, lying flat, the back of my head meeting Cashel's hindquarters. The wooden blade narrowly misses the tip of my nose. During the split second that I no longer see the brown blur of her sword, I spring up, toss my sword to my left hand, and strike her.

One more point for me.

But now we are side by side, both of our horses dancing in place like drunken soldiers—full of vigor and ready to fight.

Petra swings. I attempt to lean away again, but her sword smacks me square on my shoulder, sending a sharp pain through my arm.

One point for Petra.

I grit my teeth. Petra has a longer reach than I do. I'm better off when we're moving fast.

I wheel Cashel around and set him into a sprint straight for a wide trench of water, still laid out from one of the previous jumps. Over my left shoulder, I see Petra and her horse are right on our tail. I slow Cashel just enough for us to be side by side, a split second before the jump, switching my sword into my left hand and holding the reins with my right.

I give Cashel his head and he leaps. Petra and her horse take the jump at the same moment, and we hover there together in the air, side by side.

The crowd goes silent with anticipation.

Time seems to slow as I drop my left arm down to my side and extend at the elbow, sweeping my sword out to the left, grazing Petra's thigh with the tip. In a heartbeat, we're back on the ground.

"Aluma wins!" Egan cries out.

I slow Cashel next to a bewildered Petra. She turns her horse so we are face-to-face, and for a second I think she means to strike me. But instead she reaches out her free hand and rides closer. I extend mine, and our hands meet.

"Well done," she says on an exhale.

"You too," I tell her.

It's over. I lean down and hug Cashel's neck. "We did it," I whisper to him.

The crowd is still clapping when Cashel and I make our way out of the mock fighting arena. And somehow an energy—an excitement is pulsing through me now, like the war drum in my heart has become a steady beat, guiding me to the place I was always meant to be: the sky.

But my excitement diminishes as fast as it comes. Thayer is next—against Xander.

⁓

After my win, I'm directed to wait with Cashel in the finalists' circle: a newly enclosed ring, bordered by green and yellow flowers. And since I won my round first, I'm alone in the circle—for now. I do my best to avoid glancing up at the king or Prince Sutagus. I didn't win for them, after all.

As Thayer rides Yulla to the mock fighting arena, his face is blanched and his lips are pursed together in a hard line. He doesn't turn to meet my eyes. A selfish part of me wishes he would, so we could silently celebrate my advancement. But then I quickly remind myself that his dread is probably building and his confidence dwindling.

"You've got this, Thayer," I yell, my voice escaping me, somehow projecting straight to my target. I know we're supposed to remain neutral throughout the competition, but I can't help myself. If I get in trouble for supporting my best friend, then so be it.

Thayer turns to me, trying to fake a smile. But he's not fooling me. For the moment our eyes meet, I sense the wave of fear washing over him. And as much as it pains me, I realize there's nothing more I can do to make that go away.

"Our second two competitors are Xander Corellius, formerly of Sceilaran," Egan says, "and Thayer Pridfirth, of Cintrenia."

Xander smiles at the audience, but Thayer is staring straight ahead at the ground, blank-faced. It's as if he's blocked out the noise, the people, and the arena; like he's forgotten what he needs to do.

"Please select your weapons," Egan orders.

Xander chooses a large wooden sword. He whips it around in a smooth circle at his side. The crowd claps in response. The cameras zoom in on Thayer while he selects a bow and a quiver of arrows. He keeps his head down as he walks back to Yulla.

"Are we ready?" Egan screeches.

The crowd stomps their feet.

Thayer and Xander mount their horses and enter the mock fighting arena. They face one another from either side of the ring, just like Petra and I did moments before. Xander stretches his sword out in Thayer's direction. Thayer nocks an arrow.

The buzzer rings.

Xander doesn't waste any time. He and his perfect jumping horse race across the ring toward Thayer.

My teeth wedge together, just like my fists. I'm helpless, and I hate it.

Using only his legs, Thayer directs Yulla to the right, behind a large fake rock. He gallops out on the other side, releasing an arrow at Xander.

He misses.

Xander weaves his way through a rocky path, coming face to face with Thayer in a corner. Xander swings his sword, and Thayer leans forward on Yulla, escaping the sword's wooden edge by mere inches.

I hold my breath as Thayer springs up, nocking his bow. In one swift motion he turns, draws, and releases the arrow, hitting Xander square on the leg, leaving a yellow paint mark.

One point for Thayer.

I exhale a little.

Xander whips his sword around, charging at Thayer. Before Thayer can nock another arrow, Xander strikes him in the side with his sword. For a moment, Thayer dangles off one side of Yulla before yanking himself back into his saddle.

My breath catches—that was too close.

Thayer sends another arrow at Xander. It hits Xander's left shoulder.

I bite my lip. Two points for Thayer. He only needs one more hit.

Xander charges Thayer from the side. Thayer reloads and shoots. Xander dodges it, swiping his sword at Thayer as his horse sprints past Yulla's hindquarters. Thayer takes the blow to his side and loses his balance, tumbling hard to the ground.

No, no, no.

"Xander Corellius wins!" Egan blurts out.

"No—" I whisper. Thayer can't be out. He's trained so hard.

Thayer pops up, dusting himself off. He's unharmed, but I can see the look of defeat spreading across his scrunched face. He lowers his head as he scurries over to Yulla. The cameras stay on him the whole time, capturing every moment of his embarrassment and shame.

Xander rides over to Thayer and dismounts his horse. He pats Thayer on the shoulder and says something, eliciting a tiny smile from my friend.

The crowd cheers.

Thayer places his hand on Xander's opposite shoulder, acknowlededging the fair battle, and my hopes sink. He's really out. Xander has won.

"Our final two competitors are Bodrin Deuland, of Cintrenia, and Cloveman Ki, of Cintrenia," Egan announces.

Thayer rides Yulla to the arena tunnel, and my heart aches. I want to rush over to him, tell him everything will be all right. But I can't leave the finalists' circle, per the rules of the Tournament. There are no words to comfort him with anyway; he won't be going to Galghesworp. He won't be an Empyrean Rider. And he won't be with *me*.

This morning, I thought it was he who might leave *me* behind. I never fathomed it being the other way around. And it's not easier this way. We will be separated—unless he gets the wildcard. But there's only a one in three chance at that.

Xander rides his horse into the finalists' circle next to me. He glances over and smiles apologetically, but I can't really be angry with him, even if I'd much rather have Thayer here next to me. It was a fair win.

The final round goes to Cloveman Ki. It's a complete blowout. Cloveman's bow skills are unmatched. Bodrin didn't stand a chance.

After the final round, Xander, Cloveman, and I wait in the finalists' circle. We are all advancing. We've made it.

I should be happy, but an overwhelming guilt is flooding through me. Maybe if I hadn't competed today, Thayer would be in here now instead. He might not have had to compete against Xander. I could be the reason he's out there, and I'm in here.

Petra, Thayer, and Bodrin line up beside their horses in front of the king's stage, awaiting their fate.

"It's now time to find out which lucky competitor the king will select for this year's wildcard," Egan says, standing on the field next to the three hopefuls.

The crowd has fallen silent. Thayer stands by Yulla, his head lifted to face the king. Bodrin and Petra do the same. When I glance away from Thayer and up at the stage, Prince Sutagus moves close to the king and whispers something in his ear. The king and the prince both glance at the three competitors, all hopeful for a second chance.

My shoulders tense. *Thayer... Thayer... Thayer...*

After a long pause, the king stands and draws his sword.

"The king has decided," Egan says. "This year's wildcard selection goes to..." Egan trails off as the king lifts his sword—the cleanest steel I've ever seen. The king directs his blade back and forth between the three competitors. I squeeze my eyes shut; this is the part where the king stops on the winner and raises and lowers his sword in confirmation of his choice.

I can't watch.

"Petra Sardsen!" Egan exclaims, and the crowd erupts, the noise like daggers to my ears. I keep my eyes closed, blocking out the grimace that I'm sure is taking over Thayer's face. This isn't how I imagined today going. It should be Thayer.

95

"Wait," Egan says, his voice prying my eyes back open. The crowd goes silent as Egan rushes over to one of the king's soldiers who has descended the stairs. The man whispers something into Egan's ear.

My eyes narrow, zooming in on Egan as he hurries back over to Thayer and the others.

"My sincerest apologies to all," Egan says, catching his breath. "The king did *not* select Petra Sardsen. My eyes misled me—an honest mistake." He shakes his head, and Petra's expression wavers between confusion and anger. "The king was pointing his sword at Thayer Pridfirth, the *official* wildcard selection."

My mouth drops, and then I'm grinning.

Thayer turns his head, glancing around the arena as the spectators roar their approval. He looks in my direction, and we share a moment—of joy, of gratitude, of everything.

We won't be apart.

I thank the stars as Thayer turns back to the king and bows his head. He mounts Yulla and rides her over to the finalists' circle next to me. When he's close, I feel the urge to reach out to him and take his hand. But with all the cameras and eyes on us, I don't.

"People of Eirelannia—our winners!" Egan declares. He waves his hand at Thayer, Xander, Cloveman, and me.

Me. I did it. And Thayer is going with me.

I take a deep breath and close my eyes again, this time trying to absorb the energy of the exuberant crowd. I let my breath out slowly, opening my eyes to the world around me once more. It looks so different from this morning: the lights are still bright, but not blinding; the noises are loud, but not deafening. Somehow it's not as overwhelming. It's as if a damper has fallen over the Empyrean arena, allowing me to soften the edges and melt into it all.

But one thing still stands out, still stings like a deep scratch from the old tabby cat that lives in the stables.

My father's empty seat.

It sticks out in the distance, a reminder of why I just did what I did. I wish he could see me now.

Back in the tunnel, the cheers are dwindling down in the arena as

Egan wraps up the event. As soon as I dismount Cashel, I'm rushing to Thayer. To my surprise, he's hurrying toward me, too. Our arms wrap around each other, two best friends who've just realized the other doesn't have to face all that's coming alone; that one of us won't have to wait for the other to come home. We'll be together.

"You did it," Thayer says, his voice filled with awe.

"Did you ever have any doubt?" I ask, but I'm grinning.

"Never." He pulls me closer. "I've never doubted you, Aluma Banks." When he says my name, my tense muscles soften, and I relax against his warm chest.

"We're going to Galghesworp," I say, still in shock that the day played out this way. "You and me."

"You and me," Thayer whispers into my hair before stepping back.

We stand side by side, peering out at the arena field. The same field my father fell on earlier today. The same field where I jumped Cashel, battled, and won my spot to join the Cavalry.

Something tells me, from here on out, nothing will ever be the same. I'm finally going to become an Empyrean Rider. But I may lose my father in the process.

 FOURTEEN

By the time I push myself out of bed the next day, the sun is already rising over the crowns of the Green Hills. Yesterday is a blur. I was so exhausted last night that the emptiness in our house didn't hit me as hard. But it's hitting me now—now that I have to prepare to leave.

Leave my home.

The painful thought sinks in as I dress myself in my father's old gray sweater, my riding tights, and the trusty boots my mother left behind. I walk through the house, feeling as if I'm being dragged to the bottom of Turtle Pond with heavy rocks tied to my ankles. I can't breathe. My father and brother are gone. My father is lying in a medical bed somewhere in Tarmensil. All I want is to go to him—I should be there. But the karrier for Galghesworp leaves in less than an hour, and I have to be on it.

There's a knock on the door. I open it to Farann and Lermyn standing outside. Farann's eyes are heavy, yesterday's makeup smudged under her bottom eyelashes. She half smiles when she sees me.

"Morning," she says, almost like it's an apology.

"May we come in?" Lermyn asks with a pained expression.

"You two know each other?" I ask, my eyes darting back and forth between them as they enter.

Lermyn nods. "Miss Ross and I met at the end of the competitions last night."

Farann fidgets with her hands, rolling her cupped fingers over a fist. "I have news about your father."

I inhale sharply. "Is he okay?"

"I received word from Tarmensil." She shakes her head slowly. "He's in a coma. I'm so sorry, Aluma."

A ball forms in my throat as my heart thuds. Her words aren't registering fast enough. *He's in a coma.* "Will he wake up?"

"They don't know," she says, her eyes trained on the floor.

I turn to Lermyn, hoping he has different news. He doesn't.

The room is spinning, and each beat of my heart is loaded with blades of pain. The events from yesterday trickle into my groggy mind. My father told me to become an Empyrean Rider. He told me I had to do it. But still I want to be by his side. I want to be there with him in Tarmensil.

"There's a chance, though. And—" Farann stops herself.

"And what?" I search her face.

"Your brother is still there with him." Her tone is strange, like she's uneasy about it.

"Kase is with him," I say aloud, confirming it to myself.

"I wanted you to know. Before you left," she says.

I should be comforted. Kase is with Father. But my stomach is gnawing at itself. I should be with him, not Kase. Whatever was going on between Kase and Prince Sutagus—I just can't shake the feeling that Kase may have had a hand in putting Father where he is now.

I glance at Lermyn, and he exhales.

My chest caves inward. "What if I never see him again?"

"Don't think like that." Farann places her hand on my shoulder.

I lean forward and cradle my face, trying to calm myself. I have to leave soon, but I'm broken. And there's no comfort in knowing my father may never wake up.

"Did you find out anything about that box?" I ask, lifting my head. My eyes refocus on Farann.

"Nothing," she says.

I let out a sigh. I don't know what I was expecting—it's not as if there's been much time for her to investigate.

"I have to pack," I tell her at last.

Farann nods. She heads back to the front door, and I follow her. She turns to hug me. Tears well up behind my eyes, but I fight them back.

"It will be okay," she whispers.

"Thank you," I say, squeezing her tightly one last time.

She releases me with a sigh and smiles sadly at Lermyn before she leaves. Once she's gone, he and I go to the barn.

"I'm so sorry," Lermyn says as I make my way into Darwith's stall.

I hug Darwith around his thick neck, laying my head on him. The front tip of his wing edges behind me, as if he's hugging me back. He's the closest I can be to my father now.

"There's no time today," Lermyn says from outside the stall, "but when you return from training, I'll explain everything to you."

"The old will soon be made anew…" The words spill from my mouth, as if they've been there the whole time, waiting to be said.

"Yes. But there's no point in explaining it all now. You have enough on your plate. You're going into training—you'll need your focus for that."

I blink at him. I wish he would explain it now. If it has something to do with my father, I deserve an explanation. There's nothing I can't handle after what happened to him yesterday. But I'm too mentally exhausted to protest.

Lermyn sighs, as if he can read the frustration on my face. He probably can—I've never been very good at hiding my feelings.

"Since your father's accident, things will be put on hold for a while," he says at last.

"What will be put on hold?" I ask, halfway expecting he might answer me with something less vague. But he just presses his lips together, and I know there's no point in questioning him further. If I wasn't confused enough before, I certainly am now.

I shake my head, turning my attention back to Darwith. "Take good care of him?" I ask Lermyn. I kiss Darwith's muzzle, his tiny hairs tickling my face. He whickers after me as I move away. I don't want to leave him.

"The best," Lermyn assures me. "Now, go finish packing. The karrier will arrive soon."

I'm not ready to leave, though not just because I haven't packed.

I'm not ready to leave my *home*.

Once I've packed my few belongings into my knapsack, I stand in the center of my bedroom for a moment, trying to memorize all of its nooks and crannies. I notice the way the floorboards are buckled from years of humid summer days, the way my bed sinks more on the left side where I always sleep like a log. The faded white paint on the windowsill, chipped from all the times I've snuck out to fly Darwith to the Gray Forest. I can only hope I'll be able to return to touch the wavy floors beneath my feet, sleep in my slanted bed, and sneak—or perhaps I won't have to sneak next time—out my window.

I decide to leave the rest of the pompidorris I collected in the Gray Forest under the loose floorboard, in the drying box I've been using to store the fruits. I doubt I'll have much use for them where I'm going, and I don't want to be caught by the Empyrean Cavalry with goods from enemy territory. The pompidorris should stay preserved until I'm able to return. And even if the flesh of the fruit is no longer edible, the seeds will still be useful.

When I walk through the kitchen, for a split second, I expect my father to be sitting there, waiting for me at the table with Kase. But he's not. The silence swallows me whole, then spits me back out, bringing tears to my eyes as I survey the empty house for the last time.

Back outside, I scan the horizon. On the main road, coming from Cintrenia, sunlight glares off the black metal sides of a large land karrier. I've never seen one like this: long and narrow, like two rows of stalls, side by side, on wheels. It's nearly the length of our barn. I stare at the karrier, wondering how such a bulky machine is moving at such a quick speed—or at all.

The ground rumbles beneath me as I hurry to meet Lermyn and Cashel. The karrier stops just outside our fence line. After a moment, a suited man descends from a set of stairs near the front of the karrier.

"It will be okay," Lermyn says, a reassuring smile crossing his face as I take Cashel's lead rope. I smile back at him before leading Cashel over to the suited man, meeting him halfway.

"Aluma Banks," the man says, more than asks.

"Yes," I reply, taking a swift gulp of air.

"Follow me." He turns on his heels, leading me to the back end of the karrier.

The suited man presses a small button on the back panel, and the karrier opens. A solid sheet of metal folds out onto the ground, lowering to create a ramp.

I take one last look at our farm, attempting to soak it all in. I've never left home like this before. I've never left without a clear return date in mind—or without the reassurance that my father and Kase will be here when I get back.

Lermyn stands by the barn. He smiles again before waving me off, and I almost wish he'd call out to me, saying I can stay after all. Suddenly, I want none of this to be real. I want to be stuck at home with my daily chores, pining for the opportunity to train in Galghesworp. I would happily give up my chance to be an Empyrean Rider, if it meant my father would be all right.

"Please," the suited man says, ushering me and Cashel onto the lowered ramp.

My eyes readjust to the dim interior light as Cashel and I walk into the karrier. There are two other horses in stalls. I recognize one of them—Xander's perfect bay jumping horse. The other has a dark brown coat and a white star on its forehead. I give Cashel a pat on his neck and leave him in an empty stall.

"This way." The suited man leads me through a door.

When we enter, I take in my surroundings. Tinted windows line the walls on either side, and the cushioned benches below them face inward, with two small tables flanking each. Xander and Cloveman Ki are staring straight at me, sitting at the far side of the karrier.

"We have one more stop before we depart for Galghesworp. Please make yourself comfortable," the suited man tells me before going out the same way we came in, leaving me alone with Xander and Cloveman. Behind me, I hear the ramp closing with a soft *thud*. I squash down the urge to escape—to get Cashel and run back to the barn.

The karrier moves. I stand frozen in the same spot where the suited man left me, my hands tightening into clammy balls, my eyes trained on our farm, my home becoming smaller and smaller until it's a tiny speck in the distance.

There's no turning back now.

FIFTEEN

Even when our farm is no longer visible, I strain my eyes, as if I could somehow pull it back into focus. But it's useless. We're moving down the road to Galghesworp at a rapid speed—a speed I've only experienced flying on Darwith's back.

"Care to have a seat?" Xander says, a winsome smile spreading across his face. He moves over on the cushioned bench, even though there's already plenty of space for me.

"Thank you." I place my knapsack on the ledge above, beside two other bags, before I sit beside him.

"Thayer is our last stop," Cloveman Ki says, leaning forward from the other side of Xander. "I'm Cloveman, nice to meet you." He reaches his hand out to shake mine, and I realize we never formally met at the Tournament. I only heard his name over the speakers when he won his rounds. "I was impressed by your performance yesterday," he adds, raising his black eyebrows. "You've got skills."

"Me?" I snort. "I've never seen such a skillful archer." My mind darts back to last night, when Cloveman beat his opponent in three back-to-back shots. He could have won with his eyes closed.

"Why, thank you." He bows grandly in his seat. His dark brown eyes peek out from behind his straight black hair before he jerks his head to the side, shaking the strands off his face. His skin is fair and smooth, like porcelain. He isn't dressed like most Cintrenian boys with their traditional garb of denim pants, a plain shirt, and boots. But he's not dressed like a Uladmondian, either, with their tailored suits and polished everything.

"Ah, yes, these," Cloveman says, pointing to his pants as he catches me pondering them. They're gray with black patches around the knees and snug at his calves. "These are my creation." He grins with pride. "Made them myself."

I raise an eyebrow. I've never heard of a boy making his own clothing, at least not anywhere in Eirelannia.

"My mother is a seamstress." Cloveman shrugs. "She's from across the sea."

"Oh," I say, and it makes sense. Many people from across the sea have what some people call *style*—something that continues to fly right over my head. In Cintrenia, we wear simple clothes made by the king's approved seamstresses, or whatever we're handed down from our family members.

"Yeah." He chuckles, pulling on his pants at his knees where the different material is stitched in. "They make pants this way where she's from. It helps with your grip while riding."

My eyes land on his laced boots, not slip-on boots like we wear in Cintrenia.

"And *these*." He lifts his feet off the floor. "I like to stay looking sharp. Clean them all the time. I find it calming."

Xander nods at Cloveman's spotless black boots. "Your boots are *almost* as clean as mine," he chimes in with a chuckle. Xander's boots really are even shinier and cleaner than Cloveman's—however that's possible.

I attempt to tuck my own dirty brown boots behind me. Have I ever cleaned them? Can't say I have. I don't see much point in it anyway; they'll only be covered in mud, manure, or something else by the end of the day.

The karrier slows as the Pridfirth farm comes into view. A twinge flickers in my chest, like a small bird taking flight.

Thayer.

Pull it together.

The karrier comes to a halt at the end of the tiny road leading to the Pridfirth farm. In a moment, Thayer and Yulla are emerging from the barn, his parents trailing behind. His mother and father stand with him, their mouths set, but their eyes flitting back and forth as if they're saying a difficult goodbye, even though it's only a temporary absence for training. Both of his parents exchange a solemn hug with Thayer, and then he's leading Yulla to the end of the karrier. It occurs to me that I would have been saying goodbye to Thayer today, too, if yesterday had played out the way it should have.

Thank the stars I don't have to say goodbye.

Thayer's parents wave, but he's already out of sight. A small pain taps at my heart as I imagine what it would have been like to hug my father goodbye this morning. My eyes are blurring when the back door opens and the same suited man from before walks in, with Thayer following close behind.

"Aluma," Thayer says, acknowledging me, but his voice is reserved. He barely meets my gaze, looking away a split second later. He does the same to Xander and Cloveman before taking his seat next to me. His eyes stay on the floor, avoiding the view of his farm—his family—just outside the window.

He doesn't want to say goodbye to his home, either.

"Our next stop is the Galghesworp training base," the suited man says before he turns and leaves, repeating the same process of closing the doors behind us. As the karrier moves, the urge to escape floods through me once again, but then I look to my left at Thayer, and I know I'm exactly where I need to be.

"Are you okay, Thay?" I whisper to him, still surprised he's not even glancing up to see his family farm receding in the distance.

"I'm fine," he says, barely letting the words escape his mouth. His eyes stay fixed on his boots. After a long pause he turns to me, his eyes finally meeting mine. "Did you hear anything about your father?"

My shoulders slump. "He's in a coma," I tell him, the pain in my heart growing like a rampant weed. It's not getting any easier to face.

Thayer places his hand on mine. "It'll be okay." He tries to sound positive, but his voice quivers.

"Thank you." I say softly. My eyes linger on our hands until he removes his, and I miss its warmth at once.

We ride along the road to Galghesworp for what seems like hours. Cloveman and Xander sit on the opposite side of the room playing *Catchda*, an old board game from Tarmensil. Thayer reads a book in the other corner; he's kept to himself most of the ride. I sit on a cushion, reading a book I found about the Dark Wars—the battles that resulted in the electric shockwaves that decimated most of the technology in Eirelannia. It's a wonder any tech was salvaged at all. The Uladmondians ultimately won the war against the Laithlanners, and were able to save some bits of technology. Laithlann didn't fare nearly as well—the shockwaves destroyed most of their cities, and their people are said to have physical mutations.

I can't seem to figure out what we were fighting for in the first place. Uladmond didn't take the land or seize any resources, and much of the Old World is rumored to be toxic now. So what was the point of it all?

I glance out the window at the unfamiliar countryside. The green grass closer to Cintrenia has given way to the rockier ground of the southern part of Ivernister. There are still a few barren trees, tall and scraggly—similar to the trees of the Gray Forest.

"May I?" a voice asks from beside me.

I glance up to see Xander watching me with raised eyebrows, gesturing at the open seat next to me.

"Sure," I say.

"It looks different..." Xander nods at the landscape of blurred beiges and browns as he sits. "There is nothing quite like the green of Cintrenia."

"There really isn't," I agree.

"Did you know our fathers once trained together?" Xander asks, turning to me.

My eyes widen. "No, I didn't."

"They did. And they fought side by side." His eyes light up as if he's remembering something exciting. "My father told me many stories about the great Hearn Banks."

I can't help but smile with pride. The *great* Hearn Banks.

He shakes his head slowly, his expression growing solemn. "But things were not always easy for them, you know. The war ate away at my father. He is not the same man he once was."

"My father hasn't been the same since he retired, either," I say sadly. "I can't tell which was worse for him—the war itself, him fighting in the war, or him having to sit idly by as everyone else fought it for him once he retired."

"I understand what you mean," Xander says. "It is as if once someone fights, they transform into someone else—someone harder, less *there*. But if they make it home, and they drop that hard shell, there is nothing pure left on the inside…not like before. All that is left are shattered fragments of who they once were."

I stare at him, taken aback by the striking reality of his words.

"He was going to come out of retirement…" I say, and Xander blinks at me. "It was up to me or my brother to join the ground army, or try out for the Cavalry." I scoff, remembering Kase's indifference. "But my father would never put us in harm's way. He was ready to rejoin the ranks himself."

Xander shakes his head before glancing around, as if someone might be listening. "The king's new law?"

"Yeah, that's the one," I say, bitterness rolling off my tongue.

"Your father did not want you to join the Cavalry?" Xander asks.

"No." I exhale. "He wanted to protect me. He said it wasn't safe."

Xander lowers his chin. "I do not know a good father who would not want to protect his child." He gives me a gentle smile, the type of smile you try to comfort someone with. "And perhaps those who have been to battle, like our fathers, figure they can carry the burden more easily than we can."

I press my lips together, thinking about how many people we sacrifice to fight—and often die—all in the name of the king's wars. It makes little sense. And it's not right. But it's our reality.

"Look!" Cloveman blurts out as he bumps into my shoulder, jolting me from the darkness I was sinking into. He points out the window.

In the distance, a pale stone wall juts into the sky. It's as tall as the Empyrean arena, large enough to block out any sight of what's behind it. As Xander and I rise from our seats, Thayer takes notice and joins us.

"We are almost there," Xander says. "That wall borders the Galghesworp military base."

My eyes dart to Xander, questioning him. My father never mentioned such a fortress existing in Ivernister.

"I visited my father here, years ago," Xander clarifies as he stares out. "This wall surrounds the whole base."

The karrier slows as we near the wall. There's a loud noise, like the clanking of steel, and we resume our previous speed. I glance back to see we've passed through an open gate. Armed ground troops stand to the side, staring straight ahead, blank-faced.

"They look friendly," Cloveman says with a serious expression, but a chuckle escapes from his throat.

"I think we would all feel similarly if we were told we would never have the chance to fly," Xander says darkly.

In that moment, an abundance of gratitude falls over me. I've flown, many times, but Xander, Thayer, and Cloveman haven't yet. Sometimes I forget that other than the Empyrean Cavalry, no one in Eirelannia has ever flown, or ever will—unless they sneak out, like me.

We drive past field after field full of wingless horses and the winged Empyrean steeds, all grazing on small patches of grass amongst the rockier terrain. For a second, I wonder why the Empyrean steeds don't just spread their wings and fly to greener pastures, full of lush grass. But then I remember my father explaining that they *lock* the steeds' wings in place, so they can't extend them unless the device is removed. We've never used such a contraption on Darwith; I can't imagine not allowing him to stretch out his beautiful feathered wings and shake them to his heart's content. That's like clipping the wings of a butterfly or a bird—it's cruel, and wrong. Having wings to fly but not being allowed to spread them freely is what nightmares are made of.

The karrier rolls up onto a steep hill and another gate comes into view, this one narrower than the first. But it still looks impenetrable.

"They sure have this place on lockdown," Cloveman mutters. "No one is getting in here without an invitation."

"Or *out*, for that matter," Xander adds grimly.

Great. There's nothing I love more than being trapped behind thick walls, with no Empyrean steed to fly out with.

We drive by another group of solemn-looking guards. This time we slow enough that I can make out their faces; they look a little older than us, and the lines in their skin are deeper, like they've been staring at the sun.

"They are the king's ground army," Xander says. "They are the ones who could not compete to become Empyrean Riders, drafted to stay on the ground since they turned eighteen."

I glance over at Thayer. It could have been him. Or in the near future: Kase…or *me*.

"Hey, at least we won't be confined to the ground like those guys." Cloveman blows out a puff of air and shakes his head.

"You are right. We can thank the stars for that," Xander says. "And they are called Watchers—or the King's Watchers—here."

"What are they watching?" Cloveman snorts.

"Watching to make sure we are all safe, for one." Xander darts a look at Cloveman.

Cloveman forces his lips together, seemingly understanding Xander's shift in tone. This place is no joke.

The karrier slows once again as we drive between identical-looking buildings: square fronts with one door and a sign above each. People march by on both sides of the road, some of them dressed in uniforms different from the guards we saw at the gates.

"We have arrived," Xander says as the karrier enters a circular drive in front of a vast two-story building. The sun reflects off the smooth tawny walls, and a broad set of stairs ascends up to an arched doorway where the entry is wide open, like the mouth of a cave.

When the karrier stops, Thayer glances at me, his expression remote.

A door I hadn't noticed before opens at the front of the karrier, and one of the Watchers steps in. "This way, please." He gestures for us to follow him out through the door. "Your horses will be brought to their stalls and cared for."

Cashel. I don't like the idea of leaving him with strangers. But per usual, I have little choice in the matter.

The Watcher opens another door on the exterior wall, leading to the outside. A rush of dry air blows in. The breeze feels arid against my skin, but my hands are clammy like a washrag that's been wrung out. A short set of stairs leads down to the ground. It's not until I'm descending them that I notice three other karriers lined up in front ours, all of them now empty, I'd bet.

The Empyrean Cavalry winners from the other cities must have arrived before us. We're here last.

Thayer and I walk next to each other, behind Cloveman, Xander, and the Watcher. More Watchers stand on either side of the open doors as we head up the wide staircase of the building. Cloveman glances back at us, mocking the same stony look the Watchers have on their faces.

I smirk at his impression, thankful for the moment of playfulness before we enter the cavernous structure.

We pass through the large wooden doors and into an entry room full of chatter. A blast of heated air meets us. The ceiling is arched, and a wide staircase sticks out at the back of the room, leading up to another set of doors like a giant marble tongue, sprawled out on the floor in the middle of a big, open mouth, ready to devour us whole. The walls are adorned with tapestries in Galghesworp's city colors: dark blue and gray. And next to them, an array of portraits of the Uladmondian kings, including the current king who threatens to take all we have—King Breasal Molacus.

My gaze trails down the walls to the floor level, where four long tables are set up, two on either side of the room. Twelve people— the winners from the other cities, I presume—stand divided in their groups of four, around three of the tables, with one table still vacant. The room falls silent as the others take notice of our presence. My body tenses and pulls inward, like a turtle retreating into its shell.

But it's too late.

All eyes are on us.

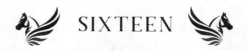

SIXTEEN

For a few long moments, the other three groups of winners evaluate us from afar, like we're fresh produce for sale at the market. Then their chatter picks right back up and most of them turn away. I'm immediately thankful for it.

"Dinner will be served soon," the Watcher tells us, leading us to the vacant table on the left side of the room, which I can now see has refreshments and name tags with our first names laid out for us. "After dinner, you will meet your training commander. Then you will be escorted to your living quarters. Please find your nametag and wait here until you're called into the dining hall."

Before any of us can speak, he turns and walks away, leaving us to fend for ourselves in a room of twelve other tired Eirelannian teens.

"You four must be the *Cintrenians*," a snide voice says from our right. A well-dressed young man with slicked-back dark blond hair and tanned white skin stands with his arms crossed. He smells like he's sprayed himself with a full bottle of men's cologne, and I immediately have to quell the urge to plug my nose and step back.

"Xander Corellius," Xander says, extending his hand.

"Barston Frost, Tarmensil," the stinky boy says, shaking Xander's outstretched hand.

"What gave us away?" Cloveman asks, smirking at Barston.

"Sceilaran, Tarmensil, and of course Galghesworp are already here," Barston says, peering down at Cloveman like he could burn through him with his eyes. He stares at Cloveman's pants, but with a sort of contempt, not a fascination like I had.

"Last, but *not* least." Cloveman shakes a playful finger back and forth.

Barston rolls his blue eyes before turning to me. "And you must be Aluma Banks. We've all been rather curious about *you*." His voice sounds as if it's being filtered through his nose before entering his mouth.

News travels quickly, apparently—faster than I'd hoped. My famous father fell from the sky, and I became the thirteenth rider. I'm sure they're curious *now*, though they'd probably never heard of me before the Tournament.

"Well, here I am," I say simply, holding my breath as if I have to be careful not to catch whatever he's spewing.

He scans me up and down, and I want to cover myself even more than I already am.

"Perhaps you'd be surprised to hear you're not the *only* girl who made it here this year." His thin lips form a hard line, as if he's displeased to announce this.

"And why would I be surprised about that?" I ask him with a shrug. He may not like female riders, but I know better than anyone that we can be as tough and skilled as any male rider.

"Feisty, this one." Barston snorts.

Thayer clears his throat, and Barston's eyes leave me for a moment. I scan the room, trying to locate the other young women who made it this year, suddenly feeling the desire to band together with them—away from Barston Frost.

Then I spot her—the only other young woman on the same side of the room as us. She's facing away, talking with three young men by their table. Her long black hair falls to her mid-back. She's similar in stature to me, maybe a little taller.

"Three other girls are here from Uladmond—one from Tarmensil, and two from Sceilaran. But *she's* from Galghesworp," Barston interrupts, following my gaze with a strange look of disgust. "You know, you Cintrenians are a lot like those four from Galghesworp—terribly simple," he says, looking me up and down again. "And harboring all the new *transplant* families. You Ivernisterians really are all the same, aren't you?"

"My family first settled in Sceilaran before we chose to move away from the kingdom of Uladmond to Ivernister," Xander says calmly. "Cintrenia is our home, just as Tarmensil is yours. It makes no difference now, as we are all here for the same reason, are we not?"

Barston rolls his eyes again—he should really stop doing that. Xander raises his brows, and without another word Barston turns and crosses the room back to his group. Xander glances over at me with a smile, and I want to hug him for making the stinky boy leave.

The four of us affix our name tags to our shirts and make our way over to the Galghesworp table. The young woman with the black hair turns as we approach. She's beautiful—one of the prettiest girls I've ever seen. Her eyes are piercing, dark like the night, standing out in stark contrast to her pale, sand-colored skin. And for some strange reason, a sense of relief comes over me when we lock eyes.

Xander, Cloveman, and Thayer greet the three boys from Galghesworp. The young woman stands waiting, watching me, and I suddenly feel awkward and excited, as if I'm meeting someone famous.

I rub my arms and clear my throat. "Hello," I say to her. "I'm Aluma."

"I know who you are," she says, her near-black eyes searching mine, as if she really does know me.

My eyebrows dart up. "You do?" I rack my brain, but can't remember meeting her—and I *know* I would recall a face like hers if I'd seen it before.

She lowers her gaze to the top of my shirt, and I follow. *My nametag.* It's right there.

I shake my head and sigh. "Right," I say with a self-deprecating snort.

She taps her nametag, which I'd failed to notice. "I'm Wolkenna." She smiles, and at once the pressure falls away from me. My shoulders relax.

The three young men from Wolkenna's group and the three from mine join us. Cloveman's eyes widen when he comes face-to-face with Wolkenna. He eagerly extends his hand to her. "Cloveman Ki," he says.

Wolkenna smirks as she shakes his hand.

Then it's Thayer's turn to meet her. I can't tell if it's because I think she's so pretty and I assume he will think the same, or if it's because his jaw unhinges more than normal, but there's instantly a burning in the pit of my stomach. I cross my arms in front of me as my throat goes dry, like I've forced down a mouthful of dust.

"Attention," a soft voice calls out, prompting us all to turn toward a thin, red-haired woman in a blue uniform, standing by the now-open door at the top of the stairs. "Please follow me into the dining hall."

Thank you to the woman in blue.

The dining hall is even larger than the entry area, with a peaked ceiling looming above the entire room. A row of sparkling chandeliers hangs from the front of the room to the back, like miniature clusters of stars. The walls are windowless, painted a dark blue with a diamond design painted in gray, lined up perfectly side by side. The floors are wooden, with different hues of brown laid out in arrow-tip shapes; the whole room seems fit for one of the king's celebrations, not for military trainees. There are four round tables spaced away from each other with four chairs set around each.

It appears the divide between cities will continue throughout dinner.

"Welcome, welcome!" a boisterous and familiar voice calls out. At the front of the room, the king's announcer from the Autumn

Tournament, Egan Frye, is standing in an all-white ensemble. His tight white pants hug his long, skinny legs and a billowy white blouse makes his upper half look like a fluffy cloud balancing on stilts. I imagine he must have the most fascinating outfits back in Tarmensil, where I'm sure he lives in an equally fancy abode.

The other winners from each city are taking their seats at their assigned tables. Wolkenna sits with the three boys from Galghesworp. I'm momentarily grateful that at least I won't have to watch Thayer blush while he eats.

There's a sign at the center of the only table left—*Cintrenia*. I take my seat with the rest of my group, pulling my chair closer under the draped white tablecloth until my foot bumps into something—someone else's foot. I glance up, and Thayer's lip lifts on one side.

"You all must be famished from your journeys today," Egan says from the front of the room. He clasps his hands together. "Please, enjoy your dinner. Afterward, you'll meet your commander, Rinehart Quin."

My mouth falls open as the room seems to shrink in around me. *Rinehart Quin*—the person my father told me to find is our *commander*? I turn to Thayer, expecting a reaction. He glances at me in a silent question, strangely unaware. Then it hits me—I never told him.

Another door opens, and a group of finely clad servers enters, carrying trays. A silver plate full of colorful food is set in front of me, but despite the delicious smell wafting to my nose, I've lost my appetite. Thayer, Xander, and Cloveman dig in right away, leaving me sitting there staring at my plate. I have so many questions, but no one to ask. My father told me to find Rinehart Quin, but I never expected he'd be placed right in front of me as soon as I arrived here.

"Is the food not to your liking?" a soft voice whispers beside me, jolting me from my thoughts. The same red-haired woman who showed us into the dining hall is watching me intently. Her pale, olive-green eyes meet mine. "I worked with our cooks to create a meal that would appeal to all of you."

"It looks delicious," I say. And it does. The woman blinks at me, as if waiting for me to say something more. Thayer and the other two boys glance up at me from their plates. Cloveman makes a shoveling motion with his fork, mouthing the words, *try it.*

The woman smiles. "You'll need your strength."

I pick up the fancy silver fork beside my plate and plunge it into some kind of pink-colored fruit sauce. I'm guessing it's the portion of the meal designed for those from Sceilaran; they have an abundance of fruit near the beachside city. The sauce tastes sweet and sour at the same time as it passes over my tongue.

"Mmm," my voice escapes me. It *is* good.

The woman grins, her fair skin blushing pink at her cheeks. "You like it?"

"Yes, it's as good as it looks," I manage between bites. "Thank you." Turns out I'm hungrier than I thought, and the unfamiliar dish seems to suppress my darting thoughts.

"I'm Moninne, one of the base medics," she says.

I press my lips into a smile with a mouthful of food behind them.

"Enjoy your dinner," she says with a light chuckle. "I'll see you tomorrow for your physical." Moninne nods to all of us before heading to the Galghesworp table.

"Thank you," I mumble over my shoulder, now fully invested in devouring everything on my plate. Sweet and savory, back and forth, flavors that transport me to places I've only imagined, and some flavors that taste like home. With the food shortages in Cintrenia, this is a feast. There's more on my plate for one meal than I'm used to eating in two days. Most of the food here was probably grown by farmers like my family or Thayer's family, who were forced to fork it all over to the king's soldiers for *redistribution*—distribution away from the people who made it, who earned it. It's no wonder so many people from the Otherside are rotund if they get to eat like *this* every day.

Cloveman glances over his shoulder, watching Moninne as she leaves. He clutches his jaw. "I think I have a toothache," he jokes. "I need to see a doctor."

Thayer chuckles, and Xander shakes his head.

"She was nice. Not what I expected for a military medic," I say.

"Nice on the eyes," Cloveman says, trying not to laugh.

"Yes, and at least twice your age," Xander tells him.

"And?" Cloveman pats his lips with his napkin.

"Perhaps there are more appropriate choices in the room," Xander says.

My cheeks warm, thinking for a split second that he's referring to me. But then Xander peers over Cloveman's shoulder at the Galghesworp group—at Wolkenna—and I want to hide under the table.

Cloveman turns to look at her. "I wish. Have you *seen* her?"

Xander nods playfully.

"Plus, I think she has her sights set on someone else," Cloveman adds, elbowing Thayer.

Thayer's eyes widen. He's quiet—too quiet. And there's that dryness in my throat again. I take a big gulp of water and hope I'm not turning red.

"Well, we are not here to meet women," Xander says.

Cloveman raises an eyebrow. "Speak for yourself."

When we finish eating, the same servers who brought our food take our plates away, leaving us with a cleared table and full middles. I wish I could just lay my head on the tabletop and shut my eyes, block out all the noise and newness. But then I think better of it and adjust my posture so that my overfilled stomach isn't pressing against my pants quite so much. What I'd give to be in my bed at home and out of these clothes that suddenly feel too tight.

"I hope you all enjoyed your meal." Egan's voice interrupts my thoughts as the rest of the voices in the room hush around me. "And now, the time has come to meet your training commander."

My eyes dart to the front of the room where Egan is standing.

A man who looks slightly younger than my father, clad in dark blue military attire, emerges from the side door. *Rinehart Quin.*

No one makes a sound as Rinehart trades places with Egan. He pauses at the front and looks out at everyone, his eyes skimming over each of us Cintrenians until he's looking right at me. There's a pause before his eyes jump to the next table—a heavy pause, one that makes me feel like he can see me. Like he *knows* me.

"I am your training commander, Rinehart Quin. But you shall

address me as *Commander Quin*," he says in a firm voice, continuing to scan the room. "Your training begins tomorrow. I expect all of you are qualified and *deserving* of your place here." He pauses. "This isn't a retreat, or a place for you to play with your friends."

He peers at the table of boys from Tarmensil in front of him—at Barston Frost. My lips press into a hard line. Commander Quin need not worry—it's impossible that Barston would have any friends.

"We are under a real threat from Laithlann, and your loyalty and service to the king is of the utmost importance." He hesitates for a moment, his eyes darting back and forth, as if he's going to catch someone having second thoughts, or trying to run. "If, at any time, I find any of you are not here for the right reasons, you will be sent home immediately."

Home. I realize the prospect of going home isn't meant to sound so good. But right now it feels like it would be a reward.

"You are here because you are the best of the best," Commander Quin says, spreading his hands. "And I expect all of you to act as such." He stops his gaze on Wolkenna's table and looks right at her, which isn't surprising—I'm sure she's the best at everything she does. "That is all for tonight. I will see you tomorrow after your medical exams."

The best of the best.

Great. And I have to find a way to talk to this guy.

After Commander Quin leaves the dining hall, sixteen Watchers enter to lead us to our rooms; mostly men, with a few women, and all with buzzed haircuts, dressed in identical charcoal uniforms. There's one for each of us, which seems unnecessary; no one is trying to escape. It was hard enough to get here in the first place.

I'm one of the last to leave the dining hall, which makes it even more awkward when the Watcher who approaches me says nothing other than: *follow me.* He can't be more than a few years older than me, but his beige skin is weathered and tanned, like worn leather that's been left out in the sun.

The Watcher leads me out through a side door, not the same one we entered through earlier in the evening. He walks in front of me by only a stride or two, but not so much that I'm out of his periphery. There's a bounce in my step, even despite everything that's happened. I just can't believe I'm actually *here*.

When we exit the building into an enclosed courtyard, the sun has gone, and the sky is dark. The air is cold and dry—much drier than it is up north, making the cold somehow not as intense. In Cintrenia, with all the moisture in the air, the chill seeps through my pores and cools my core. But here and now, the brisk air feels invigorating, even without a jacket.

We follow a path lit by small lights hanging in the branches of half-barren trees; handfuls of brown, red, and yellow leaves still cling on, reminding me of home. When I was younger, my father would rake up piles of leaves for Kase and me to play in. Then we'd sip apple cider by the fireplace while Father read to us. I smile at the memory, then realize how alone I feel, walking under the moon and stars. Thayer and the others were all led out before me, and the Watcher hasn't proven to be much company.

When we reach the other end of the narrow courtyard, the Watcher opens a door for me, waiting for me to pass through. Inside, there's a dimly lit hallway full of closed doors on either side. The Watcher takes the lead and doesn't stop until we reach the last door on the right.

He opens it. "Your room," he says, stepping to the side.

I stand like a statue as it all sinks in. I'm here, and this is everything I've always wanted.

Isn't it?

"Your bag is inside. Please." He gestures to the open door.

I enter, and he closes the door behind me before I can turn back to face him.

I'm alone in the silence, all of my thoughts rushing at me, all at once, like a raging river.

I am away from home. My father is in a coma. Find Rinehart Quin. Keep the light…

I blow out a puff of air and move at a turtle's pace down the short hallway. There's a closed door on the left, and I can hear a shower running on the other side. My new roommate, I assume. At the end of the hall, the space opens into a square room. There are two small beds, a nightstand beside each, and a window with dark maroon curtains between them. My knapsack is on the bed to the right, and there's a gray bag on the bed to the left.

I move to the window and cup my hands around my eyes, then press them against the glass, but it's too bright inside the room and too dark outside to see much more than some shadowed shapes. I pull the curtains closed and plop down onto the bed beside my knapsack. My body feels heavy, like I've been carrying a sack of grain around all day.

A door clicks open. *My new roommate.*

A face emerges from the hallway—a beautiful face. *Wolkenna.* She's dressed in flowy white pajamas and she's scrunch-drying her wet black hair with a towel. She doesn't break her stride, smiling as she sits on the edge of her bed. "Didn't see that one coming," she says.

Of course *she's* my roommate. The other three new girls are from Sceilaran and Tarmensil—both cities from the kingdom of Uladmond. No doubt they would've requested to room together.

"It's fine with me," she continues. "Seems like we may have some things in common." She opens her bag and pulls out a brush, and then she's brushing her hair and smiling at me with pearly white teeth. She's a dark rose in a garden of weeds, and I don't understand why she'd want to join the Cavalry when she looks like a queen.

Wolkenna waits, eyebrows raised, before clearing her throat.

I suddenly realize I've been staring at her like an owl, wide-eyed. I force a smile and try to remember how to respond to what she's said. "You're right. It's good with me, too."

She offers an amused smile and resumes taking items out of her bag. "Plus, this will give us time to get to know one another."

"It will," I echo, turning to my bag to unpack a few items myself. I place an old photograph of my father, brother, and me on the short nightstand beside my new bed. My eyes get stuck on my father's smile; he looked so happy that day.

"Nice family," Wolkenna says from behind me, making me startle.

"Thanks." My hands scramble over the remaining items in my bag.

"Where's your mother?" she asks.

A tightness pulls across my chest, and I freeze up like a sharp icicle, ready to break and shatter. *That's a great question.*

"Oh—sorry. I understand," she says, braving the silence. "I haven't seen my mother in a long time, either." She crosses the room and lies on her bed. "We should call it a night. We have a big day tomorrow. Goodnight, Miss Banks." She turns off the lamp on her side table and rolls away to face the wall.

"Goodnight," I say, my eyes returning to my family photo.

My father said to find Rinehart Quin. Well, I've found him. Now it's time for me to figure out what to do next.

SEVENTEEN

My eyes open a split second before a piercing alarm fills the room, screeching at me like an angry bird protecting its nest. My body jerks up and I sit, straight as a board, before glancing over at Wolkenna's empty bed.

The alarm stops, and my mind settles. Training starts today.

The floor is icy beneath my bare feet as I scurry over to the restroom door. It's locked.

"Almost done," Wolkenna calls out.

"Oh, sorry," I say, moving back into the bedroom. My gaze lands on my family photo, and last night comes rushing back—Rinehart. I have to talk to *Commander* Quin.

I change out of my pajamas and into the same outfit as yesterday: gray sweater, riding tights, and boots. Then I open the dark maroon curtains, expecting to see sunlight, but it's still pitch-black outside, as if no time has passed from the moment I entered the room last night.

Wolkenna emerges from the bathroom, her long black hair tied back in a smooth ponytail. She's also dressed in the same clothes she wore yesterday.

Glad I'm not the only one.

SHINA REYNOLDS

She eyes my outfit. "They're giving us our uniforms today."

"I didn't bring my—I don't have much else."

"Me either," she says, shrugging. "Don't worry about it."

In the bathroom, I wet my hair, attempting to pull it into a ponytail like Wolkenna's. I frown at myself in the mirror, seeing that my eyes are filled with tiny red lines. I clearly didn't sleep much.

A loud knocking on the bedroom door makes me flinch.

I exit the bathroom to find Wolkenna opening the door to the same Watcher who showed me to our room last night.

"Breakfast is being served in the cafeteria," he says, stepping aside. "If you will both follow me, I will escort you."

Wolkenna and I follow the Watcher back through the courtyard. The air is cooler than last night, causing goosebumps to rise under my loose shirt. The light of dawn is just trickling its way in through the row of trees, and a few birds are practicing their morning calls.

"So, what should we call you?" Wolkenna asks the Watcher, breaking the silence.

He glances at her with a stony expression.

"You've got to have a name, right?" She raises an eyebrow.

"It's unnecessary for you to call me anything," he says, continuing along the path.

Wolkenna smiles mischievously at me, and I realize this is the first time the Watcher has spoken out of turn.

"But if you have to call me something, you can call me Huffman," he says over his shoulder.

"Huffman," Wolkenna repeats.

He has a name. Huffman gives us both a sliver of a grin as we enter the main building.

"Progress," Wolkenna says.

A rare giggle bubbles up inside of me. "Progress."

While Huffman's name mystery was a nice distraction, my real concerns are coming back into clear focus as we slow to a halt outside of a noisy room.

"The cafeteria," Huffman says, gesturing inside. "Please meet me out here when you're finished, and I'll escort you to your physicals."

The cafeteria is enormous—fit for an army. There are many people who weren't in the dining hall last night. People older than me.

Empyrean Riders. But no Commander Quin.

As I join the serving line, I notice a familiar face at a nearby table. The same woman, now in a uniform, who showed Lermyn and me into the Empyrean Cavalry Committee room. I remember her piercing golden eyes.

Zarshona.

Wolkenna nudges me with her elbow. "Do you know her?" she asks, subtly gesturing toward Zarshona.

"I met her two days ago, right before I competed," I tell her.

She tilts her head and pauses. "But you don't know *who* she is?"

"Her name is Zarshona." I edge closer to the serving window.

"Zarshona Mund," Wolkenna whispers.

I raise my eyebrows and take my tray of food, then head to an empty table.

"Who is she?" I ask once Wolkenna is sitting across from me.

Wolkenna looks past me to where Zarshona is seated. "She's an Empyrean Rider. She was a last-minute nomination a few years ago, in Sceilaran. Now she's part of the prince's inner circle—a lieutenant." There's a bitterness in Wolkenna's voice, as if she's trying to push a bad memory away.

"She was with Prince Sutagus when I saw her before," I say.

She stares at me, a look of disbelief washing over her face. "You saw the prince? In person?"

"Yeah. I had to meet with him for my last-minute nomination."

She blinks.

"What?"

"Nothing, it's just…we have a lot to learn about each other. A lot to talk about," she says, her eyes scanning the room.

"Can we sit with you?" a familiar voice asks from over my shoulder.

I turn to see Thayer standing behind me with a tray of food, another thin young man about our age waiting awkwardly beside him.

"Of course," I say.

"Us too," Cloveman says as he and Xander approach. Cloveman

plops down beside Wolkenna and grins. Xander sits next to Cloveman, exchanging hellos with Thayer and me.

"This is my roommate, Devlin," Thayer says, nodding to the scrawny boy sitting next to him.

"Where are you from, Devlin?" Cloveman asks, taking a bite of toast.

"Galghesworp. Here," Devlin says. His eyes dart around like a lost lamb. It occurs to me that this young man somehow beat out other hopefuls to make it here, though I can't for the life of me figure out *how*.

"Dev and I live in the same area," Wolkenna chimes in. "Our parents are friends."

"Then who are the *transplanters*?" Cloveman asks.

Xander darts a look at him.

"What?" Cloveman shrugs. "That Barston guy from Tarmensil said there were transplanters from Galghesworp. I'm just curious, because we're transplanters, too." Cloveman points at himself and to Xander. "We aren't from Eirelannia—not originally. We're from across the sea. We're outsiders."

Xander shakes his head as Cloveman takes an oversized bite of eggs.

"It's okay. He was talking about Nuser and me," Wolkenna says. "Nuser's family came from across the sea, and I was adopted."

Cloveman rests his chin on his hand and smiles at Wolkenna. "Do tell."

"My adopted family found me abandoned by the border when I was young," Wolkenna says. "They took me in as their own."

Cloveman purses his lips at Xander. "See?"

Xander merely raises an eyebrow.

Cloveman turns back to Wolkenna. "So, you're like us. A transplant, too, in your own sort of way."

Wolkenna shifts in her seat. This is the first time I've seen her look uncomfortable. Somehow it makes me feel like I'm witnessing something rare and heart-wrenching, like a bear who's left its cave to explore for the first time, only to realize it wasn't quite ready to leave—not ready to be exposed. But now it can't find its way back to shelter. There's a squeezing in my chest, like someone has reached in and gripped my heart. My mother leaving, my brother I can't relate to, my father's fall; it all hurts. And seeing someone as strong as Wolkenna open up like this reminds me of that pain we share.

She and I do have some things in common—more than I could've imagined.

She turns to me. "I'm just glad I'm rooming with another Ivernisterian. Looks like Frille and Nuser got stuck with some boys from Uladmond." She jabs a thumb in the direction of the cafeteria line.

Barston Frost stands in line with another tall young man, both of them dressed in fine clothing: ornately decorated shirts, tucked into clean, ironed slacks. Behind him, two smaller young men wait, dressed in clothes much more like my own—presumably Frille and Nuser, the other two from Galghesworp.

"What's his deal, anyway—is it a *Uladmondian* thing?" Cloveman says to the others at our table, staring at Barston.

"Not everyone from Uladmond is like him," Xander says. "We are technically from there, too. Our families landed there before moving to Ivernister."

Cloveman shakes his head. "You know what I mean. We're not like them."

"Barston's father was an Empyrean Rider," Xander says, leaning in. "Damon Frost. My father fought with him during their Empyrean Cavalry days. Let us just say, this is not the first time a Frost has left a negative impression."

I glance over at Barston as he grabs his tray and I wonder—did Barston's father know my father, too?

We all turn away in silence as Barston, the other tall Uladmondian, and the two young men from Galghesworp sit at a nearby table. Devlin furrows his brow at Frille and Nuser as they sit with the Uladmondians. One of them, Frille or Nuser, shrugs his shoulders and nods toward an unaware Barston Frost, as if trying to communicate that it would be bad news for them if they ditched their new roommates.

"Can he even ride?" Cloveman mutters under his breath. "Or did his father just score him a free pass?"

Xander's eyes dart over to the other table, then back to us. "According to my father, the Frosts are skilled Riders."

Cloveman rolls his eyes. "I can't wait to see it for myself."

"Aren't you the confident one?" Wolkenna smirks at Cloveman, and his cheeks fill with color.

Finished with my breakfast, I set my fork down and stand. "I'm going to go get this physical over with," I say.

Thayer halfway smiles at me, and I realize we've barely spoken since we arrived. I miss him. I miss his comforting playfulness. He's been quiet since the drive yesterday, and even though he's sitting right there, it's like he's not all the way *here*. Like he's still waiting back at the farm for me to return. Or he's so caught up in the newness of the base and the people here that he's forgotten everything else. Either way, he doesn't seem to see me. Not the way he did before we left home.

"I'll join you," Wolkenna says, standing beside me.

"Have fun, ladies." Cloveman winks at us. I can't imagine a physical will be *fun*, but it's one step closer to training. And that means I'll be one step closer to speaking to Commander Quin, as my father wished.

We place our trays in a bin and walk back to the door we came in through. Zarshona is gone, along with many of the Empyrean Riders from previous years. Only us new arrivals are left in the cafeteria.

It suddenly sinks in, a mix of fear and gratitude.

I'm one of them. An Empyrean Rider.

EIGHTEEN

Huffman is waiting with the other Watchers against the wall when we exit the cafeteria, and I wonder: when does he eat his breakfast, or does he get one at all? He leads us back through the courtyard and down a hall different from the one leading to our room.

"The medical wing," Huffman tells us when he catches us wide-eyed. Shiny white floors mirror stark white walls, and the lights overhead emit a faint, high-pitched ringing noise, making me feel like there's a swarm of angry bees inside my ears.

He pauses outside an open door. "Please wait in this room to be called for your physical," he says.

Wolkenna and I step inside. Chairs line the plain walls with one small sliding window on the right. The sliding window opens and a woman's round face pops up. "Names?"

"Wolkenna Quin," Wolkenna tells her.

My brows scrunch together as I dart a covert look at Wolkenna. *Quin*, like Rinehart Quin? A coincidence, I'm sure. It must be a common name in Galghesworp. But come to think of it, I'd never heard that name before my father mentioned it.

The woman—I assume she's a nurse—turns to me. "And you?"

"Aluma Banks," I say.

The nurse shuffles behind the wall, then opens the door beside the window. "Miss Quin, you can come back now."

Wolkenna glances at me and arches an eyebrow before she disappears into another hallway.

I sit in a chair. It's hard, squeaking on its joints as I lean back. There's a newspaper from Tarmensil on a small end table next to me. The cover is a photo of the king—it's the same article Kase read aloud the day our father was injured. I swallow down the lump forming in my throat. It was only two days ago that I sat at breakfast with my father and Kase. And now, here I am.

I stare blankly into space as my mind wanders to my father, Kase, Cashel, Darwith, Lermyn. Then a small movement catches my eye, and I glance over to find Zarshona's piercing golden eyes peering back at me. She watches me knowingly and walks straight past, not saying a word.

"Lieutenant Mund," the round-faced nurse chirps, a hint of apprehension in her voice.

"This is for Dr. Penson. See that she receives it right away." Zarshona's voice is toneless. She hands an envelope to the nurse, glancing over her shoulder at me. My eyes dart to the newspaper, and I pretend I can't hear everything she's saying. "The prince expects an update later today," Zarshona tells her.

My eyes stay fixed on the paper as Zarshona turns to leave, my body utterly frozen, as if I've fallen into a pond of ice. Something inside of me is afraid of her.

A few more minutes pass before Wolkenna struts back into the waiting room wearing a new uniform. It's a form-fitting ensemble with a black, long-sleeve jacket, three round buttons fastening it closed at her waist. Underneath the jacket is a white shirt with a winged collar. Her riding tights are stark white, standing in contrast to her perfectly shined black knee-high boots and belt. The uniform hugs her athletic curves.

She's stunning, somehow even more so than before.

Wolkenna furrows her brow when she sees me. "Are you okay?"

"Yeah, I'm fine," I say, rubbing my clammy palms on the tops of my legs, trying to dismiss the sense that Zarshona's golden eyes are still watching me.

"It's not *that* bad in there." She smiles, but she's still questioning me with her gaze. "Plus, look at these." She gestures to her new clothing.

"Pretty nice," I tell her.

"Much better than the rags I had on before," she says. "And with Galghesworp's colors, no less. Guess they're going to keep us color-coded." She points to the two small horizontal stripes sewn onto the jacket over her left arm; the stripe on top is dark blue, the other gray.

Huffman steps into the room. "Miss Quin, I'll show you back to your room now."

Wolkenna follows Huffman out, walking confidently. But she glances back, flashing me a look of concern, as if I'm not off the hook yet—like she knows I'm not telling her something.

"Miss Banks, you're up next," the nurse says.

The round-faced nurse leaves me in a room with a fancy medical bed and a tray full of various unfamiliar-looking medical instruments. Our medical care in Cintrenia just doesn't compare. Uladmondians, on the other hand, are accustomed to it.

"Please change into this gown." The nurse hands me a piece of what feels like folded white paper. "Put all of your clothes, including your shoes, into the bin." She points at a container. Then she's out the door before I can mutter a word, closing me inside.

It's silent, except for the obnoxiously bright light buzzing above me. I slide my boots off and the chill from the tile floor immediately penetrates my worn socks. I yank off the rest of my clothes and pull the gown over myself as best I can, but the measly bit of fabric is no match for the frigid air. I place my belongings in the bin and take a seat on the chair near the side of the room.

My hands slip beneath my legs as I attempt to stay warm. An

uneasiness sweeps over me. I feel exposed. I've never had a physical before.

My mind races to Zarshona and the way she looked at me in the waiting room. The way *she* makes me feel exposed.

The door opens, and Moninne—the kind red-haired woman from last night—enters the room. She smiles at me. "Aluma, good to see you," she says, closing the door behind her.

I try to hide my nerves. I'm nearly naked in this poor excuse for a gown and shaking from the cold.

"How are you feeling today? Did you get some rest?" Her voice is soothing, like honey being poured into hot tea.

"I fell asleep right away, but I still feel exhausted," I tell her. I haven't had a good night's sleep for days—not since before my father's accident.

"That's understandable," she says sympathetically. "You've been through a lot lately."

My gaze falls to the floor, and I imagine my father lying there. Tears well up in my eyes.

"Well, how about we get you up here," Moninne says, patting the medical bed. I glance up to see a look of concern crossing her face. "I promise I'll make this physical go as fast as possible," she says.

I waddle over to the medical bed, tugging at the gown, attempting to keep some of my dignity intact. The bed is clearly designed for tall Uladmondians; I have to hoist myself onto it, only noticing after the fact that there's a pull-out step.

Moninne runs a slew of tests on me with instruments I've never seen. She listens to my heart and lungs, taps under my knee with a miniature hammer, and has me follow her finger with my eyes.

"You're doing well," she says, tying a band around my arm, just above my elbow. She presses her gloved pointer finger against the different veins under my skin, until one of them is bulging. She reaches over to the tray of instruments and picks up a needle.

I suck in a breath. The silver needle is long and narrow like a thorn.

"Continue to breathe." Moninne's voice is calm. "You're going to feel a small poke," she says, and for the first time since I entered the medical wing, I no longer feel cold. A wave of heat passes through me as I close my eyes and clench my sweaty hands into fists.

There's a sharp pinching in my inner elbow.

"You can let your breath out—*breathe*," Moninne says.

I exhale, opening my eyes.

"There we go," she says, pressing a small white tissue to my inner arm. She steps away with a small tube, full of my blood.

"What do they need my blood for?" I ask her.

Moninne places the tube on the tray and turns to me with another needle—a larger one.

I tense. *Another one?*

Moninne places her hand on my arm. "It's okay," she says, and for a moment I think of my mother, and the way her touch felt when I was younger. "The tests are to make sure everything inside of you is functioning well," she tells me. "And this last one is an injection to keep you healthy. You'll need it when you go to the Old World."

She stands over my left shoulder area. Another pinch and a sting, like an angry bee from the buzzing overhead lights has finally come down to get me. I squeeze my fists together again until the pain subsides.

"Sorry," she says. "Are you okay?"

"Yes," I tell her. *As long as there aren't any more needles.*

She clasps her hands together. "Well, you're all done."

I sigh, relieved to be done with the painful, sharp tools. But I'm still in a paper gown.

"I'll be right back with your uniform," she says, exiting the room.

In a few moments the door reopens and Moninne slides back in. She places a pair of shiny black boots on the ground.

"Here you are," she says, handing me the rest of the uniform: a white shirt, black belt, white pants, and a black jacket. I turn the jacket over. It has two stripes on the upper left sleeve, green on top, and yellow on the bottom. Cintrenia's colors. Moninne peers out into the hallway before closing the door once more. She takes a seat on the chair against the wall and leans in as if she's about to say something, but she pauses instead.

"Should I get dressed now?" I ask. I'm freezing and half naked, but I feel slightly uneasy about dressing in front of a near stranger.

"Yes," she says. "But, Aluma—if you need to talk about anything, anything at all, I'm here for you." Her voice is serious, but kind. And when our eyes meet, a sense of comfort falls over me, like she means every word she's said. Like she cares about me.

"Thank you."

She shifts in the chair as if she has something more to say, but she doesn't let it out.

"Okay, I'll leave you to it." She crosses the room and opens the door, turning back to me. "You're in great health." She drops her chin. "You'll make a fine Empyrean Rider."

I smile. Me, an Empyrean Rider.

"Your father would be so proud of you," she says in a hushed voice, as if she's reminiscing—like she *knows* him. Like she knows *me*.

She leaves before I can speak, my mind reeling with unanswered questions in the wake of her words.

I walk into the hallway feeling much warmer, thanks to my new uniform. It's exactly like Wolkenna's, except with my city's colors. The uniform moves with my body, hugging my frame with each step. My boots are polished to perfection, and I have the urge to show them off to Cloveman and Xander, only they'll have the same boots soon enough.

When Huffman leads me back through the courtyard, the sun is much higher in the sky. I relish the sunlight, the autumn rays warming my cheeks like little bits of dough sitting out to rise. I even find myself grinning for a moment, feeling confident for the first time since I arrived.

Huffman pauses at the door to my room. "You're to wait here until the remaining trainees are finished with their physicals. Then you will be escorted to the stables for training," he tells me. As he turns to leave, he does something I haven't seen him do more than once: he cracks a smile. A small smile, but a smile all the same.

When I walk into the room, Wolkenna is sitting on her bed, scribbling something. She looks me over. "Nice, the jacket suits you."

"Thanks," I say. "I never knew clothing could be this comfortable." I run my hands over my jacket arms, the fabric smooth beneath my fingertips.

"Flight-friendly, that's for sure." She arches an eyebrow.

"I'll say." I chuckle, sitting on my bed.

Wolkenna drops her pen on top of the paper and stares over at me. "So?" Her tone is different, more serious.

"So, what?" My feet plop together as I admire my new boots.

"What happened in the waiting room in the medic's office? You looked like you saw something that scared you." She moves to the edge of her bed.

More like *someone*. "Zarshona came into the room," I tell her.

Wolkenna juts her chin out. "Did she say something?"

"No, but she gave something to the woman behind the window. Told her to give it to the doctor. It was from the prince."

"Anything else?" she asks, her eyes wide.

I tilt my head to one side. Why is she so curious about this? "She said something about needing an update later today for Sutagus. Why?"

Wolkenna falls silent and stares out the window.

"What is it?" I ask.

After a moment, she turns back to me. "You remember when I said we have a lot to learn about each other? To talk about?" I nod, and she sighs. "Well, it would be good to do that now."

"Okay..." I tell her, wondering where this is leading.

Wolkenna crosses the room and sits beside me. "I know what's going on here," she says, almost in a whisper. "I know why you're here."

I stare at her, dumbfounded. What does she know? "To be an Empyrean Rider?" I suggest, noticing myself blinking much more than normal, like someone's just thrown dust in my eyes.

She shakes her head. "It's okay, you can tell me."

"I'm sorry," I say, shrugging. "I honestly don't know what you're talking about."

"Look, we don't have much time." Impatience rises in her voice. "I know what happened to your father—"

"What do you know about my father?" I ask quickly.

"About his *accident*," she whispers.

"Yeah, so does everyone else." The image of my father lying unconscious in a bed somewhere flashes through my mind as my eyes blur.

"Didn't his accident seem a little unexpected to you?"

"Most accidents *are*."

She nods. "Exactly, but it was too unexpected—almost like it was *planned*."

I search her face. "What are you talking about?"

"Think about it. Your father perfected that move years ago with his Empyrean steed—"

"*Darwith*," I tell her.

She looks at me strangely, tilting her head.

"Darwith is my father's steed."

"Right. Well, your father and Darwith knew what they were doing," she continues.

My mouth falls open. "Were you there?"

"No, but I didn't have to see it to know something was off." She stares at me. "Did you notice anything that seemed strange?"

My lips press together as my mind races. I have a hundred questions I want to throw right back at Wolkenna. But my father told me not to trust anyone. I can't tell her what I know. I can't tell her about the box I saw Sutagus with, or how Darwith's wings seemed to stop working and then start again for no reason…or the dark shadow and the bright light I saw.

So instead I ask her the one question that's been stuck in my head, like a painful splinter I can't seem to pluck out: "Do you think someone planned to hurt my father?"

Before she can respond, a loud knock on the door makes us both jump. Wolkenna stares at me with a pained expression, and I furrow my brows at the sound of another, even louder knock before hurrying to the door.

When I open it, Huffman is standing there, looking at me like he's overheard our unfinished conversation.

"Miss Banks, I'm here to escort you and Miss Quin to the stables," he says.

I turn to tell Wolkenna, but she's already walking past me, avoiding my gaze. I want to stop her right there and ask her again, but I know that wouldn't be wise.

"This way," Huffman says, his eyes narrowing before he takes the lead, Wolkenna catching up beside him.

I trail behind them, thinking of Wolkenna's face when I asked her my question. It's as if I'd answered all of her questions and received an answer to my own, confirming my suspicions without her saying a word.

Someone did want to hurt my father. But who? And why?

NINETEEN

Huffman leads us on a new route, one that takes us outside, to where there are wide spaces between one building and the next. The air is cool and dry on my exposed skin. Dust whips around my new boots, escaping from the cracked ground. Unlike my old clothes, my uniform keeps the covered areas of my body comfortable, both inside and outside the building—an improvement, for sure.

We approach a steel-framed building with a large sliding door. Horse whinnies call out from inside of what I assume is the main stable. After my discussion with Wolkenna, I welcome the sense of calm that washes over me when I walk in. The scent of horses fills the air, reminding me of home. I breathe it in and sigh as we walk down an aisle between two rows of stalls. Horses stick their heads out through the openings: a chestnut, a palomino, a paint. I would love to stop and say hello to all of them, but my eyes are darting from side to side, trying to locate Cashel.

Huffman leads us to an open area within the building, where the roof is much higher than the rest of the stable. Chairs sit in front of an indoor arena. A few other Empyrean Riders are standing near the fence, watching someone riding a wingless white horse.

"This is where your training will be held every day," Huffman says as we approach the fenced area. "Please stay here until the commander has given you leave to retrieve your horses." He turns away, then pauses for a moment and glances over his shoulder at me. "Good luck."

"Thank you," I say, smiling as he departs. Wolkenna has already gone over to chat with Frille and Nuser, who are standing closer to the fence, watching the horse and rider in the arena.

I make my way over to the fence as well, climbing up onto the metal bars for a better view. A man rides the wingless white horse on the far end of the arena, steady on its back, like he's sitting in a rocking chair. As the horse and rider glide around the edges and move closer, it registers who I'm watching—*Commander Quin.*

The man I need to talk to now more than ever.

Commander Quin and his white horse ride past the others on the fence, closer to me. The horse's hooves hit the ground, each hoofbeat echoing in my ears, like the rhythm of a heart. *Thump thump, thump thump.* The vibration grows stronger until they ride past. He directs the horse to the middle of the arena, toward a series of jumps, taking the first with ease and grace.

"He's impressive," a voice says, startling me. Thayer steps onto the fence beside me, wearing his new uniform. It's just like mine, except his riding pants are black, he has four buttons instead of three on his black jacket, and he has a white tie with his white winged-collar shirt. His eyes stay trained on Commander Quin. I pause for a moment, noticing the way the green and yellow stripes on his left arm bring out the soft brown of his eyes, before my gaze drifts down to his chest and his arms. He looks lean and strong beneath his jacket.

"Very impressive," I say. But I'm still thinking of Thayer when the words leave my mouth. I turn back just as the commander lands the second jump.

"You—your uniform fits you well," Thayer says, and I catch him watching me from the corner of my eye.

"Thanks," I say, hoping my cheeks aren't flushing. "I don't miss my old clothes half as much as I thought I would. And this jacket is surprisingly comfortable, being so fitted and all."

"You look like an Empyrean Rider," Thayer says, making me smile.

"You too," I tell him, thankful he's finally being more open again. Thankful we've made it *here*—both of us, together.

After finishing the jumping course, the commander circles his horse back to the gate, which a Watcher opens. The commander rides into the opening near the chairs and dismounts. We all hop off the fence and scurry toward him.

"Take a seat," Commander Quin says, his low voice echoing out. He gives his flawless white horse a pat on its neck and hands the reins off to the same Watcher who opened the gate.

We all scramble to our chairs; I count sixteen—all the new recruits, including myself. With all of us sitting lumped together, it's like a wave of colors on our arms: Cintrenia's green and yellow, Tarmensil's red and black, Sceilaran's purple and white, and Galghesworp's blue and gray.

Commander Quin strides to the middle of the group. "Today you will begin training to become Empyrean Riders."

I try to keep an even expression as Commander Quin's gaze meets mine for a moment. He has light brown hair with a thick gray streak, tanned beige skin, and hazel eyes. His face is clean-shaven, without so much as a hint of stubble on his chin. There's a stern look on his face and a darkness around his eyelids, like he's the type of man who doesn't sleep more than a few hours a night.

"Many of you may have assumed you're done competing," Commander Quin says. "You may have assumed that because you won one of the four spots in your city, you're an Empyrean Rider. That assumption is false. You will only become an *official* Empyrean Rider once you have *earned* your place in the sky."

I shift in my seat, and Thayer does the same. I haven't earned my place? What about the Autumn Tournament? We're here to fly. But we aren't Empyrean Riders? From the looks of fear and surprise spreading across everyone else's faces like a plague, I'm not alone in this assumption.

The commander pauses, glancing at the three boys and one girl from Tarmensil—Barston Frost and his crew—all matching with their red and black stripes, sitting together, each of them a flame in a unified blaze.

"Before any of you take your first flight, you must be approved by me." Commander Quin's eyes land on the four of us Cintrenians. I stay as still as possible, not wanting to seem guilty of anything. There's no way he knows I've flown before. No way. His gaze moves to the four from Galghesworp—to Wolkenna. "I will approve those who are here for the right reasons. Those who are here to serve our king."

Serve our king. I scoff inwardly. This can't possibly be who my father asked me to find. I'm not here to serve the king. I'm here for my father.

I'm here because he told me to talk to you, *Rinehart Quin.*

The commander peers over at the Sceilaran group of two boys and two girls, dressed in their matching uniforms with purple and white stripes. "And those who will follow orders," he adds.

Orders. It's sinking in. The selfish, cruel king who orders people's livelihoods away will be the same man ordering me to risk my life in battle. And I'll have to go along with it.

The commander turns and glances at the stalls behind him. "Go find your horses. And keep in mind that everything you do—and don't do—will determine whether your horse will get its wings."

My heart is picking up pace, like I've been climbing a tall tree, and I've just noticed there's no safe way down.

"Go on," the commander urges.

I hurry toward the aisles of stalls with everyone else, my mind trying to keep up.

"He's tougher than I thought he'd be," Thayer murmurs. "I had no idea there was more left to prove."

I exhale, the truth of the matter becoming clear. "There's *always* something left to prove."

Four name tags hang on the outside corner of a stall at the end of an aisle. My name's not there. I walk to the next aisle. Thayer's name is on the first tag and mine is on the second. Yulla sticks her head out of the first stall, whickering at Thayer.

"Hey, Yulla," he says, patting her neck.

Cashel appears at the opening of the next stall, arching his muscular neck up and over the edge of the door, and I can't help but smile. He's just as stunning as I remember. I rub his dark muzzle and press my face against his. His long eyelashes brush my cheeks like the soft wings of a butterfly.

I slide the stall door open. "It's good to see you," I whisper, and he lowers his head. I breathe in through my nose against his neck, taking in his earthy scent, and for a moment, I'm transported back home.

After I saddle Cashel with the polished tack and fine leather that's laid out for us, I lead him into the arena. Most of the other riders are already warming up their horses, taking wide laps around the edges of the oval-shaped enclosure.

I mount Cashel, sinking into my seat. It's good to be back in the saddle.

As I bring him to a trot at the edge of the indoor arena, another horse's black nose catches my attention: a buckskin horse with a golden coat and black mane, and Wolkenna on its back.

Wolkenna glances down at Cashel. "Taima seems to like…"

"Cashel," I tell her, patting his neck.

"She doesn't like many." Wolkenna raises an eyebrow and cracks a smile.

I bring Cashel into a smooth canter—the same smooth canter I experienced when I first rode him. Wolkenna does the same on Taima. We ride side by side in rhythm, like the breeze rolling through the tall grasses of the Green Hills. Cashel stretches out his long legs, reaching for each stride. I feel like I'm floating, falling in sync with his every move.

"Looks like we're going outside," Wolkenna says, pulling me from my dreamlike daze. She nods at the others, who are exiting through a sliding door on the other side of the arena.

We follow the rest of the group, making our way out into an out-door arena bordered by another fence, a row of dark pines, and what appears to be the Galghesworp base wall. The sky is empty and blue; the dry air blows dust into small spinning clouds. And it's quiet, not at all how I'd imagined a military base would be.

We all ride to the center of the arena and gather around Commander Quin, where he sits atop the same white horse from before.

"Now that you're warmed up, it's time for your training," Commander Quin says. "Since all of you are skilled horsemen and horsewomen, you don't need any basic training." He looks around at everyone else. "Today you will learn to fly, given you pass the upcoming tests."

A few muffled chirps escape some of the other riders' mouths. Commander Quin twists around, trying to locate the source of the excitement.

"Don't be mistaken," he continues. "Flying requires a great deal of self-control. How you handle yourself in flight will either save your life or destroy it."

Thayer shifts on Yulla. None of these other riders have flown like I have. I'm the only one who knows what it's like in the sky. Any of us could take a fall like my father did. But I've experienced how free it feels to fly. I *know* it's worth the risk.

Something catches Commander Quin's attention, and we turn to follow his gaze. An Empyrean steed and Rider are flying straight at us, too fast and too low for comfort. The chestnut steed nearly grazes us with its hooves as it passes overhead and touches down behind Commander Quin, near the edge of the arena.

"The first skills you must learn are takeoff and landing," Commander Quin says, glancing over his shoulder at the Empyrean steed and Rider. The steed's long, black wings stretch out on either side of its body before it pulls them close to its sides.

"This is Lieutenant Mund," Commander Quin says as the steed and Rider trot closer. "She will teach you these skills."

Zarshona's golden eyes burn with a fiery intensity as she gives us a once-over, making my hands sweat. I wipe them on my pants as discreetly as possible. Of course, it had to be her—the only person I've ever met who makes me feel like I'm under a magnifying glass, burning in the sun. When she looks at me, it's as if she sees something that I don't quite understand—something I don't even see myself.

I catch Wolkenna glancing over at me from the corner of her eyes, and I remember the frustration in her voice when she talked about Zarshona.

"Most Empyrean Rider accidents happen during takeoff or landing," Zarshona—no, *Lieutenant Mund*—says, her voice sharp, like a blade. "Similar to jumping, with flying you must be ready, but you must not fight it. You need to be in sync with your steed at all times. Your steed is your partner up there." She juts her chin toward the sky. "Your lifeline."

I glance up at the blue above, feeling my confidence break down. Darwith is the only steed I've ever flown on. Cashel's a wonderful wingless horse, but how will he perform when we take to the skies together?

"Once your horse has its wings, there's no turning back," Commander Quin says, his eyes passing over each of us. "Your steed will know what to do and how to fly. It's in its blood. You're the one who must learn."

And learn, we do.

The commander and Lieutenant Mund take us back inside to the indoor arena, where we all take our turns at the jumps, one by one, focusing on our takeoffs and landings. From having flown before, it's hard for me to see how this training is that helpful for actual flight takeoff and landing. But despite my nervousness about flying a new steed for the first time, I'm still looking forward to it. I go through the motions like the others, hoping I don't appear too comfortable or excited by the prospect of flying soon.

Barston Frost proves to be as good of a rider as Xander claimed earlier. I was halfway hoping he *was* just a shoo-in because of his father's connections, but it's clear from his posture and confidence that he got here all on his own.

There are two riders who don't fare as well as the rest of us, including Devlin, the young man from Galghesworp—Wolkenna's friend. He's definitely sitting in the middle of the not-so-skilled department.

"Focus is required at *all* times," Lieutenant Mund says after we've completed our jump training.

"The competitions in your individual cities were your first test. This was the second," Commander Quin says. "And at this point, there's only a small margin for error."

I grip my reins. This was a test? My lips form a hard line as I replay my jumps. I was solid; there's no way I didn't pass this test.

"We are looking for great riders who will become fierce warriors." Lieutenant Mund glances at the young man who flubbed a jump, and he shrinks in his saddle. "We haven't even started discussing your fighting skills," she says warningly, peering straight at me.

I hold my breath, trying to appear more confident than I feel. Finally, she turns away, and I exhale with relief.

"Today, some of you will be transferred to ground patrol," Commander Quin says. Wait—does that mean some of us will become Watchers? Huffman's face flashes through my mind, and I wonder: was he once an Empyrean Rider hopeful, too?

I shift in the saddle. Some of our number might be denied their dream, but I'm determined to realize mine. I need to be here.

"Attend to your horses, and you will be escorted to the cafeteria for lunch," Commander Quin says. "We will notify those of you who will be sent to ground patrol. The rest of you, be ready to move on to fight-and-flight training later today."

Everyone is silent as we take the tack off our horses. The energy in the stable has shifted from excitement to worried anticipation, and the joy we once felt has completely dissipated.

After we put our tack up, Thayer and I lead our horses to their stalls, not saying a word. Devlin walks ahead, shaking his head to himself. A wave of pity falls over me—he was one of the weakest on the course. And though I feel guilty about it, I silently thank the stars that I'm not in his boots.

"Only the strong survive," a strident voice calls out from behind us.

I twist around. Barston Frost chuckles with the other tall boy from Tarmensil as they mock Devlin with wobbly arms. Barston is wearing his usual smug expression when he catches me glaring at him. He starts toward me, his eyes narrowing.

I turn my back to them and continue walking Cashel, hoping to avoid what appears to be coming next.

"Isn't that right, *Aluma*?" Barston asks. And there it is.

"Don't even bother," Thayer whispers to me, before I can react.

I follow his advice. I don't turn around. I don't acknowledge Barston at all.

"Your *father* wasn't one of the strong ones, was he? Falling off his steed like that." Barston heaves an exaggerated sigh, laced with mock disapproval.

I whirl on my heels to face him. An ugly smirk is stretched all the way across his ignorant face. He's loving this, and it makes me want to punch him.

"You know nothing about my father," I snap back, my fists clenched and ready to attack.

He holds my stare. Thayer touches my arm, and I flinch. "Come on," he says, his warm eyes attempting to calm my anger.

"The truth hurts," Barston taunts.

I keep my eyes on Thayer and take a deep breath in.

Thayer shakes his head slowly. "Don't. He's not worth it."

"Mr. Frost—a word," a booming voice calls out from behind Barston.

Commander Quin.

"Yes, sir," Barston says, giving me an unapologetically smug smile before walking away with the commander.

My boots press into the floor, as if it will steady me from the tremble rolling through my body.

"Let's go," Thayer says.

I lead Cashel into his stall. His lunch is already laid out for him. I'm not accustomed to people taking care of my horse for me, but Cashel happily hurries over to his meal. I give him a kiss on his neck before I leave, breathing in deeply, letting his scent ground me once more.

"Don't pay any attention to him," Wolkenna says, walking over to me.

I snort. "You heard?"

"It was hard not to."

Thayer is waiting by the front of the stable for me. Cloveman and Xander join us, and from the looks on their faces, I imagine they overheard Barston, too. Devlin scurries to walk with us from an aisle of stalls.

"Maybe the commander will put that guy in his place," Cloveman says as we all walk together.

"Or maybe," I say, "he'll get thrown out of here like the stinking pile of manure he is."

TWENTY

Back in the cafeteria, we go through the same motions as we did in the morning: get in line, take a tray of food, find a seat. My mind is thinking about too much all at once, and nothing at all. I barely notice how quiet I'm being until we're all sitting together at the table again.

Thayer peers over at me. "Are you okay?"

I take a break from staring at my food to glance at him, and when our eyes meet, my heart feels a little less pain, and the tension inside of me diminishes. "Yeah, I'm all right," I say.

The other boys and Wolkenna are all digging into their lunches like they haven't eaten in days. I take a bite of the sandwich in front of me, the bread disintegrating in my mouth until I remind myself to chew.

"I'm going to be put on ground patrol," Devlin blurts out.

"Don't say that," Thayer says.

Cloveman shoots a glance at a nearby table. "The guy from Sceilaran did a lot worse than you did."

Xander glances over at Cloveman and raises his eyebrows. We all know Devlin and the guy from Sceilaran are the main two who had any real issues. At least I hope they're the only ones. Maybe I landed poorly on a jump or two? I swallow, and a remnant of bread sticks in my throat. I take a large gulp of water, trying to wash away the uncertainty boiling up.

"Maybe it would be better anyway," Devlin mumbles.

Wolkenna tilts her head. "With *that* attitude, yes."

Devlin shrugs, as if he's already given up.

"Your family is counting on you, Dev," she says.

Devlin stares at her for a long moment, then abruptly stands. "I can't do this," he says, grabbing his tray. He exits without another word, leaving us all in stunned silence.

Wolkenna sighs, shaking her head.

"What was that all about?" Thayer asks her.

"He's *your* roommate—you tell me," she snaps back at him.

Everyone at our table stops chewing mid-bite, waiting for the tension to break.

"Hey." Cloveman nudges Wolkenna. "It's no one's fault." He glances around the table. "The pressure is real for everyone here. All we can do is stay hopeful, encourage each other, and try our best. Right?"

All eyes shift to Cloveman. He's said something serious, something valuable, something true. A smile spreads on Wolkenna's face, and she looks at Cloveman as if she's just seeing him for the first time. There's a palpable energy passing between them, like they're connecting on a new level.

I glance over at Thayer, and his eyes are right there to meet mine. He smiles his Thayer smile. And despite everything—the pressure, the uncertainty, the sadness—for a moment, I'm smiling inside. He dips his chin, as if to say, *everything will be all right*, reminding me of when he last looked at me with the same expression: the night he patched my arm up after I fell, trying to fly for the first time.

Sure, we knew each other before then, but things after that were different. *We* were connected—on our own level. We shared a secret. If Thayer hadn't found me hiding in the Empyrean stables after I fell that night, holding my bleeding arm, trying to figure out what I was going to do next—well, I might not have been able to continue flying. We wouldn't have had winter jam that year, or any to follow. And things would be different between me and Thayer.

I silently thank the stars I fell that day. And that he found me, and accepted me, just as I was—gashed arm and all.

~

The fight-and-flight training room is intimidating. There's a raised area in the center with benches surrounding it—a fighting stage of sorts—with weapons lining the lower walls. Four targets are placed on the outer walls of the room, each with a tapestry hanging above in its city's coordinating colors.

"Have a seat," Lieutenant Mund says.

I sit on the end of a bench as Commander Quin and Lieutenant Mund watch us from the middle of the stage. I glance around at the others, noticing that Devlin isn't present, and neither is the other boy who flubbed a jump earlier. They didn't make it.

"None of you have been to battle," Commander Quin says. "And none of you have been to battle on an Empyrean steed. *I* would know."

I gulp inwardly, hoping he doesn't know I've already spent *plenty* of time flying.

"Fighting from an Empyrean steed differs greatly from hand-to-hand ground combat or combat from regular horseback," Lieutenant Mund says. "As you experienced during the combat portion of the Autumn Tournament, it's difficult to maintain composure, balance, and focus." She gives Thayer a side-eye, and he sits up straighter, like someone has slapped him on the back.

"All of you can fight, but all of you must improve your fighting skills. If you want to survive, that is," Commander Quin says. He looks around at everyone before he continues. "Laithlann is not like the rest of Eirelannia. You can't expect to survive without your Empyrean steed."

Reality kicks me in the gut. *Survive.* Fighting is not what I signed up for. But I *will* have to fight other people—possibly kill them. Am I even capable of that?

"The Scalers—" Lieutenant Mund starts, then pauses and glances over at Commander Quin. "The *people of Laithlann* have adapted to their surroundings, hence their name. Scalers are ruthless, and they know their kingdom better than any of you."

"Since none of you have ever seen, nor set foot, in the Scaler cities—Nammden and Knarrno—none of you can fully comprehend what you'll see when you travel to them for the first time," Commander Quin says. "Their cities were once larger than any other cities in all of Eirelannia, with great structures, reaching high into the sky." His hands lift, as if he's illustrating his memory onto an invisible paper.

I've flown on Darwith over the Gray Forest. I've been in Laithlanner territory. But I yearn to know what the Old World looks like beyond the trees, where the Laithlanners still live.

"Since the wars, the people of Laithlann have survived, all in giant buildings, *scaling* their walls and traversing between the tall stacks of rubble," Commander Quin continues. "The ground is not walkable; the spaces in the city that were once streets are now covered in toxic water. The Scalers navigate the ground water, leaving and returning to the cities by use of their special water karriers. But for us, the *sky* is the only way in, and out."

The Scalers have water karriers? I thought every bit of technology was destroyed in the Old World and that only Uladmondians still had karriers. I guess I don't know nearly as much as I thought I did.

"You must learn to handle yourself in the sky. Between those giant buildings is where you will fight." Lieutenant Mund's eyes narrow. "We have developed a special bow that we've started using against the Scalers." She selects a longbow from the raised area. "This bow has good range and great accuracy if used correctly."

Of course it's a bow—my weakest weapon.

Lieutenant Mund sets the bow down and selects a sword from the rack. She swings the blade around in a few quick rotations on either side of her body, with the speed and dexterity of a seasoned fighter. My breath catches in my throat.

"For those of you who wind up too close to a Scaler, you'll want to be quick with your sword." Lieutenant Mund peers over at me. "They *will* use theirs."

Maybe I'll learn how to use the bow after all. I wouldn't stand a chance fighting against anyone who can wield a sword like Lieutenant Mund.

Commander Quin clears his throat. "Let's begin, shall we?" He scans over all of us. "I heard a few of you are already skilled and trained." His eyebrows raise, as if asking whether anyone is brave enough to claim the titles of *skilled* and *trained*. "Cloveman Ki, you're up first."

Cloveman's eyes widen before he stands and ascends the small set of stairs to the center of the stage. The commander hands him the longbow and a quiver full of arrows. He gestures at a target on the far wall on the other side of the room. Cloveman surveys the bow, holding it out with one hand and readying an arrow. He pauses, his focus zooming in on the target.

"Go ahead," Commander Quin instructs, keeping his eyes on the target.

Cloveman releases the arrow, and it blurs across the room, hitting the target on the lower end. His shoulders slump forward slightly, enough that I think I see him deflating a little.

"Again," the commander says.

Cloveman draws another arrow and releases. The arrow flies straight, hitting the target at almost dead center.

The commander nods. "Thank you, Cloveman."

Cloveman sets the bow aside and walks down the stairs with a small smile creeping across his face.

"Let's see...*Barston Frost*," Commander Quin says, his voice lower than before.

Lieutenant Mund smirks as Barston trudges up the stairs.

"Barston, we'll have you demonstrate your sword skills with Lieutenant Mund." Commander Quin hands him a sword—a *real* sword.

"Okay, Mr. Frost," Lieutenant Mund says, raising her wicked-looking blade in front of her. "Let's see what you've got."

Commander Quin leaves Lieutenant Mund and Barston Frost—my two least favorite people in Galghesworp—on the stage to duel it out. This is good for me, no matter which way the match ends.

Lieutenant Mund circles Barston with slow intention—a storm building momentum, just before lightning strikes. Barston swings his sword. She dodges his advance, spinning around on the other side of him. He passes with another forceful swing, and again as he turns. This time her sword meets his sword with a loud *clang*. They both glare at each other as the metal screeches. They pull away—*clang, clang, clang*.

Barston swings low and fast, and Lieutenant Mund jumps in the air. She moves in with her sword outstretched, swinging it toward Barston's neck. At the very last moment, she halts her strike, her hands holding the sword steady less than an inch from his throat.

Barston freezes, but even from my seat I can see his throat move up, then down as he swallows—his *pride*.

Lieutenant Mund nods. "Not bad—"

His smug grin returns as he laps up her praise.

"—but not quite good enough," Lieutenant Mund finishes with a shrug. Barston's grin disappears.

I have to fight back the urge to clap. *Only the strong survive, Barston.*

Barston makes his way off the stage with a little less pride. And for that, I am thankful to the golden-eyed swordswoman, Zarshona Mund.

"Now, for the rest of you," Commander Quin says as he takes the stage again, gesturing to the color-coded targets, "there's little time and much to prove."

My heart thumps in my chest. Like it or not, it's my turn to claim my place.

Training with skilled fighters doesn't make me feel any better about my own skills—or lack thereof. At the station beside us, Wolkenna demonstrates that she's adept with both a bow and a sword. My new roommate seems to excel at everything she does, and I secretly hope some of her talent will rub off on me.

At our station, Xander works with Thayer on his sword skills. Cloveman approaches me, carrying a bow while I tinker with another.

"Here," he says, offering me an arrow. "Looks like you could use some practice."

I snort. "You don't say?"

Over the last couple of years, Thayer and I had a few target practice sessions. I wish I'd taken those sessions a little more seriously. I feel my cheeks warm as I remember how he used to stand behind me, his hands lightly guiding my arms into position. Even back then, I was already getting lost in the moment—focusing on the wrong target.

Cloveman holds his bow in position. I fumble, trying to follow his lead as I pull back on my bowstring. The arrow wobbles, and I wish I could put this thing away and work with the sword instead.

"And release," Cloveman says, releasing his arrow. It blazes straight to the middle of the target.

"*Seems* simple." I lower my bow and arrow, blowing out a puff of air.

"Try it—and keep your torso straight. Your stance and correct posture are both essential to improving your shot."

I move my feet, adjusting my stance. I nock an arrow and stand straighter. Lifting my bow into position again, I set my sights on the target. I exhale and release. The arrow hits the target before I can even lower my bow, right on the outside of the center circle.

Whoa.

"There you go." Cloveman nods. "I'll leave you to it."

My confidence grows as I practice, but my mind wanders. I imagine the colorful target against the wall is not a target at all, but another person. I push my eyes shut and try to clear my head.

When I open my eyes, Thayer is standing beside me with a sword. "Care to spar?"

I raise my eyebrows. "Like old times?"

He nods, smirking at me. So sure of himself.

I set the bow on the rack and select a long, thin sword. I twist it around the way my father showed me and Kase.

"Are you ready to be defeated?" Thayer moves in front of me with his sword outstretched to meet mine, a grin forming on his lips.

I laugh from my gut, holding the blade out in front of me, admiring its luster. "Are you?"

I strike first. He meets my sword with a *clang*, pushing mine away. We move in a small circle, in a dance of sorts. I dodge his advance and bring my sword to a quick stop next to his abdomen.

He lowers his weapon. "You always were better than me with a sword."

"And you with your bow." I smile.

Past Thayer, Lieutenant Mund's eyes are on us. I lower my sword as she nears, hoping to avoid any interactions.

"Don't mind me," she says, stopping next to Thayer. "Continue."

"We're finished," I tell her, feeling the blood drain from my face.

"We're *never* finished, Miss Banks." Her eyes burn into mine. "Not until our last breaths."

Every little hair on the back of my neck stands upright, the way I imagine it would if I were about to rush into battle. She elicits a deep sense of fear in me—the kind that makes me feel like every bad part of me is on display, and I must do whatever I can to hide my flaws—to hide *myself*—from her. I don't get it, but it's as real as the deadly blade in my hand.

Thayer's brow sets into a hard line. Lieutenant Mund doesn't seem to notice I'm glancing at him, pleading silently for him to intervene.

She looks over at Thayer and reaches for his sword. "If you don't mind."

Thayer shakes his head, handing her the weapon. He steps away and mouths an apology to me. Behind him, Xander and Cloveman are tuning in and making their way over.

Perfect—an audience.

"Shall we?" Lieutenant Mund—sword extraordinaire—asks in her smooth voice.

I instinctively raise my sword to meet hers, not thinking about the repercussions. She pulls back and swings as soon as our blades meet. The steel nearly grazes one side of me; she's too fast. "There goes your arm." She smirks, lowering her sword.

My heart pounds in my chest. I try not to make eye contact with her glowing eyes as I glance down at my arm. Thank the stars—still intact.

"Again," she says, raising her sword.

I attempt to swing as fast as I can, but she blocks me with ease. I swing lower. She blocks me again. With a quick movement, she brings her sword close to my other arm.

"There goes your other arm." Her eyes are like golden embers of fire. "Now, how are you going to fight without arms?"

"Again," I say, my voice squeaking out from behind my teeth. Before I know it, I'm raising my sword to meet hers.

Her eyebrows raise. She's as surprised as I am for keeping this absurd match going.

We bring our swords together in a similar swing. I pull my blade away and dodge. I'm getting faster. I jump toward her and manage to almost graze her side. She brings her sword to meet mine, twisting my blade in a small circle. My weapon flies out of my hands, clanging onto the floor.

Taken aback, I stare at the sword, lying on the ground. I haven't dropped a sword since I was first learning to wield one. I've just made a complete fool of myself. I can't bear to look at Lieutenant Mund's face; I'm sure she's smiling the most wicked grin.

"You're a fast learner." In one fluid movement, she slides her foot under my sword, pops it up into the air, and catches the grip with her other hand. "You'll make a fine opponent someday." She hands me the weapon. "Just make sure you keep both arms."

I take my sword, still avoiding her gaze. She complimented me, and yet I still feel the sting of shame. I wouldn't have made it past the first round in the Autumn Tournament had I been matched against her.

She turns and walks to the Galghesworp station. That's when I notice Wolkenna and the others are looking in my direction. She, and everyone else in the large room, saw me drop my sword—saw me lose to the best swordsperson I've ever met.

Thayer nudges me. "You did well."

"It wasn't good enough," I whisper, disappointment coursing through my veins. I thought I was better than *that* with a sword. "I blew it."

Thayer shakes his head. "Stop. You didn't blow anything. This is practice."

But it's not just practice. This is real. I'll be fighting in a real battle, with real people. Against someone like Zarshona. Someone who won't stop short of taking my life if I drop my weapon.

TWENTY-ONE

By the time Commander Quin and Lieutenant Mund return, I'm more than ready for a break. After hours of weapon training, my body is aching all over. I don't recall the last time my arms and back were this sore; I thought I'd worked through that level. Then again, I've not trained for hours straight with live steel since I was much younger—and apparently much more agile—and never with such a heavy longbow. But now I've learned a few new tricks, and I'm faster and more skilled than before. I hope my father would be impressed.

Commander Quin and Lieutenant Mund take us back through the stable to the space in front of the arena where we sat before. Our horses are all mingling in the center of the arena, with Watchers holding their long lead ropes. My eyes scan over the assortment of horses until I spot Cashel, who is standing next to Wolkenna's buckskin mare, Taima.

"You've all done well with your first day of fight training," Commander Quin says once we're all situated near the fence line. "Each one of you has shown you're worthy of being here." Commander Quin glances in my direction, and all at once, I realize that I still haven't spoken to him. "Now, it's time for your horses to prove their worth and their connection to you—the rider."

"Not every horse will receive its wings," Lieutenant Mund says, eliciting a few gasps from our group. More bad news. "This isn't something you can change. If your horse isn't deemed worthy to become your Empyrean steed, we will all know shortly—in which case, you'll both be assigned elsewhere."

"What you're about to witness is something you're forbidden to speak of—to anyone. This is part of your oath to the king," Commander Quin says, his eyes trailing over each of us. "If you aren't prepared to commit yourself to the services of the king and swear you will never reveal what you see here today, then this is your last chance to leave. This oath stands, regardless of whether your horse becomes a steed or not. To break it is punishable by death to both you and the person you've told."

I turn to find everyone else looking around at each other. Thayer and I lock gazes, and for a moment, I think of darting my eyes across the stable to suggest we bail, but then I think better of it and turn the other way. Wolkenna glances at me, and she lowers her head slowly into a nod, as if she's saying, *stay*.

I swallow, gulping down a stone—no, the boulder that's lodged in my throat. I'm not prepared to commit myself to the services of the king. I'll never be ready for that. But my father sent me here. This must be part of his plan—it has to be.

My gaze shifts back to Commander Quin.

"Good," he says to everyone. "Let's continue."

A Watcher enters from the front of the stable, carrying a rectangular tray. When he reaches us, he stands next to Commander Quin like a statue, the tray held out in front of him. On the tray is a collection of locket necklaces—one for each of us, I assume.

"Line up," Lieutenant Mund says, and we all follow her order. "When you reach the front, step forward and receive your locket, then take a seat."

Before I know it, it's my turn to step to the front. Commander Quin hands me a locket necklace, and for the first time, I'm close enough to him that I could whisper why I'm here, explain what my father asked me to do. But then there's Lieutenant Mund and the Watcher, standing equally close, staring right at me.

When I turn back, the others have taken their seats. I sit next to Wolkenna, and her eyes meet mine for a split second, as if she wants to tell me something, but there's no way for her to do so without being heard. My gaze falls to the gold necklace in my hands. There's a small circular locket at the end of the chain. I fidget with it until it pops open. Inside, there's a tiny piece of white canvas.

Commander Quin's voice pulls me away from my locket investigation. "When I come around with my sword, press your right thumb against the tip of the blade until you break the skin. Then place a drop of blood on the inside of your locket, press firmly, and repeat after me."

I want to glance around, to see how everyone else is responding to the news of a *blood* oath, but I can't move. I'm stuck watching the commander draw his sword from his scabbard, leveling it out to the seat closest to him. I don't see who goes first—or second, or third. But I can hear the words Commander Quin says loud and clear, just before they're echoed back to him.

"By my blood, I swear my allegiance to the king of Uladmond, King Breasal Molacus the Third. By my blood, I swear to honor his name, fight for his glory, and protect his kingdoms. By my blood, I swear my life to the king."

The process is repeated until Commander Quin is standing directly in front of me. The Watcher is next to him, wiping the end of the blade with a cloth, clearing any traces of blood from the glistening steel. The commander lowers his gaze when he lifts his sword out to me. I lift my hand so my thumb is in line with the pointy tip.

Commander Quin's hazel eyes lock with mine; the light catches his steel, reflecting off the red halos around his pupils—red like the blood he's asking me to seal my fate with.

I touch my thumb to the tip of the sword. The sting is instant, just like the single drop of blood that appears. I lift the locket and press my thumb to the white canvas. When I remove it, my blood remains on the canvas, wavy circular lines like the inside of a chopped-down tree. And just like that tree, I too will be remembered and measured by these red lines.

"Repeat after me," Commander Quin says.

Before I know it, I'm swearing my allegiance to an unworthy king I never wanted to serve—a blood oath to the same king who has taken nearly everything my family has to give. I swear my very *life* to him, and I do it all willingly.

What am I doing? What's wrong with me?

The closed locket, now secured tight around my neck, weighs heavy, like a lock and chain binding me to my new duty. My thumb is sore, but it's nothing compared to the sickness building in my gut, like I ate a batch of old eggs and there's nothing to do but wait until the queasiness subsides. But something tells me this feeling won't go away. Not now, not ever.

When the commander and the lieutenant lead us into the arena, I finally see Thayer's face. It's pale, all the blood drawn away from his skin, as if he's not seen the sun for years. He reaches for the locket, fumbling with it like it's choking him.

"Now that you've taken your oaths, we can proceed with your mounts," Commander Quin says as he stands in front of us, our horses, and the Watchers still waiting behind him. "Are there any questions, before we move on?"

I raise my right hand, my thumb throbbing as I do.

"Miss Banks," Commander Quin says just as Lieutenant Mund reaches his side. She's carrying a small silver box, with four open triangles—mountain peaks, perhaps?—etched in black on its side.

I shift my gaze back to the commander. "Will it hurt them?" I ask, Cashel coming into my view behind the commander.

"A valid question," Commander Quin says, glancing at Lieutenant Mund. "One that Lieutenant Mund is more suited to answer, as she will be handling the transition."

Lieutenant Mund looks at me with her piercing eyes. "Hurt—no. Quite the opposite," she says, holding the small silver box closer to herself. And right then, I remember the last time I saw a box like this—albeit an even smaller black one, with three vertical silver lines—but a fancy-looking box all the same. It was the day my father's accident took place.

I shift my weight, confusion coursing through my veins.

"Any more questions?" Lieutenant Mund asks. No one else says a word, and I don't have the guts to inquire about the box in her hands. "Right then, let's continue, shall we?"

Commander Quin nods to her when she turns to him.

"You will want to shield your eyes when I alert you," Lieutenant Mund says, moving closer to our horses. "Only reopen them when I say." She takes the box into one hand and places her other hand on the top. "Cover your eyes now."

I slam my eyes shut, raising my hands in front of them at the same time. Even so, a light flashes so brightly past my fingers and eyelids that all I see are oranges, pinks, and reds dancing across the small spaces inside my eyes—like dozing off while lying in the sun. An incredible warmth rushes through my body as the color show continues on for what feels like several seconds. There's no noise at first, but then I hear the distinct *whoosh* of an Empyrean steed flapping its wings. Then another. And another.

As quickly as it appeared, the brightness disappears, with only traces of light still visible behind my closed eyelids.

"You may open your eyes again," Lieutenant Mund's voice calls out.

I lower my hands eagerly, focusing my gaze past Commander Quin and Lieutenant Mund to where our horses are standing—our new Empyrean steeds. Their long, feathered wings flap in place, ready to take flight, and I realize all at once why the Watchers were necessary.

"Your horses are now Empyrean steeds," Commander Quin says.

"*Most* of your horses have become steeds," Lieutenant Mund corrects the commander, and my heart sinks.

Not Cashel. Not Cashel. My eyes scan across the steeds until I spot Cashel's face. At the top of his shoulders are long *silver* wings. I squint, attempting to verify that my eyes aren't fooling me.

"No!" I hear someone shout to my left. I turn to see one of the tall young men from Tarmensil shaking his head in protest. "No, no, no! It's a mistake—try again!"

"Control yourself, young man," Lieutenant Mund cuts him off, nodding toward a nearby Watcher. "As you were forewarned, not every horse receives its wings. Your horse hasn't proved to be worthy of becoming an Empyrean steed with you as its Rider. You will be reassigned to a more appropriate position."

The Watcher approaches the tall boy from the side.

"Worthless horse," the young man snaps. "Give me a new one— *I'm* worthy of this, broken horse or not." He crosses his arms and widens his stance.

Lieutenant Mund's eyebrows are high on her forehead, her lips pursed together. She nods to the Watcher again. This time the Watcher takes the young man by his arm, leading—*dragging*—him away.

"Do you know who my parents are? You won't get away with this!" the young man yells, until his voice is but an echo.

I turn back to face Lieutenant Mund and Commander Quin, and all I can think is: what will happen to his horse?

Another Watcher approaches Lieutenant Mund. He's the biggest Watcher I've seen yet, built like a brick wall. His uniform is the same as the garb other Watchers wear, except for one additional detail: gloves. Lieutenant Mund hands the Watcher the silver box, and he exits with it.

What's in that box? And why is the Watcher wearing gloves?

"Now that we've tied up the loose ends, would the rest of you care to meet your Empyrean steeds?" Lieutenant Mund says, gesturing to the row of steeds. The wingless horse belonging to the young man who was reassigned from Tarmensil is being led away, and a twinge of sadness falls over me for the horse, realizing it will never know the sky.

"Go on," Commander Quin says, bringing me back to the moment. And just like that, I'm hurrying over to Cashel, like I've finally finished my chores and am free to do what I please. I'm nearly running, moving with ease—without any soreness at all. Somehow my aches and pains from training have diminished. It's strange, but

I'm too excited about Cashel's transformation to ponder the idea for long.

Everyone else follows suit, hurrying to their steeds. From the corner of my eye, I spot Thayer running up to Yulla, who's now sporting black wings. I feel myself smiling. How often have Thayer and I talked about this moment? And how many times had I thought it would *never* be possible for me?

"Taima!" Wolkenna rushes past me with a grin plastered on her face, reaching her buckskin steed with black wings.

And then I'm standing in front of my horse—my Empyrean steed. Cashel bobs his head and stretches out his new wings.

They *are* silver. Just like I thought.

"Whoa," I whisper, moving my hand to his neck, giving him a rub as he whickers. I run my fingers over his silver wings—they're soft and feathered, just like Darwith's, but with an iridescent sheen, unlike any I've ever seen. He's magnificent.

"Well, well, it appears we have the rare pleasure of meeting a silver-winged steed," Lieutenant Mund says, approaching. I turn to see everyone else looking in our direction, their own steeds beside them.

Commander Quin nears, looking Cashel over. "A rare pleasure indeed," he says.

My eyebrows scrunch together.

Lieutenant Mund tilts her head. "You must know the legend?" she asks, her eyes watching me closely.

I shake my head. All I've heard is that a silver-winged steed is the rarest type of steed. In fact, come to think of it—I've never seen one myself.

"The legend says that whoever rides the Silver-Winged Steed will free Eirelannia," Commander Quin says in a lower voice, his eyes on me now, just as intense as Lieutenant Mund's.

There's a sudden tightness in my chest, as if my muscles are pulling apart in both directions. Before I can stop myself, the words burst out of my mouth. "Free Eirelannia from what?"

Commander Quin raises his eyebrows as if he's about to speak.

"It's only a legend," Lieutenant Mund says, laughing it off. "Nothing more. You've just got yourself a good-looking steed, that's all."

The commander turns to Lieutenant Mund, his eyes narrowing and a hand coming to cover his mouth, as if he's trying to conceal his expression somehow. Then, in a quick moment, he resumes his rigid posture and faces everyone gathered around.

"Right," Commander Quin says, clearing his throat. "All that's left to do now is fly your new steeds."

Fly. The strange tension building in my chest disappears, replaced with the anticipation of taking to the skies again.

"As you can see, your steeds are eager to use their new wings," Lieutenant Mund says. "It's important for them to use them right away, with *you* on their backs. They will connect flying with you."

"We'll practice outside," Commander Quin says. "Tack up and meet in the outdoor arena."

I have the same flutter in my stomach that I get every time before flying. But this will be the first time I fly without Darwith.

And it's the first time I won't have to fly in secret.

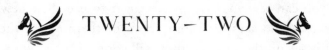

TWENTY-TWO

The sun is on its descent to the horizon. The wind from earlier is gone, leaving the sky motionless. It's a perfect time to fly. I've only flown at night, under the cloak of darkness, never when the sun is still in the sky. Never when the blue above seems to go on forever.

Cashel walks beside me, his neck in a perfect arch. The anticipation builds in my chest like a drum, ready to take on a faster tempo.

Ready to fly.

Thayer and Yulla walk beside us. Thayer's head is held high, his gaze trained on the sky.

"It's time," I whisper to him.

He turns to me with a smile on his face. "I'm ready."

Lieutenant Mund and Commander Quin ride over to us on their Empyrean steeds. Lieutenant Mund is on the same chestnut steed she flew in on before, and Commander Quin is riding the same white horse from this morning, which now proudly bears a pair of white wings, pure as fresh winter snow.

"This is Elro," the commander says as he stops in front of us. "He also just received his wings earlier today. I thought I'd put myself in a similar position to all of you."

"Mount your steeds," Lieutenant Mund says, and no one hesitates.

I hoist myself onto Cashel, brushing up against his wings; they're so soft, for being as powerful as I know they are. He prances in place with unbridled enthusiasm. He's ready to be in the sky, and so am I. Thayer glances over from Yulla's back. His eyes are wide, his cheeks round and pink.

"It's simple," Lieutenant Mund says. "Your steed already knows how to fly." Her chestnut stretches its dark wings out to its sides. "Hold on and trust its instinct. And remember to use the takeoff and landing skills we went over earlier. As you can imagine, falling from the sky is a lot worse than falling from a jump."

She gives her steed a kick, and they gallop off toward the other end of the arena.

Falling from the sky is a lot worse. I find myself blinking back tears once again, wishing I didn't know firsthand how devastating a fall from the sky can be.

Lieutenant Mund's steed's wings flap as it moves faster, and in a heartbeat, they're in the air—flying. She does a large loop in the sky, circling back in our direction.

"Who's first?" Commander Quin asks.

Everyone's eyes are fixed on Lieutenant Mund as she soars through the sky. A few moments pass, and no one jumps at the opportunity. I glance over at Thayer. His smile has disappeared.

"I will," my voice creeps out.

Everyone turns and stares.

"Go ahead," Commander Quin says, arching an eyebrow. "But don't forget to come back down."

I drag in a deep breath as I pat Cashel's neck. I position my reins and gather some of his mane, intertwining the two. Cashel trots forward when I give him the go-ahead. Another squeeze and he canters, releasing his wings out to his sides. His wings glisten blue and silver in the sunlight, like a mirror to the sky, as they push the air away. We edge closer to the end of the arena. I give him another squeeze, and he gallops. I lean forward slightly and squeeze him once more, and his hoofbeats stop beneath us. His wings propel us into the air, over the fence line.

We're flying.

The base walls fall away below us. A flock of birds flies in the other direction, to the south. Everything is open. And for the moment, *I am free.*

With our increasing height, I can see beyond the base walls, beyond a string of near-barren trees. The city of Galghesworp is in the distance. It appears larger than Cintrenia from the sky, but not by much. Their Empyrean arena sits in the middle of the city, much like at home.

We soar through the cloudless blue sky. Cashel breathes steadily, as if he's still running on the ground, but smoother. His wings flap with ease, pushing us higher. He stretches his wings out and holds them in place, and we coast.

I relax my grip and enjoy the view. I've never seen the sky so clear and bright. It's brilliant.

As we circle back to the arena, I spot Thayer taking off on Yulla for the first time. I direct Cashel toward them, and we hover in place. Thayer's eyes are wide and glistening, like a dark pond absorbing all the light, allowing me to see the wonder that lies beneath the surface. He's holding on tightly, crouched low and close to Yulla's neck.

Thayer shouts out at me in a combination of excitement and fear as he and Yulla speed past us. I give Cashel a squeeze, and we follow. The air rushes by my face as Cashel's wings flap vigorously, and soon we're flying neck and neck with Thayer and Yulla.

"How does it feel?" I call out to Thayer.

"Like I could thank the stars myself from these heights!" He peers up at the darkest blue, where the sky meets the edge of the world.

"Thank the stars," I echo, a smile starting on my face and deepening as I am overwhelmed with gratitude for this moment—Thayer and I, flying together for the first time.

We continue to fly away from the arena where we took off, until we're almost past the tall walls bordering the edges of the base and what lies beyond. The land to the south is even more barren and dry than the land we passed through in the land karrier. It's nothing like the Green.

"Head back to the arena," a voice calls out from behind us.

I turn as Lieutenant Mund catches up with us. Thayer nods, and we circle back. We pass over the many buildings and fields within the base. Everything below is small and bright as the sun reflects off the metal buildings.

The other steeds and riders hover over the arena we took off from. Commander Quin and his steed, Elro, make a smooth circle back to all of us. Elro moves more like a well-oiled machine than a steed as he glides through the sky, white wings slashing through the air like blades shaped from angular clouds.

"Congratulations, *Riders*," Commander Quin says, hovering between us. "You have now officially joined the ranks of the King's Empyrean Cavalry."

My fellow recruits whoop in celebration, congratulating one another from their newfound places in the sky. I glance over at the unaware Commander Quin, remembering the other thing my father told me to do.

Find Rinehart Quin. Find him.

But then a warmth fills me as the commander's words sink in, distracting me from my original mission, like taking the first sip of one of Father's hot teas after a cold day of working in the stables. I exhale deeply, patting Cashel's neck and wishing my father could see me now.

I've done it, just like he asked.

I'm an Empyrean Rider.

⌒‿

I spend the next few weeks either in the sky, appreciating Cashel and his new gift of flight, or on the ground, learning to fight. I've steadily improved my weaponry skills, and I haven't lost an appendage yet. Thankfully, Lieutenant Mund hasn't challenged me again since I first dropped my sword. She leads us through our flight lessons, though, in which I try not to appear too comfortable about being so far away from the ground. We practice takeoffs and landings, using a bow from the sky, and shooting at fixed targets. And most days, after fight-and-flight training, we're given a break to fly around within the Galghesworp base boundaries.

My father's request continues to lurk in the back of my mind, but now that I've found Rinehart, I'm not sure what I'm supposed to say to him. I wish I could talk to my father and ask him what to do, but word from Uladmond is that he's still in a coma. So, I throw myself into training instead, relishing the feeling of being in the sky again. That, and I've grown closer to Thayer than ever before, more than I'd realized was possible. We spend all of our free time together, enjoying the views from the sky. It's as if we're both drawn to each other. As if he's become a part of me.

When Wolkenna and I return to our room after dinner, I'm exhausted. My legs are as heavy as bricks, sore from the fight training, jumping, and flying. I'm ready to collapse. After a long shower, I lie on my bed, my body stretched out on the firm mattress, thanking me for stopping for the day.

After Wolkenna returns from her shower, she sits back on her bed, head resting against the wall, watching me.

I've had questions since our interrupted conversation about my father and his accident—about what she knows. There haven't been any free moments where I wasn't consumed by exhaustion or surrounded by others. And now, despite my best efforts to stay awake, my eyelids flicker to darkness.

"You know, with how busy we've been, I haven't had the chance to tell you about my adopted parents," Wolkenna says, her voice startling me from my daze.

"No," I say sleepily.

"More like adopted *parent*—the man who took me in."

"Mhm," I mumble, trying to remain alert.

"*Rinehart*—Commander Quin."

My eyes pop open. And just like that, my mind is wide awake, racing wildly.

"Rinehart Quin is your adopted father?" I push myself up onto my elbows. "I thought your last name was just a coincidence."

"No, not a coincidence." Her voice is quiet. "He took me in a long time ago."

I stare at her, not registering what she's saying.

"I've lived with Rinehart's friends for a couple of years now. They're friends of Devlin's parents." Wolkenna exhales. "Rinehart is always here on the base for training, so he had me stay with them." She pauses. "Devlin was the only person here who knew that Rinehart is my—well, he's like a father to me."

"Why are you telling me this?"

She hesitates. "Rinehart knew your father."

I shake my head, acting as if I don't understand. Acting like my father didn't tell me to find *him*.

"He told me what happened to your father. He made sure we were roomed together," she tells me, lowering her head.

"Why would he want us to room together?" I ask, eyeing her warily.

"In case you hadn't noticed, it's pretty much impossible for Rinehart to talk to you without being seen."

"Why would he need to *talk* to me?" I don't know how much longer I can keep my own secret hidden. And some of this is news to me.

"Aluma, you have to trust me." Wolkenna crosses the room and sits beside me.

I stare at my hands, full of newly formed blisters. I have to tell her. There's no way she's making this up. I turn to her, and her dark eyes lock with mine, waiting.

"My father, before he lost consciousness, he told me..." I take another moment, still unsure.

"He told you what?"

"He told me to find Rinehart Quin." I let out a puff of air. There, I said it. Secret's out.

She scoots closer, seemingly unfazed by my revelation. "Did he tell you anything else?"

"He said..." I trail off, remembering my father's words as he lay in the middle of the Empyrean arena, the life draining from him. *"You're the only light."*

She swallows.

"And he said I had to find Rinehart. That I had to become an Empyrean Rider."

"Anything else?" Wolkenna asks.

"No—is there something more?"

She stares off.

"Wolkenna?" Now I want to know.

"Did you ever hear your father say, 'The old will soon be made anew'?"

The words hit me like a punch to the gut. I shake my head. "My father never said it, but his friend, Lermyn, told me those words. He asked me to relay them to my father."

Her eyebrows furrow. "Did you?"

"Yes, I told him the day of the Autumn Tournament. Before his accident."

"What do you know about it?"

"'The old will soon be made anew'? Nothing," I tell her, wishing Lermyn hadn't been so secretive that day. Wishing he'd told me what he knew.

"Hey." Her voice softens as her hand lands on my shoulder. "I'm sorry about your father. But you need to know—he was a part of something. A movement."

"A movement?" I echo.

She nods. "He was working with Rinehart. There's a lot you and I both don't know. But I do know they were planning something. Something big."

"My father never said anything."

"Of course he didn't. He had to protect you," she says.

"Protect me from what?"

"From the truth."

"What *truth*?" I ask, thinking back to the morning of the Tournament. Then a swift realization dawns on me. "The king's new law," I whisper. "My father was worried they'd take our farm. He thought he'd have to come out of retirement. Maybe that's why he wanted me to become an Empyrean Rider, to save our farm."

Maybe I *am* the only hope to save our farm. But that can't be right. My father wouldn't want me to join the king's military just for that. No matter how much our home means to him, my safety has always been more important in his mind.

"It goes deeper—*much* deeper," Wolkenna whispers. "It's a lot to digest, I know." She moves back over to her bed and sits. "Look, let's continue this tomorrow. We're both exhausted enough already."

I nod slowly, attempting to settle my racing thoughts. I *am* exhausted. This is too much for my tired brain to process. Nothing is clear, and I need sleep.

I lie back on my bed and roll onto my side, gazing at the photo of my father and brother. My father looked so happy. My eyes flicker closed as his face roams through my sleepy mind. A happy face with so many secrets.

What else was he hiding?

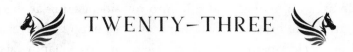

TWENTY-THREE

My eyes fly open at the sound of a blaring alarm. I bolt upright in my bed and turn to face Wolkenna as she flips on her lamp and sits up, straight as a stick, looking over at me.

"What's going on?" My heart thumps as a wave of heat rushes through my body.

"I have no idea," she says, moving to the window and pulling back the curtains. It's still dark outside.

"All Empyrean Riders, report to the main stable immediately," a loud voice orders over the speakers in the hall.

Wolkenna and I share a look as we begin pulling on our uniforms.

"Report to the main stable immediately—this is not a drill," the voice continues.

Wolkenna slides into her boots. "Strange," she says, a perplexed expression crossing her face.

I lean over to slip my own boots on. My stomach is achy and my body is worse off than it was when I fell asleep. The one night I could've used a good night's sleep, and it's *not a drill*.

Wolkenna and I exit our room, both of us glancing at each other when we realize Huffman, our Watcher, isn't anywhere in sight. We hustle outside into the darkness toward the main stable. Hurried voices follow us. The moonlight trickles through the low-lying clouds like little spotlights, illuminating the rushing bodies of the older Empyrean Riders I saw in the cafeteria and the new Riders from our group, all moving in the same direction. The temperature has dropped considerably, and the air is cold on my face.

"It's not a drill," Wolkenna mutters as we scurry over to the others.

The lights are on, bright as day, when we enter the stable. I squint, attempting to adjust my vision. I spot Thayer running over to me, his eyebrows drawn together.

"What is all this?" Thayer asks, his voice hoarse.

I shake my head and shrug. His guess is as good as mine.

We all move to stand in a group by the arena, and then the crowd parts, making way for Prince Sutagus Molacus.

My hands clench into fists as the little hairs on my neck rise.

The room goes silent as the prince marches in, stepping onto a platform in the middle of everyone. He's wearing his military uniform, and his hair is slicked back as if he hasn't slept a wink. His eyes are a frigid blue. He looks the same way he did during my nomination, when he mentioned my mother.

My nails dig into my palms.

Lieutenant Mund stands on one side of the prince. Her eyes are intense under the lights, golden and glowing. The prince stands higher than her on his makeshift platform. But there's still one person missing—Commander Quin.

"At approximately 0200 hours, we were attacked on the Ivernister–Laithlann border, five miles east of here." The prince's voice is husky, as if he's been yelling. "The attackers—Laithlanners—killed three of our border guards while attempting to infiltrate Ivernister. Some of our night scouts followed the attackers back over the border and reported them heading east toward Knarrno, by water karrier, with a sizable group."

A few Empyrean Riders murmur.

"We perceive this as an act of war." The prince's eyes narrow. "By the king's orders, we will track down and eliminate the perpetrators. *Tonight*."

War. I'm going to war.

"Where's Commander Quin?" Wolkenna blurts out.

Prince Sutagus narrows his eyes at her, his nostrils flaring before he answers. "The Commander is currently indisposed. I will be leading tonight's mission, along with Lieutenant Mund."

Out of the corner of my eye, I see Wolkenna clenching her jaw. The situation does seem a little unusual. The prince has extensive combat experience, to be sure, but why is he showing up here in the middle of the night? And what's going on with the commander?

Before I can consider it further, a hand touches mine. I look up at Thayer and see his face is blanched, his eyes still on the prince. I squeeze his hand, feeling the dampness of my own—or maybe his, too.

"We leave immediately. Prepare your steeds and meet in the outside arena." The prince clears his throat and marches through the parted crowd. Lieutenant Mund follows.

As he passes me, the prince turns his head, and his eyes meet mine for a split second. His gaze, full of anger and violence, sends a shudder down my spine, and I suddenly feel like I'm going to be sick.

The crowd disperses as the other Empyrean Riders scramble toward the stalls. Thayer, Wolkenna, and I stand frozen in place. Thayer's hand falls away from mine.

"Come on," Xander's voice calls out from behind us.

This must be a nightmare. I need to wake up.

I turn, shaking my head back to reality, hurrying to Cashel's stall. He's awake, and stomps the ground as I open the door. I give him a quick neck rub while simultaneously leading him to the tack area. I saddle him as quickly as I can and head to the outdoor arena.

Outside, a few ground soldiers are handing out weapon-packs to the Empyrean Riders: a bow and a quiver of arrows, a sword, a rope, and a saddlebag. Another group of soldiers slides armor over the Riders. I fall into line with the others, my legs feeling weak.

This can't be happening.

I scamper over to one of the soldiers handing out weapons, realizing at the last minute who the person is—*Huffman*. His eyes lock with mine.

"Miss Banks," Huffman says, handing me my weapons. He attaches the rope to my saddle before turning and glancing around. "Be careful," he whispers, frowning as he steps over to the next person in line.

My body is trembling as I mount Cashel, weak and nervous—the worst combination for what I'm likely facing.

The rest of the Empyrean Riders are waiting for the last of us to collect our weapons. I ride Cashel over to Thayer, where he sits on Yulla, his face still devoid of all color. Wolkenna trots up to us on Taima, peering over at me with a strange look. Then she glances past me, toward someone else.

I turn, following her gaze. The prince is staring at me. A bitter chill runs through my bones, like I've fallen through the ice at Turtle Pond during midwinter.

I twist away to see a look of concern settling over Thayer's face. Xander and Cloveman ride their steeds over to join us. Despite the battle to come, Xander somehow seems calm and collected, while Cloveman fidgets nervously with his weapons.

"We will fly in two packs," the prince announces. "One group flying with Lieutenant Mund, and the other with me."

Lieutenant Mund stares out at us, her eyes flickering like fire under the moonlight.

"On our command, you will attack the enemy," the prince says. "Unless it's a last resort, maintain your distance. You don't want to end up on the ground using your sword."

I clench my reins, as if I'm clinging on for my life.

The prince eyes us. "New Riders fly with Lieutenant Mund. The rest with me," he orders, turning his steed away.

The veteran Empyrean Riders follow Prince Sutagus to the middle of the arena. The prince and his steed sprint into a gallop, and in moments they're flying. The other Empyrean Riders follow him into the abyss of the night sky, while the rest of us wait for Lieutenant Mund's command.

"If you want to stay alive, obey my orders," she says. "Stay in the pack. Don't attack until I say." With that, she turns her steed toward the middle of the arena.

Attack. My body clenches as I force myself to prepare for what's to come.

"Let's go!" Lieutenant Mund calls over her shoulder. She kicks her steed and takes off toward the edge of the arena and into the sky. The recruits from Tarmensil follow next, then the group from Sceilaran. Wolkenna and Taima take off into the darkness, and the other two from Galghesworp follow.

And then it's just the four of us from Cintrenia.

"Be safe, my friends," Xander says before taking off at full speed.

Cloveman glances over with a wilted expression, then follows after Xander.

Thayer shakes his head. "This isn't right—I'm not ready." His eyes search mine, as if I can somehow stop this.

"We have to go." I say the words, but they don't sit right with me, either.

Thayer struggles to nod. I give Cashel a squeeze, and we take off into a gallop. Thayer and Yulla catch up beside us. Together, we move to the edge of the arena, in perfect sync with each other.

"I'm right beside you!" I call out to Thayer.

The blurred ground grows darker as we lift off into the night sky. I'm shaking all over, as reality finally sinks in: this *isn't* a nightmare.

TWENTY-FOUR

The air is frigid on my exposed skin as Thayer and I fly through the dark sky, following the other new Riders. Lieutenant Mund leads the group, and the rest of us move into a *V* formation behind her, like a flock of migratory birds.

"Stay close!" Lieutenant Mund shouts to us.

Moonlight breaks through the clouds as we follow her over the walls, leaving the base and the city of Galghesworp far behind. The lights of the training yard disappear in our wake, fading into the darkness that envelops the countryside. I lean closer to Cashel's neck as we enter the cloud cover, blocking the icy air as it rushes past. We ascend higher and higher, until we finally burst through the clouds to find the prince and his group hovering in place, waiting for us.

"We are about to pass into Laithlanner territory," Prince Sutagus says. "From this point on, we go into stealth mode." He looks over his shoulder at the open sky above the clouds, where the unobstructed light from the moon makes our path much clearer. "Watch for our signal to attack." The prince turns his steed and starts off toward Laithlann. The rest of us follow.

Our flight through Laithlanner territory is silent. No one makes a sound, each Rider taking stealth mode as seriously as the next. When the clouds separate and the moonlight shines through, there's land, water, and I can't tell what else below—it's still too dark.

My mind tries to drift, but the cold air slapping my face keeps me in the present. I'm alert and distracted at the same time.

Lieutenant Mund holds her left fist high and signals below. She directs her steed in a steep dive toward the ground, and we follow, water droplets wetting my face as Cashel and I descend.

When we exit the last of the cloud cover, a wide river comes into view. In the distance, small lights float on top of the moonlit water—a water karrier. Prince Sutagus and his group halt, hovering in silence. Lieutenant Mund and the rest of us slow until we're hovering in place beside them.

I glance at Thayer, his face red from the cold wind. Wolkenna peers over at me, and I catch a hint of apprehension in her expression—or is it fear? Up until now, I didn't think Wolkenna was afraid of anything.

"That's our mark," Prince Sutagus tells us, pointing at the water karrier.

My heart thumps like a war drum in my chest, and the swishing sounds of our Empyrean steeds' wings flapping in place pulse in my ears.

I'm not ready for this.

"On my signal, we attack." The prince takes his reins and wraps them around the front of his saddle. He readies his bow in his left hand. The rest of the Empyrean Riders follow, and soon all of us are ready to fire.

Ready to kill, if necessary.

I hold my legs firmly around Cashel, steadying myself as I nock an arrow in my bow. All the balance work I did on a horse as a child—learning to canter and jump small streams without using my hands—is finally proving useful.

Thayer stares at me, fear coating his face like bloodstained mud. I try to swallow, but my mouth is bone-dry.

The prince and his steed dive toward the river, and before I know it, we're all flying low and close to the dark water. The clouds part, allowing the moonlight to bounce off the river again, and our reflections take shape for the first time. Cashel's wings stretch out, long and wide, straight as arrows on either side of us. The shape of my head stays close to his neck. And in this moment, it's as if he and I are one unit, gliding precariously toward our fate.

The floating karrier comes into view, its deck lights flickering as it moves on the water. Small figures stand watch on different levels.

I draw in a ragged breath.

The prince raises his string hand vertically, then drops it sharply to his side, signaling us to fire. Lieutenant Mund gives the same signal. I watch as the prince nocks and releases an arrow, targeting a man standing at the end of the karrier. The man yells out before tumbling over the edge, falling into the swirling water.

I can't exhale.

Arrows whistle through the air as they're sent at the water karrier and back at us. I trail behind Lieutenant Mund and the rest of our group as they shoot their arrows at rapid speed. We fly past on the left side, coming to hover beside it. Laithlanner voices shout out as they shoot in our direction.

It feels unreal. What if one of those arrows hits me? My body clenches up as I realize for the first time: I could die out here. Tonight. Right *now*.

My bow is in position, but I haven't sent an arrow at the karrier yet. My mind goes blank as Thayer fires another arrow beside me.

"Attack!" Lieutenant Mund yells at me between shots. Her eyes glare into mine. "That's an order!"

I draw my bow, shut my eyes, and release my first arrow at the karrier.

Don't hit anyone. Don't hit anyone.

My eyes open as a man fires an arrow from the karrier, right in my direction. A burning rush of air rips past my neck.

Thayer flies closer, his eyes wide. "Aluma, defend yourself!" And it hits me all at once—that burning air was the *arrow* the man just fired, inches from my throat. Thayer sends a string of arrows at the man who shot at me. The man drops when at least two of Thayer's arrows hit him.

Blood pumps through my veins, hot and fast, as I snap out of my stupor. *I don't want to die.*

Another armed man on the karrier turns his attention to Thayer, readying his weapon.

"Thayer!" I yell, releasing my arrow straight at the man. He tumbles over the karrier railing and into the water.

I wince, useless regret churning in my stomach like sour milk and razor blades. I just took a life. I'm a killer now.

"This way!" Lieutenant Mund shouts.

We circle around the front of the karrier after her. On the other side of the karrier, the prince is shooting toward the top level. A group of men are positioning a large, ball-shaped weapon. We shoot at them in unison, firing arrow after arrow as they engulf the ball in flames. The fireball launches into the air and hits two Empyrean Riders that I don't recognize. They scream as both steeds and Riders crash into the water in a fiery mess.

I reach for another arrow, but my hand grasps at nothing. I'm out.

My eyes dart around. What do I do now?

Lieutenant Mund draws her sword. She hovers, looking at the prince, waiting for an order. Cloveman and Xander fight side by side, sending their remaining arrows at the karrier. Cloveman grabs thin air as he reaches for another arrow, finding his quiver empty. As he draws his sword, an enemy arrow strikes his right arm. He yells out in pain. Wolkenna flies Taima between him and the water karrier, sending her remaining arrows at the person who shot Cloveman.

Another fireball flies toward Lieutenant Mund and a boy from Sceilaran. The boy's face is full of fear as he tries to fly straight up, but the fireball strikes his steed. He screams as he falls into the river, his steed falling beside him.

"We're out!" Lieutenant Mund shouts to the prince.

"Pull back!" the prince orders over the sounds of arrows and the screams of the injured. Bodies litter the river, some flailing for help, others drifting like logs, stiff and lifeless in the water.

Despite the chaos ensuing around me, everything goes quiet for a moment, like I'm in the eye of a storm. Arrows streak by in slow motion. Those that don't hit a Rider or their steed slice up through the cloud line, heading toward the moon.

Cashel's wings are still flapping, keeping us in the air, but I'm frozen in place, an easy target for enemy arrows. I'm trapped—unable to scream, unable to make myself move an inch.

I'm as good as dead.

In a quick moment, an arrow from the karrier strikes Lieutenant Mund in the side of her abdomen. She fumbles her sword and clutches her side as her steed flies higher into the cloud cover.

Cashel throws his head with a loud snort, his mane hitting me in the face like a whip. I snap back, my mind now fully alert. Through the dimly lit sky, a white steed breaks through the clouds, rushing straight for us, its rider wearing a silver mask, a dark cloak, and holding a bow. A traitor—or a Laithlanner? But then, Laithlanners don't have steeds.

I draw my sword and give Cashel a squeeze. Everything inside of me is now screaming to get out of here.

"Thayer!" I yell out frantically, searching for his face. I turn Cashel in a circle midair, realizing there's no one left in the sky around me, except for the masked person on the white steed.

"Come on!" Thayer's voice calls from above. I thank the stars as my eyes dart upward, finding Thayer just as he disappears through the cloud cover with the others.

An arrow buzzes past my head. I turn, squeezing Cashel, and time slows down once more.

A man on the karrier has his weapon aimed at me. The masked person on the white steed blazes toward me on my left side as I try to direct Cashel up to the clouds. But before I reach the cloud cover, a sharp pain hits my right leg. I lean into the pain, dropping my sword. An arrow is in my thigh.

My eyes blur as the pain tears through my body, every nerve in my leg burning like fire.

I lift my head as the same man on the karrier readies another arrow, trained right at my chest. The sound of wings draws near. I turn as the mystery white steed and rider fly between the karrier and me, blocking the arrow's path. But before the man on the karrier releases his arrow, my weakening body betrays me. I sway in the saddle, tumbling off Cashel.

And then I'm falling with my back to the water.

Cashel swoops down toward me, his wings outstretched, his nostrils flaring. The moonlight trickles through the clouds behind him, illuminating his long silver wings. It's breathtaking.

Maybe this is just a dream, after all—some kind of beautiful nightmare.

But then my body breaks against the hard water, and the world goes dark.

TWENTY-FIVE

D*rip…drip…drip…*
   My eyelids are heavy, like they've been painted over with mud. I don't have the energy to push them open. There's solid ground beneath me and some kind of heavy fabric draped over the top of my body, and yet I'm still freezing cold. My right thigh aches. I slide my hand onto my leg, scared of what I might feel. Something is wrapped around that part of my thigh, where the pain is radiating like a sharp needle has pierced my skin.

The arrow.

In a moment, everything rushes back. The battle, Thayer flying into the cloud cover with the other Empyrean Riders, the masked rider on the white steed, the arrow sticking out of my thigh, the moonlight, Cashel trying to reach me as I fell.

I'm alive.

I force my eyes open to darkness. I'm in a tunnel—*a cave.*

A few pieces of burnt wood glow red and crackle just to my left, the heat warming my cheeks like a welcome ray of sunshine. Beyond the dying fire, a dim light trickles in at the end of the cave. Water droplets fall from the tops of jagged rocks into puddles. My mind races as I realize that the only caves I've ever heard of are the *Knarrno Caves*.

I'm in Scaler territory.

I push myself up onto my elbows, and the heavy fabric—a dark cloak, by the looks of it—that was draped over me falls to my lap. Pain throbs through my leg with each careful movement. Pushing the cloak off to the side, I look down to see my thigh is wrapped in a bandage. There are other pieces of cloth scattered around me, all with dried blood on them—my blood.

"You're awake," a voice says.

I freeze, motionless. It's silent except for the water dripping. It won't stop dripping.

The little light coming in from the mouth of the cave frames a figure. I drag myself in the opposite direction, attempting to stand. A stabbing pain hits my leg again and again until I collapse, gasping for breath.

"You shouldn't," the figure—a young man—cautions me as he approaches. He can't be but a few years older than me. His hair is black and slightly wavy, resting near his shoulders, with skin the color of sandstone. He crouches beside me—dark eyes, high cheekbones, and a strong jaw.

I catch my breath.

He holds my gaze for a few moments before he reaches out to my thigh.

I swat his hand away. "Don't—"

"I need to check your leg," he says, his voice deep and steady. He waits, not touching me. "I'm the one who fixed it."

I sit for a moment. Do I have any other options?

"Go ahead," I say finally, my voice cracking.

"I applied a healing paste to fight infection," he tells me, carefully unwrapping the material around my leg. His warm hand grazes my skin, and I flinch. He stares at me, his eyebrows pulling together.

"Are you a Scaler?" I ask, wondering if he's a Laithlanner. A sharp pain shooting from my hip to my knee makes me jerk. "Ow!"

"Hold still," he says, watching me. His lips curl up on one side.

"A *Scaler*," he scoffs, shaking his head. "Why am I not surprised?" He glances at my now-exposed wound.

I grimace, the pain somehow increasing when I see it. A white paste has been dabbed over the top. I can't help but imagine him smearing it on my leg; his hands were on me, and I didn't even know it.

"Yes, I'm a Scaler," he says. "But we refer to ourselves as Laithlanners."

I'm sitting with a Scaler, the only person from the Old World I've ever seen. I search his eyes and glance him over, trying to figure out which part of him could ever be considered *grotesque*—the way we've always been told a Laithlanner would look.

He's the very opposite of grotesque. I flush at my train of thought.

The young man finishes covering my wound with a new cloth and glances at me. "Are you all right?"

My cheeks burn even hotter, and I turn away to hide my embarrassment. "Where am I?" I ask, attempting to divert attention from any blushing on my part. Thank the stars for the dim cave lighting.

"Knarrno," he says, rubbing his hands together in front of the fire.

"How did I get here?" My eyes follow him as he sits across from me. He lifts the thick cloak that I'd pushed to the ground and drapes it back over my legs. His shoulders are broad and strong, but he's otherwise lean.

"You were already here," he says with an odd expression.

My brows furrow.

"What?" He snorts. "You didn't know you were in Knarrno?"

"I—I thought I was still a good distance away."

"When I got to you, you had fallen into the Knarrno River."

So he was there. At the battle.

"After your people attacked us—" He pauses, his jaw clenching. "After *you* attacked us."

I lower my eyes, feeling a ripple of shame. Though it's not as if I had much of a choice. "Where's Cashel—my steed?"

He turns his head toward the cave opening and sighs. "Your *Empyrean* steed?" He peers over at me with intense eyes. "He's here. He wouldn't leave you. He followed me all the way."

Cashel is here. I try to stand, ignoring the pain as best I can. "I want to see him—"

"Hold on, not so fast," he says, rushing to my side, lifting me underneath my arms, his hands finding my waist.

I swallow hard as I try to steady myself, keeping the weight off my right leg, all the while keenly aware of how close he is to me.

My eyes dart to where I was just lying. "Where are my weapons—my sword, my bow?"

"At the bottom of the river, I assume."

I stare at the ground as I replay my fall. He's right—I dropped my weapons. So I'm unarmed, with a stranger—an *enemy*.

Great. This is the perfect way to wake up from a nightmare.

"We need to get going," he tells me. "You've been out all day." He keeps one hand around me, scooping up his cloak from the ground with the other.

"Where?" I ask, inching forward, my teeth gritting together. My leg still feels like there's an arrow sticking out of it.

His strong hand cups my lower back as he steadies me once more. "Let me carry you."

"I can walk," I object, trying to take another step forward, but the pain is overwhelming.

"No—I'm carrying you," he says, and in one fell swoop, he's holding me in his arms. He carries me to the opening of the cave, my face awkwardly close to his neck. He smells like the ocean, and for a moment, I forget about the throbbing pain in my leg.

A loud, crashing sound greets us as we near the entrance of the cavern. He carries me out onto the black rocks, and I see that we're by the ocean. The waves clap against the jagged cliffs, and the wind drags the salty water toward us, traces of it painting my lips. The sky is so overcast it might as well be night; gray clouds meet the inky sea, all in a blur.

We turn a corner, away from the turbulent water. The sounds of the waves become muffled as the boulders outside the cave create a barrier. A soft rain falls as he carries me with ease, not saying a word, over the rocky ground.

I turn my head to see where he's carrying me. Dark green, majestic trees—a forest sprawls out in front of us. Tall grass leads to a path. As he carries me down the trail, there's a rustling somewhere to our left.

I tense, my eyes darting around wildly until I spot Cashel. His wings are tucked by his sides as he trots over to us. He extends his neck and touches his muzzle to my outstretched hand, whickering.

"Can you put me down now?" I ask, attempting to squirm out of the young man's arms. He sets me on the ground without protest, and I immediately regret my request to stand. The weight on my leg makes my fists clench. Still, the pain is better than letting a stranger carry me around like a small child.

I rest my head against Cashel's warm neck, steadying myself. I breathe in his earthy scent, instantly feeling closer to home. Another steed approaches—beautiful and white, its wings tucked to its sides. It's remarkably similar to Commander Quin's Empyrean steed, Elro. My mind races as I remember the battle and the white steed flying toward me with the masked rider...right before I fell.

"*You,*" I say, blinking. "It was you?"

He scratches his neck and nods. "I tried to save you."

"Why?" I shake my head. "And how do you have a steed?" My mind is whirling in every direction.

"There's a lot to discuss, Aluma."

My mouth falls open. "How do you know my name?"

A loud howling noise emerges from somewhere deep in the woods. Chills run through my body as I squint into the nearby trees. Cashel stomps in place and blows out a puff of air.

"We need to go—*now*," the dark-haired stranger says, peering past me into the forest. "We don't want to wait for what's coming out of those woods."

"Why? What's coming?"

"Jeklers," he says, lifting me onto Cashel.

"*Jeklers?*" I echo, an incredulous smirk forming on my face. Then I remember that horrifying growl I heard on my trip to collect the pompidorris.

"They're no joke," he tells me.

189

"I thought those were just made-up stories to keep us out of the Gray Forest," I say, my eyes scanning the trees, just in case.

He frowns. "Unfortunately, they're very real."

I stare at him in disbelief, but he doesn't seem the type to make up tales.

"Can you ride?" he asks.

I nod. *Let's hope so.*

"Good," he says, turning to the white steed, swinging his leg over its back. "Follow me." He directs the steed back the way we came, through the woods, and toward the clearing of tall grass before the cliffside.

I hold Cashel in place for a moment, considering my options. I don't know where I am. He knows my name. And there's something howling nearby in the woods. Not great options, either way.

I give Cashel a squeeze with my left leg, and we follow the stranger on the white steed out of the woods. The howling noise behind us grows louder, sounding closer and closer as we ride away from the trees. There's definitely something out there, and I'm not keen to find out what it is.

"We have a long way to fly. We have to go now," the stranger says. "I promise I'll answer all of your questions soon enough." His dark eyes meet mine, and for some reason, I feel as though I can trust him.

"Will you at least tell me your name?" I ask.

"Gattacan."

# TWENTY-SIX

We fly in silence for what feels like hours. The air is wet with cold; a constant drizzle rolls off my frozen cheeks, and I long for the firepit back in the cave. Wherever we're going, it's taking longer than it did when I flew with the Cavalry into Laithlanner territory. The small glimpses I catch between the cloud cover look unfamiliar. The ground below is dark and tattered, the way I always expected Laithlann to look beyond where I've seen.

"We're getting close now," Gattacan calls over the sound of the rushing air.

I lower my head closer to Cashel's neck, attempting to absorb some of his warmth. The clouds break apart again, and I catch the first familiar marker—the Gray Forest—the farthest I've ever been into Laithlanner territory before today.

"We're going to Nammden?" I blurt out.

He turns and nods.

Nammden—the capital city of Laithlann.

Excitement and fear wash over me as the forest begins to thin out, the somber trees giving way to a barren wasteland. The surface is charred—darkness everywhere. The air is even more frigid than it was closer to Knarrno. I wiggle my nose, or at least I try; I can hardly feel it now.

Gattacan descends through the air on his steed. I follow him down until we're much lower and I have a better view. The darkness is not only on the ground, but also in the sky. A low patch of cloud cover creates a ceiling above us. The air is thick and wet, but strangely, the earth looks as though it's been burned to ashes. Within moments, the ground passing below is no longer dry and solid, but water—*murky* water.

As we glide through the gray mist, my gaze shifts until I realize I'm staring at Gattacan's dark hair blowing behind him. The strands almost seem to dance, moving apart before clashing back together, much like the waves outside the cave. It's mesmerizing.

When we fly through another cloud, I snap out of my daze. And as we emerge on the other side, I see it.

The city of Nammden.

I can't believe my eyes. Off in the distance, large structures jut up into the dimly lit sky—tall buildings reaching high, like steel giants standing frozen in place.

As we fly closer, the buildings become much clearer. Verdant moss decorates the metal walls, growing up from the murky water surrounding the bases of the towering structures like green tentacles racing to the sky. Most of the windows on the lower levels are gone, their frames filled with shards of glass. The windows that remain reflect the other buildings, like huge mirrors. Large black panels line the tops of some of the shorter buildings, like the panels on karriers. Many roofs also boast lush green gardens, planted between the black panels, and every tower contains a wide silver barrel.

I follow Gattacan past the first large building, through a maze of even taller structures. I occasionally catch glimpses of our reflections in the intact windows. Cashel is beautiful—wings flapping effortlessly, markings like a storm. My face appears distorted, then clear, like a warped version of myself. It's an accurate portrayal of how I'm feeling inside: while nothing is making sense right now, there's a glimmer of hope that soon, some of it will.

Gattacan navigates through the buildings as if he's done it a thousand times, weaving in and around them effortlessly. He's a veritable compass—the perfect companion for someone as lost as I feel right now.

My eyes catch movement to my right. There's a person—a Scaler—sliding across the side of a building, holding on to a wire above and standing on another wire below. It's no wonder they're called *Scalers*—they can literally scale the buildings.

We turn, flying over what I imagine was once a busy street. I notice all the Scalers traversing the buildings, with wires attached to the metal frames, running parallel to the ground, but up as high as us. Pairs of wires stretch from one building to the next. A few Scalers cross the open spaces on the lines between the buildings, attached by ropes that slide along the top hand wire. But it looks as if they're floating in mid-air—a terrifying feat. We weave above and below a few different sets of wires between the buildings, and now I'm close enough to make out their faces; they're as varied in appearance as the rest of the people in Eirelannia. They turn from the lines on the buildings they so effortlessly cling to, staring at me as we pass, bags on their backs, full of what looks like fresh produce and other goods.

Gattacan turns again, flying his steed straight toward one of the tallest buildings we've seen so far—a dark gray structure with a peaked roof. I slow Cashel as Gattacan directs his steed through a huge hole that's been gashed out near the top of the building. I take a deep breath and follow him in as he disappears through the opening.

My eyes slowly adjust to the darkness inside the building. Gattacan lands his steed ahead of me, and I direct Cashel in the same direction. His hooves strike the ground like a loud clap of thunder, rousing me from my exhausted state.

Gattacan dismounts and rushes to my side. "Here, let me help you," he says, reaching for my waist. Normally, I'd prefer to dismount on my own, but with my leg aching so badly, I decide not to protest.

I lift my right leg over Cashel; it's stiff from the long ride. I let myself lean over into Gattacan's outstretched arms, and he pulls me toward him. His warm body presses against mine, offering an instant relief from the cold.

"Thank you," I say as he lowers my feet to the ground. He stays by my side as I adjust to my shaky sky legs. Then he loops his arm underneath mine, supporting me as I hobble beside him.

"Cashel will be taken care of," he says, gesturing over to the side of the open space, where Cashel and Gattacan's white steed have already found a large trough of water. There's a skinny man in dark garb tending to them.

I nod, although I'm hesitant to leave Cashel with a stranger. "Can you tell me what we're doing now?" I ask.

"Gattacan!" a woman's voice calls out from behind us. We turn, and I study the woman's face as she comes closer into view. Once again, she is the opposite of grotesque; her skin is the color of pale sand and her hair is straight and black.

"Mother," Gattacan says, letting go of me briefly to give her a hug. In a moment he returns to my side, steadying me.

She gazes at me, then turns back to Gattacan, a silent question in her eyes.

"This is Aluma Banks," Gattacan explains. "Rinehart…he thought she would be safer here."

Rinehart Quin? They know each other? And he thought I'd be safer *here*, with the enemy? Why would he think that?

Gattacan's mother gives him a quick nod, and then her expression turns grave. "What about your sister?" she asks.

"I saw her retreat with the other Empyrean Riders. She's fine," Gattacan tells her. "No one would have suspected a thing."

"Your sister?" I ask, finally mustering up the courage to speak.

Gattacan looks to his mother, and she nods. "Wolkenna," he tells me.

"Wolkenna?" I echo, nearly falling away from his grasp. "Wolkenna Quin?" My roommate, Rinehart's adopted daughter, is Gattacan's *sister?*

"Yes, Wolkenna is my daughter," his mother says with a smile. "And I'm Delna. It's a pleasure to meet you." Her voice is soft, her eyes dark as night.

My eyes dart to Gattacan, my mind racing. He raises his eyebrows, reminding me to respond to his mother. I smile as much as I can manage.

A look of concern crosses her face. "Are you afraid?"

Of course I'm afraid. I've never been this far into Laithlann—until recently, when I almost *died* in the Knarrno River. Now I'm with a Scaler in his own territory, standing with two people claiming to be my roommate's family near the top of a colossal building.

Still, I shake my head. Until I know more about these people, I can't afford to show any weaknesses. My injured leg makes me vulnerable enough.

Delna places her hand on my shoulder, seemingly detecting my lie. "You're safe here."

I try not to pull away, even though I'm sure I should; she's a Scaler. But her eyes are kind and somehow comforting. And for a second, it feels like I'm looking at Wolkenna. I'd be a fool not to notice the resemblance between them—and between Wolkenna and Gattacan as well. His looks are as striking and unforgettable as his sister's.

"Your father has been anxiously awaiting your return," Delna says, glancing at Gattacan. "We've received word from a few of the crew who've returned from Knarrno." Her gaze shifts downward, lingering on the leg I'm favoring. "Gattacan, why don't you take Aluma to the medic and have that wound properly treated?" she suggests. "I'll go find your father—we have much to discuss. Meet us in the dining room once she's been looked after."

Gattacan nods, and his mother smiles at me.

"Welcome to Nammden, Aluma."

⁓

The medic is quiet as he assesses the wound on my leg. He cleanses it, applies a new healing paste, and wraps my thigh with clean white material. He offers me a tonic to ease my pain, but I refuse—I'd rather remain sharp and aware for now. Despite Delna's friendly welcome, I'm still uneasy about being in Laithlanner territory.

When we're done, Gattacan balances me as we walk down a long corridor. Rows of candles light the walls, flames flickering. We turn into a smaller hallway and pass through a doorway into a large room. There's a massive steel table inside, and the room itself is well-lit, with candles hanging all around. Tapestries adorn the walls, gray with green stripes, colors I haven't seen together. One tapestry stands out more than the others—a single silver wing outstretched.

"Where..." I ask, my voice escaping me as I recall the last few times I've seen that silver wing. Then I remember the legend Rinehart spoke of when Cashel received his wings—that whoever rides the Silver-Winged Steed will free Eirelannia. But that would mean...

"My son!" a low, booming voice calls out. A tall, dark-haired man walks through the door at the opposite end of the room. He strides over, his arms open. "I'm glad to see you've made it home safely," he says, embracing Gattacan as I once again wait awkwardly to the side.

"Father, this is Aluma," Gattacan says, turning to me.

"Aluma Banks," his father says knowingly, offering a smile.

I blink. He knows my full name. A hundred questions dart through my head as I stare at him blankly.

"Vikmal. Vikmal Gray," Gattacan's father says, pointing to himself, as if I should recognize the name. His face is older, but striking, like Gattacan's.

I nod and smile politely.

Vikmal pulls out a chair for me. "Here—sit! You must be famished," he says. He's right; I am. I haven't eaten anything since yesterday.

Gattacan helps me over, and I plop down as gracefully as possible. The chair is cushioned and comfortable, much more so than my saddle. My body sinks into it, thanking me for the rest. Gattacan sits beside me as his parents take their seats across from us. Moments later, two other men enter the room, each carrying a tray of steaming food. They place the trays in front of us, and the aroma hits my nose like the smell of fresh-baked bread wafting in the breeze.

My mouth waters.

"Help yourself," Delna says. The Grays reach out, scooping a bit of each type of dish onto their plates. I select a slice of bread and a few pieces of dark, leafy greens, spooning a creamy sauce over them. Gattacan grins.

"What?" I whisper.

He pushes a bowl toward me. "*That* one is a soup." He chuckles, nodding his head at the sauce—the *soup* I just mistakenly put on the greens.

My face flushes.

"But I'm sure it tastes just as good," he says, attempting to ease my embarrassment.

"Gattacan!" Delna shakes her head. "It's fine, Aluma. We should have explained." She scoops more of the soup into a bowl for me. "Here."

"Thank you," I say. Naturally, I put soup on a plate full of vegetables. I take a spoonful of the soup. It's perfect: hot, creamy, and flavorful—something I've never tasted before. It runs down my dry throat and coats my empty stomach. "Mmm." The sound escapes me involuntarily.

"Do you like it?" Vikmal asks, leaning forward.

"It's delicious," I say, between the most mannerly mouthfuls of soup I can take.

"It's a family recipe—Delna's mother's." Vikmal raises his bushy black eyebrows and smiles. "The white fish are caught right outside these buildings, along the coastline."

"It's been years since I tasted fish," I tell him, realizing I haven't had any since I visited my grandmother in Sceilaran as a child. Only registered fishermen are allowed to fish the Tarmen Canal back in Cintrenia, so this is a real treat.

We continue to feast, and the Grays take turns making small talk. I try each of the dishes, all of which are as tasty as the one before. After I finish another bowl of soup, I notice the others have finished eating. I wipe my mouth with the cloth laid out beside my empty bowl and sit back in my chair with a full stomach.

"I'm sure you have many questions," Vikmal says to me, opening his hands. "Shall we go sit by the fire?"

He stands up from the table, gesturing toward the door.

"I do have questions," I say. Lots of them. I'm so tired of being left in the dark.

But finally, someone is ready and willing to answer all of the unknowns that have been floating around my head like lost sheep.

It's time for transparency—for truth.

It's time to step into the light.

TWENTY–SEVEN

I follow the Grays into another room. Orange and red flames rise in a grand fireplace on the far wall. A few large armchairs and a long couch surround it. Gattacan's parents take their seats in the chairs. The warmth of the fire hits my skin as Gattacan leads me to the couch. He helps me lower myself to the dark, plush cushions, and the tension in my body releases as I sink into them.

"Here," Gattacan says, lifting my legs onto the end of the couch, so I'm resting across nearly the length of it. His touch is gentle, yet firm. My cheeks warm as I glance over at Gattacan's parents, who are gazing at the fire. *Thank the stars.* Gattacan places a pillow under my feet. "This will help."

"Thank you," I say as Gattacan sits just past my feet at the end of the couch.

Flames crackle to my left as I lean against the armrest, my legs outstretched and warming by the second. The pain lessens in my leg as my back relaxes. My eyelids are heavy. And somehow, despite all my pressing questions, I'm strangely comfortable here.

"Where shall we begin?" Vikmal asks, glancing over at me. "There's so much to tell you before you go."

"Before I go?" I ask cautiously.

Gattacan's parents both turn in their seats so they're facing me. They look over at Gattacan, who shakes his head.

I turn to his parents in confusion. "What is it?"

"We weren't sure how much Gattacan had filled you in on," Delna says.

"I was just trying to get her back here safely," Gattacan tells them.

"You did well," Vikmal says to his son before looking back at me. "Aluma, you can ask us anything."

"How do you know my name?" I blurt out.

"We know who you are," Vikmal says. "You are an Empyrean Rider. We know Rinehart Quin and—"

"Commander Quin—how?" I ask.

Vikmal shares a quick glance with Gattacan. "Rinehart is a Laithlanner," Vikmal tells me. "He's lived undercover as a Uladmondian for most of his life, a sacrifice he made for Laithlann."

Rinehart is a *Scaler*—and he's been working for his enemy. A sacrifice indeed.

"Your father is also a friend of ours, and a friend of Rinehart's, too," Vikmal says. "Before your father's accident, we were communicating with him through Rinehart."

"*My father*—you know my father?"

"Yes," Vikmal says. "Since we were much younger than we are now." A small, nostalgic smile crosses his face, then rests, like a water karrier returning to harbor.

"And you have Empyrean steeds here?"

"No," Gattacan says. "The steed I have now is Rinehart's."

"So that *is* Elro," I whisper.

Gattacan nods. "Rinehart told me to take his steed during the attack."

"What attack?! When?" I ask.

"I went to meet with Rinehart," Gattacan tells me. "Near the border, like we have many times before. But someone found out about our meeting and attacked our people, and then Rinehart."

I shake my head. That's not what we were told back at the base.

"Rinehart instructed me to take Elro, return home, and warn everyone that the Uladmondian forces were planning a large-scale attack on Laithlann. He said to find *you* as well, before it was too late—before you were hurt, or worse. He described you and your silver-winged steed." Gattacan pauses. "I saw them take Rinehart prisoner as I hid nearby. They called him a traitor."

My eyes narrow. "Who took him?"

"Prince Sutagus," Gattacan says, "and a golden-eyed woman. They were both on Empyrean steeds. They killed many of our men." He swallows. "The same woman who took an arrow later while she was killing more of our men on the water karrier."

"Zarshona Mund," I say, her name escaping my mouth. I pause a moment. "I don't understand. We were told the Laithlanners—that *you* had attacked us over the border in Ivernister."

"We didn't. We were only there to talk to Rinehart, in secret. They attacked us in *our* territory," Gattacan says.

I glance over at Vikmal and Delna. Their eyebrows are furrowed as they listen to their son.

"After they attacked us and took Rinehart into custody, our remaining crew turned around on the water karrier, attempting to flee. I waited until I was sure they had escaped. One of our men was still alive, but wounded. I heard him when I was leaving. There was nothing I could do, other than stay with him until he passed," Gattacan says, his expression remote. "He was a friend."

Gattacan's parents both wear pained expressions at this news. I stare at my wrapped leg, realizing I could be in a much worse place right now. "I'm so sorry."

Gattacan clears his throat and continues, "Later, before I took off, I saw the Empyrean Cavalry flying over the border toward Knarrno, following after our remaining crew on the water karrier. I trailed all of you from behind." He glances at me. "I didn't know you were with them, not yet. But when I reached the battle, and I spotted Cashel's silver wings, I knew I'd found you. You looked just like Rinehart's description. I tried to get to you when I saw you were being targeted—before the arrow hit your leg. But I was too late, and you fell before I could." Gattacan draws in a ragged breath, deep creases forming between his eyebrows.

"Thank you...for saving my life," I say, locking eyes with him.

"I brought you to the caves, at least until you woke," he tells me. "It wasn't safe to ride with the surviving Laithlanners on the water karrier. They wouldn't have been too keen to see me with an Empyrean Rider."

"And Wolkenna?" I ask, leaning forward, looking over at Gattacan's mother.

"Her real name is Wolkenna *Gray*," Delna says. "She's been undercover in Ivernister for a long, long time. She volunteered to do so. Rinehart took her in for us. He told everyone she had been abandoned." She pauses, taking a deep breath. "You don't understand how hard it's been for us. We only see her on very rare occasions. She sneaks out sometimes to meet Gattacan at the border, to give us updates. Tell me, how is she? Have they been mistreating her?"

"She's doing well," I tell her. "She's my—well, she *was* my roommate, back at the base. My friend."

I realize again just how similar Wolkenna looks to her parents and Gattacan: black hair, intense eyes, and high cheekbones. They're all stunning.

How did I not notice the minute I met Gattacan?

I attempt to process what I've been told, my legs now warm like I've been sitting in the summer sun. But my mind is still racing. Who *are* these people? What are they trying to do?

And what do they want with me?

"Now that Rinehart has been found out," Vikmal says, "we must evacuate Wolkenna at once." He stands and moves behind Delna's chair, placing his hands on her shoulders. "It's not safe for her there anymore."

"What were you planning with my father and Rinehart?" I search my mind for clues. "*The old will soon be made anew*," I mutter. "Was that you? Do you know Lermyn Githah, too?"

"Yes, it was all of us," Vikmal says. "We were planning to take back what is ours—our kingdoms. Our freedom."

"Freedom?" I blink.

Vikmal moves back to his empty chair and sits, letting out a deep sigh. "The king, the prince, and the nobility in Uladmond have been lying to the people for a long time. We Laithlanners haven't been fighting anyone. We've been trapped here with diminishing resources—resources that were destroyed when the Uladmondians first attacked our families, generations ago."

A shiver runs through me. It doesn't sound so different from what we've been going through back home.

"Not so long ago, when our people stood their ground and refused to bow to the previous kings of Uladmond, they attacked Nammden and Knarrno, killing most of us." He pauses, peering into the fire. "And now, generation after generation, each king has become more intent on forcing those of us who remain to submit—*or die.*"

My body tenses. Everyone is forced to submit in Cintrenia, too. We'd all starve, be persecuted, or killed if we didn't.

"We want to live, and live free. Free to use the land, which was once our home, full of life and light," Delna says, opening her hands.

Vikmal stands and moves in front of the fireplace. "Your father and other Ivernisterians have been coming together, to join us Laithlanners in the fight. They, too, want to attain their freedom and keep their land in Ivernister, without being stripped of every crop they grow and everything they earn."

"The king's new law..." I murmur.

He nods. "Many of your people don't want to end up the way we have here. We all want to live without the nobility of Uladmond taking everything from us, or killing us if we don't obey."

My tired mind attempts to process everything. All these years, and I knew none of this.

"My father's accident," I say, hoping to be wrong, "was it—"

"It wasn't his fault. It was a silent attack," Vikmal says. "Someone sold your father out." He looks at me, his dark eyes peering into mine. "Someone knew something."

"The box..." I whisper.

Gattacan's eyes shift between me and his parents. "A box?"

"Yes, there was a small black box…" I say, trailing off as I imagine Kase giving it to Prince Sutagus on the day of the Autumn Tournament as I listened from Darwith's stall. "It must have belonged to my father. My brother—he gave it to Sutagus."

Delna gives Vikmal a look, and he nods at her.

"That box," she says, turning back to me, "is much more than what it seems." She leans forward. "It's a relic—*one* of the relics. Was that the last time you saw it?"

"Yes—what do you mean, *relic*?"

"Relics contain power. Some relics have the power to give, and others the power to take," Delna says.

My eyebrows pull together in confusion.

"They have the power to give your horses their wings," Delna says. "And some have the power to take them away." She glances at her son, whose eyes are darting between his father and mother.

I blink, remembering the silver box Zarshona Mund held when our horses became Empyrean steeds.

"Among other powers," Vikmal says. "You must have seen a relic of darkness just before your father's accident."

I remember the black box Prince Sutagus held in his spindly fingers, right before my father fell.

"Outside of the nobility—and those who tried to protect the relics before they were stolen—most people in Eirelannia have no idea that the relics even exist, or the power they hold," Delna says.

"Did you see a symbol on the side of the relic of darkness at your father's accident?" Vikmal asks.

The etched design on the small black box flashes through my mind. "Yes. It had three silver lines standing upright. And I saw another in Galghesworp—when Cashel received his wings. Except it was a larger silver box, with four open triangles etched in black."

Vikmal glances at Delna and then back at me. "That black relic of darkness belongs to Ivernister. The three lines represent the tall, fertile grasses in your kingdom. The larger silver box was a relic of light. The four triangles represent the mountains in Uladmond."

Powerful boxes—*relics*? I push myself to a more upright position, trying to keep everything straight in my mind. "What now?" is all I can manage.

"Once we've finished our discussion and you've gotten some sleep, you must go back to Cintrenia," Vikmal tells me. "No one knows you've been here. For all they know, you were left in Knarrno at the bottom of the river."

"They don't know if I'm alive?" I ask, wincing. *Thayer*. He doesn't know I'm safe.

"It's highly unlikely," Delna says sympathetically. "So, when you go home to Cintrenia, to your farm, if anyone catches you, you must say your steed brought you back." She pauses. "And then you can help your people and us, the way your father had planned."

"How?"

"There's another relic," Delna says. "The last free relic of light—that we know of, that is. There were originally four of them," she continues, opening her hands. "Each kingdom in Eirelannia possessed one, and each brought new life to the area. From your description, it would seem that Uladmond still has their relic of light. And I'd assume they have the relic of light from the fourth kingdom as well. No one knows where the remaining one is. We've always assumed it had been destroyed, or that Uladmond had found it."

More confusion sets in. "I only know of *three* kingdoms in Eirelannia," I say. "Ivernister, Uladmond, and Laithlann."

"There were once four kingdoms, long ago, before the wars," Delna tells me. "Each kingdom was peacefully ruled by its own leader, free to live how they saw fit."

"And as there are four relics of light, there are also four relics of darkness," Vikmal says, chiming in. "Balance was to be maintained. No one was to use a relic of darkness in the ways people have used them. They were to be a safeguard if ever there was a violent invasion from across the sea—not to attack and destroy others in Eirelannia. They were for protection. Each kingdom had one relic of light and one relic of darkness. There was balance."

"What was the other kingdom called?" I ask.

"Samduh," Delna says. "It made up the southern half of what is now Ivernister and Uladmond. The story is, the king of Uladmond sent spies into the kingdom of Samduh, stealing their relics, both light and dark. The king used the relic of darkness to subjugate the Samduhians, killing anyone who tried to fight for their land. Without their relic of light, they couldn't defend themselves against the darkness. Eventually, their main city fell and became present-day Sceilaran. And since there were so few survivors, the truth was hidden away, or lost entirely from them. Our elders told us these stories as a warning: the kingdom of Uladmond has a thirst for power, and they'll stop at nothing to dominate us all.

"If the king collects all four of the relics of darkness, it will be impossible for us to defend ourselves ever again," Delna continues. "That is a force we've never faced. Three of them were combined during the Dark Wars—that's what destroyed most of our kingdom."

"Your father had the relic of darkness from Ivernister," Vikmal tells me. "He was planning to hide it, in the same location where he hid Ivernister's relic of light. And the Uladmondians already possess the other three relics of darkness, including Laithlann's."

Dread creeps down my spine. "But now Sutagus has my father's, too."

"Exactly—or worse, he's already given it to the king," Vikmal says.

"He may have…" I mutter, staring at the ground. "Sutagus was carrying the relic near the king right before my father was hurt."

"Then it's true," Vikmal says with a sigh. "A relic of darkness *was* used against your father and Darwith. Just enough for it to appear like an accident. And now they have all four relics of darkness." He glances at Delna, fear filling his eyes.

There's a sinking feeling in my gut, and it's dragging me down with it. I remember Farann telling me that they were collecting the boxes, and that a message would be sent *loud and clear*. Now I know what her words meant—they attacked my father in order to send a message to the resistance.

"But the last known relic of light is still safe—the one your father hid," Vikmal says. "You *must* retrieve it and bring it back here, so we can protect it."

"Me?" He can't be serious.

Vikmal nods. "The last relic of light is our only hope to protect ourselves from the darkness."

"But why do you need *me?*" I ask.

"Because you're a Light Keeper, Aluma," Vikmal tells me.

"A Light Keeper?" I echo, my eyebrows lifting on my forehead.

"You're Hearn Banks's daughter. Your father is both Empyrean Rider and Light Keeper," Vikmal says. "You have the power inside of you, too."

A nervous laugh erupts from my nose. "Are you sure you have the right person?"

Vikmal smiles and bobs his head. "There's so much more for you to learn, but there are only a few who can carry the light and shut out most of the darkness. Many let the darkness consume them as they extinguish the light, eventually forever. You and your father are both Light Keepers."

"What about my brother, Kase?"

"Light Keepers can run in families," Vikmal says, "but as far as we know, Kase doesn't share your ability."

"Then how do you know I'm one?" I ask.

"Your father found out by accident, when you were a child," Vikmal tells me. "Before your father hid the last relic of light, he said you were in the barn with him. He said he had the relic sitting out next to you. He left for a moment, and when he returned, he said it was open."

"And *that* makes me a Light Keeper?" As I say it, I remember my father's words, right before he lost consciousness: *Keep the light.*

A rush of warmth courses through my veins.

"Relics of light only open for Light Keepers," Delna says. "There's really no other way to know if someone is a Light Keeper until they're near a relic of light."

"What about relics of darkness? Do they have keepers, too?" I ask, unsure if it's even a valid question.

"No," Delna says. "Anyone can open a relic of darkness. But only Light Keepers can wield or open a relic of light."

My mind is not keeping up with *any* of this. I glance over at Gattacan, hoping for more clarity, but he just watches me, a confused look on his face. It appears most of this information is new to him, too.

"We will have more time to discuss these matters, I hope," Vikmal says. "But for now, you're the *only* Light Keeper who isn't incapacitated."

"So there are others—other Light Keepers?" I ask.

Vikmal nods. "Each kingdom has at least one Light Keeper."

"Who is yours?" I ask.

"Rinehart," he says.

So *that's* why my father wanted me to find Rinehart. Because Rinehart knew what I was—what I *am*. And because Father knew Rinehart was a Light Keeper, too.

"At the moment, you're the only one who can get to the last relic of light. But you'll need Darwith," Vikmal tells me.

"Darwith?" I imagine my father's Empyrean steed, and Lermyn taking care of him at home. *Home.*

"Your father hid the last relic of light years ago. Darwith is the one who flew him there. He'll know where to take you," Vikmal says. "You must fly home to Cintrenia, early tomorrow morning."

My father's fall flashes through my mind. Darwith's wings failing. The warmth I felt when I saw the light.

"Wait," I say, trying to remember the details. "I saw a bright light when my father fell. I'm sure of it. A light shined from somewhere, and then Darwith's wings started working again." Concerned eyes stare back at me. "And then again, when our horses received their wings, the lieutenant—Zarshona Mund—had a silver box. The one I mentioned with the four mountain peaks. There was a bright light when she opened it." Then I pause, realization dawning. "Wait—does that mean Zarshona is a Light Keeper, too?"

"Yes," Delna says grimly. "Rinehart discovered that for us years ago."

"But why would they use their own relic of light to save your father?" Vikmal asks himself more than anyone else, his face set in a grimace. "Was this all part of their plan?"

"They tried to *kill* him—then save him?" I mutter. "That doesn't make any sense—"

"They must've planned it that way, to render him powerless, to take him in," Vikmal says. "So they could interrogate him about the location of the last relic of light."

My mind spins. The image of my father falling from the sky replays in my head, over and over again.

"It's late," Vikmal says, breaking through my nightmarish thoughts. "Tomorrow you must fly back to Cintrenia for Darwith." He stops, staring at my neck. "And keep that on, for now."

My eyes enlarge, my hand finding the gold locket at my collarbone. "If that's what I think it is?" he says.

I nod. *It is*—the blood locket. My oath to the same king I'm about to betray.

"At least until you return." He dips his chin. "Then you can remove it." With a weary gesture, he adds, "Now, get some rest—you'll need it."

I exhale, rubbing my arms with my warmed hands. Everything I've heard here is overloading my mind.

I glance over at Gattacan, who is staring at me, his eyes more intense than ever. I remember my father's words the day he fell from the sky. *You're the only light...*

He wasn't able to finish his sentence before, but now I know what he meant to say.

TWENTY–EIGHT

When I open my eyes, Gattacan is standing beside the bed, watching me, and for some strange reason I don't startle, or worry about how long he's been in the room. I stare into his midnight eyes for a moment before pushing myself up to my elbows.

"Is it time?" I ask, stifling a yawn.

He nods.

I'm still exhausted, but at least I got *some* rest, and my leg is a little better, thanks to the Laithlanner medic who attended to it yesterday. I'm still in yesterday's clothes—no point in changing out of my Empyrean uniform if I have to go back home in it. Wearing anything else, or even cleaning up too much, would signal that I was rescued by someone, and not just any someone—a Laithlanner. But attending to my leg was a necessity. Otherwise, who knows if I'd make it home before an infection set in.

Still, I can't help but imagine how nice a hot shower would feel right about now.

I ease my leg off the bed and onto the floor, slipping into my dirty Empyrean boots. Gattacan reaches his hand out to steady me as I stand.

"Thank you," I say, taking it, his fingers gently bracing mine.

"Thank *you*," he echoes in a husky breath.

"For what?"

"For what you're about to do." He's still holding on to my hand.

I swallow, letting it go so that I can pull my hair up into a pony-tail. As soon as I do, I remember what lies ahead. All the revelations the Grays shared last night flash through my mind like a lightning storm. I'm a Light Keeper, like my father. But what does it all mean?

"I wouldn't thank me just yet," I mutter.

Gattacan tilts his head to study me.

"I mean, I don't even fully understand what I'm supposed to do." I run my hand over the top of my head, attempting to smooth down any stray hairs that might be sticking up.

"You will soon enough. These things take time." He offers me his arm. "My parents will tell you the plan over breakfast."

I loop my arm through his, though the weight on my leg isn't nearly as painful as it was. Still, it's nice to have his support.

"Cashel is ready for you. He was fed and groomed last night," he says, leading me out of the room.

"Thank you. I was so tired, I should've—"

"I told you he'd be fine. I'm starting to think you don't trust me," Gattacan says, a smile forming under his perfect angular cheekbones.

"These things take time," I joke. He chuckles, and his arm flexes against mine when he does.

After an information-filled breakfast, during which Gattacan's parents go over the detailed plan I should follow, I'm full of even more questions. But at least I know enough now to move forward.

Gattacan and I make our way back into the large landing area where we arrived last night. Cashel is waiting, saddled off to the side, looking clean and well-fed, just like Gattacan said he would. His ears flick forward, and he whickers as I approach.

I give him a hug around his neck and breathe in his scent, instantly feeling relieved.

"He's loyal to you," Gattacan says, patting Cashel's shoulder.

I gaze at Cashel's face, his marbled eyes peering out from behind his gray mane like dark moons.

"If—" Gattacan stops himself.

"If what?" I ask, glancing at him. He presses his lips together.

"*If* I ever had my own steed, I'd want him to be like Cashel," he says, somehow looking younger and more carefree. "Plus, he has silver wings. I've never seen a silver-winged steed."

I smile as Gattacan boosts me into my saddle and hands me the reins, hoping that someday he *will* have his own steed.

"Be careful out there," he says, peering up at me, his eyes intense and full of hope.

My stomach flutters for a moment, the way it does when I'm taking off into the air after being on the ground for too long—almost the way it feels when I'm with Thayer. "I will," I say, turning Cashel toward the opening of the building.

"I hope we meet again." A serious expression crosses Gattacan's face.

"Me too," I say, giving Cashel a squeeze.

We take off at a gallop. Cashel's wings stretch out and flap, forcing us into flight as his hooves leave the ground—just as we run out of building. I catch my breath—we're higher than I remember, and the water-filled streets below are obscured by a dense white fog.

We fly toward the Gray Forest, the way Gattacan instructed, navigating through the steel giants as if he were leading the way. When the trees appear in the distance, I imagine Gattacan's face—*Gattacan Gray*. Was the Gray Forest named after the Gray family, after their dark and mysterious ways?

The forest appears beneath us, tree after tree until it's so dense, the ground disappears, and all I see are shadowy greens and grays. My mind wanders as I stare down at the skeletal trees. My father is lying somewhere in Tarmensil in a coma. *If* he's still in a coma. Maybe he's not even alive. I shudder at the thought, shaking my head, feeling the cold air slap each side of my face. He has to be alive.

I can't bear to lose him.

~

By the time I snap out of my mindless worry, the morning sun is rising behind me, casting light on the disappearing bony trees below. I recognize these parts—we're close to the Ivernister border. The last time I was on this side of the border looking over at Cintrenia was before the Autumn Tournament.

The Empyrean arena is on the horizon. It's probably best if I head straight to our farm—then I can go on foot or by wingless horse to the Empyrean stables to fetch Darwith. If the king's soldiers notice me, I'll be sent back to the base until our training is over—or worse. But after the battle the other night, I can't help but wonder if training *is* over.

I don't want to find out either way.

I fly the long way home, avoiding being seen as best I can. I've never seen Cintrenia from the sky during the day, not until now. It's green, it's beautiful, it's home. I've missed it.

Our family farm comes into view: our house, our barn, our chicken coop. This is all I have. But with my father in a coma, and me a fallen Empyrean Rider who's joined the enemy, there's no way we can keep any of it.

My grip tightens on the reins as my fingers form into fists. How can the king and the nobility justify taking what isn't theirs? It's theft. And it's wrong.

We land on the field by the chicken coop. And despite the frustration winding up inside of me and the fear of the king's soldiers seizing what is ours swirling through my mind, I can't help but smile for a moment.

I'm home.

I leave Cashel behind the coop, hoping to keep him out of sight. When I dismount, relief falls over me—the ache in my leg is lessening by the hour. This is the first time I've done much walking without Gattacan's aid since my accident.

As I circle around the front of the coop on foot, my smile vanishes. The gate is wide open. My eyes narrow as I investigate inside—not a hen or egg in sight. But there's no sign that a wild animal came in for a feast, either.

No. Someone stole them.

As I approach our house, an uneasiness rushes through my body like a strong gust of wind—the front door is open. I dart to the side of the house, pressing my back against the wall. Maybe it's Kase. That has to be it. I don't want to consider any alternatives, not if I want to keep up the courage to look inside. I inch along, closer to the door, until our kitchen window is on my left. I blow out a silent breath and lean my head over until I'm looking through the window. My eyes move back and forth, scanning the kitchen, but there's no movement. I don't see Kase.

I slide past the window until I'm at the open door. The door handle is broken, hanging from the frame like it's been hit hard. My muscles clench; Kase wouldn't cause that kind of damage. That means someone else has been here. The door swings in the breeze, its hinges creaking every few moments like a high-pitched howl. I nudge the door open all the way, waiting to hear if anyone is rustling inside.

Nothing—no one. Not a sound.

I enter slowly, glancing around behind me as I do, hoping I'm not a complete fool for going in. Someone could be waiting to catch me. This could be a trap.

The kitchen is a mess. I didn't see it through the window, but it looks like a storm blew through our entire house, dragging all of our belongings to the floor. The cabinets are open, our plates and bowls are broken, and our table has been flipped over.

My throat is dry like I haven't had a drink of water in days. "Hello?" I croak, accepting that I'm as good as caught if there's anyone inside.

Silence. Thank the stars.

I make my way into my father's room. It's just as bad as the rest of the house, with everything torn through. Even his mattress is ripped apart.

A photo lying on the floor catches my eye—it's of me, Kase, and my father. It's a similar photo to the one I kept beside my bed in Galghesworp. I take the photo before I leave the room, realizing I may never see the one at the base again.

My room is no better. I push my scattered books away from the area near the window. The floor is still intact. My fingers find the crevice between the wall and the loose floorboard, and I lift it up. Underneath, the pompidorris I collected are still inside the drying box. They've started to wrinkle a little, but the flesh might still be good inside, and the seeds will be fine either way. I snatch one and carry it out, along with the photo.

Before I leave our house, I grab my water canteen off the kitchen floor and fill it at the sink. I take a long gulp, the cold liquid coating my throat. For a moment, I have the urge to clean up our house, imagining I could just hide in my room after that, and wait for my father to return home.

But I know better. Nothing is going back to normal now.

When I go back outside through the kitchen door, I spot Cashel. He's moved from the coop and is now stomping the dirt near the front of the barn. I hobble over to him with as much speed as I can muster.

"What is it?" I ask, patting his neck after placing the pompidorri, photo, and my water canteen in the saddlebag.

A noise comes from inside the barn, and a loud whinnying. My eyes narrow. That doesn't sound like my mother's old mare, Blossom. But she's the only wingless horse that was left at the farm for Lermyn to care for. She's who I was planning on riding into town.

I slide the door open on its tracks and hurry in. My heart skips a beat as Darwith trots to me from the other end.

"Darwith?" I say, my mind beginning to race. He should be at the Empyrean stables with the rest of the Empyrean steeds—how did he get here?

As I near Darwith, there's another noise. A faint groaning coming from inside the tack room.

I stiffen in place. Another groan. I move cautiously to the door and ease it open.

Lermyn is lying on the ground, his upper body propped up against the tack room wall. Blood trickles from his abdomen like a leaky faucet. He coughs, raising his head to look at me. "Aluma…"

I rush to his side. "I'm here. Hang on, Lermyn."

He strains to keep his head upright as he stretches out a shaky arm, placing his weathered hand on my shoulder. His attempt at a smile dissolves into a pain-filled grimace, and he drags his other hand to his abdomen as blood seeps out faster from the hole in his shirt.

I press my hand over his, applying pressure over the wound, but the blood keeps coming. "What happened?" I ask. Who would do this to an old man—to *Lermyn*?

He coughs. "They know…"

"Who?" My eyes dart around for something—*anything* to help stop the bleeding.

He tries to speak again, forcing each word out. "The king…the prince…they *know*—"

"They know my father hid the remaining relic of light?" I ask, finishing his sentence.

Lermyn looks startled for a moment, then nods.

"I met the Grays," I tell him. "I know about the relics—about Light Keepers."

"Then it's not too late, " he says. "You must take Darwith, *now*. I had him fly off when the soldiers came earlier. He returned after they left." He looks past me to where Darwith is standing by, watching. "And they took Blossom—I'm sorry."

I press my lips together, the image of soldiers stealing my mother's frightened paint mare rushing through my mind. I exhale, shaking my head—I'd love nothing more than to go after her, but I can't do anything about Blossom right now.

"They know about Darwith? That he knows where to go?" I ask.

"Yes. I'm not sure how they figured it out. Maybe your father is awake," he says, his head thudding against the tack room wall. He coughs again, and blood trickles from the edges of his mouth.

I swallow hard, realizing Lermyn isn't going to survive this. "What will they do to my father?"

His gaze falls to the floor. "I'm sorry, Aluma…"

"Stay with me," I say, fighting back tears.

"You must find the relic…" he whispers, his voice fading.

"Where is it?" I grab his shoulder, steadying him as he slumps forward.

"Darwith knows the place—past the Green Hills, inside the Gray…" he stammers, before his voice finally gives out.

I shake his shoulder. "Lermyn?"

He doesn't flinch. His eyes are still, looking nowhere.

I stare at the floor, a pain radiating in my chest. Right in my heart. My hands form into tight fists.

They killed him.

A new energy pulses through me as I glance again at Lermyn's lifeless body. Such a kind old man; he didn't deserve this. He died protecting my father's secret—protecting the relic. He died fighting for our freedom.

Something inside of me shifts as the wheels in my mind spin, like I'm racing a horse and cart over the Tarmen Canal. But I'm not just going fast—*I'm focused*. I won't let Lermyn die in vain. I won't allow my fate to be controlled by the king, by the prince, or anyone else. My hand moves to my heart—to the locket around my neck.

I rip it off, throwing it behind a box of tack.

"Goodbye, Lermyn," I whisper. "And thank you." I cover his body with a horse blanket, because I don't know what else I can do.

When I leave the tack room, Darwith is watching me, his dark eyes peering out from between his long black mane.

"It's you and me again," I say to him. I don't bother saddling him; there's no time to waste. There's no need. I can ride bareback.

Darwith follows me out of the barn and into the sunlight. I take a deep breath of the cool, fresh air, allowing it to coat my lungs with new possibilities. Cashel and Darwith touch noses, reacquainting themselves. I lead Darwith to the fence line and step onto the first and second pieces of wood, lifting my injured leg up with me each time. Darwith bends one of his front legs, bowing, the way my father taught him. He waits until I pull myself onto his back and push my hurt leg over the other side of his thick frame before he stands.

I wrap my hands through his thick mane. "Bring me to the relic of light," I whisper, and his ears flick back at me in recognition. He whickers, stretching out his wings and giving them a shake.

I glance over at Cashel. "Follow us," I say, and Cashel mimics Darwith, shaking out his own wings, preparing for flight.

My uninjured leg presses against Darwith's body, and he breaks into a trot onto the tall grass near the house. With another nudge, he smoothly flows into a canter, then a gallop. I glance back over my shoulder. Cashel is following us, his wings flapping. And before I know it, we are lifting off the ground, leaving our home and Lermyn behind.

Cintrenia lingers off in the distance as our farm shrinks beneath us. I lean in closer to Darwith's warm neck as he takes us higher and higher, back toward Laithlann. The Green Hills are as vibrant as ever in the early dawn light, and an energy fills me like never before—as if I'm absorbing all the power of the sun.

This is my home. And no one can take it away from me.

I won't let them.

TWENTY-NINE

The Green Hills disappear as the Gray Forest emerges. Trees reach into the sky like skeletal soldiers, standing guard on the border, protecting the secrets of the Gray. Somehow, the charcoal tone of the forest isn't as harsh as it seemed before. The small amount of sunshine trickling through the clouds highlights the specks of surviving green foliage, intermixed with autumn's oranges, reds, and browns. Green specks of life—specks of *hope*.

After flying past the area where I would normally land to collect pompidorris, we soar further over the forest for a while longer. I hold on to Darwith's mane as he swoops down past the tree line and into a wide clearing the size of an arena, long and narrow. His hooves hammer the murky ground, shifting me forward closer to his withers until he comes to a stop.

I pat Darwith's neck as he pulls his wings in. When I look over my shoulder, Cashel is landing behind us. He gives his wings a shake and folds them to his sides as he catches up.

I glance around at the bordering trees, dense and dark, and not as welcoming as they appeared from the sky. And it's quiet, eerily so. A chill runs up my neck, like a hundred spiders are crawling up my spine.

I hope this is the right place.

Excess water from the constant drizzle drips onto the puddled ground. Scattered fallen logs lie rotting throughout the clearing, with fungi growing from their bark.

A branch snaps somewhere in the bordering trees.

My body tenses, and I pretend the sound was from a small animal. It better have been.

I pull my leg over to dismount. Darwith bows again, allowing me to slide off with minimal impact. My feet sink into the mushy ground; it's wet, and squishy with dead leaves. I turn in a complete circle, scanning the clearing. My nose scrunches in, avoiding the stench of rot that fills the air.

"What now?" I whisper.

Darwith moves toward the bordering trees at the narrow end of the clearing. I hobble behind him and Cashel follows. As we near the tree line, a horse-sized opening comes into view—a path.

A low howling echoes from somewhere behind us, like a strong wind whipping through a vast canyon. I whirl around to face the noise, expecting to see something terrifying, but there's nothing, save for the clearing from which we came.

My mind races back to the woods near the caves in Knarrno, when I was with Gattacan. This sounds like the same type of howling. I remember Gattacan's face when he heard it. And I remember what he said: *jeklers.*

My stomach twists into a tight knot as Darwith and Cashel both stomp their hooves, splashing the murky water onto their legs. I turn back to the trees, hurrying onto the path. Only it's not a path—it's a tunnel. A tunnel of trees. We move through the narrow passage, the spindly branches creating a domed shape around Darwith's and Cashel's lowered heads. It's strange and unnerving, yet somehow fascinating and wonderful, all at once.

A dim light breaks through ahead, luring us forward. We trudge out of the tree branch tunnel and onto a small stretch of open ground, just a few horse-lengths long.

"Whoa," I hear myself say. In front of me, the roots of a massive, twisted tree form a staircase, leading to a vast opening below. Like the passageway behind us, the bordering trees create a roof of sorts. Only a small amount of light trickles in through the tightly woven branches above, as if I'm under an enormous wicker basket, trying to block out the sun. The base of the trees forms a tight border, almost like an enclosed arena sealed off from the outside world by towering tree trunks. I quickly realize there's only one way in *and* out—the opening behind us.

In the middle of the enclosed clearing, there's a tall hedge, at least as high as my chest. It's curved, following the same circular shape but smaller than the tree border on the outskirts. Farther in, there's another hedge. It's even taller than the first. And then another hedge, and yet another beyond that. It's like a giant practice target facing upward, with its rings made of hedges, getting progressively higher as the hedges get closer to the center—to the bullseye.

In the distance, past all the hedges, a light flickers. A warmth washes over me, and somehow I know. I can feel it instinctively, just like Cashel knew how to fly.

It's the relic of light.

We can fly to it—*I hope.*

I shuffle to Darwith's side to remount, but he stomps his hoof in protest. I glance back over to the hedges and then up to the low ceiling of hanging tree branches, realizing why he's resisting my idea: there's no room to fly. Not even enough to hover. And there's no way I can climb the hedges. They're too tall, and even from this distance I can see they're full of long, sharp thorns.

Cashel nudges me.

That's it—*Cashel.* He's an even better jumper than Darwith.

I lead Cashel over to a wide tree root step just beneath the top ledge. I lift my good leg and place my boot into the stirrup, then pull myself up, swinging my injured leg over. I sink my heels in as I give Cashel a squeeze. He moves carefully down the massive set of tree stairs as I lean back in the saddle. I glance over my shoulder to see Darwith trailing us.

As we descend, I catch my breath. It's the grandest staircase I've ever seen. The roots of the ancient trees twist, spiraling into the ground like waves of wood, crashing into themselves. It must have taken lifetimes for them to grow this way. It's hauntingly beautiful.

From the bottom of the stairs, the hedges in the distance appear taller than ever, and I begin to doubt that even Cashel can clear them.

A low growl echoes out behind us, from what sounds like the top of the stairs, near the hallway of trees.

I freeze on Cashel's back, not wanting to look.

Another growl, and it's unmistakable this time. It *is* coming from the same type of creature I heard while with Gattacan in the woods near Knarrno, and before that while I was collecting pompidorris, not too far from here.

We're not alone.

I slowly turn Cashel to face the staircase, thanking the stars when I see nothing but darkness near the tree tunnel.

A few branches snap. My eyes catch movement, and I hold my breath. A pair of glowing red eyes are staring straight at me, like small orbs of fire. The beady red eyes grow larger and larger as they creep toward us from the same opening we came in through at the top of the stairs. Our only way out.

I don't move. I don't breathe.

Darwith stomps at the base of the steps as the creature fully emerges from the tree tunnel and moves to stand at the top of the stairs. Bared, yellow fangs; drool dripping off the sides of its open growling mouth; its snout long, like a wolf. Its body is as large as a bear, covered in dark, matted fur. The creature edges forward on stocky legs and huge paws, with jagged black nails jutting out of each one.

A jekler.

A nightmare out in the day.

I shudder on the inside, remaining as still as I can, attempting not to scream. The jekler stalks closer, slinking its way down the stairs, like a hunter that's been spotted, but is still thirsting for its prey. Darwith rears up, lashing his front hooves out in the beast's direction. The jekler stops in its tracks, lowering its head, its fangs on full display, like a collection of sharp daggers. It crouches menacingly, growling at Darwith.

Cashel steps in place beneath me as a light to our left catches my eye, flickering beyond the tall maze of hedges.

The relic. This may be my only chance.

I turn Cashel toward the hedges, giving him a squeeze, and we take off at full speed. I look over my shoulder to see the jekler lurching down the steps, straight toward where Darwith is standing guard at the bottom. Everything in me wants to turn around and fight beside Darwith, but I'm weaponless, and he seems to be creating a blockade to help me reach the relic. I can only hope the jekler doesn't get past Darwith—and that it doesn't hurt him.

I press Cashel on. *Faster.*

Before the first hedge, I glance back to see Darwith rearing up, his black wings stretching out as he and the jekler collide, hooves against claws.

I face forward again, slowing Cashel into a collected canter. He lifts his front legs off the ground, and we're leaping over the first hedge. I was right: it's at least chest-high on me and full of thorns. I'd never have been able to climb over without being stabbed by its wooden spikes—especially not with an injured leg and a jekler breathing down my back.

We land on the other side and sprint toward the next hedge—about ten horse-lengths away. I look once more over my shoulder, glimpsing Darwith's long wings peeking up behind the wall of thorns we just cleared. The jekler snarls. Darwith squeals.

A pain rips at my heart—*Darwith.*

Cashel snorts as we approach the next hedge; this one must be as tall as my head. His wings stay tucked to his sides. I give him a firm squeeze, and he jumps. The top is wider than the previous and, once again, full of sharp spikes.

Cashel clears the top and we land on the other side, picking up speed.

The next hedge is farther out in front of us and taller than me by far. I've never jumped Cashel over anything as high as these, not even during training in Galghesworp.

The branches above us are slightly higher, leaving more room to jump. But they're still not high enough for the flapping wings needed to fly. When my father hid the relic, he must have planned for it to be accessible only by jumpers, and not by Empyrean steeds, at least not one using its wings.

But he taught me to jump.

I can do this—Cashel can do this.

We take the jump, and I hold my breath, glancing down as Cashel's hooves graze the top of the thorn-covered hedge. He stumbles as we land, regaining his composure at the last second, breaking back into a gallop. I rub his neck encouragingly with my loose finger—the only one that's not gripping the reins and his mane with all my might.

Up ahead, beyond the final hedge, the light seems to be shining brighter. But the hedge is too tall—Cashel barely made the last. And the tree roof is still too low.

Nevertheless, we have to try. We *have* to jump the final hedge. It's the only way.

I squeeze my legs around Cashel as tight as I can, ignoring the pain that's making itself known again in my right leg. I crouch, ready for whatever happens next as Cashel blazes toward the final hedge.

"You can do this," I whisper, Cashel's ears twitching at the sound of my voice.

Right before the final—and tallest—hedge of thorns, Cashel raises his front hooves as if he's about to fly, quickly extending and flapping his wings once, pushing off the ground and leaping into the air at the same time. He closes his wings as we ascend, tucking them in just before they clash with the thick branches above. We're jumping higher than ever before—we might as well be flying.

As we soar over the final hedge, I see a small silver box sitting on a large boulder up ahead. There's a warm light radiating out from it, flickering in front of us.

The relic of light.

The air rushes past my ears as we descend, clearing the impossible jump. Cashel lands hard, but quickly recovers. My arms wrap around his neck as he trots toward the relic.

"You did it," I whisper, in awe of my steed. But as I survey the clearing, turning Cashel in a full circle, my heart sinks. That impossibly tall, unbroken hedge completely surrounds us. There's no way out, except for back over.

If my father did indeed construct this place, then he designed these protections well—*too* well.

We reach the relic, perched on top of a reddish-brown boulder at least as tall as me, and equally wide as it is tall. The silver relic has three upright black lines etched into it, like the tall grasses in the Green, just like Vikmal described. It's similar to the one I saw when Cashel received his wings, but with a different symbol.

This one belongs to Ivernister, then.

I lean down from Cashel's back, my hand reaching out toward the relic. Before I even touch it, I feel a warmth, as if an invisible ray of sunshine is reaching back for me.

A rush of heat flows through my hand as I lift the relic. It's about one hand-length high and half the width. It's not as heavy as it looks, but it's solid, with sharp metal edges. My eyes dart upward as the light trickling in from the dense tree branch cover above us becomes brighter and brighter. The relic pulses with warmth.

A piercing squeal rips through the air. *Darwith.*

We need to get back to him, but those daunting hedges are standing between us, blocking our only path. I hold the relic in my hand, its heat moving through my arm like a wave of liquid honey. And all at once, I sense it—there's something *inside*. My other hand finds the top of the box, as if it's luring me closer. I use my fingertips to slide one edge of the top, just a little, and it retracts. A bright light emits from the opening, beaming up—up through the tree branches above.

And then the branches are moving—expanding higher and

higher, raising up—while still not revealing the sky above, but creating a taller dome.

A *flyable* dome.

I hurry, sliding the relic shut and placing it in the saddlebag. I give Cashel a squeeze and he gallops toward the hedge.

"Fly Cashel—*fly*!" I tell him, and in a quick movement, his wings stretch out and flap. His front hooves lift off the ground as he pushes his wings downward with extreme force, right before we would run straight into the hedge.

And we're jumping—*flying* above the tall hedge of thorns.

I lean close to his body as his wings continue to flap. Instead of landing on the other side of the hedge, we fly low, gliding over the remaining three hedges as well. We land on the other side of the first hedge, the roof branches collapsing in behind us, reverting to the way they were when we first arrived. I exhale in relief, glancing at the relic in the open saddlebag.

What just happened?

No time to ponder that now. *Darwith*—where is he? My eyes dart to the base of the tree root staircase to find Darwith's black frame, lying motionless. Bright red blood litters the ground around his body, and the jekler's mauled form lies lifeless on the other side of him.

Darwith isn't moving. He's not moving.

Cashel whinnies at Darwith as we near. Moments pass. Nothing. Then a faint whickering noise echoes back, and one of Darwith's tattered wings twitches.

He's alive.

Darwith extends his wings, forcing himself to stand. He wobbles in place, barely able to hold himself steady.

I slide off Cashel and hurry over to Darwith. Much of the blood scattered around is his own. He lowers his head as I reach out for him.

"Darwith…" I whisper, touching his neck; it's soaked with a mixture of blood and sweat. Gashes cover his body, and his shredded wings go limp at his sides.

He's broken.

I swallow hard, attempting to push away my fear of what's sure to come next. I can't handle it.

"I'm so sorry," I whisper, my eyes blurring. He sacrificed himself to protect me.

He rubs his muzzle on my arm, and my tears flow. And then he's kneeling back down, one front leg at a time. But this time, he's not bowing for me to get on his back—he's too weak to stand.

"No, Dar…please, stand up…" I whisper, realizing my efforts are futile. I put a hand on each side of his jaw, turning his head to face me. "It's all right. It's all right."

A small light reflects off his dimming eyes. It's coming from behind me. Choking down my sobs, I turn.

My saddlebag is aglow.

The relic.

I gently release Darwith, rushing over to my saddlebag to retrieve the relic. As I touch its metal sides, the warmth reaches out for me, until it's flowing through my hands.

The power to give. Gattacan's mother said it had the power to give. I lift it, its warmth stronger than before. I have no clue what I'm doing, but if there's any way I can save Darwith, I have to try.

I rush back to Darwith as he lowers his head to the ground, his life fading fast.

An energy passes through me. It's coming from the relic, just like it did before I opened it moments ago. A heat—a *power*. My fingers instinctively find the top of the box once more.

I slide it open.

A light as bright as the sun shines out. I turn my head and shield my eyes as the warm glow swirls all around me. It encompasses me, like a cloak of sunshine, holding me in pure warmth. I feel like I could stay this way forever. As if I am one with the light—as if it's a part of me.

A silent moment passes.

Then Darwith whinnies.

From behind my closed eyelids, the glow of the light diminishes. I slide the top of the relic, and it snaps shut.

I open my eyes. Darwith moves with ease back up to his hooves, standing tall and proud, his black wings mended and strong. His black coat shiny, with no traces of blood or gashes.

My jaw drops. He's healed. The relic can heal. It can *save*.

"Dar!" I yell, scurrying back over to him. As I do, I suddenly realize my leg is no longer in pain. My eyes dart to my thigh, and I quickly unwrap my bandages. My arrow wound is completely gone—no sign of any injury at all.

My mind rushes to my father—if the relic healed Darwith and me, it could heal him, too.

I lay my head against Darwith's neck for a moment, thanking the stars he's all right. When I pull away, he rubs his muzzle on my face, his warm breath and long whiskers brushing against my cheek. I smile at the light in his eyes. He's full of life once more.

The relic continues to hum with power in my hands. I stare down at it, dumbfounded. This is one powerful metal box—*relic*. I must keep it safe. I can't let it fall into the hands of Sutagus and the king.

Reverently, I return the relic to my saddlebag, then mount Cashel. All three of us hurry up the giant root staircase and back through the tree tunnel. When we reach the open clearing where we first landed, a feeling of intense relief washes over me.

"Take me back to Nammden, back to the Grays," I say, feeling more than alive as we take off into the sky. And despite the constant chill in the air, a warmth embraces me.

I hold my head high. I have the last known relic of light. It will be protected now, away from hands belonging to evil minds.

I feel myself smiling. Lermyn would be proud. My father would be proud.

I did this for them. For our home.

For our freedom.

THIRTY

The cloud cover thickens as we near Nammden, the air damp like a wet towel has been wrung out. Water fills the ground beneath us, covering the old streets. The giant buildings stand out like metal islands, stretching up into the overcast sky.

As we approach the steel structures, my mind races back to Gattacan, remembering how I followed him through these buildings just yesterday. I imagine his black hair streaming away from his angular face, and my heart beats a little faster.

Then I picture Thayer flying beside me. The way he smiled being up in the sky for the first time. The way his eyes smile every time his lips do.

Thayer.

I hope he's all right. I miss him. More than I ever thought I could. And I don't know when I'll see him again.

I'm not okay with that. I need to see him again. I need to know he's safe.

Darwith flies close beside us as we enter the maze of buildings. The sun shines between them during fleeting breaks in the cloud cover, the light reflecting off the colossal steel beams and the remaining glass.

Scalers—men, women, and children—scale across the exteriors of the buildings, high in the air, with skilled ease. They traverse the sides of open windows with the same wires and ropes I saw the first time I flew in. Belongings hang from the wires and from their backs. They pivot to watch me as we fly past, not changing their courses, or their expressions. Steely faces—like the buildings they inhabit. Faces much like most of the people in Uladmond and Ivernister. And some of them just as intense and beautiful as the Grays.

My eyes trail down the sides of the buildings until I spot a bright green hue on top of the murky water. A few small water karriers move back and forth across the liquid streets. I wonder what it would have been like to stand at the base of one of these buildings and look up, before the city was flooded—how small it would make someone feel, to be next to an unwavering giant.

We approach one of the tallest buildings in the city, the same charcoal-gray building where I slept last night. Despite its color blending in with the silvery sky, it stands out among the rest. The large hole at the top where we flew in before looks as if something exploded, long ago, through the whole upper center of the building. But it didn't collapse. It's not fully broken—just damaged. And still serving its purpose.

We fly into the opening of the building, my eyes adjusting to the dimmer light. I glance over my shoulder to make sure Darwith follows. In the landing area, a few people are standing on either side, watching as we descend.

I dismount and give both Cashel and Darwith a pat on their necks, thanking the stars we made it back in one piece. One person scurries off—perhaps to alert the Grays of our arrival—while another approaches me.

"I'll take care of them," the man says, his eyes looking past me to Darwith and Cashel. I glance around for any sign of the Grays, hoping to first confirm I should leave both steeds with him.

"I was the one who cared for Cashel before," the man tells me. "No need to worry."

I smile politely, remembering that he did a good job with Cashel last night. I detach my saddlebag and secure it under my arm. "Thank you," I tell him, watching as both Cashel and Darwith follow him to the water trough.

"Aluma," I hear from behind me. I turn in place as Wolkenna strides toward me from the other side of the corridor.

"Wolkenna!" I run to meet her, wrapping my arms around her slim frame.

She hugs me back, squeezing my shoulders as we pull away. "Didn't expect to see me, did you?" she asks, giving me a sly smile.

"No, but I'm glad you're here. Are you okay?" I check her over, making sure she's not injured. Her long dark hair hangs with no restrictions, unlike the tight ponytail she usually wore at the base.

"Yes, yes, I'm fine. Are you?" She glances at my legs, a perplexed look crossing her face. Her parents or her brother must have told her about me being shot.

I snort. "Better than ever."

"And now you know—you know *everything*?" she asks, raising an eyebrow.

"Your family filled me in, yes. I had no idea," I tell her, shaking my head as we amble through the corridor. Scalers shuffle past us, some glancing at me with odd expressions, others keeping their eyes to the ground.

"It's good you didn't know," Wolkenna says, peering over at me. "You were safer that way."

"But you…you attacked your own people?" I ask hesitantly. If my memory isn't skewed from my fall, then she shot at least one armed Scaler on the water karrier during the battle over the Knarrno River.

She stops, her eyes darting side to side to check that we're alone. "I had to keep my cover for as long as possible," she murmurs. "And the crew didn't know who I was." She blows out a puff of air. "I had to defend myself…and my friends."

I take a deep breath. I can't imagine having to do what she did.

"What about Thayer?" I ask carefully. My last memory of him was his face as he disappeared through the cloud cover during the battle.

Her eyes narrow as she pivots toward me.

My blood turns to ice, and I grip her arm. "What? Wolkenna, is he okay?"

"Thayer is—well, he's here," she says.

"He's *here*?"

She nods, continuing down the hall. "As I was sneaking out, Thayer saw me. He hadn't been doing well since we returned—he wasn't talking to anyone. He thought you weren't coming back. When he saw me leaving, he asked where I was going. I knew he was your close friend, and it seemed like he could tell I was hiding something. So I told him I was going home. Told him you were likely there, too." She looks me in the eye. "He risked everything to leave—to see you. Neither of us can ever return across the border again. They'll have our heads if we do."

A jumble of emotions rushes through me like an avalanche. "Where is he?"

She gestures down the hall where I slept last night. "This way."

Thank the stars. Thayer is here. He's safe.

"Is everyone else okay, back at the base?" I ask as we move down the corridor. "And how did *you* get here?"

"At the battle, when I saw Rinehart's steed, I knew it wasn't Rinehart flying on Elro. He would've come to the arena when the alarms sounded," she says, staring at the ground. "I knew something was wrong. And I recognized my brother's silver mask." She pauses. "I assumed Rinehart told Gattacan to find you. So I knew you'd be in good hands. That's the only reason I left when I did."

"You don't need to explain," I tell her. "I'm just glad you're safe."

She forces a wavering smile, then continues. "When we all arrived back at the base, it was different. An arrow grazed Cloveman's shoulder during the battle, and he was sent to the medic. Lieutenant Mund was badly injured and disappeared as soon as we landed. And Prince Sutagus was completely out of control—he was furious. He ordered that everyone be interrogated, so he could find out who was behind the mask.

"We all went to our rooms to wait. I knew I was probably on their short list, because of my connection to Rinehart, and that my cover would likely be blown. So I snuck out, with Huffman's help. He got me to Taima, and he told me the prince had sent Rinehart straight to Tarmensil, to serve as an example of what happens to traitors. They're going to torture him."

"*Huffman* helped you?" I ask.

"Yes," she says. "He said he knew about me, and about you, and he wanted to help."

"But Huffman is one of the King's Watchers," I protest, attempting to process.

She shrugs. "He switched sides. Joined the resistance."

"And Rinehart is in Tarmensil, being—" I can't utter the next word.

"As far as I know." Wolkenna takes a shaky breath. "What could I do? He was gone, taken before we ever left the base."

"Nothing," I tell her. "It's not your fault."

She presses her lips together, pain welling up behind her dark eyes.

"What about the others? Xander and Cloveman?" I ask.

"They're here, too."

My jaw drops in surprise.

"And Moninne—Dr. Penson," she adds.

"What? How?"

"Thayer convinced me rather quickly to offer Xander and Cloveman the chance to get out of that place—that *prison*—too. And Moninne, well, she's a Laithlanner—she's always been with us."

Moninne is a Laithlanner, too? Who else isn't who they say they are?

I clutch the saddlebag closer to my side, and Wolkenna's gaze falls to it.

"Is that what I think it is?" she asks, her eyes widening.

I nod as we stop in front of a door down the hall from the room I slept in the previous night.

"Thayer's inside. I'll notify everyone else you've returned," she says, glancing at my saddlebag again. "And I'll tell them about your success." The awestruck look on her face remains as a light fills her eyes. "Thank you, Aluma."

I smile. "Thank *you* for bringing Thayer here."

She nods once and turns, hurrying back down the hallway, leaving me in front of the closed door. I draw the saddlebag to my waist, checking for the relic. It's still there, warm as ever.

I take a deep breath, knock twice, and turn the handle.

⌒

When I step into the room and shut the door behind me, there's no one in sight. The bathroom door is closed, and I hear running water. I set the saddlebag on a small side table and sit on the bed. Something tells me it's safe to put the relic down for a minute, especially around Thayer.

The water shuts off, and the bathroom door clicks open. Thayer stops in his tracks, his eyes on me. He's still in his Empyrean Rider uniform, but he's no longer wearing the gold blood locket that was around his neck.

He's broken his oath, too.

A warmth rushes through my body, and it's not from the relic this time. I stand, and Thayer rushes over to me, pulling me into his arms and holding me close to his chest. His scent fills my nose—fresh rain on trees. Clean and warm, like the forest when the sun peeks through the canopy after a storm.

"I'm so glad you're okay," he breathes, brushing my hair out of my face, his fingertips trailing on my cheek.

A hundred butterflies flutter through me as I gaze into his brown eyes.

"I didn't know if I'd ever see you again." He pauses, dropping his hand and stepping away. "They—they wouldn't let me turn around. They said you were gone."

"I'm here, Thay," I say, reaching out for him.

His eyes well up with tears. "I'm sorry it wasn't me. *I* should have saved you—I should have been there. I swear I didn't know. I didn't know you were still...*alive*." He lets the word fall out of his mouth in a whisper, as if to forget the thought.

I shake my head. "You couldn't have known."

He runs a hand through his hair. "If I had waited for you to come through the clouds and made sure you escaped when we did—" He pauses, dragging in a ragged breath. "I thought you were right behind me."

"Hey." I step closer, lifting his chin. "Stop beating yourself up. We're both alive. And we're both here *now*. That's all that matters." I lean in toward his full lips, wanting to feel their touch. I gaze into his eyes, and then his lips are pressing against mine, soft and warm. I kiss him eagerly, a deep fervor rushing through my bones.

I take a deep breath as our lips part, as if this is the first time I've ever felt air rush into my lungs, giving me life, giving me strength. Thayer rests his forehead against mine, his lips curling up on the sides.

I'm grinning, too.

His smile spreads to his eyes, and he pulls me into a hug again. "They told me about you," he says. "They told me you're special—a *Light Keeper*."

"That's what I was told," I say. "But I'm still not sure what it all means."

"I've always known you were special," he whispers. "You're a light—a light in the sky." His breath dissolves on my neck like a soft breeze, making my skin tingle. "My light..."

I smile with my face pressed against his chest, and for a moment, I feel as if I'm glowing—radiating warm light.

The bedroom door clicks open behind us, startling me. I turn away from Thayer as Wolkenna walks in, leaving the door wide open.

"Hey, you two," she says, her mouth pulling into a knowing smirk. I can feel myself blushing as she approaches.

A few seconds later, Gattacan emerges behind Wolkenna, his eyes locked on me. My skin goes hot as I brush my hair out of my face. Thayer glances over at me, his eyebrows furrowing. Gattacan looks at Thayer, then back over to me, and suddenly I feel as if I've been caught in a spotlight, with every part of me exposed.

"Gattacan, this is Thayer," Wolkenna says, seemingly oblivious to the awkward tension that has consumed the rest of us.

Gattacan stays close to the doorway, but nods in a silent acknowledgment. Thayer mirrors his gesture.

"You two haven't met?" I ask, shifting my weight, my eyes flickering back and forth between them.

"No," Thayer says, his voice suddenly deeper.

"When Thayer and I arrived, my brother was still out collecting supplies," Wolkenna says, shooting a strange look at Gattacan. "Isn't that right?"

"That's right," Gattacan says coolly.

Wolkenna crosses her arms. "I only caught up with him after I left Thayer here."

"Oh," I say, wishing I could somehow escape this uncomfortable conversation.

"But I told Thayer that *Gattacan* is the one who found you," she says, turning her gaze to me. "The one who *saved* you."

I glance at Gattacan, my cheeks flushing as I remember the way he carried me from the cave—and how nice it felt to be in his strong arms.

What am I thinking? I was just kissing Thayer.

A look of curiosity flashes across Wolkenna's face, as if she can read my mind. "Our parents will be waiting for you in the dining room. We should go," she says.

"Do I have time to change?" I ask, pulling at my dirty uniform, realizing I must smell as bad as a I look.

"Oh—yes. Sorry," Wolkenna says, darting a look at her brother before nodding at me. "Let's head back to your room. I'll get you some fresh clothes, and I'll let my parents know you need some time to freshen up."

"Thank you," I tell her, then hesitate, noticing the staring contest going on between Gattacan and Thayer.

"We'll come back to fetch Thayer before dinner," Wolkenna says, noticing my hesitation.

"Go—I'm fine," Thayer says, crossing his arms in front of his chest.

I give Thayer an awkward smile as I snatch up the saddlebag from the side table and walk back to the door. Wolkenna heads out into the hallway, leaving Gattacan standing there, looking between me and Thayer.

"After you," Gattacan says.

Thayer keeps his eyes on me until Gattacan closes the door behind us, and regret immediately washes over me. I should explain—I should tell Thayer. But I don't know exactly *what* to tell him.

Wolkenna leads the way through the corridor, with me trailing behind her. I hold the saddlebag close to my side, hearing Gattacan's footsteps right behind me. I feel as if I should say something to him, but I can't even think straight right now.

"How was your supply run, big brother?" Wolkenna says over her shoulder.

"Fine," Gattacan says flatly.

"Oh?" Wolkenna turns on her heels, bringing us to a quick halt. "What about this?" Wolkenna pulls on Gattacan's loose sleeve, revealing four large gashes on his left forearm, all in a row—a giant claw mark.

My eyes go wide as Gattacan yanks his sleeve back down, glaring at Wolkenna.

"It's nothing," he says, his nostrils flaring.

"Still like to hide things, I see." Wolkenna shakes her head. "And after all these years, I thought maybe you'd be a little less... secretive." She turns, striding ahead again.

I stay motionless, staring at Gattacan's covered arm. He's hurt; that's no small scratch. My brows furrow, silently asking him what happened. His dark eyes lock with mine, and then I'm reaching out to his arm, gently placing my hand over his wound. He barely flinches.

"Wow—*interesting*," Wolkenna says, startling us both.

I drop my hand and turn to see her watching us from a few steps away. She raises an eyebrow. There's no judgment in her expression, just a sudden understanding that while I care deeply for Thayer, I'm also undeniably drawn to Gattacan—to *her brother*.

And I have no idea what to do about it.

We continue to walk in silence. Every step more awkward than the last.

"Here we are," Wolkenna says finally, opening the door to reveal the small but comfortable bedroom I slept in last night. She points at another door on the far wall of the room. "You can shower in there. I'll have someone bring you new clothes." She turns away, then faces me once more. "I'll have them bring Thayer some, too."

"Thank you," I say, ignoring the shift in her tone as best I can. She eyes me for a moment and glances at her brother once more before she leaves.

I step into the room, avoiding eye contact with Gattacan. I've had enough humiliation for one day. I push on the door to close it, but he pushes back.

"Wait," Gattacan says, sliding in through the door behind me and closing it himself.

My body is tense, and I can't help but hate myself as I take in his features without distraction for the first time since I've returned: black hair, dark eyes, angular jaw, and skin that I know smells just like the ocean. My heart thumps faster, and I wish I could slow it down. I look away, hoping that will help.

"I'm sorry about my sister." He huffs. "She's always been like this. I'm not surprised that her time away hasn't changed her much. She's as perceptive as they come."

"Yeah, I've noticed that about her," I tell him with a wry smile.

"I'm glad you're back," he says, and the fervent sincerity in his tone sets my heart racing again.

"What happened to your arm?" I ask, hoping he can't hear the drumming in my chest.

"It's nothing," he says, his hand resting over his covered wound.

"It looks like you were *attacked* by something."

He hesitates, suddenly looking a little sheepish. "I was there."

"Where?"

"In the Gray Forest," he says, moving closer, wringing his hands. "I followed you."

"You *followed* me?" I echo, my jaw dropping.

He nods. "I took Elro and waited outside of Cintrenia." He pauses, running his hand through his long hair. "I didn't know where the last relic of light was, but I had a feeling it might be in our territory, given the history between your father and mine. When I saw you flying, I trailed you." A look of shame crosses his face.

"Why? You could've been killed—"

"It wasn't right for you to go alone. I should've gone with you in the first place."

"But that's what needed to be done, right? I'm a Light Keeper, remember?"

He stares at the ground. His silence is answer enough.

"Now, what happened to your arm?" I demand, realizing he still hasn't responded to my original question.

"A jekler—the same one that attacked Darwith."

My hand flies to my mouth at the thought, holding back an internal shriek.

"I didn't want you to know," he says, shaking his head. "I didn't want my family to find out."

"Did *you* kill it?" I ask cautiously.

"No, Darwith did."

"How—"

"By the time I made it through the tree tunnel, you were already jumping over the hedges. I saw the jekler attacking Darwith, and I rushed in to help. The jekler turned on me." He inhales sharply. "Darwith—he attacked it from behind. He saved me." He lowers his eyes. "I ran back out of the tree tunnel while Darwith fought the jekler, and I took off on Elro. I waited in the sky until I saw you leave."

"And you followed me back here?" I imagine him trailing behind me on Rinehart's steed, bleeding out from his arm. I could've helped him.

He steps closer, his hands open. "I'm sorry I left Darwith. But I knew once you found the relic—I knew you'd be able to save him—*if* he needed saving." His midnight eyes peer into mine. "Maybe I shouldn't have followed you, but I was...worried about you."

"Thank you," I say, attempting to step back from the intensity in his eyes, feeling the drum in my chest growing loud again. "I should probably clean up now."

"Of course, I'll leave you," he says, moving toward the door.

"The relic—it can heal you, too," I blurt out, glancing at the saddlebag, remembering the light. The pure warmth that surrounded me in the forest.

"I know," he says, turning back to me. "But its powers must be preserved. Plus, I'll heal all on my own." A small smile crosses his lips, as if he finds excitement in the challenge.

He's stubborn, but he has a point.

"Wait—at least take this," I say, remembering the pompidorri I stashed. I open the saddlebag and lift the fruit out for him. "Eat a handful of its seeds. It will help ease the pain."

"Thank you." His hand grazes mine as he reaches for the pompidorri.

"I hope it helps. You can eat the rest of the fruit—or, I like to make jam with it," I say, rambling on like some strange bird chirping away, wondering why the touch of his hand has left a cool tingle on my skin.

He smiles at me once more before leaving. The door clicks shut, and I let out a long sigh. Alone at last. Carrying my saddlebag, I trudge into the bathroom and drop it in the corner, shutting the door behind me. I turn on the shower, leaving the water to run until the bathroom is steamy.

As I pull off my jacket, it occurs to me that I may never wear it again. All those years I wanted to be an Empyrean Rider...and now, the only thing I want to do is take this uniform off and leave it all behind me.

I step into the shower, the hot water running over my head like summer rain, washing away all other distractions, until only three things are circling in my mind.

The last relic of light. Thayer. Gattacan.

What have I gotten myself into?

THIRTY-ONE

There are new clothes laid out on the bed after my shower. I pull on the soft, long-sleeve sweater and warm pants. The outfit is looser than my uniform, but comfortable all the same. I slip into my Empyrean Rider boots and catch a glimpse of myself in the mirror. My cheeks are still rosy from the hot shower, but at least I look as if I no longer smell like a murky forest floor.

There's a knock at the door. I grab the saddlebag and scurry over to open it.

A frail older woman is standing in the hallway. Her eyes are dark like stone, a deep brown that's on the verge of obsidian. Traces of black linger in her silver hair, perhaps from her younger days.

She looks me over approvingly. "The clothes fit you well, Aluma," she says. She must have been the one who delivered them so stealthily while I showered. "I'm Nadie, Gattacan and Wolkenna's grandmother. I'll walk with you to the dining room. If you're ready?" She dips her chin.

"Yes, thank you."

The old woman leads me through the long corridor. She walks with a limp, leaning to the left each time her right foot hits the floor. It reminds me of Lermyn and the way he hobbled around. Another pang of sadness hits me at the loss of him. He was a kind man—one I wish I would've had more time to get to know.

The scent of food fills my nostrils before we even step into the dining room. Naturally, I'm hungry again. Everyone is sitting around the large table: Gattacan, his parents, Wolkenna, Thayer, Xander, and Cloveman.

"Mother, Aluma, join us," Delna calls out, standing and hurrying to her mother's side. "I take it you two have been introduced?"

I nod to Delna, then smile at Nadie, the kind old woman. She smiles back at me, and I realize her eyes are the same shade as her grandson's.

Xander and Cloveman both stand to hug me as I approach the table. The tension in my shoulders lessens when they do. I didn't realize just how worried I had been about them.

"It is good to see you again," Xander says. "I am relieved you are safe. We were all quite worried about you."

"It's true." Cloveman nods. "We all thought the worst."

"Thank you." I smile. "I'm so happy you're both here now, too."

I take a seat in the empty chair next to Thayer. He glances over at me, and I notice Gattacan watching discreetly from across the table. Vikmal, Delna, Nadie, and Wolkenna all turn to look at me, too.

All eyes are on me.

I clutch the saddlebag closer in my lap, the weight of the relic suddenly heavy with importance.

"Tonight we feast," Vikmal says. "Aluma, we were told you were successful on your quest." He holds a glass in the air. "To your bravery."

Everyone else lifts their drinks, and I follow their lead. We all tilt our glasses toward one another's, and they clink together as they meet.

"To her bravery," everyone echoes.

Gattacan nods in my direction before taking a sip, his eyes somehow saying, *thank you.*

We're served an assortment of delicious foods. Thayer's eyes widen as he tastes some of the same dishes I tried for the first time just the night before. I take a bite of each item on my plate, savoring them all. Laithlanners sure know how to combine flavors well.

Vikmal stands as we finish our meals. "Let's continue our evening by the fireplace," he says.

Wolkenna, Cloveman, and Xander decide to break off and head to their individual rooms. I stay with Thayer, Gattacan, his parents, and Nadie.

In the fireplace room, I sit next to Thayer on the couch, setting the saddlebag on the top of my thighs. Gattacan takes a seat on the other side of me. My body warms, from both the relic and the crackling fire. Sitting sandwiched between Thayer and Gattacan has nothing to do with my increasing body heat, I'm sure.

"Tell us about your journey," Delna says, leaning forward in her armchair.

Everyone is watching me again. The relic sits obscured by the saddlebag in my lap, but it's as if they can all see right through the fabric, to the silver box inside. My mind races through the events of my journey today. *Lermyn.* My shoulders slump, and a familiar ache in my chest returns.

"Lermyn Githah," I say, "my father's friend—*my* friend—was killed." My eyes stay on the floor.

"No—" I hear Vikmal say. "What happened?"

I take a deep breath in, and let it out. I'm not sure I'm ready to relive this. But I explain it all, recounting every detail of what happened from the moment I arrived back at the farm.

"There was nothing anyone could do," I tell them, feeling my eyes blur. "He was a good man."

"And a true friend," Vikmal adds. "This news comes as a shock. Unfortunately, like the rest of us, Lermyn knew the risks. But we will miss him greatly." He glances at the saddlebag in my lap. "This only makes me more thankful that you were successful on your journey."

Gattacan shifts beside me as the memory of the thorny hedges flashes through my mind. The dome of thick branches opening above me. *The jekler.*

"Darwith led me to it. He made it all possible," I say. "And Cashel—he's how I reached the relic. It was well protected."

I wonder if Vikmal knew about the hedges—or the beast.

"And now you've brought it here for us to protect." Vikmal stands, taking a pair of black gloves from his pocket and pulling them on.

I nod, squeezing the saddlebag, the relic still warm on the tops of my legs. I don't want to let it go. My eyes linger on his now-covered hands—what are the gloves for?

"I will keep it safe. Hidden and secure," Vikmal says, elongating his gloved fingers as he approaches.

I glance around to see everyone else's eyes are still on me. Slowly, I open the saddlebag and reach my bare hands inside. The relic is hard and rectangular, a heat radiating off of it, flowing through me like a warm river. When I take it out, it glows faintly in my hands. I remember the last time it glowed: when it healed Darwith and me.

"It can heal," I tell Vikmal. "You didn't mention it could do that." I glance over at Gattacan, his hand draped over the top of his sleeve, hiding the large gashes on his arm. Something tells me he's not planning to reveal that he followed me into the Gray Forest.

Vikmal watches me intently, his eyes narrowing. "Yes, it can. Did it open for you again?"

"It did," I tell him. "I didn't know, and…Darwith…he wasn't going to make it." My stomach churns at the memory. "I opened it twice. The second time, Darwith was better. And my leg—it healed me, too."

"Now that you've experienced the power of the light, you know how important it is for us to protect it," Vikmal says, placing his gloved hands around the relic and carefully pulling it away from my grasp. The warmth fades. "We'll be able to keep it safe here."

Vikmal leaves the room with the relic of light, the only thing left I could use to save my father's life. I run a hand through my hair as a stream of emotions courses through me like a stampede. If Vikmal can keep the relic safe, then that's much more than I can hope to do.

As we sit by the crackling fire, the attention in the room shifts to Thayer. The older Gray women seem fascinated by him. With his gentle, personable manner, it's no surprise he draws them in. He tells them about his family farm and the crops they grow—things the Laithlanners haven't been able to cultivate for generations.

I sit quietly, thanking the stars the focus isn't on me for a moment. My eyelids are heavy as I stare into the fire. I feel like I'm in a bit of a daze, after everything that's happened. I'm in Scaler territory. I just gave the last known relic of light—one I never knew existed—to a Scaler, who until recently was my enemy. My father is far, far away, and possibly not even alive.

I shake my head until my eyes refocus on the undulating flames. *Stop thinking that way. He's alive—he has to be.* I imagine him lying peacefully in a medical bed, waiting for me to come to his aid. And my brother, wherever he is.

"We still have much to discuss," Vikmal says, reentering the room, "but it can all wait until tomorrow." He clasps his now-ungloved hands, glancing over at Delna and Nadie.

I snap out of my daze, out of my tiresome thoughts, back to reality.

"But we were just finally getting to know Mr. Pridfirth," Nadie says, beaming at Thayer with her eyelids creasing up.

"I'm sure he's tired." Vikmal raises his brows at Thayer, as if offering a sly reprieve.

"I am," Thayer says with a knowing smile.

"Then it's settled. Talking resumes tomorrow," Vikmal says, placing his hands on the back of his armchair.

"Thank you," Nadie says to me, her wrinkled hands covering mine as we leave the room. "For bringing us some light. Sleep well, my child." She hobbles off past Thayer, who is waiting for me in the corridor.

Someone clears their throat behind me. I turn, surprised to see Gattacan looking expectantly at me.

"Goodnight, Aluma," Gattacan says, his eyes burning into mine like the hot flames we just moved away from.

"Goodnight," I say, blushing a bit under the intensity of his stare. I glance once more at Gattacan's arm, hoping he'll remember to use the pompidorri seeds for the pain.

When I turn around, Thayer is watching us, his face pulled taut.

I offer him a reassuring smile, trying to mask the tension building in my body.

Once we're alone in the corridor, Thayer and I fall into wordless step. His hand reaches out, his fingers interlocking with mine. A warmth passes through me, much like the warmth from the relic, but with a different energy—one I can't quite explain. It feels good—great, even. And I wonder: why didn't we do this before, back at home, when things were still simple?

Thayer stops at the door to my room, giving me a long hug before planting a soft kiss on my waiting lips.

"I hope this is okay?" he asks, his face inches from mine.

"Yes," I breathe.

"Before today, I've been wanting to kiss you...for a long time," he whispers.

When he leaves, I smile to myself, laying my hand flat against my chest, trying to keep his warmth with me for as long as I can, realizing all at once: I never want to let it go.

 THIRTY–TWO

The room is still dark when I open my eyes, but I can't sleep any longer. I slide off the bed and shuffle over to the window. The glass is still intact—perhaps it was reinstalled. Either way, I'm thankful it's there at all. It's a long way down through the thick clouds stretching out in the darkness.

The air is chilly on my skin. I pull on the clothes Nadie gave me last night and tiptoe in the direction of the fireplace room. Maybe I'll be able to warm up a bit in there.

Someone is sitting on the couch with their back to me when I enter. I clear my throat, and Wolkenna glances over her shoulder before looking back to the flames.

"Couldn't sleep?" she asks.

"Guess not." I trudge my way over to the front of the couch and plop down beside her.

"One drawback of being a Light Keeper, I suppose. *Lots* of pressure," she says.

"Yeah, I'm still not sure what being a *Light Keeper* even means."

She shrugs. "Lots of pressure, that's what it means."

"Great." I reach my hands out toward the heat of the flames. "Is it always this cold here?"

"Yes. Especially at night. *Almost* makes me miss Galghesworp." She grabs a blanket off the side of the couch and tosses it to me.

"Thanks."

We sit in silence, side by side. My eyes stay on the fire; yellow and orange flames dance to the crackling beneath them. The warmth of the blanket and the fire gradually lull me into a dreamy state, relaxing my tense muscles. Here, in this moment, it's so easy to forget everything that's happened.

"They killed Huffman, you know," she whispers, pulling my attention right back into the room.

My heart clenches. "What? Are you sure?"

"I heard his screams." She shakes her head sadly. "He died for us. He's the only reason we all made it out alive."

I glance at Wolkenna. A shadow falls across her pained face.

Huffman. He sacrificed himself. First Lermyn, now Huffman. And Rinehart has been taken to Tarmensil as a traitor. We can't lose anyone else.

"I keep thinking about what they're doing to Rinehart," she says, finally. "I'm going to go find him. I have to."

"In Tarmensil? But you said—you can't cross the border again. Wolkenna, you said they'll have your heads."

"I know what I said, but I can't leave him there. I have to do something."

"What will your father do?"

"*My father* is the reason I haven't gone sooner." She runs her hands through her dark hair. "I've been begging for him to let me go since I returned. He's forbidden me to try. He says Rinehart can handle himself. But the prince is an evil man, and a powerful one at that. And according to my father, the king of Uladmond may already have all the relics of darkness. And if he does..." She inhales, barely letting the air escape again. "I may be too late."

I sit for a moment, imagining Rinehart Quin bleeding in a cell somewhere—or worse. My mind races to Lermyn, remembering how he died in front of me.

The prince *is* an evil man. And every part of me knows it.

"Well, let's go get Rinehart, then." The words fall out of my mouth.

Wolkenna turns to me. "Are you serious?"

"Yes," I say, warming to the idea. "And my father, too. I don't want to leave anyone else to be tortured or killed. Enough has been taken from us."

And now that I know there's a power that can heal my father, I can't leave him in the hands of Prince Sutagus and the king. I may not have the relic of light in my possession—*that* would be helpful—but if I can get Father back here, surely Vikmal will let me use it to heal him.

Wolkenna rubs her hands together, the flames reflecting in her eyes. "Okay, let's do it. But we have to leave before my father finds out. We'll go first thing in the morning, before he wakes."

She's right—he can't know we're leaving. There's no way he'll let us go, not with how dangerous this mission is bound to be. I hid flying from my father for a long time. I'm not proud of it, but it was necessary for my family to survive the winter.

This is necessary for our survival, too.

"Just us?" I ask, leaning forward.

Her eyes narrow. "Can you trust Thayer?"

"Of course. What about Cloveman and Xander?"

She shakes her head. "Cloveman is still injured. And I don't want to leave him here without anyone he knows. So Xander should stay and keep an eye on him."

I agree, realizing she means to keep them in the dark. But she's got a point—I doubt either of them would be too keen on staying behind while we try to rescue Rinehart and my father.

"What about Gattacan?" I ask.

"Gattacan will come," she says, rising to her feet. "But if we're going to do this, we need to prepare now."

"I'm ready," I say, standing, hoping I'm telling the truth.

"I'll go find my brother. You get Thayer. Meet us in the landing area before dawn."

And just like that, we're going to Tarmensil.

⌒〰

I creep through the hall, past my room, knocking on Thayer's door as quietly as possible before pushing it open.

"Thayer," I whisper, leaning inside.

"Aluma?" Thayer's voice is groggy.

"It's me." I step in and close the door.

"Are you okay?" he asks, clicking the light on beside his bed. He sits up, the blanket falling to his lap, leaving his bare chest and abdomen exposed. His hair is disheveled and his lips are extra plump from sleep.

I remember our two kisses yesterday, and I instantly warm all over. I want nothing more than to crawl into the bed next to him and feel his lips on mine again. But we have a mission, and I need to focus. "I'm fine," I tell him.

He rubs his eyes. "What's going on?"

"Wolkenna and I are going to the capital—to Tarmensil."

"What?" His eyes widen.

"We're going to rescue Rinehart and my father."

"You're serious," he says, more than asks.

"We're leaving soon."

He shakes his head. "Why didn't anyone say anything?"

"Because we're not telling anyone. Only Wolkenna, Gattacan, *you*, and I can know about this. Will you help us?"

"I—Aluma, it's not safe."

"Nothing is safe anymore. You don't have to come, but I'm going," I say, realizing I haven't even considered he might not want to come with us.

Thayer waits a moment, exhales, and nods. "Then I'm going, too."

A half-smile crosses my face.

I wait in the hallway as he gets dressed. Then we make our way down the long corridor to the landing area.

Our steeds—Cashel, Yulla, Taima, and Elro—are all saddled and waiting.

Wolkenna steps out from the hallway where they lead the steeds after we ride—their makeshift stable area, I'm sure. She smirks when she sees Thayer standing beside me. Gattacan emerges, too, watching me with a wary expression.

"Here—we'll need these," Wolkenna says, handing each of us a bow and a quiver of arrows. "Swords are over there." She nods to a selection of steel leaning against the wall.

I sling the bow and quiver across my back and select a sword.

"Wear these," Gattacan says, handing us each a mask—just like the one he wore when I first saw him. That silver mask—like liquid metal—was one of the last things I glimpsed before I fell.

A chill runs through my body, remembering the way everything felt like a nightmare as my back hit the water that night. I hope I never have to experience something like that again, but I thank the stars I survived and that I'm here now.

I walk over to Cashel, giving him a pat on his neck. Taima stands quietly beside him, her muzzle rubbing against his. Cashel whickers softly, clearly enjoying the attention.

"These two," Wolkenna says as she mounts Taima.

A light chuckle escapes my nose. "No kidding."

"Wolkenna!" a booming voice echoes out in the landing area.

I turn to see Vikmal storming toward us, anger written all over his stern face.

Great—we're caught. There goes our plan.

THIRTY-THREE

"Where do you think you're going?" Vikmal growls through gritted teeth.

"You know *exactly* where, Father," Wolkenna barks back.

Xander and Cloveman catch up from behind Vikmal, confusion on their faces. I shake my head, alerting them to stay quiet.

"You disobeyed me." Vikmal scowls. "And you put others at risk." He glances at Cloveman and Xander, then narrows his eyes when he faces Wolkenna. "Don't you think you've done enough, bringing in these outsiders."

"*People*, Father. They're *people*," she snaps, dismounting Taima. "Like Aluma and her father. Like Thayer. Like Rinehart. Like *us*."

"You're not like everyone else, and Aluma is a Light Keeper," Vikmal tells her. "When will you learn your place?"

"Maybe you're right. Maybe that's why *we're* ready to save Rinehart and Aluma's father when you won't even try." Wolkenna juts her chin out at him in defiance.

"They knew the risks," Vikmal says evenly. "We all did."

"They took him to Tarmensil!" Wolkenna shouts. "You know what awaits him there. He's a *traitor*—they'll torture him. And they'll do the same to Aluma's father if he ever wakes up."

Vikmal swallows hard, darting a glance over at me for the first time. "It's too dangerous," he says, but his tone is uncertain.

I take a step toward him. "Please," I say softly. "How will we ever be able to forgive ourselves if we don't try?"

He looks away, his eyes finding those of his son. "Gattacan, you're in on this, too?"

"Yes," Gattacan says.

Vikmal's jaw flexes. "The rest of you—we *all* need to have a discussion, but not here." He scans the opening and our steeds, now impatiently stomping in place. "Meet me in the dining room after you've seen to your mounts." He pauses, glancing back at Xander and Cloveman. "And Wolkenna and Gattacan—make sure these two take those vile things off." He gestures to the gold blood lockets still around their necks.

Wolkenna watches until her father turns the corner, then shifts to face us, raising her eyebrows at Xander and Cloveman. "Welcome to Nammden," she says with an exhausted sigh. "Come on, I'll help you get those off."

"I'll see to them," Gattacan says, eyeing the steeds, his voice strangely neutral.

"*A Light Keeper?*" Cloveman asks Wolkenna as they walk away with Xander. I'll let her explain that one.

Gattacan glances at me and Thayer before he leads the steeds toward the hallway to their makeshift stable area.

Thayer walks with me back to my room, giving me a hug before he leaves. I let myself sink into his arms, realizing how much better it would be if I could stay this way, wrapped in his embrace, shielded from everything else that I know I need to face.

Once I'm alone, I close the door behind me and shuffle over to my bed. My tired back thanks me as I lie down and stare at the ceiling. My mind races to my father and Kase. My father has been found out, but what's become of my brother? I remember him asking Sutagus what was in the box. At least he didn't know it was a relic of darkness or what the prince would use it for. And Rinehart is being held somewhere in Tarmensil. Rinehart and my father—and Kase, if he's still with my father—could all be in the same place. And in grave danger. They could all be subjected to torture.

Something stirs inside of me, like a windstorm picking up speed.

I can't let that happen. I have to save them.

As I leave my room, an energy jolts through my body, as if I've had a good night's sleep and I'm not actually running on empty. When I march into the dining room, Vikmal is sitting alone at the table, his head in his hands.

I clear my throat, and he looks up at me with distressed eyes.

"I need to speak with you," I announce, walking over and pulling out the chair next to him. I turn it and take a seat, so we are sitting face-to-face.

He stares at me blankly.

"I'm going to save my family," I tell him.

His eyebrows furrow.

"But I need your help."

He stays motionless, observing me. "Your father..." he begins, any traces of anger in his voice from before now gone.

"What about my father?"

"Your father, Rinehart, Lermyn—all of us, we agreed a long time ago," he says. "We agreed that if any of us were ever captured, we would do whatever was necessary to protect our cause."

I shake my head. "I don't understand."

"Your father may still be incapacitated, but Rinehart—he'll do whatever it takes to keep our secrets safe, to keep himself from leaking information."

My mind twists to a dark place, one I don't care to visit. "Are you saying he'd *hurt* himself?"

"To keep his silence? Yes." Vikmal lowers his head. "You see, there's no point in going to save Rinehart. There likely won't be a Rinehart to save. Wolkenna knows this."

"What about my father?" I ask, my heart sinking like a rock. He'd *never* do something like that. He can't.

He exhales. "If your father wakes, it won't be to anything good. They'll try to force the same information out of him."

I stand, my hands pressed firmly on the table. "I can't leave him there to die. I saw what the relic of light can do. We can rescue my father and bring him back here. We can wake him."

Vikmal stares at the table.

"I won't give up on my father, my brother, *my family*." My voice grows louder. "I'm a Light Keeper. Doesn't that mean I'm supposed to *do* something?"

"What's going on?" someone asks from behind me. I glance over to see Gattacan standing in the doorway. Vikmal waves his hand, dismissing the concern in his son's voice.

"We were just having a discussion," Vikmal tells him.

I nod in agreement, my heart thumping in my chest, still waiting for Vikmal's answer.

Wolkenna slides in through the doorway behind her brother. A look of surprise fills her eyes as they dart between me and her father. Vikmal's hardened face softens a little at his daughter's presence. And then, as if on cue, Thayer, Xander, and Cloveman all enter, standing side by side against the wall just inside the doorway.

"You were right," Vikmal says, glancing at Wolkenna. "You were right to want to try."

Wolkenna's eyes narrow, clearly skeptical of his sudden approval.

Vikmal continues, "I shouldn't have forbidden you to go to Tarmensil for Rinehart and Hearn. Regardless of the agreement we all made, many years ago."

Wolkenna and Gattacan move closer to the table.

Vikmal looks over at me. "Hearn is lucky to have you as a daughter." Then his eyes meet Wolkenna's for a moment. "As I am lucky to have you. We shouldn't give up on family, or the ones we love."

I glance over at Wolkenna and see a small smile forming on her face.

"If you decide to pursue this quest to Tarmensil, you have my approval, and any resources I can offer," Vikmal says to his children. "But Wolkenna, you know Rinehart may no longer—"

"I know," she says, not allowing him to finish his sentence. And I'm thankful for it; I don't want to think of that possibility. Rinehart and my father *have* to be alive.

"I must stay here to protect Nammden, and the relic of light," Vikmal says. "The rest of you are free to do what you will."

Determination spreads across Wolkenna's face, and Gattacan's. Thayer smiles in my direction. Xander and Cloveman nod at me, too. *They're all in.*

"It's my understanding there will be a grand celebration in Tarmensil in three weeks—an ideal occasion to get in and out without being spotted," Vikmal says. "And this will give you all ample time to prepare."

"But they could both be dead in that time—" I object.

Vikmal looks stricken. "I know. Unfortunately, anything before that would be too risky. The lot of you are far too conspicuous under normal circumstances, but the celebration provides the perfect cover. There will be plenty of strangers going in and out of the city that night."

"I don't like it either," Wolkenna says, turning to me. "But I think it's the best option we have. We'll be no use to anyone if we get caught."

Three weeks before I can get to my father—that's too long. But what else can I do? I have to wait. I can't rescue him by myself.

Three weeks it is. Then we're going to Tarmensil.

⌒

We don't waste any time.

Our first task is to visit Nammden's supply room. We follow Wolkenna and Gattacan down the long corridor, past the landing area, and through the makeshift stable area. Darwith and Cashel are standing side by side, munching on hay. It's the first time I've seen them both relaxing together.

We continue until we arrive at an old staircase chamber. I peek over the railings. There are a few floors above us, and an endless abyss of stairs below—a dark drop beyond where my gaze can reach. My hands go damp on the cool metal as I clutch the rail tighter. Though I've flown even higher than this on Cashel and Darwith before, I somehow feel far more vulnerable to falling than I ever have on a steed.

We walk down a few levels, our footsteps echoing in the cold chamber. As we exit the stairs, we enter an open floor where there are no interior walls, no doors, and no glass left in any of the windows. The wind howls through the empty level like a sad song. No one is around but us.

"We'll need to *scale* a little," Wolkenna says as she leads us to the wall of open windows.

A light drizzle blows in as we approach the opening. My hands start sweating again—we're *in* the clouds, and without any means to fly.

"Might as well let the steeds eat and rest," Gattacan says. "Plus, this way you can see the sights, and experience more of *Scaler* life." He raises an eyebrow in my direction. "Don't worry—it's a short trip."

Xander walks to the window and peers over the edge, jerking back inside with wide green eyes.

Cloveman sighs. "That bad, huh?" He nudges Wolkenna on her arm. "I take it there's no other way to the supply room?"

"We'll tie you in, harness to rope—rope to wire. Just in case." She winks at him.

Gattacan strides over to the open window. He holds on to an exposed beam as he reaches out and grabs ahold of a rope that's dangling above. A thick wire comes into view, stretched out parallel to the ground. He holds on to it while stepping out backward onto what looks like thin air.

I inch forward to see better. Gattacan is standing on a large beam, with another thick wire below. He glances at me, his eyes dancing with excitement. My body tenses as I realize he's only inches from falling, with no way for any of us to save him.

"You'll face the building. It's easier to get back in that way," Wolkenna instructs as Gattacan demonstrates.

Gattacan steps onto the wire below the beam, his back to the open sky. I want to reach out for him—he isn't tied in. But he quickly swings himself back into the building with ease. "I'll give you a hand," he says, looking over at Xander first, unaware of the scare he just gave me with his bold move.

Xander steps forward, mustering up a brave face as Gattacan grabs a harness from the wall and hands it to him.

"Step into it, like this," Gattacan says, pulling another harness up to his own knees, and then raising it until it's resting around his athletic frame. Xander pulls his harness on around his waist, and Gattacan shows him how to fasten it.

"All right." Gattacan gestures to Xander to come to the window next, then reaches for a latch connected to the rope that's hanging from the parallel wire above. "Attach this latch to your harness, make sure it clicks, and you're good to go." He attaches it to Xander's harness with a *click*.

"Follow me," Wolkenna says to Xander, pulling her own harness on with ease. She attaches herself to a latch connected to a dangling rope to the left of Xander's with a *click*. Still facing us, she steps out backward onto the wire, not even glancing below, while simultaneously grabbing the wire above. Does she know *any* fear?

"Here," Gattacan says, tossing a harness each to Thayer and Cloveman, as Wolkenna and Xander disappear from the window. "I think you two can manage." Gattacan holds the last harness open and glances at me. "Step right up," he says.

I glance at Thayer, who is adjusting his own harness and watching me with a tight jaw.

Gattacan stands behind me, his hands brushing the outside of my legs as he pulls the harness up to my waist, sending a cool rush through my body. "Hold it here, I'll tighten it," he says in a husky voice. I grab the harness at my hips, and Gattacan tugs on either side until it's snug.

Someone clears their throat. My head pops up to see Thayer, now near the open window, his eyes on me. Cloveman clicks in and slides across the wire and out of view.

Gattacan places his thumbs between my waist and the harness. "A good fit."

Is he talking about the harness, or something else? The way he's looking at me makes me think it's the latter.

Thayer's nostrils flare as he huffs. He clicks the latch to his harness and scales past the window to his right, out of my sight, following Wolkenna, Xander, and Cloveman.

"Are you ready?" Gattacan asks, his intense eyes peering into mine. I feel his hands lingering on my hips, steady but gentle. And I can't help but remember how strong his arms felt around me when he carried me into the forest. Or the way his scent made me feel so *alive*.

"I guess so?" is all I can manage, my heart thumping, like it's ready to jump out of my chest.

We move to the open window. I don't look down—I keep my gaze fixed on Gattacan instead, which I'm finding far too easy to do. It's nearly impossible not to stare at his features in appreciation. His eyes are so dark, like the cave I met him in, but deeper, like there's something waiting at the end. They narrow when he smiles.

"Here, let me," he says, his hands reaching for my waist again. He pulls softly on my harness and grabs another dangling rope with a latch, securing it near my navel. *Click.* He glances at me. "You'll be safe. I'll be right beside you." He smiles again.

I move closer to the ledge. The wind brushes droplets of water across my skin as I step out onto the beam. I glance down, then up, checking that my harness is indeed secured to the latch and the rope, and then making sure the rope is attached to the thick parallel wire above before grabbing hold.

"I've got you," Gattacan says, his voice smooth and calming. And he does—his hands are still reaching out to guide me.

I step onto the bottom wire, wobbling. I steady myself, drawing in a deep breath, then slowly shift to face the building.

"That's it—now all you have to do is *scale*," Gattacan says encouragingly. He drops his chin and gently releases me.

I take a small step to my right. And then another. And another.

Thayer is not too far ahead, and the others are just past him. I glance back at Gattacan as he clicks in—he's grinning.

"You're scaling," he calls after me.

I peer up at the gray sky. Never in a thousand years did I think I'd be moving across the outside of a steel giant. And never did I think I'd start falling for a *Scaler*—and Thayer, at the same time. I'm not sure which scenario scares me more. Either way, I'm facing them both now.

A vibration buzzes through my hands, and I squeeze the wet wire above with all my might. I twist to my left as Gattacan steps out beside me. He smirks, and I realize the wire is still intact—I'm not falling.

"Not so bad, is it?" he asks.

I let out a shaky laugh. "It's different, that's for sure."

I turn to my right and keep moving. Thayer is waiting ahead, his eyes trained on me.

"You've got it," Thayer says.

I smile at him as my hands slide along the top wire, hoping he can't sense my confusion about him and Gattacan. I scale faster, my feet side-stepping below on the bottom wire. I glance over my shoulder and see other Laithlanners scaling the buildings across the way, like us, but much more smoothly and confidently than me, I'm sure.

I turn to Gattacan. "Why scaling?"

"Look down," Gattacan says.

I squeeze the wire before I dare glance below. We're just as high as I thought. My eyes follow the side of the gray building down—down to where I have to squint to make out the ground level. Dark green water covers the streets, but I can't tell how high the water level is above the foundation.

"Water karriers are scarce," Gattacan says. "Plus, over the generations, we've become accustomed to living life up here. The wires connect every building to the next. Scaling allows us more freedom and time efficiency between buildings." He nods past me to my right.

I turn to see Wolkenna, Xander, and Cloveman are now between the buildings past Thayer. The wires stretch out across the gap. Nothing beneath except the water-covered streets far below.

My mind races back to when I fell from Cashel, the dark water breaking beneath me. I tighten my grip, the steel wire digging into my palms. The wind and rain blast against me as I scale out into the open area between the buildings. My hair whips across my face, shielding most of my view. Between mouthfuls of my locks, I catch a view of deep blue, off in the distance.

The ocean.

It's beautiful. Dark and turbulent. So close I can taste it: wet droplets of sea salt saturating my lips.

I turn back to Gattacan. "I didn't realize we were *this* close to the ocean."

"Where did you think all that water came from?" He gestures below.

"*That's* ocean water?"

"A mix," he says. "The ocean water is untainted until it washes farther ashore and mixes with the rain, chemicals, and sewage around the city." He raises his eyebrows. "Not your typical day at the beach."

The green tint from the street water is visible even from this height. I imagine the beach in Sceilaran, in Uladmond, where I visited my grandmother when I was a child. The ocean there was light blue and calm—a tranquil paradise. This is no paradise around us. But somehow, it's beautiful in its own broken sort of way.

"But that's not where you catch the fish, is it?" My stomach curdles at the thought.

"No, no." He chuckles and takes a hand off the wire to point out the buildings closest to the open sea. "That's where we catch fish. Fisherman work from the buildings that face the ocean. Most of the lower floors are completely submerged. The third or fourth floor usually works great for a place to cast out, though. Otherwise we take our more powerful water karriers—the ones that can get past the break—out to sea and fish there."

"How do you get clean water?" I ask, remembering the long shower I took, that was thankfully *not* tinted green.

Gattacan points up at one of the large silver barrels I noticed on the roofs when I first arrived in Nammden.

"What is it?" I squint at the barrel, raindrops blurring my view.

"A rainwater collector," he says. "Every building has at least one."

I feel the wire go taut. I check to my right. The edge of the next building is near. Wolkenna, Xander, and Cloveman have disappeared—they must have gone in through a window up ahead—but Thayer is still scaling toward the steel building.

"They've been there since before our time," Gattacan continues from beside me. "Whenever it rains, we get more water—and it rains *a lot*." He chuckles, glancing up.

"No kidding, it seems to rain here even more than it does in the Green," I say, glancing to my right just as Thayer steps through a large window into the building in front of us. Peering over my shoulder, I notice another rooftop across the water-filled street is full of vegetation—of green. I turn back to Gattacan and point. "What about that—are those crops?"

"They are," he says with a proud smile. "We grow what we can from the rooftops—vegetables, berries, and even wheat. We forage for the rest in the forest—mushrooms, mainly."

My eyes are wide as I take in my surroundings.

"Do you collect pompidorris, too?" I ask, wondering if we could've already been at the same place at the same time before.

"No—the one you gave me is the first I've ever seen of its kind. They must grow closer to the border, and we don't venture too far that way...unless we have to."

"Well, it seems like you've done quite well with what you've got." I glance around, admiring their ingenuity.

"Luckily Nammden was already prepared for what would happen here," Gattacan says, as I turn back to him. "We just didn't know it would work out that way. But sometimes things just fall into place." He swallows, his eyes peering into mine, and I wonder if he's still talking about the rainwater collectors.

There's a tug at my waist.

I twist back as Wolkenna reaches out to me. I grab her hand

and step through the open window, instantly relieved to be back on solid ground. Xander, Cloveman, and Thayer are already taking off their harnesses.

I exhale, pushing my wet hair off my face.

"How was it?" Wolkenna asks, unhooking my harness from the rope dangling from the wire.

"Not so bad," I tell her. "But I much prefer flying."

I step out of my harness as Gattacan swings in from behind us.

"Okay, let's get going," Wolkenna says.

We follow Wolkenna across the open level, much like the one in the first building, and head into another stairwell. We descend a few floors, and as we exit the door from the stairwell, we hear voices—*lots* of voices.

A colorful market bustles with activity before us—small stands with people selling food, clothing, and trinkets. An upbeat melody of soft drums and a stringed instrument plays somewhere out of sight. People shuffle around us, carrying bags on their backs, full of vegetables and goods. The smell of fish wafts out to my nose, making it wrinkle. Then the scent of fresh-baked bread. For a moment, I can almost imagine I'm back home in Cintrenia, walking through the city.

Wolkenna leads the way through the crowds, the rest of us trailing behind. A few people notice her, and then more and more, until they're parting on either side, like she's walking down an ever-clearing sea of people.

I get it—she's *that* beautiful.

And then people start bowing their heads.

"*Princess,*" a few people say in quiet voices.

More and more people halt to stare.

"*Your Highness,*" someone says from behind me.

I turn as more people bow their heads—to Gattacan this time.

My eyes dart back to Wolkenna, but she won't make eye contact with me. Neither will Gattacan.

Princess? Your Highness?

Wolkenna glances at us with a harried expression before stepping through a doorway. Xander, Cloveman, Thayer, and I follow. Gattacan closes the door behind us.

The room is empty and quiet—and clearly *not* the supply room.

Cloveman stops behind Wolkenna, opening his hands. "Anyone care to explain?" he asks.

Wolkenna sighs.

"Princess?" I ask incredulously. "You're the princess of Laithlann?"

She shrugs, so I turn to Gattacan. He scratches his neck self-consciously.

"Prince Gattacan," I say, connecting the pieces. "The son of the king—the *future* king of Laithlann?"

His dark eyes meet mine, and it all sinks in. I was saved by the prince of Laithlann.

The Scaler Prince.

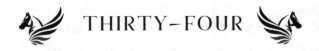

THIRTY-FOUR

The room is silent.

Wolkenna pulls her dark hair behind her shoulders. Cloveman stares at her, his jaw unhinged. Gattacan walks over and stands next to his sister.

"It all makes so much sense now," I muse, eyeing the two of them.

Thayer glances over at me, furrowing his eyebrows.

"My father, Rinehart, Lermyn—they had to have a strong support system here," I add, thinking aloud. "And they *did*—they were working with your father. The *king*. I can't believe I didn't figure it out sooner." I turn back to face the royal siblings. "Why didn't you tell us?"

Guilt spreads across Gattacan's face. "I'm sorry," he says. "But if you had found out about us before you retrieved the relic of light and then been captured, you would have been at risk. We'd all have been at risk."

"We were going to tell all of you," Wolkenna says.

"Oh, really?" My hands find my hips. "When? Before or *after* Tarmensil?" I ask, realizing my sarcastic tone may no longer be appropriate, given their royal status.

Gattacan drops his head.

"After," Wolkenna says. "Now you know, but it puts us all in greater danger. If any of us are captured..." she says, trailing off. "Until now, no one outside of Laithlann, other than our few allies, knew who's been leading the way here."

I drop my hands from my hips.

"It was safer that way." Wolkenna sighs.

"Safer?" I repeat, shooting her a skeptical glance.

"Look, this doesn't change anything," Wolkenna says. "Except now we really have to make sure none of us get caught."

"You shouldn't go to Tarmensil," Cloveman says to Wolkenna, his eyes pleading with her. "You're the *princess* of Laithlann. It's not safe for you."

Wolkenna smiles and pats his arm. "That's sweet, really it is. But I've been a spy for years. Being a Laithlanner princess doesn't mean I can't fight or defend my people. It means I *must*."

Gattacan nods, agreeing with his sister. "Prince Sutagus has attacked our people by King Breasal's orders, repeatedly. I wouldn't be fit to be the prince of Laithlann, or the future king, if I didn't fight back," he says, standing taller somehow. "We will fight for our freedom from Uladmondian rule—we will *never* stop fighting for that freedom."

Freedom. We all want the same thing.

"I will also fight for it," I say, nodding in agreement.

Xander clears his throat beside me. "I will fight, too," he says.

Cloveman nods. "I'm in."

"Me too," Thayer says.

We all stand in silence for a few moments, affirming our pact. The frustration inside of me toward the secretive newfound prince and princess dissipates, as quickly as it emerged.

We're all in this now. And we have to work together.

Wolkenna claps her hands once, breaking the silence. "Okay, let's stick to the original plan and head to the supply room."

In the market area, I notice the way every single person glances at Gattacan and Wolkenna, admiration crossing their faces. The deference to them is obvious—it all makes so much sense now.

We walk through a long hallway, away from the loud marketplace, toward a black door. A guard stands in front of it. As Wolkenna and Gattacan approach the man, he straightens his posture and steps to the side.

"Here we are," Wolkenna says.

Inside, rows of weapons fill the space: bows, quivers full of arrows, ropes, knives, and swords galore. We walk along the right side of the room, swords and bows to our left, ropes and bags on the right near the wall. Past the swords and bows, there's a section of knives, of all different shapes and sizes. It's an entire gallery of weapons and gear.

Wolkenna selects a knife and twirls it around. "Take what you need, but only what you can carry."

Xander holds a large knife, observing the well-honed blade. "We are not planning on needing to use any of this, are we?"

"If we have to use any of it, we're already in trouble, in which case we'll need it." Wolkenna raises an eyebrow. "The plan is to get in and out without being spotted, like at the base."

"But that's not what happened..." The words slip out of Cloveman's mouth.

Huffman. He must be talking about Huffman.

Wolkenna turns to him, tilting her head. "No, it's not," she says coolly. "But we'll take more precautions this time. And we'll try not to cut it so close." She turns and starts toward another door at the end of the room. "Plus, we'll do things a little differently this time." She gestures for us to follow her through the now-open door.

The next room is much smaller than the first and lined with racks of clothing, all color-coded by the cities of Eirelannia.

"We're going in disguise," Wolkenna says. She selects an Empyrean Rider uniform jacket with purple and white stripes—Sceilaran's colors—holding it up to herself. She glances at the mirror on the wall.

"As Empyrean Riders?" Xander's voice raises.

"I *think* they might recognize us," Cloveman snorts.

"No, not as Empyrean Riders," she says. "I wanted to see if purple was my color. It's not." Wolkenna shrugs as she hangs the jacket back in its place. She strides over to another rack and selects a lavish dress. "We're going as Uladmondians."

Gattacan eyes Xander before grabbing a white suit off the rack and handing it to him. He selects another suit for Thayer and one for Cloveman.

"Here, try this one," Wolkenna says. She holds out a long golden dress and a fancy pair of heeled shoes for me to take.

"A dress?" My eyes go wide. I haven't worn a dress since my mother was still around.

I hold it up to myself in the mirror, gazing at my reflection. The light overhead hits the golden sparkles, making them flicker like stars. Almost like they're moving—dancing, even.

"Yes, a dress. Clearly you haven't been to Tarmensil in a while," Wolkenna says.

"You're telling me they dress like *this*?" Thayer says, inspecting his teal suit with uncertainty.

Wolkenna nods. "Not always, but everyone will get dolled up for the king's celebration. The only other option is to dress like the King's Watchers. But we'll be able to get around a lot easier posing as guests, not guards."

"I have only been to Tarmensil a few times during some of the king's festivities, but it is true, this is how they dress," Xander says, shrugging on his white suit jacket to check the fit.

"We'll change once we arrive, outside of the city," Wolkenna says. "Obviously these aren't the best riding clothes."

She's not kidding. I've never ridden in a dress, let alone flown in one.

"How many times have you been to Tarmensil?" I glance at Wolkenna and Gattacan.

"A few missions like this," Gattacan says. "Haven't had an issue."

Hopefully that doesn't change.

"Let's pack it up," Wolkenna says as she heads back into the weapon room, a black dress and some shoes draped over one of her shoulders. We all take our clothing and follow her.

I select a small knife and a holster I can wear on my lower leg under the dress Wolkenna has given me. She throws me a bag, and I slide the dress, shoes, knife, and holster inside.

"One more stop before we formulate our plan," Wolkenna says, striding out the main door, past the guard in the hallway.

We walk back through the market area. But instead of going back to the stairwell, we come to an opening in the wall. It's wider and higher than a doorframe, and a man is waiting on a platform inside.

"Seventeenth floor," Wolkenna says to the man after we step in. The man nods and presses a button on the wall with a tiny seventeen etched into it.

"Watch yourself," Gattacan says to Thayer as two metal doors close in from either side.

The small platform moves—or drops? I grab ahold of Thayer's arm, noticing Gattacan's eyes on me as a whooshing sound fills the small space.

We're *dropping.*

"Never been in a lift before?" Wolkenna smiles at Cloveman, who's grasping on to a rail on the wall, holding on for dear life.

He shakes his head.

"It's a faster way to get up and down so many floors. Better than the stairs," she says.

The lift comes to a stop, and the doors slide open.

"This way," Wolkenna says, passing us. She leads us along a stark white hallway until we arrive at a small sitting area, and beyond that, another door—almost like the waiting room in Galghesworp before my physical, but more inviting. Wolkenna presses a small button by the door. A few moments later, it opens.

A familiar face stands before us.

"Dr. Penson!" I say, and she smiles.

"Please, call me *Moninne.*"

Moninne's kind eyes brighten, like the first night I met her at the base. And despite my mind filling with questions, an immediate wave of comfort washes over me.

We follow her into the next room. There are empty chairs, medical instruments on trays, vials full of different liquids, and a desk in the corner.

"Did you get them?" Wolkenna asks as we gather.

"I did," Moninne says, hurrying behind the desk.

"Get what?" I ask, turning to Wolkenna.

"Blood pockets," Wolkenna says.

I squint my eyes. "Blood *what?*"

"Here we are," Moninne says, carrying a small tray, pausing in her tracks. "I take it you haven't explained this to them yet?" She takes in the blank stares of Xander, Cloveman, and Thayer.

Wolkenna shakes her head. "We weren't sure we'd get to use them."

Cloveman's eyebrows raise. "We're all ears."

"Everyone who comes and goes out of Tarmensil is tracked by blood," Wolkenna says. "And since they already have records of most everyone's blood—except for Gattacan's, since he's never been registered—we need these." Wolkenna takes one of the small pockets off the tray and places it on her finger. "This is how we get in and out without being traced."

"Whoa," Cloveman says, stepping forward. He takes the blood pocket out of Wolkenna's hand, turning it this way and that.

Moninne holds the tray out in front of him. "Careful, we don't have many extras," she says. Cloveman places the blood pocket on the tray, and Moninne uses a small metal tool to move it back into place.

My mind wanders back to when Moninne took my blood during my physical at the base. How could I forget the needles?

She has my blood. *They* have my blood.

"The day of our physicals..." I say, looking at Moninne. "I saw Lieutenant Mund bring an envelope in. It was for *you.*"

"That's right, she did," she says, placing the tray on a stand. "The prince was monitoring you because of what happened with your father." She clears her throat. "After that, they were playing it safe. They wanted to make sure they had you on record."

"On record," I echo, my hand covering my inner elbow where my blood was drawn. "I'm on record now?"

"No," Moninne says, giving me a crafty smile. She glances at

Wolkenna before looking back at me. "I swapped your blood, along with Wolkenna's, with stored blood we had at the base, blood from people who won't be checking in or out of Tarmensil anytime soon."

Thank the stars.

"And these—" Moninne holds up one of the small pockets. "These are full of different blood samples that won't arouse any suspicion if they're recorded checking in or out. You must always use one at the checkpoints, especially if you're not registered, as an unknown sample will trigger their alarms."

"They are tracking us?" Xander asks.

Moninne nods. "Unfortunately, they do have your blood. Thayer and Cloveman's, too."

Thayer's eyes go wide.

"I apologize for that," Moninne continues, glancing over at Wolkenna and me. "I didn't realize they were with you."

"We didn't exactly know that then either," Wolkenna tells her.

"Those of you who disappeared from the base will be tracked," Moninne says. "And they'll be tracking more diligently in case any of you show up anywhere."

"But these pockets will disguise it? As we won't be using *our* blood?" Thayer asks.

"Exactly," Moninne says, grabbing a short needle. "It works like this." She pokes the tip of the needle into the pocket resting on her hand. A drop of blood pops up into the tube of the needle. "They'll get the blood of someone else, not yours. So long as you use the finger it's attached to."

Thayer nods.

"I'll go first," Wolkenna says. She sticks her right pointer finger out, with her palm facing the ceiling.

Moninne squeezes a tiny amount of clear paste from a tube onto the top of Wolkenna's finger. She places the small blood pocket on top of it, pressing the edges around Wolkenna's skin, making an unnoticeable seal.

"Let it dry and it should stay put," Moninne says. "Wear them around to get used to how they feel. They'll fall off in a few days, at most. Come back on the day of your departure and I'll apply fresh ones."

The others admire Wolkenna's new blood pocket as Moninne makes her way over to me. I take a seat, lifting my hand to her, and she applies the sticky clear substance onto my finger.

"It's nice to see you again without all the false pretenses," Moninne says to me, smiling.

"Likewise," I tell her, remembering all at once when she said my father would be proud of me, back at the base. "Do you know my father well?"

Moninne's green eyes meet mine, warm like summer grass in the sun. She nods.

"How?"

"From the base," she says. "Before he retired."

"Oh," I say, staring at my finger as she presses the sides of the blood pocket into sealed edges.

"I wanted to tell you." She exhales, a glimmer in her eyes. "Your father—he's special to me." A small, almost apologetic smile crosses her face.

My eyebrows raise. Moninne and my father know each other—and he's *special* to her. She releases my hand, and her red hair falls around her soft face, framing her fair skin. She likes my father. Probably quite a lot. And I can see why he would like her in return. She's nurturing and kind. And pretty, like a delicate flower.

Moninne continues to attach the blood pockets onto everyone else's fingers, and my mind jumps from my father and Moninne to my mother.

My mother—I can't remember the last time I thought about her. Only a few things remind me of when she was still around—her horse, Blossom, and the riding boots she left me. That's about it. Well, that, and how Kase was undoubtedly her favorite; how I so often felt invisible to her. When all I ever wanted was her love and acceptance.

I imagine Moninne would give her love freely, if she ever had a child. She would be a good mother—the kind who helps her daughter to bloom. But I can't go back; I'll never be a child again.

I'll never have a mother like Moninne.

A warm hand lands on my knee, and I turn to see Thayer sitting beside me, his eyebrows pulling together. "What's wrong?"

I stare at my boots. "Nothing," I whisper, realizing my feelings must be written clearly on my face.

"Hey," Thayer says, squeezing my knee gently. "You're not alone. You're *never* alone."

My eyes meet his, and a warmth passes through me, reaching to the depths of my core. Sometimes, it's as if he knows me better than I know myself.

"We're all done here," I hear Gattacan say. I glance up to see him standing on the other side of the room, his gaze trained on Thayer's hand on my leg.

Everyone else heads through the doorway where Wolkenna is standing, tapping her foot impatiently. Thayer exits in front of me, and Wolkenna follows him, but I linger behind for a moment.

"Moninne—" I stop myself, choosing my next words carefully.

She looks up at me. "Yes?"

I take a deep breath. "My father is lucky to know you."

A smile spreads across her slender face. I want to tell her I'm lucky to know her, too—that she's made me remember that motherly kindness can still exist in my life, even without my own mother. But I don't tell her. It's enough that my father had her in his life. All those years I thought he was alone, without my mother—but he was never alone.

And neither am I.

THIRTY-FIVE

Over the next three weeks, we train with the prince and princess of Laithlann. Their fighting instructors teach us hand-to-hand combat moves that can take a person down with one hit. We practice with weapons, too, so much so that I begin to feel as if the sword is an extension of my body. I spend time learning to scale with Gattacan when Thayer is out learning to fish with everyone else. And I somehow manage to hide the guilt that's building in my chest, sitting on me like a brick.

I have feelings for both Gattacan and Thayer. Each of them reminds me of the different things that I love best in this world. They both bring me comfort. But I have no idea what I'm doing, and a part of me is terrified that I'm being a complete fool.

On the morning of our planned rescue trip to Tarmensil, we meet with Moninne to apply our new blood pockets. Then we spend the rest of the day refueling with food and sleep, as much of it as we can get. The steady rain helps me drift off, despite my mind running a mile a minute.

As the sun goes down on the night of the celebration set to

happen in Tarmensil, we gather around the fireplace to review our plans.

"We will fly to Tarmensil," Xander says. "But once we arrive, we continue on foot."

"You know your way around, right?" Wolkenna asks. "You can get us to the prison chambers, where they're keeping Rinehart?"

Xander nods.

"And my father and brother?" I ask.

"Your father could be in the palace clinic. They will have a heavy guard on him if—" Xander stops himself.

I blink. "If what?"

Xander lowers his head. "If he is still alive."

A sharp pain twists in my stomach. I can't imagine my father being gone for good, not before, not now, not ever.

"The disguises should help." Xander pauses. "But our faces could very well be posted all over the place." He eyes Wolkenna, Cloveman, and Thayer. "At least, everyone but Aluma, who people assume is dead, and Gattacan, because no one there knows he exists." He exhales. "There is always a reward for traitors in Tarmensil."

"That's a chance we'll have to take," Wolkenna says.

"No, he's right," I say, turning to Wolkenna. "No one will be looking for me or him." I turn to Gattacan. "*We* should be the ones going to get my father and brother out."

Thayer's face contorts. "Are you sure?"

I nod, and the others agree.

"I can get us past the guards at the prison," Cloveman says. "Or arrange for a suitable distraction." A mischievous grin crosses his face. "I could even wear one of those silver masks." He raises his eyebrows with excitement.

"Someone should stay with the steeds. Distracting the guards shouldn't be an issue," Wolkenna says, glancing at Thayer and Cloveman.

Thayer shakes his head. "I'm going into the city with Aluma," he says, his eyes holding mine for a moment before shifting to Gattacan. "At least until you two break off to get into the palace."

I don't want to be separated from Thayer, either, but this is our best bet. He knows it as well as I do.

"Cloveman?" Wolkenna drops her chin.

"Fine, fine, I'll stay with the steeds," Cloveman says, glancing around at everyone. "I guess *my* skills aren't in very high demand." He sighs dramatically.

"Thank you," Wolkenna says to him. "And don't worry, you make a fine distraction."

Cloveman lifts his chin and smirks. "Can I still get one of those masks?"

"Don't push it." Wolkenna chuckles.

"We should leave soon," Xander tells us.

"We get Rinehart, Aluma's father, Kase, and we get out," Wolkenna says. "Aluma, we'll need to bring Darwith so we can fly everyone back."

"And some of us can fly doubles, if necessary," I tell her.

"We need to try to get in and out without raising the alarm. If we get into a fight, we cannot win," Xander says, looking specifically at Wolkenna.

She tilts her head. "I'll do whatever I need to do to get Rinehart back."

"He's right," Cloveman says to Wolkenna. "Tarmensil is their home—we don't know it like they do." He locks eyes with her. "Let's just get everyone out safely."

Wolkenna exhales. "Fine," she says to Cloveman, before looking around at the rest of us. "It's settled. Cloveman will stay with the steeds outside the city. Xander will lead the way and be a lookout. Thayer and I will rescue Rinehart. Gattacan and Aluma will go into the palace to find Hearn and Kase."

We all nod in agreement.

"Meet by the landing area as soon as you collect your supplies," Wolkenna says, standing.

An energy rushes through me like a brisk breeze in the morning—I'm going to see my father soon.

⁓

When I get back to my room to collect my supplies, there's a soft tapping on the door. I open it to find Gattacan's midnight eyes on me.

"May I come in?" he asks.

I step out of the way as he enters and shut the door behind him. He crosses the room and takes a seat on the edge of my bed, sighing as he stares at the floor.

"What is it?" I move to the middle of the room, then stop, uncertain.

"You shouldn't do this," he says. "It's not safe."

"I have to. I'm going to get my father. There's *no way* I'm not doing this."

Gattacan looks up at me, stands, and closes the space between us. "These last few weeks…" He exhales. "Ever since I saw you fall into the water…" His strong hands land on my arms and slide over my sweater, causing goosebumps to rise on my skin underneath. "Ever since I met you, I've felt something for you. I've wanted to protect you—to keep you safe." He stares into my eyes, lifting one of his hands to my face, caressing my cheek.

My heart thumps faster—a drumbeat in my chest.

"I can't bear to watch something happen to you again," he says, cradling my jaw. He shakes his head. "I *won't* let anything happen to you."

His face inches ever closer, and I can't breathe. I can't breathe.

Then his lips are on mine, and we're moving to the beat of my heart, our heads dipping to either side as we kiss feverishly. My hands lift of their own accord, my fingers twining through his thick hair. Gattacan pulls me even closer, deepening the kiss.

I inhale sharply and step away.

"Aluma…" He whispers my name like a breathless song. And I don't know what to say. I don't know what to do. There's an irresistible pull between us—an urgent desire for his lips to be back on mine.

But…

"We should really get going, don't you think?" I ask abruptly, hurrying over to the door and swinging it open.

Gattacan waits in the same spot I left him, staring at the ground. He scratches his neck. "I'm sorry," he says, peering over at me.

I nod so fast I almost give myself whiplash. Then I'm shaking my head. "No, don't be sorry."

Why would he be sorry? For *kissing* me?

He kissed me...

After Gattacan leaves, I close the door behind him. My back presses against the wood, and I exhale like someone is jumping on my chest. I brush my hair out of my face and my fingertips land on my lips—lips that were just kissed by the prince of Laithlann.

The image of his mouth inches from mine won't leave my head—a snapshot refusing to disappear. I don't want it to disappear. The way it felt to kiss him, like I was flying high through the sky at lightning speed, the cool air rushing past my skin, making all of my senses come alive.

I shake my head and force myself away from the door, snatching up the jacket I've been wearing for the last three weeks—thanks to Gattacan's grandmother. As I hurry through the corridor, Thayer steps out of his doorway. I stop in my tracks for a moment, my face hot with confusion. He smiles, his brown eyes bright and happy to see me, but as I get closer, his expression changes.

He searches my face, his eyes narrowing. "What's wrong?"

"Nothing." I shrug.

"Your face..." He raises his eyebrows. "It's so...*rosy*."

"Hm." I squeeze my lips together, attempting to hide any evidence of my kiss with Gattacan. "Well, I'm fine."

He nods. And I thank the stars he doesn't *actually* know me better than I know myself. But the brick of guilt lands right back on my chest again.

"Let's go," I say, taking off like we're in a race. "Don't want to keep the others waiting."

When Thayer and I reach the landing area, everyone else is already standing around their steeds. Vikmal, Delna, Nadie, and Moninne are waiting close by. Vikmal—*King* Vikmal—steps over to me as we approach. It's been weeks since I found out he's the king of Laithlann, but I'm still adjusting to all that it entails. He opens his gloved hand to reveal a small glass vial.

It's glowing.

He gestures for me to take it.

"What is it?" I lift the clear glass tube from his hand, and a warmth runs through my arm like a stream.

"Power. It's *light*," Vikmal says. "But be careful with it—it's the only light we have left that your father had extracted for us." He folds my hand around the vial with his own.

The warmth amplifies, pulsing through my veins. This is *all* they have. I try to open my hand, but Vikmal keeps his hand on top of mine.

"When you find your father, open the vial. It should revive him," he says. "And keep it safe until then."

"Thank you, Your Majesty."

Vikmal tilts his head to one side, raising an eyebrow. "As I've said before, please, call me Vikmal."

I smile and nod, acknowledging his request.

"Let's go," Wolkenna calls out from Taima's back. Everyone else mounts their steeds.

I put the vial in my pocket, and its warmth radiates like sunshine clearing the shadows. I give Cashel and Darwith each a rub under their manes and glance over to see Gattacan on Elro. Gattacan's hair falls around his face, and I imagine the way it would feel in my hands again—the way it would feel to kiss him once more.

My heart thumps, and I turn away before it beats any harder.

I glance over at Thayer on top of Yulla. He looks back at me, a confused expression on his face. Guilt washes over me again, filling the spaces around me like an overflowing bathtub.

I'm sinking fast.

Moninne hurries over to me, her green eyes bright with emotion. "You know," she says, breaking me away from my racing mind, "you remind me of your father. You're brave like him, *strong* like him." She places her hand on my shoulder. "Be safe on your journey, and bring him home."

"I will," I say, basking in the warmth of her words, attempting to forget about everything else.

I mount Cashel and survey the crowd that's gathered. It's not just Moninne, Vikmal, Delna, and Nadie seeing us off—quite a few other people hover near the openings to the hallways and on the sides of the landing area. And everyone's eyes are on us.

Before I give Cashel a squeeze, I glance around at the other riders, each of us from different places, with different lives. We are all riders, but not like the Empyrean Riders I once thought I wanted to become.

No, we are something more.

Something better.

THIRTY-SIX

The chilly night air beats against my skin like the crack of a whip. Fall has firmly set in, each night colder than the last. As we weave through Nammden, the lights shining from the steel giants brighten the dark sky, creating a soft glow beneath the clouds. When we reach the city limits, the water-filled streets blend and disappear into the Gray Forest.

The Gray Forest—which I now know *must be* named after the Grays—is darker than ever beneath us. I glance over at Darwith and the others flying in silence. I imagine jeklers lurking somewhere below, ready and waiting to devour anyone or anything.

When the Gray Forest thins out, Thayer flies Yulla closer to me and Cashel. He glances over and smiles before pointing out ahead of us. I follow his hand; the lights of Cintrenia sparkle in the distance. The Green is just as beautiful at night as it ever was. I try to spot our farm—*our home*—but we're flying too high and too fast to make out the smaller details of the landscape below.

It was so different the last time I was down there. No father. No brother. Only a torn-through house. It just wasn't the same.

But now *nothing* is the same.

We stay close to the snake-like Tarmen Canal—the only body of water that flows all the way across Eirelannia. It was constructed before the wars, when all the kingdoms were still working together—independent, but connected. Now the canal is only accessible between Cintrenia and Tarmensil. The Uladmondians don't want any of us floating into Laithlanner territory.

We fly away from Cintrenia, following the canal toward the Uladmond Mountains, a place I've only traveled through as a small child. The clouds thin out around us and the moonlight shines onto the canal; water karriers cruise in both directions. A chill runs through me as I realize Uladmondian eyes could be on us, right now.

The plan was to fly southwest to Cintrenia from Nammden, and then follow the Tarmen Canal to Tarmensil—that way if we *were* spotted flying, it would appear we were coming from Cintrenia, given the flight path. We figured it was safer than flying the shorter route straight between Nammden and Tarmensil and risking getting caught. Plus, the terrain farther north is far less forgiving than flying over the canal if someone were to fall.

"Are we good?" I ask Wolkenna, trying to keep my voice as quiet as possible, but loud enough for her to hear me over the sound of the air rushing past.

She nods once. I hope she's right.

The terrain changes as the ground climbs higher into the Uladmond Mountains. Colossal, sharp rocks jut into the night sky, like angry pieces of earth, trying to escape into the moonlight from the dark crevices below. They're intimidatingly beautiful.

The snow-capped mountains and the Tarmen Canal fill the space beneath us. Rock face after rock face, slicing into the darkness. I wind my fingers through Cashel's mane, gripping his thick charcoal-gray strands even tighter as we follow the canal.

As fast as they appeared, the Uladmond Mountains disappear, giving way to a broad valley. It sprawls out toward the twinkling lights in the distance: the capital city of Uladmond—Tarmensil.

The moonlight shines on farms, fields of crops, and sleeping animals. A valley full of life. The opposite of how Nammden is with its toxic waters. I glance over at Wolkenna as she stares at the fertile landscape, and my heart sinks. She's never known the rich soils that spark life, that grow green—not like me, not like anyone in the kingdoms of Uladmond or Ivernister.

I return my gaze to the sparkling lights ahead. A towering wall of pale stone surrounds the city, much like the one at the Galghesworp base. I trace the Tarmen Canal with my eyes—it looks like it might be the only way in.

Xander flies out in front, gesturing for us to fly closer. We move into a tight pack behind him. He leads us down and away from the canal, to a field without lights or people. We descend to the ground, where an old barn stands in the middle of an empty field, near a burned-out shell of what appears to have once been a house.

I grip Cashel's mane as his hooves hit the ground, Darwith landing beside us. As we approach the barn, Xander raises his hand and comes to a stop. We wait in the moonlit field as he rides his steed ahead, scanning the area. He dismounts, slides the barn door open, and disappears inside.

My eyes dart around the empty field. The air is dry, but not as cool as I expected; it's much warmer than Nammden, but still chilly enough to keep me alert.

A few moments pass. Xander peers out from the barn and gives us the all-clear signal. We hurry over to him, scanning the dark fields. He slides the door open wider, and we ride straight into the darkness.

My eyes adjust to the dim interior of the barn. The moonlight finds its way through the cracks and holes in the roof, and the wood creaks as the breeze rustles through the dilapidated walls. This place must have been abandoned long, long ago.

Xander slides the barn door shut behind us as everyone else dismounts their steeds. I pat Cashel's neck before sliding off onto the dirt floor.

"This will work," Gattacan says, nodding with approval.

"I know this barn," Xander tells us. "No one will be coming here."

We all peer over at him, waiting to hear more.

"An old man used to own this farm. He knew my father." Xander glances around. "I came here a couple of times with him to look at potential horses."

"What happened to the man?" I ask.

Xander shakes his head. "My father told me he disappeared. Said his land was left to waste."

I peer around at the many empty stalls. "What about the horses?"

"That could be why he disappeared," Xander says. "I heard the prince had confiscated them for the king. Took them all to Tarmensil."

My fists tighten as the image of our now-empty barn in Cintrenia fills my mind. Lermyn protected Darwith from whoever ransacked our home and stole Blossom. Thank the stars I didn't lose Darwith or Cashel, too. But the king is still destroying lives, like the livelihood of the old man who once tended to this barn. The king continues to suck the land dry with his incessant wars, draining its people by taking all they create and earn, and then claiming it as his own to do with it as he sees fit.

But the king can't take *everything*.

He can't control our thoughts—our *true* freedom. That's why we're here, after all.

"We need to get moving," Wolkenna says, opening her bag and pulling out her dress.

I swing my bag around and open it. The golden dress shimmers in the dim moonlight. I look over to the boys, already dressing out in the open. Thayer pulls a white undershirt over his head while Gatta-can straightens his dress pants over his long legs. Wolkenna makes her way over to a stall, disappearing inside with her black dress. I follow her lead and claim a stall of my own, closing the door behind me. Taking the small vial of light out of my pocket, I place it beside my bag for safekeeping. It's still warm, and I wonder: does it ever grow cold?

I pull off my borrowed clothes and slide into the golden dress; it's soft against my windburned skin. My hand searches for the small knife and holster I stowed in my bag. I tuck the vial of light between the knife and the holster; it's a snug fit, but at least I won't have to worry about losing it. I pull the long dress up past my knees, attaching the holster on my outer right calf, and let the golden fabric fall back over my legs. I take the fancy shoes out of the bag and carry them with me; no way I'm wearing these until it's absolutely necessary. They're pretty, but not at all practical.

When I exit the stall, I spot Thayer in his teal suit. My lips part. I've never seen him wearing one. He looks so much more...mature. And strange, but good strange. The fabric hugs his chest and his arms, making his lean body seem broader and more defined. And the blue-green color makes his brown eyes stand out. He looks so handsome.

"What, you don't like?" Thayer says, walking closer to me, brushing his hand over his suit jacket.

"It looks great," I tell him, stepping into a patch of moonlight, making the sparkles on my dress dance.

Thayer clears his throat. *"Wow,"* he says. His eyes are wide, and he's staring at me as if he's never seen me before.

My face warms.

I turn to see the others all looking at me, too. Gattacan peers over from near the steeds. He's wearing a black suit with a golden shirt underneath; it matches my dress. His long black hair is pulled back in a low ponytail, like a curtain drawn to reveal the most eye-opening window—his face. His jaw tightens and releases as his eyes meet mine.

"You look beautiful," Gattacan says. My lips press together as the heat in my face increases. Thayer shoots Gattacan a look, and suddenly I want nothing more than to go back into the stall until they simmer down.

"He's right. You clean up nicely," Wolkenna says as she strides over.

"Not so bad yourself," I say, thankful for her ability to pull me away from Gattacan's and Thayer's burning glances. She looks like a princess in her black gown—oh wait, that's right.

She is.

"Here." Wolkenna opens a small bag. "I got this from Moninne. All the women here will be wearing it, and we need to blend in." She pulls out a tiny tube and opens it to reveal a pale pink paste.

I eye the creamy substance as she squeezes it onto her finger, recognition tickling the back of my mind. "Is that...makeup?"

"Very astute, Aluma," she says with a chuckle. "Now hold still."

I remember my mother's makeup. All the different colors and textures. I remember her sitting in front of her mirror applying a similar paste to her lips. She told me it was called lip gloss, and that someday I should wear some to help me attract a proper husband.

I scoff under my breath. If only my mother could see me now. She'd be so proud.

Wolkenna applies about four different unknown substances to my face, with swift, expert hands. By the time she's done, I'm sure I must look ridiculous. Then she fusses with my hair for a bit, tucking it this way and that until it's arranged to her satisfaction.

She steps back, observing her work. A large grin fills her face. "I'm good, I'm really good," she says, gesturing for Thayer to look.

My face warms all over again, but this time because I'm *sure* I look utterly absurd.

Thayer smiles. "You look...different."

"Bad different or good different?" I ask, alarmed.

"*Good* different," he says, his cheeks pinker than moments before.

Wolkenna finishes applying makeup to her own face. I'm not sure how she does it so well, what with no reflection to see herself. She places the tubes and palettes back in her bag and turns to face us. "Now, who's ready for a party?" she asks, swinging her black hair behind her shoulders.

I snort—*party*. Right. Is that what we're calling this mission now?

Still, there's no time to waste. I hurry over to Cashel and Darwith. "Take care of them," I say to Cloveman, who is standing close by.

"Don't worry, I've got this," he says with a reassuring smile, patting Cashel's neck.

"Thank you," I say. But I still don't want to leave them.

Xander pulls the large barn door open, and Gattacan and Thayer make their way out first. Wolkenna steps into the light beside me, and Cloveman's jaw drops to the barn floor.

"I—uh—you look *stunning*," he says to Wolkenna.

A smile spreads across her perfectly made-up face, and I swear she blushes. "If we don't return, fly back to Nammden with the steeds and warn the others," she tells him.

Cloveman shakes his head rapidly. "You're coming back, Princess. I'm not leaving without you."

Wolkenna smirks. "Thanks for staying here to protect the steeds," she says to him, leaning closer to his face. "What you're doing is just as important and brave." She kisses his cheek and steps away.

Cloveman's face lights up the darkness like a candle.

"Thanks again, Cloveman," I say, grinning, before scurrying after Wolkenna and out the door.

The dress isn't as heavy as I expected, but I can imagine it would be difficult to ride a steed in. I hike it up to my knees, with my shoes still in hand, and we trudge ahead through the high grass toward the Tarmen Canal. The wall surrounding the city looms in the distance to our right.

Soon I'll be on the other side of that wall. And one step closer to finding my father.

THIRTY-SEVEN

We stop behind a line of tall shrubs by the canal. A well-lit rock pathway leads from a land karrier parking area to a loading dock, where an impressive water karrier is waiting in the canal with its ramp set out, ready to be boarded. It's much like the water karrier I saw on the day of the Autumn Tournament: rectangular, nearly the size of our barn at home, with black sun panels lining the top. Men and women mosey along the path to the dock, arm in arm, the men in suits, the women in gowns.

"That is our way in," Xander whispers, nodding at the water karrier.

Wolkenna looks at my bare feet and raises an eyebrow. "*Now* would be a good time to put your shoes on."

She's right, but I've been dreading this moment. I slide into the narrow contraptions, the bottoms of my feet arching as if I were standing on my toes—highly impractical.

"From this moment on, you are all Uladmondians, visiting from the countryside, or Sceilaran, for the king's festivities," Xander says. "We should pair up now—everyone but me."

"Aluma, you're with Gattacan," Wolkenna says. "And I'm with Thayer—like we planned."

I nod, but my back stiffens as Wolkenna interlocks her arm with Thayer's. It's the first time I've seen him arm and arm with anyone else, let alone a princess. Gattacan lifts his hand to me, and I take it, realizing how much of a hypocrite I am when I welcome the prince's strong but gentle grip.

The shoes are more walkable than they looked, but still not fool-proof. Gattacan helps me stay on my feet as we walk through the grass. We all make our way along the line of hedges until we reach the karrier lot. Rows upon rows of land karriers fill the space. I've never seen so many all in one place at the same time; I didn't know so many remained after the wars.

A Uladmondian couple chats by one of the land karriers. We slip into our roles before they lay eyes on us. Xander breaks away, leading the pack. He looks confident in his white suit, like a nobleman. He's sure to turn heads.

Gattacan and I follow next, his arm supporting me across my lower back as I glide along with as much grace as I can. Yet part of me knows it wouldn't be the worst thing if I stumbled and Gattacan had to catch me.

I glance over my shoulder. Thayer and Wolkenna stroll behind us, neither of them noticing me. Thayer's shoulders are pulled back, and his head is held high. He smiles at Wolkenna, and I think I see his cheeks flush.

My lips press into a hard line as I remember how Thayer seemed awestruck when he first met Wolkenna. The memory leaves a bitter taste in my mouth, and I can't get it out. Thayer is either the best actor ever, or he's really enjoying this stroll, arm in arm with a beautiful princess.

I inhale sharply and turn my head so I'm looking forward again. It's better not to look behind me.

Just stay focused.

King's Watchers stand frozen on the sides of the rock pathway, all wearing identical dark uniforms. My muscles tense as we walk past the first Watcher, a sword at his hip and a bow on his back. Gattacan pulls me closer to his side, putting pressure on my outer hip. He smirks at me, no fear in his eyes, his cheekbones like smooth ridges over sand. And right then, I forget about the Watchers standing guard. I forget about the bitterness in my mouth—about Thayer walking arm in arm with a princess.

As we near the water karrier, a Uladmondian couple walks up the ramp. Ahead, the canal cuts through the large wall off in the distance. I'd heard there were very few entrances into the capital, and so far, that seems to be true—this is the only one I've seen. Tarmensil must be completely surrounded by that wall—that could be why all the land karriers are parked on the outskirts of the city.

My throat goes dry. We don't have our steeds, we don't have a water karrier, and we don't have an escape—unless we come out the same way we go in.

When we ascend the ramp to the water karrier, the Uladmondian couple in front of Xander stops. Both of them take a turn placing one hand onto a metal plate. A King's Watcher stands behind the apparatus. After a moment, he gives them each a nod, and they board the karrier.

Xander steps over to the Watcher next, and we edge closer. From here I can see the metal plate is sticking out from the side of the entrance of the water karrier. Xander places his pointer finger over it, and there's a faint clicking noise.

The blood pockets.

Xander pauses as the Watcher looks at a screen beside the hand plate. A few seconds pass, and a green light flashes. The Watcher nods and Xander boards.

My pulse quickens. Gattacan and I are next.

Gattacan goes in front of me, placing his finger over the plate first. The green light flashes for him, but he doesn't board yet, instead he steps back by my side.

I'm grateful for it.

Calm, calm, calm. I reach out and place my pointer finger on the plate, hoping the Watcher doesn't see my hand shaking. In a quick moment, there's a small pressure on my fingertip, and my eyes lock on the plate, waiting, waiting, waiting…

Please, let this work.

I hold my breath. The light flashes green—thank the stars.

The Watcher nods, and I smile with as much nonchalance as I can muster. Gattacan interlocks his arm with mine, and we step into the karrier.

Inside, there are seats lining the walls beneath the windows, facing the water. Uladmondian couples are sitting, talking amongst themselves, drinks in hand. One couple eyes us, and right then I'm sure we're only a glance away from being found out. The woman scrutinizes my dress and raises her chin with a smirk—or a smile, I can't tell. I shift my attention to a suited man standing in the middle of the karrier, surrounded by a high counter; bottles, drinks, and fancy glasses line the top.

Xander sits by a window, peering out at the water, feigning disinterest.

I glance up at Gattacan. He nods at me as we make our way toward the suited man waiting behind the countertop.

"My lady," the suited man says as we approach.

My eyes dart side to side. *Me?*

"A drink, perhaps?" the man asks.

"We'll both have a Tarmen Tonic," Gattacan says, filling the silence with his low voice. I admire his unshakable confidence—I'm everything but unshakable right now.

"Yes, sir, coming right up," The suited man says, grabbing two glasses.

A small smile creeps across Gattacan's lips. At least *he's* amused by my ignorance.

Out of the corner of my eye, I watch as Thayer and Wolkenna enter, their arms still interlocked. The bitterness in my mouth returns, and I'm ready for something to wash it down with.

The suited man hands us our drinks. The liquid is a reddish hue, garnished with a black olive. *Fitting*—Tarmensilian colors.

Gattacan escorts me to an area of empty seats along the front of the karrier. He holds my drink as I take a seat, attempting not to rip the golden dress. He sits next to me, handing me my glass.

I take a small, experimental sniff of the blood-colored liquid and try not to grimace at the burning sensation filling my nostrils. Whatever it is, it's too strong for me; I need to keep my head as clear as possible.

Gattacan leans closer, brushing my hair out of my face, his soft fingers tracing over my skin. "You don't have to drink it," he breathes into my ear. "Just pretend." Another curious smile crosses his lips as he relaxes into his chair.

I return the smile, thankful that I can just pretend to drink. Just in case it's as potent as it smells.

I glance over to catch Thayer staring straight at us from the drink counter, his jaw clenched. I imagine he has a similar bitterness in his mouth right about now. Wolkenna notices Thayer's expression and lays a flirtatious hand on his arm, drawing his attention back to her. It's a smart move; everyone here is supposed to think they're a couple, after all.

I remind myself again that it's fake—just for show. Still, I turn away and stare out the window, attempting to push aside these unwanted feelings of jealousy.

"I know you two have a history," Gattacan says quietly.

I keep my gaze fixed ahead. He must have noticed me watching his sister and Thayer, and I'm not sure I'm ready to hear what he's about to say. But I *am* ready to crawl into a hole now.

"Still, sometimes it's a good idea to just pay attention to what's right in front of you."

Before I can react, a sudden jerk of the water karrier and a loud clicking noise startles me, as the vessel juts forward beneath us. The water breaks past the sides of the window, splashing out into waves. I hold my drink steady as the karrier speeds ahead toward the massive wall looming in the distance. I turn to Gattacan, my lips pressed together, like I'm hiding them from the memory of his lips against mine. The drum that was my heart.

I'm paying attention to you, Gattacan Gray. Trust me.

As we near the giant wall, the opening comes into view—it's a tunnel. Far above, Watchers line the top, scanning the area like hawks perched in a tree, searching for prey.

The front of the karrier enters the darkness. I feel Gattacan's hand land on my knee, and for a moment, I feel calm—as if I'm in the eye of a storm.

Whatever lies ahead, I won't have to face it alone.

⁓

Light flickers from the outside of the tunnel as we near the other side, a sharp contrast to the surrounding darkness. The water karrier exits, and Tarmensil, in all its splendor, spirals up before us.

Colorful city lights play off the water of the canal, creating elaborate designs, like moving paintings. Narrow cobblestone streets, not large enough for land karriers, curve up the sides of the rock hills. Stone houses and shops fill each level, surrounded by fruit trees and vibrant flowers. Fancily clad Uladmondians stroll along the sides of the canal, some lounging around street tables.

I catch my breath and try to keep my jaw from dropping at the grandeur of it all.

The canal winds through the city, allowing me a first-class view of the beautiful sights. Peak after peak of manicured everything, nothing out of place. As the canal curves again, one rock face rises higher than the rest.

The palace.

The grandest structure in the city by far. Sparkling lights illuminate the stone walls, set high above the rest of the buildings. Red and black tapestries blow in the breeze.

The water karrier stops at a landing dock at the base of a steep hill, the palace walls rising in the distance. Gattacan clears his throat as the karrier door opens. Across the way, Xander straightens his jacket before exiting. Thayer and Wolkenna leave after Xander. Gattacan stands next to me, offering his hand. I set my untouched drink on the table as we wait a moment to follow.

As we step out of the karrier and onto the ramp, I hear music playing off in the distance. More Uladmondians than I've ever seen all in one place roam the streets, making their way to the palace. Their clothing is more lavish than anything I could ever imagine. As glamorous as the golden dress I'm wearing now.

We make our way onto the street. It's so clean it glimmers, even at night. Xander leads the way, the rest of us following as couples. Gattacan interlocks his arm with mine again, and in this enchanting place, I feel like *I'm* a princess, too. This *must* be what it would feel like.

I catch my reflection for the first time as we pass by the glass front of a shop. The silky dress hugs my body, draping down to the floor as if it were a golden flower petal. It shimmers in the city lights, like stars in the sky. My gaze raises to my face, and my eyes go wide. I've never seen myself look like this. The dark makeup Wolkenna applied makes the blue-green colors of my eyes pop brighter than ever. I smirk at the pale pink gloss covering my lips. I look different, like an adult. Like someone who belongs here.

Gattacan's arm squeezes around mine. "You really are beautiful," he whispers.

I purse my lips into a smile, realizing I'm now staring at him, thinking the same thing. He looks like a dream tonight—all the time, actually.

Up ahead, Xander turns off to the right, behind a building. Wolkenna and Thayer follow after him a few moments later. Gattacan and I walk faster to catch up, but when we take the corner, there's no one else in sight. Gattacan peers over at me, looking as confused as I feel. Did we lose them?

"This way," Xander whispers, stepping out of the darkness, startling us.

Thayer and Wolkenna stand behind him in a narrow walkway wedged between the stone buildings. Thayer's gaze lands on my arm, still linked with Gattacan's, and I realize Thayer has already disconnected his arm from Wolkenna's. The charade has paused, for now.

I gently unhook my arm from Gattacan's, feeling Thayer's eyes still lingering on us.

We follow Xander one by one along the walkway and into an empty square. A large building stands front and center, looming over the surrounding structures. Bars line the small windows at the top, but they're much too high for any of us to peer into.

"The prison," Xander says in a hushed voice.

Wolkenna nods. "That's where Rinehart will be—if he's still here."

"We should split up." Xander looks at me. "Gattacan and Aluma—the clinic is in there." He points in the direction of the palace. "You will have to go in the front, like everyone else. Play along for a while and find the clinic from there."

Gattacan snorts. "Very helpful."

"That is all I know," Xander says.

Wolkenna elbows her brother, shooting him a glare.

Thayer moves closer to me, his face blanched. He reaches out and touches my hand, and a warmth extends, like the sun giving the last of its light for the day.

"Please be careful," Thayer says to me, his voice gentle.

"You too," I whisper.

"We meet back at the barn tonight," Wolkenna says. "If anyone isn't there a few hours before sunrise, assume the worst, and get out while you still can."

Assume the worst. Get out while you still can. I take a deep breath, steeling myself for what's ahead.

"I'll wait for you," Thayer tells me.

"No need to wait for anyone," Gattacan says, eyeing him. "I'll get her back safely."

An uncomfortable silence envelops us, Thayer and Gattacan's hostilities echoing back and forth around me. Gattacan's eyes narrow. Thayer's jaw clenches. I clear my throat.

"Good, thank you," Thayer says with a curt nod to Gattacan.

"Are you all ready, or what?" Wolkenna asks, stepping closer between them.

"Ready," I tell her, my hands tensing, moisture building on my palms.

As ready as I can be.

THIRTY-EIGHT

G attacan and I hurry back the same way we came. My nerves are on high alert, but I don't say a word. My mind races to Thayer and Wolkenna. They have to find a way into that prison to free Rinehart, which seems like an impossible task. I hope they can manage it safely.

I try to direct my thoughts back to my task—*my father*.

When we reach the main street leading to the palace, Gattacan rests his hand across my lower back again. The pressure of his fingers, moving me forward, ever so slightly, helps my nerves calm enough so that I'm not visibly trembling. At least I hope I'm not. The street is even more crowded than before; hordes of high-class citizens parade toward the grand structure. We slip into the crowd, positioning ourselves between a few Uladmondian couples.

"It's all so silly," says a slender woman walking nearby. "He shouldn't *wait* to attack." She shakes her head, and her stark white hair bobs from side to side like a big ball of snow-capped hay.

"Indeed," her companion—a man in a powder blue suit—says in a snobbish voice. "You know if it were up to the prince, we would already be in control of those Scaler rebels."

Gattacan's hand tenses against my back.

"How long is it going to take the prince to get his brother to act like the king?" The woman's tone is bitter, like unripe fruit.

"*Shh*—I know, my dear," the man says in a whisper.

Gattacan's eyes are still fixed on the palace, but frustration is washing over them like dark clouds.

Have these people ever met a Laithlanner? Or are they just like I was—full of force-fed lies?

All lies.

The street curves around to the large arch of the palace gates. The King's Watchers stand guard on either side of the street and atop the walls of the structure. I consider ducking down, afraid someone might spot me, but when I glance over at Gattacan, I'm again reminded: we are Uladmondians tonight. We're supposed to be here, and no one knows who we really are.

A chorus of strings echoes out from inside the gates as we make our way under the arch. A grand courtyard opens to the palace doors in the distance. A spectacular fountain dominates the middle of the space. Soft lights shine out from behind the flowing water, casting shadows across everyone walking past. The walkway splits to the right and to the left on either side of the fountain like a snake's tongue. Green vines with red flowers crawl along the outer walls and over elaborately trimmed shrubs.

We follow part of the crowd to the left. I spot the musicians I heard from outside the gates playing their stringed instruments in the corner of the courtyard; four suited men creating a breathtaking, wordless melody.

The song reminds me of something I once heard as a child, lending a surreal quality to the air. I keep walking, but everything seems so soft around the edges, like a dream—one I want to move through slowly and quickly at the same time.

When I was younger, Farann told me that whenever she visited Tarmensil, they'd have elegant parties like this *every week*. With this kind of needless extravagance, it's no wonder the kingdom of Ivernister is starving. Our kingdom is a prisoner to the Uladmondian's opulence.

The open palace doors come into view once again as the left and right walkways merge on the other side of the fountain. We're nearly to the entrance now. My hands are clammy, and I thank the stars that Gattacan hasn't tried to hold one. If it weren't for his hand on my back, edging me forward, I'd probably need to sit for a moment and collect myself.

There's different music playing inside—a waltz. It's more intense, but still smooth, a medley of strings, brass, and drums. An extravagant ballroom sprawls out in front of us, full of men and women swaying to the steady music, striding side to side across the pristine floor, like birds floating in the breeze. Other Uladmondians select colorful drinks from suited men near the sides of the room. A grand staircase curves up on the right side, to an open crossway above, spanning across the rear of the dance floor, with a wider balcony in the middle.

"There," Gattacan whispers, nodding his head to the far-left side of the room. There's a hallway behind a drink station and a couple of Watchers standing nearby.

"How do you know?" I ask quietly.

"I've been here before—when I was younger." He eyes the hallway from where we stand. "The palace clinic is that way. If your father is here, then he'll be down there."

My father...

All at once I feel compelled to race to the hallway. I restrain myself, taking just a single step forward, resisting the emotions rising in my chest. "Let's go," I tell him.

The music softens as we make our way through the crowd, then cuts off entirely. Everyone slows to a halt, their chins lifting as they gaze up at the balcony. We stop in our tracks and turn. Perched in the center, in an all-white ensemble with a bright purple bow tie—Sceilaran colors—is Egan Frye. His hair has an unnaturally white sheen with a purple pattern on the sides. He's as fancy as I remember.

"Good evening, good evening!" Egan Frye's shrill voice rings out from the speakers and the balcony above us. "Thank you for joining us on this beautiful Tarmensilian night to celebrate the many accomplishments we've had over this last year."

I keep my head tucked behind a woman's elaborate hairdo, hoping

Egan doesn't spot me in the crowd. Not that I'm sure he'd remember my face.

"King Breasal has led us through yet another year, free of Laithlanner attacks," Egan says, and the crowd claps in unison, like big showy birds clacking away.

No attacks? No mention of the Galghesworp fight or the battle on the Knarrno River? Or the lives that were lost?

Not on *their* soil—not their problem, I gather.

I glance at Gattacan—he's glaring up at Egan. My hand finds his arm and I hold it gently, attempting to offer him support, the same way he's supported me. But when his dark eyes meet mine, they're full of anger, full of resentment. And I can't blame him.

Egan continues, "Tonight our king wishes to honor his younger brother, Sutagus—your prince—for his continued support, and his brave conquests to extinguish the Laithlanner forces once and for all!"

The crowd cheers, even more enthusiastically than they did for the bit about the king.

Gattacan pulls away from my grasp. "Come on," he mutters. "We're not waiting around for what comes next."

I nod—I don't want to wait, either.

We move toward the drink station, trying not to draw any attention to ourselves. A few Uladmondians glance at me with strange looks as we walk through the otherwise motionless crowd. I try to come up with some excuses I can use if anyone questions me—*I need to use the ladies' room. I need to take a seat. I'm tired of listening to this rubbish.*

All right, scratch that last one.

"Ladies and gentlemen," Egan announces as we continue to the hallway. *"Your king."*

The crowd erupts as Gattacan and I walk past the two Watchers near the drink station, both of them staring up at the balcony. I twist around to see the king enter, his arms spread out in welcome as he smiles at the crowd. He looks the same way he did the last time I saw him—the day my father fell from the sky.

I turn back to face the hallway, swallowing down the urge to yell—to *scream* at him. At the prince, too, if he were up there.

A few Uladmondian couples gossip amongst themselves on either side of the corridor. Gattacan and I coast past them, avoiding eye contact. We turn right, down another hallway. The walls are bright white, much like the medical wing at Galghesworp. I quicken my pace, keeping my eyes trained on the door at the end.

My father is behind that door. I can almost sense it—like an oncoming storm.

Another door swings open on the left side of the hallway and a man steps through, locking it behind him.

My stomach drops. And drops again.

Prince Sutagus.

I turn on the balls of my feet, twisting away from Sutagus. I can't let him see my face. He'll surely recognize me.

Gattacan's eyes widen when he spots the Uladmondian prince. Panic fills me as I hear Sutagus's footsteps approaching, his heels clacking against the floor.

We're going to get caught.

Gattacan stares me straight in the eyes, cupping my face in his hands. He leans in and presses his lips firmly against mine while he swivels me in a half circle, keeping my back to Sutagus. I'm frozen in his embrace, the cool rush of his mouth on mine awakening all of my senses, like I'm jumping into icy water.

Sutagus clears his throat as he passes. His footsteps grow fainter and fainter, until I hear nothing but Gattacan's breath and my own. After a few moments, Gattacan releases me.

I inhale sharply. Gattacan's face is still close enough that I can feel his breath on my skin, cool and invigorating. I peer over his shoulder. Sutagus is gone.

I exhale with relief. Gattacan scratches his neck and smirks. "Well, he didn't see you."

My lips press together, part exhilarated and part mortified. I'm *sure* Sutagus didn't see me after that. How could he? The desire for more of Gattacan's closeness swirls around with the fear of being caught—and the realization that I'm possibly just steps away from my father.

I hurry onward to the door at the end of the hallway. When I reach it, I twist the knob, hoping it's not locked. It opens easily in my hand. I step inside, into a small room with a couple of chairs against either wall and a desk in the middle. I would have expected someone to be standing guard, but there's no one around. Gattacan slides in behind me, letting the door click closed. There's another door on the left side of the room, and a faint beeping noise coming from the other side.

Father.

Gattacan reaches for my arm. "Let me go in first," he whispers.

I shake my head. "No, I've got this. You can wait here."

He looks at me as if he wants to protest, but eventually nods and steps aside.

The beeping intensifies as I enter the room. It's dark—the beeping machine with its glowing red numbers and lines illuminates the bed enough to see a figure. The vial of light warms against my leg as I move closer.

It *is* my father. Just as I sensed. He's lying motionless, wires extending from the machine attached to his body.

My eyes fill with moisture. I reach out and clutch his hand, pulling it to my face as the tears drop. "I'm here, Father...*I'm here.*" My voice barely escapes me, but I hope he can somehow feel my presence.

The vial pulses with energy, warmer and warmer against my leg. I lay my father's hand back on the bed. He doesn't move—not even a flinch. I lift the bottom of my dress to my knees. The vial of light glows between my knife and holster as I reach for it.

A door clicks open.

My body tenses as I drop my dress to fall back over my legs, hiding the knife and vial.

I glance at the open door, realizing it's another one I hadn't noticed in the darkness on the opposite side of the room. A figure stands on the threshold, not making a sound.

"Gattacan?" I whisper hesitantly.

A light switches on, revealing my brother, his eyes wide.

"Kase?" I say, my voice cracking in disbelief.

Gattacan rushes into the room from the door I came in through. He eyes Kase, sizing him up, before turning to me.

My brother continues to stare at me blankly. He's dressed like a Uladmondian. He *looks* like a Uladmondian. Despite that, I rush over and wrap my arms around him. I'm relieved to see him safe and seemingly well cared for. He's still my little brother, after all.

"They said you were dead," Kase says, pulling me to arm's length, his eyes searching mine.

"I'm okay," I tell him, offering up a reassuring smile. "Are you?"

"Of course," he says, still looking stunned. "But what are you doing here? How—"

"There's no time," I say, cutting him off. "I came to get you and Father out of here."

The vial continues to warm in the holster against my skin. It's almost hot now.

Kase's eyes narrow. "Why?"

"Why?" I echo. "Because you're not safe here, and neither is he." I turn to my father and move back to the bed. I lift the hem of my dress and reach for the vial again.

"What are you doing?" Kase moves to the other side of our father.

I hold the warm vial in my hand. "I can help him."

Kase looks closer. "What is that?"

"It's light. Now, shut your eyes," I instruct Kase, and then glance at Gattacan to do the same.

They do.

I open the top of the vial and a bright light streams toward my father's face. The radiant wave of white spills over his head and travels along his body, covering him in a soft glow.

The light stops flowing as quickly as it started—the vial is empty.

"You can open your eyes," I tell my brother and Gattacan.

The machine begins to beep rapidly, louder and louder. My father twitches.

I place my hand on his, leaning closer as he moves. "Father?"

The beeping increases. Kase's face contorts as he watches the machine, its red lights flashing in unison with the sound.

"Aluma…" my father says, his voice faint.

My heart jumps as he opens his crystal-blue eyes.

"Father!" I hug him as gently as I can.

"It *is* you," he whispers. "Where are we?"

I release him from my embrace, leaving one hand on his arm.

My father turns to Kase, reaching out for his hand. For a moment, my brother doesn't move. I narrow my eyes in his direction, and Kase takes our father's hand in his.

"We're in Tarmensil. In the *palace*," I tell him.

My father's brow furrows.

"Aluma, you need to leave—now," Kase says, peering back at the door.

"I'm not leaving without him," I say, sending Kase a stern look before returning my attention to our father. "Can you sit up?" I try to help him, but he doesn't move. "Gattacan, would you—"

Gattacan rushes over and helps me pull my father into a seated position. My father's gaze lands on the empty vial lying on the bed next to him. His eyes search mine.

"You know…you know about the last relic of light?" he asks, a hopeful smile crossing his lips. He glances over at Gattacan and back at me.

"Yes," I say.

"The *what*?" Kase asks, running a hand through his blond hair.

"I'll explain later," I tell him as Gattacan and I both attempt to lift my father off the bed. We try to help him get his feet on the ground, but his body is too weak. Why didn't the light work?

"I'm sorry," my father says. "It's no use. They must have injected me with darkness."

I glance back at the vial, as if it might somehow refill itself. But it's still empty. It wasn't enough.

I need more light.

"Whatever this is, you don't have time for it—" Kase calls over his shoulder as he runs back out the door he came in through.

"You can't carry me out of here. They'll see us." My father struggles weakly against us, collapsing back on the bed. "You can't get caught. Go, *now*. And take Kase with you."

I shake my head, in denial of his order. "Do you know where they keep the relics?" I ask, my mind spinning. "If I can find another relic of light, I can get you out of here."

"There's a place, hidden somewhere in the tack room in the palace stable," he says. "But you'll never get there in time. You need to get out of Tarmensil while you still can."

"But if I can get to it, I can save you—"

"Aluma, you have to go. You have to leave me behind."

A new, piercing alarm rips through the air, much louder than the beeping machine hooked up to my father. My eyes dart between the two doors as Kase comes barreling back into the room.

"They'll be here any moment!" Kase yells, rushing toward us.

"Go!" My father tries to push himself up, but falls back onto the bed once more.

"I'm not leaving without you!" I tell him. "We came all this way— for *you*." I squeeze his hand, not wanting to let go.

"You woke me. That's enough." He smiles as much as he can muster. "We'll meet again soon, sweet Lumi."

"Father—"

"Now go." His voice is stern this time as he gestures at the door. My heart clenches like an invisible force is squeezing it. Everything inside of me is screaming: *Don't be stubborn, Aluma—listen to him!*

Because as much as I don't want it to be true, he's right. I can't save him. Not if I want to save myself, too.

Gattacan touches my arm. "Come on, this won't work. We have to go."

"I'll always be with you...*always*," my father says, holding the empty vial out to me.

I nod, unable to process everything. I take the vial from his hand and lift my dress knee-high, sliding the tube back between my knife and holster.

Gattacan tugs me toward the door we came in through.

"I'll come back for you!" I yell over my shoulder, my voice breaking over the incessant beeping and the blaring alarm. Then Gattacan pulls me from the room, hauling me away from the one person I want to save more than anyone.

THIRTY—NINE

I have tunnel vision. Everything blurs past me at superspeed: flashing red lights, the sounds of the blaring alarm, Kase rushing ahead…and Gattacan's arm around me, guiding me back out into the main hallway.

I attempt to twist around and out of his grip. "No—my father's here. He's awake! We can't leave him!"

Gattacan holds me tighter, shaking his head. "Stop—we have to get out of here."

My nostrils flare. I want to break free from his grasp and rush back to be with my father, even if that means I'll get caught. But I know he's right, just like my father is right—there's nothing I can do. Not until I have more light.

The alarm stops.

Thank the stars.

We hurry after Kase. Gattacan interlocks arms with me, attempting nonchalance.

Two Uladmondian medics step into the hallway after my brother rounds the corner in front of us. Gattacan and I slow our pace as the medical team rushes past us toward the room where we left my father.

I feel another sudden urge to run back to my father, fearing what they might do to him when they discover he's awake. I glance over my shoulder once as the medics reach the door at the end of the hallway, and then we turn the corner, moving safely out of sight.

Uladmondians litter the wide hallway back to the ballroom in groups, glancing around and trying to figure out the cause of the alarm. My eyes dart from person to person, desperately searching for my brother in a sea of strangers.

Kase. I've lost him.

Then I hear a familiar voice. "I'm here," my brother says, stepping out from behind a group of gossiping Uladmondians and waving us toward him.

We follow Kase through another door, and he closes it behind us. We're in a large closet: mops, brooms, and cleaning supplies hang from the walls.

"What's your plan?" Kase asks evenly, but I detect frustration in his tone.

"The palace stable. Can you take us there?" I ask.

Gattacan shoots me a disapproving look. "We need to get back to the barn and warn the others," he interjects. "Now that the palace alarms have sounded, none of us are safe. Someone must have triggered them."

"The barn?" Kase asks, glancing at Gattacan and then back at me, ignoring my first question.

"It's outside the walls—near the canal," I tell him, motioning with my hand to get back to the other more pressing question: can he lead us to the relic room?

"There's only one way in and out of the city," Kase says, confirming my previous fears, but still not answering me about the stable.

I raise my eyebrows at my brother. "Can you take us to the palace stable or not?"

Kase closes his mouth, his jaw flexing.

I narrow my eyes at him, the way I used to look at him when he'd lie about taking a book from my room without asking. "*Kase.*"

"Fine—I'll show you," he says, opening the door. He peeks out before glancing back at us. "This way."

An upbeat song is playing in the ballroom, as if the alarms never sounded at all. We follow Kase across the dance floor, dodging couple after dancing couple. I try to keep my focus on the task at hand, but the room is spinning. Grinning Uladmondians with bright clothing and sharp laughter twirl around us, like some kind of lucid nightmare.

The music stops.

Uladmondians split apart on the dance floor, as if making room for someone. Kase turns back to me, his face drained of blood.

"Hurry—" Kase whisper shouts at us, then darts into another hallway nearby. Gattacan and I trail my brother, like we're tied to him, following his every step.

"Make way!" someone orders.

I glance over my shoulder and freeze. Prince Sutagus and a handful of guards barrel down the makeshift aisle through the parted crowd, toward the medical wing we just left.

Toward my father.

My mind races. Now that he's awake, will they interrogate him? Or, worse—*torture* him?

Kase grabs me by the arm. "It's too late." His voice is harsh. "You need to get out of the city."

I shake my head. "No—take us to the stable."

My brother just stares at me, his mind clearly somewhere else.

"Come on," Gattacan says. "We'll find it ourselves." He glares at Kase, and for a moment, I think he's going to punch him.

Kase juts his lips out, two thin lines. "I'll point you in the right direction, but don't blame me if you get caught." And then he's off, leading us down the corridor. Gattacan and I share a look of uncertainty before we follow behind him.

Halfway down the hallway, Kase stops in front of a door. He peers left, then right, but no one is around.

"Go through here," Kase says in a hushed voice, opening the door. "It will bring you back to the main courtyard. On the opposite side, there's another door into the palace. Take it. There's a hallway, just like this one. Follow it to your right until you hit the end. Take the door there. There's a smaller courtyard that leads to a gate. After the gate is the outdoor arena. The stable is on the other side."

I nod, attempting to memorize the steps. "Come with us," I urge him.

Kase exhales. "I can't, they'll be looking for me."

"But Father told me to take you. You have to come with us."

"I'm better off here. I can watch over him." His icy blue eyes dart back to the ballroom. *"Go—"*

Gattacan studies Kase's face for a moment before giving him a cursory nod. Then I pull my brother into a hug. He embraces me in return, but when he steps away, his eyes avoid mine.

Gattacan and I pass through the open door, leaving Kase to close it from the other side.

My shoulders tense as we make our way to the only other exit across the room. This doesn't feel right. Kase should be coming with us. We should be getting Father out of here *together*.

None of this is right. None of it.

Gattacan opens the door on the other side of the room, and the lights from the courtyard shine in. He hurries back over to me and wraps his arm around my waist.

"Come on," he says, nudging me. "We don't have much time—"

"We can't…" I whisper, feeling the frustration build inside me like a fast-growing weed.

"He made his choice." Gattacan's voice is low and cool, an echo in a cave.

He made his choice. But it's not the right one.

〜

The courtyard is nearly empty. Everyone is inside, except the Watchers up on the perimeters, whom I didn't notice on the way in. It's quiet—no more rhythmic music to distract me. But if it weren't for the sounds of the nearby fountain, my heartbeat would surely give me away.

I keep my face turned toward Gattacan. I smile at him, pretending everything is all right. We stay close to the front of the palace doors, crossing to the opposite side of the courtyard. The entrance Kase mentioned comes into view, partially hidden behind a row of shrubs. A maintenance door, perhaps? One that isn't meant to be visible to the masses. There's nothing grand about it.

We glance up, waiting for the Watchers to turn before entering. The hallway beyond is empty in both directions, thanks to the festivities and excitement resuming in the ballroom.

We hurry down the hall; it could be the same one we were in before, if I didn't know any better. It looks identical, but flipped. When we get to the end, Gattacan opens the door and peeks out first, then waves me through.

There's another courtyard, a smaller one, just like Kase promised. No grand fountain, no music, just a few rows of trees with tea lights dangling from their branches. It reminds me of the courtyard back at the base. And for a split second, I wish I was still there, still protected by my innocence—before I knew the truth about everything that matters.

Gattacan reaches the gate at the end before me. He pulls it open, the metal squeaking on its hinges, like a bat screeching in the night. I rush through, waiting on the other side, staying close to the wall, and Gattacan follows.

An outdoor arena of sorts, one without a fence but bordered by the surrounding stone buildings, separates the space between us and—*the stable.*

I glance at Gattacan. His jaw is set, his brow furrowed. "Let me go first—I'll check to make sure no one's inside," he says in a whisper.

My eyes go wide. "Excuse me? I'm going, too. With or without you."

Gattacan sighs. "You're too stubborn. Anyone ever told you that?"

"You're too bossy—anyone ever told *you* that?"

His dark eyes narrow as if he's trying to read me like a book, one he can't quite decipher. Then one side of his lips curls up, and he's smirking at me.

"Fine," he says. "Let's go."

"I was going to go anyway," I remind him.

"Oh, trust me, I know you were."

We wait for a moment in silence, listening for any movement, any signs of Watchers. But there's nothing.

I lead the way, staying close to the perimeters, rather than darting across the narrow end of the dirt expanse between us and the stable. I'm keenly aware that if anyone *is* around, they'll spot me—sparkling golden, moving like a lizard, with the backs of my arms attached to the walls. Not suspicious, by any means.

When we arrive at the entrance to the stable, Gattacan peers in first.

"It looks clear," he says quietly.

The lights are off, but there's enough illumination from the surrounding buildings that I can see what's in front of us: one wide aisle down the center of two rows of stalls facing each other, and the tack room at the end on the left. It's nearly identical to the main barn at the Empyrean stables in Cintrenia. I feel like I'm at home for a fleeting moment before I glance at the golden fabric hanging from my body like a tight curtain.

I'm far, *far* from home.

I pick up the pace, keeping to the left side, passing three stalls before I hear a whicker. And then another. The horses and steeds are waking up.

When I reach the end of the aisle, I stop outside the tack room door. A sickness bubbles up from my gut. The last time I went into a tack room, Lermyn died in front of me.

"Are you okay?" Gattacan's hand finds the back of my arm, making me flinch.

I nod quickly. Inhale. Exhale.

I enter first. It's much darker than the aisle of stalls, with only a sliver of light making its way in from where I opened the door. My hands search the edges of the room until my fingers find a switch. And...lights on.

Saddles, bridles, and blankets line the walls, just like the tack room in the main Empyrean stable in Cintrenia—only the gear here is far more lavish. Even more so than in Galghesworp, too. The saddles here are rimmed with gold and silver, and everything is polished so well, it shines.

"Seems necessary," Gattacan says, lifting a jeweled bridle with a golden bit from the wall before letting it thump back down again.

"Clearly. Horses love their precious metals."

I catch Gattacan cracking a smile as he runs his hands along the walls, searching for any sign of a hidden door. I do the same, but I feel nothing. No indentations on the walls, no lines on the floor, and no openings above. What are we missing?

My eyes scan my surroundings again: saddles, bridles, saddle blankets…and one large metal chest sitting at the end of the room.

"Gattacan—" I say, rushing over to the chest, which is big enough for me to fit into. Big enough to fit all the relics.

I open it. Brushes, curry combs, and hoof picks are on one side. Leg wraps on the other. I move everything to the edges of the chest, half expecting the relics will be hidden under the pile of bristles and metal nicking at my skin.

But then I've reached the deepest point, as far as my fingers can reach.

Solid metal. There's nothing here.

"Anything?" Gattacan says from behind me.

I shake my head, exhaling. *Useless.* I slap my hands against the inside of the bottom of the chest, frustration pulsing through my veins.

My head tilts to the side. I hit the bottom again.

It sounds…*empty*. Like a hollow tree trunk.

I pull my hands out of the chest, tapping the ground near my knees. It's solid underneath.

My eyes go wide, my hands feeling the back side of the chest next to the wall. I reach down, fingers patting left to right. Then I feel it.

A lever.

 FORTY

I pull the lever and the metal chest moves, sliding slowly into the vacant space to its left. I stand back, Gattacan stepping beside me. He glances over, his eyes flickering with excitement—or fear. I can't tell which, but *I* feel both.

Underneath the chest, an opening—a *passageway*—becomes visible.

At our feet, a staircase leads down into the darkness, like a gaping mouth ready to swallow us whole.

I take the first step. My heeled shoes slowly clack down each stair. My hands reach out to find cool stone walls, helping me keep my balance.

"I'm right behind you," Gattacan says.

The temperature drops as we descend into the darkness. I count seventeen steps until my foot extends down for the next, only to find the floor. I catch myself, my right hand reaching out to nothing, and I move back until my heel hits the edge of the staircase.

A hand touches my shoulder, making me jump.

"It's just me," Gattacan whispers.

I turn to face him, the soft glow of light from the tack room above framing his head like a crown. *Fitting.* I lean closer to him, reaching out, my hand searching the wall.

Another light switch.

I flip it on, still facing Gattacan and the stairs. His dark eyes go wide.

I spin back around to see what he's seeing, my heart thumping in my chest.

Relics.

At the end of the otherwise empty, wide room, there are eight stands, all waist-high, shaped like tall hourglasses: four on the left and four on the right.

Of the four stands on the left, two are empty. The other two each have a small black box on top. My mind flashes back to when I saw Sutagus with one just like them. The same day of my father's fall. *Relics of darkness.* The black relic on the right has a silver sun etched into it: a horizontal straight line with a half circle on top with small lines depicting the rays of the sun emitting from the curved side. This must be from Samduh—the lost kingdom, what with the abundance of sun on the southwest coast of Eirelannia. It must have belonged to them before they lost everything. The other relic has two silver waves etched into its sides—Laithlann's, if I had to guess.

My eyes dart to the right, to the other four stands; they must be for the relics of light. They're identical to those on the left, except they're all empty. There's not a single relic of light—not *one* to save my father with.

"Where are the rest?" My voice comes out in a rasp.

Gattacan moves closer to the small black boxes on the left. "The king of Uladmond—or the prince—they must have the other two relics of darkness and the other three relics of light somewhere else."

"Your father hid the relic of light I retrieved from the Gray Forest, right?" I ask, hoping it's still safe.

"He did," he says. "So once we take these two relics of darkness, we'll have one relic of light in our possession and two relics of darkness." He peers back at me, and his eyebrows raise. "We'll almost be even."

I inhale, feeling the cold air fill my lungs. He's right. We'll be closer to even—which means we'll have a chance of defending ourselves should the Uladmondians attack. We'll have a shot at restoring balance. But we can't do the one thing I want to do most right now: save my father.

"Without the relic of light..." I say, attempting to push away the dark truth that's burrowing its way into my head.

I can't save my father. Not tonight. Perhaps not ever.

Gattacan shakes his head, as if he can read my thoughts. "I'm sorry, Aluma."

"We should hurry," I say, moving over to one of the two relics of darkness, keeping my blurring eyes focused on the little black box.

As the cool air pricks at my skin, I notice one big difference from the last time I was near a relic: the lack of warmth, the lack of a pull. An absence of light. The stands must keep the relics closed and in some kind of unused state—almost as if they're dormant.

"Gattacan, wait," I say, just as he's about to lift the other relic of darkness.

He jerks his hands back.

"Something's wrong," I say, glancing at the empty stands beside it. I look closer. There's a small, raised button, the same color as the stand. A sensor or...an *alarm*. "Don't lift it."

Gattacan leans forward, seeing what I see.

"We need something to put on top of the stand," I say, my mind darting back up to the tack room. "Quick, go get two horse brushes and two leg wraps."

He gives me a confused look.

"Trust me," I tell him, and he races up the stairs.

I peer at the relics of darkness, remembering what Delna said: *Anyone can open a relic of darkness. But only Light Keepers can wield or open a relic of light.* Then I think of how Vikmal had to touch the relic of light with gloves. But Prince Sutagus handled a relic of darkness with none.

Gattacan rushes back down into the room. Like I asked, he's carrying two long brushes and two leg wraps in his arms. He sets everything on the floor next to me.

"I need your help," I say, taking one rolled-up leg wrap and unraveling it. "As I lift the relic, you slide this under, and pull down on both sides." I demonstrate, pulling the wrap taut between my hands. "That should keep enough pressure on the sensor until I move the relic, then replace the weight with a brush."

Gattacan nods quickly, taking the wrap from me.

"Are you ready?" I ask, my fingers dangling just above the relic of darkness.

"Let's do it," he says.

My hands find the edges of the relic. I exhale slowly, and Gattacan slides the taut leg wrap right next to the edge of the underside. As carefully as I can manage, I lift the tiny black box just enough for Gattacan to slide the wrap underneath, until it's directly over the sensor. He pulls down on either side of the wrap, applying steady pressure over the sensor as I exhale again, this time lifting the relic all the way off.

It's cold against my palms, chilling me to the bone—almost as if it's sucking the warmth from my skin. I rush to set it down on the floor before grabbing a horse brush and darting back to the stand where Gattacan is still holding the wrap in place.

I lay the brush over the top of the sensor, bristle side pointing up, and press my lips together as I step back.

"Should I let go?" Gattacan asks.

I nod, and Gattacan slowly lets go of the wrap. We both grimace, half expecting an alarm to sound. But there's nothing.

I tilt my head back, staring at the ceiling, sighing in relief. One down, one more to go.

We move over to the last relic of darkness, repeating the process. Gattacan pulls the wrap taut, holding it steady, and I lift the cold black box from its stand.

A stair creaks. And we turn, just as someone steps down the last stair into the room.

A Watcher.

The tall, uniformed man stands frozen, in front of the last step. For a moment, none of us move. The Watcher eyes the two relics of darkness, one on the floor and the other in my hands.

Then he's lurching at me, his arms out.

An alarm sounds just as I see the blur that is Gattacan darting in front of me to block the Watcher. It takes me a split second to realize that he let go of the leg wrap over the sensor. I trip back, my mind racing. We're caught. The Watcher will kill us, or worse—bring us to Prince Sutagus.

The Watcher and Gattacan are on the floor. Gattacan is on top of the Watcher, his fist finding the man's face in one swift movement. The Watcher punches Gattacan's ribs, and I wince in pain for him. Gattacan holds the man by the throat, pushing him down as if he could force him through the solid floor beneath us. The Watcher reaches for something at his hip—a blade. I lunge forward, kicking my foot out against the man's arm just as he lifts it to stab Gattacan in the side.

The Watcher drops the blade, searching for it with his fingers. I snatch it up, but the man reaches for another weapon at his other hip. He's going to kill Gattacan. I jump, blade-first toward the man's ribcage, thrusting the steel into his side, before he can draw his other weapon. The man bellows in pain, yanking the blade back out, red on silver. Gattacan elbows the Watcher's arm so hard that the man drops his weapon. I hurry around them, kicking the knife away, realizing it doesn't matter either way as the man falls unconscious, Gattacan's hands back on his throat.

Gattacan remains on top of him for a moment before he turns to me, noticing the blade covered with blood next to me. The one I stabbed into the Watcher. Then his eyes fall on the relic of darkness that I'm somehow still holding.

What did I just do to that man? It's as if I just went wild—lost my humanity for a moment. Is *this* what darkness feels like?

"Let's go!" Gattacan yells over the blaring alarm. He grabs the other relic of darkness off the floor, and we race back up the stairs as fast as we can.

My heeled shoes and tight dress only allow me a small amount of freedom. To my surprise, there's no one waiting for us in the tack room, but the alarm is blaring throughout the stable. With all the alarms tonight, I can't imagine anyone has a clue about what's going on in Tarmensil.

The horses are stirring, some kicking their stalls. As we sprint past, one horse is sticking its head out through the top of its stall. One I would recognize anywhere: my mother's horse, Blossom.

I hurry to her stall, her black-and-white face reaching out to greet me.

"What are you doing? Come on!" Gattacan shouts.

"This is my mother's horse—" I say, wishing Blossom had wings. I can't get her out of here without them.

"We don't have time for this!" Gattacan takes the other relic of darkness from me, placing it next to the one between his left arm and abdomen, pulling me along with his right hand.

"I'm sorry!" I call out to Blossom. "You'll be all right here."

I have only a moment to hope that's the truth before we're running out the front of the stable.

The outdoor arena between the stable and the palace is now littered with fancy Uladmondians, some entering the arena through the same gate we came through. They're all glancing around at each other, as if they've just been evacuated.

The alarms—they don't know what triggered them. They don't know that it's *us*.

Gattacan and I slow to a walk, catching our breath, pretending to be part of the masses.

"Here," Gattacan mutters, handing me the two relics of darkness. He quickly takes off his suit jacket, wrapping it around my shoulders, so it's draping over the tops of my arms, concealing the relics.

We walk to the opposite side of the arena, away from the gate we came in through. There's no chance of sneaking back through the palace that way. We need to find another path out of here.

When we reach the opposite side, I notice another open gate, through which several Uladmondians are exiting.

"There," I say, gesturing in their direction with my chin. We follow another couple through as Watchers stand guard on the other side.

I take a moment to get my bearings, then realize we've reached the main road that leads to and from the palace. My head darts to the right, toward the arched entrance of the big palace courtyard. The relics of darkness are cool against my chest, like they're willing me to bring them into the palace and see what kind of damage they could do. Maybe I could cause enough mayhem that Gattacan and I could carry my father out. This is my chance—it may be my *only* chance to save him.

"We can't," Gattacan says, as if detecting my plan. "We won't make it back to him."

"But I—"

"Shh…" His voice is low. "We'll come back. I swear it."

I search Gattacan's eyes as we move forward, past the other couples, until we're walking down the road alone. *Away* from my father.

"Trust me," Gattacan says. "We can't get in and out of there alive. Not again—not tonight."

He's right. I'm of no use to my father if I'm captured, or dead. Plus, I have no clue how to use a relic of darkness, and this is no place for a trial run—and certainly not a time for any more mistakes.

Off in the distance, the same rectangular water karrier we arrived in comes into view. It's floating by the same dock, past the shops where we landed before.

Gattacan's arm wraps around my shoulders and his jacket, hiding the relics beneath. Thank the stars it's a chilly night and I have an excuse to be cold. The alarms grow fainter and fainter as we walk. No one seems to be in a panic outside the palace walls.

We're safe. For now.

Thoughts of Thayer, Wolkenna, and Xander pass through my head. Did they complete their mission? Did they get to Rinehart? Are they all safe?

"We should go to where we all split up," I suggest. "They may still be in the area where we last saw them. By the prison."

"That wasn't the plan. They'll meet us at the barn." Gattacan's hand presses me forward to the loading dock. "We need to get out of here before anyone catches on."

I nod slowly. He's right—again. But that doesn't mean I have to like it.

A Watcher stands guard outside the water karrier as we approach. My heart thumps faster, the image of the other Watcher lying on the relic room floor flashing through my mind. We may have killed that man. I shudder at the thought, the relics of darkness icy reminders against my skin.

The Watcher by the karrier peers over at us as we walk onto the ramp. He's standing beside a small plate, much like the one the other Watcher took our blood from before. I shift the relics hidden under Gattacan's jacket to one arm, attempting to keep my face as neutral as possible.

"Exciting night," Gattacan says to the Watcher as we approach, exhaling like he's ready to hit the hay.

The Watcher gives us a polite nod. He's oblivious.

Gattacan steps forward and places his finger on the plate. There's a quick *click* and a green light. He steps to the side.

I carefully extend my left hand out, cradling the relics with my right arm. I place my finger on the plate.

Click.

A red light reflects off of the Watcher's eyes. He darts a look at the plate. He peers back at me. Then at Gattacan.

I glance down, and it hits me like a kick to the gut. There's a small dot of blood on my left pointer finger.

Wrong finger—wrong hand.

That's *my* blood.

FORTY–ONE

attacan's eyes dart back and forth from my finger to the Watcher. My heart is pounding. The Watcher reaches for his weapon, but I jut my left hand out at the man's throat before he can get to it. The Watcher falls limp into Gattacan's waiting arms.

My eyes scan the area. No one's around, and the Watcher is out cold. Gattacan grabs him underneath the arms and drags him into the karrier.

"Come on!" Gattacan growls.

As soon as I'm on board, Gattacan pulls a lever on the inside wall and the door closes. There's no one else in any of the seats that line the border of the main seating area. It's just me and the unconscious Watcher as Gattacan disappears to the front of the karrier.

"You can't be in here—" a man's voice says from the other room.

There's a scuffling sound and a loud *thud*.

I scurry to the front of the karrier as it jolts forward, finding Gattacan in the captain's seat and another unconscious Watcher on the floor.

"You know how to drive this thing?" I ask, peering out the window at the canal.

Gattacan nods as the karrier picks up speed, the water swiftly breaking past the sides. He must have driven one of these back in Nammden. Their streets *are* water-filled, after all.

"What about everyone else? They won't make it back now. We need to wait—"

"They may be out already, or they'll find another way. But we can't wait for them. Especially not now."

I shake my head, inhaling sharply. This is all my fault. I didn't use the right hand. And now, because of *my* mistake, we very well might be leaving our friends to fend for themselves.

Gattacan steers the karrier toward the tunnel in the distance.

"Take off his jacket," Gattacan says, glancing at the Watcher on the floor.

"What?"

"Give me his jacket!" he snaps.

I set the relics down and pull off the man's uniform jacket. The Watcher can't be much older than us. He might be the same age as Huffman.

Huffman. He was a Watcher, too. And he switched sides. Maybe this unconscious man, or the one lying in the seating area, or the one on the relic room floor—maybe they wouldn't follow the king, either. Not if they knew the truth.

"Here." I toss Gattacan the jacket, and he slips it on.

"Go to the passenger area and sit—they'll be watching." Gattacan peers out the window before looking behind me. "Take that, too. Put the relics in it."

I turn to find a knapsack—the Watcher's bag, I presume. I dump out its contents, then place the two relics of darkness inside before throwing the bag over my shoulders. A feeling of immense relief flows through me when the relics are no longer touching my skin. It's as if a dark energy was chilling me to my core. And I didn't even *open* these relics, as I did the relic of light.

My feet are aching from the heeled shoes as I hurry back to the seating area near the entrance. The other Watcher is lying right where Gattacan left him, next to the bar where we got our Tarmen Tonics earlier tonight. My eyes dart to the rough water erupting out behind the karrier as we approach the city wall.

Everything slows for a moment as the karrier enters the darkness of the tunnel. Then the lights shine in from the other side, and everything speeds up again as we exit through the gate. Watchers stare down at the karrier from the top of the wall, but none of them so much as flinch. And neither do I.

The karrier speeds along, water gushing out from the tail end. We're heading in the same direction where we departed from earlier in the night. I sigh as the wall and the Watchers guarding it become smaller and smaller in the distance.

Gattacan rushes back into the room. "Let's go."

I blink at him, utterly perplexed. "Who's driving?"

He ignores my question and gestures for me to get up. "We have to jump."

"What?!"

"There are a lot more Watchers where we're headed. We need to get off—*now*." Gattacan pulls the lever for the main door. "Come on."

I hurry over to him as the door opens, the sound of rushing water echoing in.

I step closer to the opening, the water swirling past below. The shore is way too far for us to jump. What's his plan?

Gattacan pulls off the Watcher's jacket.

"I'll take mine back now," Gattacan says, motioning for his suit jacket. I set the knapsack down and slide out of his jacket. Gattacan pulls it back on and snatches the knapsack up from the floor. "I'll carry it," he says, tightening the straps on the bag near his shoulders.

I nod, realizing that in moments, we'll both be swimming.

Gattacan takes several long strides backward. "We need to get a running start—jump as far as possible, to clear the wake, so the karrier doesn't suck us under."

Suck us under. Great. I won't be jumping far in this dress or these shoes, let alone swimming in them.

"Wait." I kick off my tall shoes and hike up the right side of my gown, reaching for my knife.

Gattacan's eyes widen.

I cut the dress above my knees and slide the knife back into its holster. Then I rip the fabric the rest of the way around, into a tattered mess.

"Okay," I say, realizing Gattacan is staring at me. I grab my shoes from the floor, looping the straps over my left wrist.

"Ready?" Gattacan reaches out for my free hand.

I'm far from *ready*, but I take his hand anyway. His fingers grasp mine in a firm grip.

We take off into a sprint, my body tightening in anticipation as we leap into the air. I manage to gulp in one desperate breath before the icy water breaks beneath me. A cold so bitter it almost feels like heat floods my body, as if hundreds of sharp needles are poking at my skin.

Underwater, I lose Gattacan's hand as the current rips me around. I swim as hard as I can toward the surface, hoping I'm going in the right direction.

My head emerges from the water, and I take a ragged breath. I swirl in a circle as the karrier speeds away. No sign of Gattacan.

I twist again, the current pulling me down. "Gattacan!"

"Aluma!" he calls out, his voice deep like the water beneath me.

I turn to see him swimming toward the edge of the canal. I use my arms like paddles, pulling the water past me as I move forward.

Gattacan climbs the steep embankment and reaches out for me. I lift my hand, feeling his fingers clasp my wrist. Then he's pulling me to him. Sharp rocks scrape my bare feet as I climb out of the water.

I pause at the top of the embankment, bending at the waist, trying to catch my breath. My eyes dart to Gattacan's back, where the knapsack remains zipped.

"Intruder alert!" a loud voice booms out over the alarm system.

"Hurry!" Gattacan says, dragging me behind him.

We run to the walkway and then into the grass to the large hedge, stretching all the way to the landing dock in the distance. A loud siren blares—right from where the karrier has now passed ahead of us. Where we would have been if we hadn't jumped when we did.

The *intruder alert* announcement continues, repeating over the sirens. Gattacan pulls on my hand, sprinting even faster. We dart behind the hedge and through the tall grass. A bright spotlight catches the corner of my eye, shining from the top of the main canal gate, out onto the water. Another light flashes on closer by, next to where we just jumped into the canal.

I pick up the pace, my feet burning and bruised, my legs carrying me as fast as I can go. I keep my gaze fixed on the barn, looming ever closer in the darkness.

Don't look back. Don't look back.

We finally reach the barn, and Gattacan opens the door. "In," he orders.

I run inside, gasping as I rest my hands on my knees. Gattacan hurries in behind me, his eyes glued on the canal as he slides the door closed.

A figure steps into the moonlight, startling me and Gattacan.

"Cloveman," I gasp, searching his worried face. "The others?"

He shakes his head grimly.

They're not here.

⌒ᴗ

My breathing is ragged as I make my way over to Cashel and Darwith, who are standing with the other steeds in the corner of the barn. I grab my bag and pull out my dry clothes, water dripping from my hair and what's left of my dress.

Gattacan sets the knapsack of relics down and pulls off his jacket and wet shirt, exposing his taut abdomen and chest. I force myself to turn away, even as a shiver of excitement courses through my veins.

Pull it together, Aluma—now's not the time.

"Where are they?" Cloveman's hands are fisted in his hair. "Where's Wolkenna?"

Unable to answer him, I slip into a stall and pull off the soaked dress, taking the knife and holster off after. My lips press together in a hard line when I notice the empty vial, the one I failed to save my father with.

"We don't know," I hear Gattacan say.

I pull on my dry clothes before wringing out the ruined golden dress. Then I stuff the dress, knife, and empty vial into my bag. I slip my sore feet back into my riding boots, thanking the stars for the protection and warmth they provide. Never again with those heels—never again.

When I exit the stall, Cloveman is pacing back and forth near a now-dressed Gattacan.

"I'll carry that," I tell Gattacan, dropping my bag next to him and gesturing to the Watcher's knapsack with the two relics of darkness hidden inside.

Gattacan nods, taking my smaller bag of clothes and shoving it inside his own. I pick up the knapsack, feeling the chill from the relics reaching out to me like icy fingers of despair.

"What happened—the sirens?" Cloveman asks, still pacing frantically.

"What *didn't* happen?" Gattacan says under his breath, his eyebrows raised as he watches me in the dim light.

Cloveman turns to me, stopping in place. "And where's your—" He cuts himself off.

"My father is alive," I say, hearing my voice, wishing I could've tried harder to get him out. "He and my brother stayed behind."

"What about Wolkenna? Xander and Thayer?"

"They were going to find Rinehart," I tell him. We said we'd all meet back here."

Cloveman buries his face in his hands, exhaling.

"It's not safe to stay here now," Gattacan says. "They'll find us if we do."

"But we said we'd wait until a few hours before sunrise," I protest. The others—*Thayer*—are likely still inside the walls, fighting their way out. Or worse.

"I know what we said," Gattacan snaps at me. "But now we have no choice." He lifts a hand, gesturing to the blaring sirens in the distance. But really I know he's talking about me—and *my* mistake.

I press my punctured left pointer finger against my thumbnail, the pinch of pain an unwelcome reminder of my carelessness. "I'm not leaving them," I say firmly. Those sirens wouldn't be blaring if I hadn't been so careless.

Cloveman crosses his arms beside me. "We *can't* leave them," he says to Gattacan.

The barn door slides open. We all freeze as two—three figures edge toward us through the darkness. Gattacan draws his blade. Cloveman and I don't move.

The first two figures step into the moonlight that's shining through the cracked roof.

Xander...and Thayer. Both of them dripping wet. Xander supports Thayer as he hobbles closer.

And Wolkenna, her hair sopping, her dress torn, much like I tore my own.

"Aluma!" Thayer's eyes widen. I run to him, wrapping my arms around his wet body. I take his other arm over my shoulder, supporting him as he walks.

"What happened?" I ask as Thayer shivers in my arms.

"Watchers—they are coming," Xander says.

We lower Thayer to the ground against the wall. He grimaces.

"Is it broken?" I ask, examining his left foot.

Thayer shakes his head. "I don't think so."

"He kicked a door down," Xander says.

My eyebrows shoot up on my forehead as I give Thayer an incredulous look.

He shrugs. "It was the only way out."

I glance over my shoulder at Wolkenna. Her face is pained, her posture rigid. She hasn't made a sound. Cloveman takes his jacket off and wraps it over her arms.

"We found Rinehart," Xander says. "He was in the prison, just like we thought, but the Watchers caught us on our way out. The sirens were blaring, and we had no choice but to swim the canal. They lost us when we went under the main gate."

Gattacan exchanges a grim look with his sister. "Rinehart—is there any way he could've made it out?"

Wolkenna shakes her head slowly, her nostrils flaring as tears form in her eyes. "He'd be with us now if we would've fought," she says, glaring at Xander. "You shouldn't have listened to him—"

"What happened?" Gattacan says. "What's she talking about?"

Xander sighs. "The Watchers closed in on us, and Rinehart fought back. He told us not to fight. He ordered us to take Wolkenna and get out while we still could."

"We shouldn't have left him," Wolkenna insists.

I know exactly how she must feel. It's the same way I feel—like I abandoned the one person who never abandoned me.

"The whole city was on high alert," Thayer says. "There were Watchers all over the place when we made it to the canal. Rinehart is the only reason we got out at all."

"Well, thank the stars you three are okay," I say to Thayer.

"You should all change—you'll freeze up there if you don't," Gattacan says, throwing Xander his bag, and handing me Thayer's. His eyes land on my hand, still on Thayer's foot, and he pauses for a second before going back to Elro.

Thayer works his way out of his soaking wet suit jacket while I retrieve his dry clothing. I help him pull the wet shirt off over his head and turn away as he takes off his pants, handing him his dry bottoms over my shoulder.

Xander comes out of a stall in dry clothes, Wolkenna from another.

"Where's your father—and Kase?" Thayer asks from behind me. I turn to see he has his dry pants on. I hand him his dry shirt. He studies me, the whites of his eyes red in the moonlight.

I hesitate, not wanting to relive any of it. "They're both still in the palace. My father is alive and alert...but I failed."

Thayer keeps his eyes on me, his hand finding mine. He squeezes it gently.

Xander leads his steed to the door. "We need to go—now."

"You're riding with me," I say to Thayer. I don't want him flying alone while in pain or shivering with cold. I scoop up the bag of relics, sliding it over my shoulders before hurrying to Darwith, Cashel, and Yulla.

When I lead the steeds back over, Cloveman is already pulling Thayer up into a standing position. Gattacan mounts Elro by the door, glancing back at me trying to help Thayer, his expression unnervingly neutral. Wolkenna mounts Taima beside them.

I call for Darwith to come closer—he's bigger, better for doubles. He bows low as we ease Thayer up onto his back. Then Darwith stands, and Cloveman boosts me into place behind Thayer.

I wrap my arms around Thayer's waist. His abdomen is strong beneath my hands, just like it was on the early morning of the Autumn Tournament. But this time I don't move my hands away. I'm not letting go.

Gattacan stares at me from the door. He turns away when he catches me looking. I can't imagine what he must think of me—after all, our lips were just pressed together barely an hour ago.

Cloveman mounts his steed, and we all head out of the barn and into the night. Yulla stays right by Darwith's side—as close to Thayer as she can get.

Off in the distance, searchlights are still scanning the canal as the sirens continue to blare. It's only a matter of time before they track us here.

"Wait!" a voice calls out.

I know that voice.

Gattacan darts Elro between us and the figure the voice came from. I squint into the darkness as the person runs closer, their hands lifted.

Kase.

I slide off Darwith and run to my brother. "How did you—what are you doing here?"

"They took Father—" he gasps.

I flinch away from him, dread creeping through my limbs. "Where?"

"I don't know, but you're right, I can't stay here." He tries to slow his breath.

"We've got company!" Cloveman yells out.

Behind Kase, two lights flash on, shining right in our direction.

A land karrier—and it's moving fast from near the canal. They've found us.

"Come on!" I pull Kase toward the steeds as the lights grow larger and brighter behind us. "You can ride Cashel."

"But I've never flown before," he says, fear coating each word.

Everyone watches with hurried expressions, their steeds stomping in place, ready to go.

"You can do it. Just hold on. Cashel will take care of you." I place my hand on my brother's shoulder, belatedly noticing that his clothes are somehow dry. "You've got this."

He nods and mounts Cashel. Thayer lends me his arm and pulls me back onto Darwith. I glance to my right to see the land karrier lights getting closer—too close.

"Let's go!" Gattacan takes off into a gallop on Elro. Wolkenna and Cloveman urge their steeds into gallops as well, side by side. Xander nods at me before taking off, too.

"Ready?" I ask Kase. Not that he has a choice.

"I—" Kase starts as Cashel stretches his wings out on either side.

"Good—hold on!" I yell, and Kase grabs a handful of mane as Cashel moves beneath him. I give Darwith a squeeze and he sprints into action beside them.

Gattacan, Wolkenna, Xander, and Cloveman take off into the sky ahead of us. Darwith's hooves stop hitting the ground as we lift into the air. Kase takes off on Cashel next to us, Yulla on our other side. Over my shoulder, I watch the large walls surrounding Tarmensil— the walls holding Rinehart and my father prisoner—disappear as we fly away from the city, back toward the jagged mountains.

FORTY-TWO

The frigid air bites at my skin as we soar over the Uladmond Mountains. The cloud cover parts, and all at once the night sky is on full display. Stars twinkle like thousands of fireflies. I keep my head tucked behind Thayer's left shoulder, leaning into him, grateful for his warmth—grateful for *him*. Kase flies Cashel ahead, next to the others, while Thayer and I stay in the back of the pack with Darwith, with Yulla soaring alongside.

My mind is unsettled. My father. Rinehart. They should be with us, too.

I wrap my arms tighter around Thayer to quiet my thoughts. A growing warmth from his back presses against my chest, our body heat pulsing back and forth like it's linked to the steady rhythm of our hearts. One of his hands lands on top of mine. He turns over his shoulder to look at me.

"This isn't over," he says as the air rushes past us. "We'll get your father back."

I try to speak, but there's a ball forming in my throat, dry and painful. "I failed him." My body quivers when I say the words.

"You didn't fail." His warm breath hits my cheek. "You did something brave." He leans back and twists his upper body to his left, cupping his left arm around the right side of my waist. His eyes glisten in the moonlight as they gaze into mine.

Another pulse of warmth rushes through me.

He pulls me closer until his full lips are pressing against mine. Our mouths are like two pieces of a puzzle, melting into each other until it's as if they were always one. The warmth increases throughout my body, reaching every inch of my being. And for a moment, with our lips locked, I let everything else fade away. I let go of the pain in my heart. I disregard the fact that I'm on Darwith, high in the sky, passing over jagged mountains.

Right now, I am safe.

Right now, I am free.

And I've never felt more alive.

Thayer's warm breath disappears as he turns back. And I immediately long for his lips to return, but I content myself with laying my head against his shoulder, my hands finding one of his. Our fingers interlace, and the warmth of our connection remains in my body, like a hot spring I could bathe in all night. I want to hold on to this feeling for as long as I can.

I glance up at the sparkling stars, thanking each one of them for this moment.

Then I peer far ahead at Gattacan, his black hair flowing behind him as he flies in front of the pack. I'm glad he doesn't turn around. I know I have to address this—this thing going on between Gattacan and me, and me and Thayer. But not right now.

For now, I'm going to imagine I don't have to decide.

The others ascend higher as the lights of Cintrenia come into view. We shift our flight path northeast, back toward Nammden, following them into the cloud cover until only a faint glow seeps through below.

By the time we descend again, we're well over the Gray Forest. The dim light plays off the trees below, casting our shadows into sawtoothed figures.

"We're almost there," I call out to Kase as we fly closer to him and

Cashel. He looks much more comfortable now—his face settled. I'm not too surprised, he's always been a quick study.

Kase barely acknowledges me at first, but his expression changes as Nammden comes into view, his eyes widening at the sight of the steel giants. And for a moment, I wish we weren't only siblings, but friends, too. I wish I could share the excitement and newness of this experience with him. But he doesn't share it with me, quickly resettling his face as soon as he sees me smiling at him.

When we land in the Grays' building, I slide off Darwith first, feeling the full weight of the relics on my shoulders. They're heavier than I thought. Then Darwith bows low for Thayer to dismount, and I rush to help ease Thayer down, taking some of the pressure off his foot.

I pat Darwith on his damp neck, feeling his heat radiating out toward me. Inside, without the cold wind slapping against my face, I realize just how frozen my skin is. My hands rub against my frigid cheeks, attempting to restart my blood flow.

"Let's get you to Moninne," I say to Thayer, glancing at his foot.

Kase slides off Cashel next to us. His eyes dart from side to side as he checks out the wide landing area.

"Are you okay?" I ask my brother.

"Yeah," he says. But his eyes are red—bloodshot, even.

"Flying isn't so bad, right?"

Kase pulls his shoulders back. "I prefer to stay on the ground, where *we* belong."

I shrug, unsurprised, but disagreeing wholeheartedly. *I* belong in the sky.

Cashel rubs my arm with his muzzle, his breath warm. I press my forehead to his for a moment before a few men come and take him and the rest of the steeds to the makeshift stable area. Kase follows me over to the others. I adjust the bag on my back, realizing Gattacan and I haven't told anyone about the relics of darkness.

Footsteps echo out from the corridor, and a few moments later, King Vikmal emerges with Queen Delna by his side. Their eyes survey our group, pausing on both Wolkenna and Gattacan.

"Rinehart?" Vikmal asks. "Where is he?"

Xander steps forward. "We were caught. We had no choice but to leave without him."

Wolkenna narrows her eyes at Xander, but she doesn't say a word.

Vikmal's face pulls taut. "And Hearn?"

"Still in Tarmensil," I tell him, my heart shrinking in my chest. "He's awake, but the light we gave him…it wasn't enough. He could barely stay on his feet, let alone manage the journey back."

"But if he's awake, he can be tort—" Vikmal's nostrils flare before he turns away. He exhales, loud enough for all of us to hear. I feel the weight of it on my back. Just like the relics. Because I woke my father, he is now more vulnerable than ever. A fact I had tried to bury away on our flight back, so I wouldn't crumble beneath the pressure of my own guilt.

This is all my fault.

"Father." Gattacan steps forward.

Vikmal turns to his son, his face reddened. "You went to save Rinehart and Hearn—you didn't bring back either of them, and now they know you were there? This is exactly why I didn't want you to go in the first place." His voice is controlled, but seething with anger.

Gattacan stares at the floor.

"We rescued my brother," I say, gesturing to Kase.

Vikmal studies Kase for a moment, but the kindness that once lingered in his eyes has disappeared. Delna moves over to Vikmal, placing her hand on his arm. Xander, Gattacan, and Cloveman keep their heads down. Wolkenna taps her boot against the floor, her arms crossed.

I hear another set of footsteps approaching and turn to see Moninne hurrying over to us. She looks me in the eyes, her expression hopeful, but her face falls when I shake my head.

"We couldn't get him out…" I whisper. "But he's awake."

She presses her lips together, nodding quickly.

"Thayer's foot is injured," I tell her, changing the focus away from my missing father.

She surveys him. "I'll help you to your room, then gather my supplies." She glances around once more, as if confirming my father really isn't here.

I turn to Thayer, hugging him. "I'll see you in the morning," I suggest.

His brows furrow. "Are you sure? I can stay—"

"It's okay," I say, before addressing Moninne. "This is my brother, Kase. Could you please help find him a room?"

Kase shoots me a look, one I can't fully decipher—confusion, hostility? Both?

"Of course," Moninne says, and Xander and Cloveman help Thayer hobble down the corridor. Kase follows behind them, scoping out his new surroundings.

When it's just me, Gattacan, Wolkenna, and their parents, I take a deep inhale, preparing for my next move.

"My brother isn't *all* we returned with," I say, pulling the bag around to my chest.

Everyone looks over at me, waiting. I glance at Gattacan. He nods once.

"My father told us about the hidden room, where they keep the relics." I reach into the bag and pull out one of the small black boxes. "Gattacan and I were able to find it before escaping."

Vikmal's eyes go wide.

"We found two relics of darkness," Gattacan tells them.

Vikmal takes a step forward, his entire demeanor changing. "We'll take them," he says, extending his hand. "They'll be safe here."

I place the relic of darkness back in the bag next to the other one and hand it over, happy to be relieved of the weight, the pressure, the *chill*. Vikmal accepts the bag and raises his eyebrows at me, as if asking if there's anything else I want to share.

"I'll...go get some rest, then," I say, filling the awkward silence.

Gattacan glances over at me as I dip my head to them. I turn and make my way down the corridor.

"*We're* not finished," I hear Vikmal say to Gattacan and Wolkenna.

I sigh, but keep walking anyway. This is *my* fault. If I had only used the correct hand, maybe they would have escaped with Rinehart.

Maybe Gattacan wouldn't be taking the fall—for *me*. Thank the stars we at least found two relics of darkness. I can only hope Vikmal will consider our mission a partial success, despite the lack of my father and Rinehart.

~

Kase is sitting on the edge of his bed when I enter his room a few minutes later. He looks up at me and then back at his hands.

"What happened to Father?" I ask him, closing the door behind me.

"After I showed you the way out, I went back to the clinic," he says. "I was in the hallway—I could hear the prince. He was talking to Father."

"And?"

"He called him a *traitor*. He said Father would be tried for conspiring against the king." Kase glances up at me, and I wince, trying not to think about what I know they do to traitors. "I realized they'd likely turn against me," he continues, "so I ran off. No one saw me leave."

"I shouldn't have gone in," I mumble to myself, running my hands through my tangled hair. "I shouldn't have used the light to wake him. At least they wouldn't hurt him then."

"That light..." Kase pauses, looking thoughtful. "If we had more, maybe we could use it to save Father."

I search his eyes. "You know about the light?"

"Father mentioned the last relic of light to you. And Sutagus talked about it—he was talking to the king days before Father woke up." He pauses. "They want it desperately, whatever it is."

He still doesn't know. He doesn't realize that what he stole from Father was a relic of darkness. That the one he gave Sutagus was the same one they used to cause Father's accident.

I can't tell him he inadvertently injured Father. That *he's* the reason Father is trapped in Tarmensil.

My jaw clenches. "They'd trade Father for the relic of light?"

Kase nods.

"Well, it's impossible," I tell him, thinking of the relic of light I found in the Gray Forest. "It's hidden. And the Laithlanners—the people here—they need it to defend themselves. Giving the Uladmondians that power is the last thing they'd do." I sit next to Kase and place my head in my hands.

"They're not going to let Father go. Or that commander," he says, almost as if he agrees with the Uladmondians' choice to hold our father and Rinehart as prisoners.

I scoff at him. "How do you know? How do you know so much about them and what *they* want?"

A sudden uneasiness splashes over me, blending in with my growing frustration.

"You're right…it's probably impossible." He says, turning away. "We should try to get some sleep."

"Yeah, we should," I tell him, rising to my feet. "I'll be right next door if you need anything."

"Thank you. Goodnight."

I wish him the same and close the door behind me, pausing for a moment in the hallway. Defeat seeps through me like thick sap. I should know my brother better than most. So why does he always feel like a stranger to me?

I still don't understand him.

When I get to my own room, I lie on the bed, letting it cradle my aching body. My eyes close, all the thoughts in my head floating around aimlessly until I drift into an exhausted sleep.

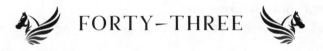

FORTY-THREE

"Wake up, Aluma."

A shadow is towering over me when I open my eyes. The clouded moon emits enough light into the room for me to see a man's jaw clenching.

King Vikmal.

"What is it?" I sit up straight in bed and turn on the lamp, still in the same clothes I fell asleep in.

"Your brother—he's gone."

"What do you mean, *gone*?"

"He took Darwith—"

My stomach knots as I stand. "Kase took Darwith?"

Vikmal nods. But I can't make sense of anything. Kase is gone? And he *took* Darwith?

"When did this happen?" I ask.

"While we slept," he tells me.

"Kase wouldn't leave—he wouldn't take Darwith. There has to be an explanation."

Vikmal glares at me. His face as hard as the steel that lines his tower. "You brought him here, but I'm assuming—I'm *hoping*—you had nothing to do with this?"

"To do with what?" I ask. "Taking Darwith? I'd never—"

"Is there any reason your brother would betray you—or your father?" Vikmal asks sharply.

"Betray?" I echo. "No, Kase wouldn't."

"Well, Darwith isn't *all* he took," Vikmal says grimly. "He found and stole the relic of light you retrieved from the Gray Forest, and one of the two relics of darkness we had."

My hands fly up to cover my mouth, muffling my cry of shock. I can't believe Kase would do this.

"He won't be able to open the relic of light until their Light Keeper—or your father—opens it." Vikmal exhales. "But now they have all the light that we know of. And with us only having one relic of darkness left, we—" He stops himself.

I lower my now-trembling hands. "This has to be a mistake," I say, but a part of me is remembering Kase's words last night. He knew about the light...

"Is it so hard to see? You're the one who told us Kase gave the relic of darkness to Sutagus—the same one they used against your father. He's already betrayed you both once before."

I shake my head. "Kase didn't know what it was then. For all he knew, he was trading some strange box belonging to our father, probably for a position in Tarmensil."

"You're saying he didn't know what the relic of light was, either?" Vikmal raises his eyebrows.

"Kase mentioned the light last night." I let the words fall out of my mouth, like something I want to be rid of.

Vikmal's eyes turn pitiless as he scrutinizes me.

"He thought," I continue, "that maybe if he had it, he could barter to get my father and Rinehart out."

"And you believe he's flying there by himself, without telling any of us, so he can try to trade the relics?" He gives me a cynical look. "Are you really that naïve?"

The room is spinning. My shoeless feet are blurring. I can't process anything.

I feel like I'm going to be sick.

"Your brother is working for Prince Sutagus," Vikmal says, his voice low and restrained. "We were set up. We were tricked. And now, since you woke your father, they can use him to open and control the last known relic of light. We'll only have one relic of darkness to defend ourselves with if—*when* they attack us."

My vision goes dark. I need to sit. My brother, my little brother. How could I be so blind? Kase is working for the prince. I take a sharp, tremulous breath, sinking back onto the bed. Images rush through my exhausted mind: Kase and my father arguing over the king's new law. Kase giving Sutagus the relic of darkness. Kase deciding to come with us to Nammden only after the prince saw my father awake. Kase stealing the relics.

It's all possible. It's all true. And in my gut, I know it.

Kase lied to me. My brother betrayed me—he betrayed our father.

"I—I don't want to believe this," I whisper, standing again as my body trembles. A flood of emotions hurls straight through me, like a dam breaking. And I can't stop any of it.

"Well, for all of our sakes, I hope you come to your senses soon. Because you have no choice but to believe it," King Vikmal says. He nods once before crossing the room, shutting the door behind him when he leaves.

My mind races. I knew something wasn't right. *I knew it.* Someone triggered the alarm in Tarmensil—it had to have been Kase. He only came with us to Nammden to steal the relics. Like he stole the relic of darkness from our father. He never had good intentions. He never wanted to save our father.

But I was too naïve, too blind to see that Kase could be so cruel—so selfish.

Anger boils up inside me—*hate.*

I sit once more, letting my head land in my hands. My breath escapes me between each painful stab in my heart.

"Aluma?" Thayer's voice calls out from the other side of the closed door, a gentle reprieve.

I try to suck in my sobs, wiping at my eyes. A few moments pass, and the door clicks open. Thayer hurries in and sits beside me on the bed. He wraps an arm around me.

"I heard," he says. "We all did—I'm so sorry."

"How could he?" I choke out. "He's my *brother*." I stare at Thayer as my body trembles.

"Come here," he says, pulling me closer, and I cry into his chest. My head aches, just like my heart.

"I shouldn't have been so blind—he's *exactly* like my mother." I spit the words out like venom, each one intensifying my anger. Kase *is* like our mother—a traitor to our family.

"None of this is your fault. You're not in control of your family. They make their own choices, same as you."

I inhale deeply. He's got a good point—but it doesn't make me feel any better. I exhale slowly, attempting to push out every bit of hurt and frustration. But there's an endless supply. I lie on my side, facing the window. Outside, the sky is dark and empty, just like the numbness falling over me.

Thayer lies behind me with his arm around my waist. I take his hand and pull it up to my chest, holding it with mine.

"It'll be okay," he whispers.

But for the first time, not one part of me believes it.

Thayer's arm is still draped over me when I wake. My eyes drift over to the window, where rain drizzles down the panes of glass. The clouds have overtaken the morning sky, leaving it an inky gray.

I sit up and move to the side of the bed, gazing out at the dense clouds, imagining Kase reaching Tarmensil with the last known relic of light and a relic of darkness.

Thayer stirs behind me. "You fell asleep," he says groggily, scooting to the edge of the bed next to me. He eases his injured foot onto the ground.

"How are you feeling?" I ask.

"Much better." His eyes meet mine. "Are *you* okay?"

"I'm okay," I say, but my teeth are digging into my bottom lip.

He raises his eyebrows, calling my bluff.

"We should go talk to the others, figure out what the plan is now," I tell him. We straighten ourselves up and head out into the hallway.

We make our way to the dining room first. I'm not positive I can stomach anything, but I'm sure everyone is eating breakfast by this time. But when we walk in, there's no one in sight. We try the sitting room next, only to find another vacant space. The flames in the fireplace once keeping the room warm have long since disappeared.

"Where is everyone?" Thayer asks.

I shrug, but then an image of Cashel and the other steeds flashes through my mind. "The landing area," I say, taking off through the corridor. Thayer hobbles along beside me.

As we approach the landing area, I hear voices. Queen Delna, Xander, and Cloveman are standing in a small circle, talking in clipped sentences. But I can't hear what they're saying.

"What's going on?" I ask as we near them.

They all take notice of Thayer and me, meeting us in the middle of the landing strip. I glance over at Xander and Cloveman, but both of their faces are blank.

"What is it?" I ask nervously. *What now?*

"Vikmal has traveled to speak with the elders in Knarrno," Delna says, her voice faint. Her face looks drawn, as if she didn't get much sleep.

I turn, glancing around for the prince and princess. "Gattacan and Wolkenna?"

"They left to fly over the Gray Forest," Delna tells me. "They'll be keeping an eye out for any incoming threats."

I inhale sharply. Gattacan didn't say goodbye.

"I should go after Kase. This is my fault," I say, peering down the hallway toward the makeshift stable area.

"No," she says, stepping closer. "Not until we have a clear plan."

Her eyebrows raise as if she's waiting for me to acknowledge what she's saying—what she's *ordering* me not to do.

I nod. I *don't* have a plan. And I've already failed enough.

"When will they return?" I ask, imagining Gattacan and Wolkenna flying out into possible danger. Without me. *Because of me.*

"Later today," Delna says. "Now that the Uladmondians will soon have the last known relic of light, we will be defenseless. We don't know how much time we have left before they attack." She pauses, her eyes boring into mine, willing me to listen to her next words. "We must think before we act. Our lives all depend on it."

Xander and Cloveman glance over at Thayer and me.

"So, what do we do now? Sit around and wait?" Thayer asks. "What about Hearn and Rinehart?"

"If the Uladmondians are planning to strike soon, we must prepare ourselves in the best way we can," Delna says. "Earlier, Xander and Cloveman informed me that they'll be traveling back to Cintrenia to find their families, before the Uladmondian forces strike."

My gaze shifts over to Xander and Cloveman. They both nod. What Delna says is true.

"You're leaving?" Thayer asks them.

"I need to speak with my father. He may be able to help," Xander says.

"My mother is alone," Cloveman tells us, opening his hands and then dropping them to his sides. "I'm not leaving her to fend for herself if another war breaks out."

My eyes move to Thayer. His family is still in Cintrenia, as well. And they have no clue that their son has been working with the Laithlanners, here in Nammden.

"Do you want to go, too?" My voice is weak, as I realize all at once what's about to happen. He's about to leave.

Thayer looks over at Xander and Cloveman then back to me. "You could come with me," he says, his eyes locking with mine.

"*Any* of you who return are taking a big risk," Delna interjects. "They've seen your faces. Especially yours, Aluma. They may have already gone after your families. We don't know."

"I can't go back. I have nothing—no one to return to, anyway," I tell her.

"A wise choice," Delna says.

I glance over at Thayer. I don't want him to go. But I can see the look in his eyes—he needs to go home to his family. I'd do the same if I were in his position.

"I'm coming back for you," Thayer says, reaching out for my hand. "But I need to make sure my family will be safe first. Maybe they'll head south, away from Cintrenia, farther away from here. But I have to warn them."

I nod, hoping to hide the mix of fear and sadness that's welling up inside of me. "When are you leaving?" I ask, glancing around at Thayer, Xander, and Cloveman.

"Now," Xander says. "The sooner I talk to my father, the better." He lowers his head. "I am coming back, though. And I *will* fight the darkness with you."

"Well, then, you should all go. Together." I attempt to sound brave, but I feel more like a mouse standing in front of a lion: vulnerable and terribly alone.

"We'll keep Aluma safe," Delna assures Thayer.

"You should get going," I tell Thayer, releasing his hand. He searches my eyes for any lingering doubt, but I stand firm. I can't show him how utterly afraid I am right now—afraid that he'll get hurt, or that he won't be able to return.

I can't lose him.

"Please, just *stay* here, in Nammden," Thayer says. "I need to know you'll be safe."

"I'll be safe…" I tell him.

Xander and Cloveman head to the makeshift stable area. When Thayer turns to leave as well, I try to keep the image of his brown eyes with me, long after he's walked away.

Delna brushes a sympathetic hand over my arm before she heads down the main corridor toward the living areas.

I wait in silence, pacing restlessly until the three boys return with their steeds.

Cloveman walks over to me with his steed, his face hardened. "When Wolkenna returns," he says. "Tell her...tell her I'm coming back."

I force a smile for him. "I will."

Cloveman hoists himself into his saddle. Xander nods at me from the landing area, where he's already mounted his steed.

Thayer's face is pale as he leads Yulla over to me. His eyes are lost. "This doesn't feel right," he says. "I don't want to leave you here."

"It will be okay. *I'll* be okay," I say, taking one of his hands into mine, wondering if I'm telling the truth. "Be careful."

He pulls me into a hug, his warmth reaching out for me like a hot summer day. I inhale deeply, attempting to memorize his scent—everything about him. Just in case.

I don't want to let go of him when we finally break apart. He walks Yulla out onto the landing area and pulls himself up into his saddle. My lips press together, holding back from yelling out for him to stay.

Thayer glances at me one last time as he, Xander, and Cloveman take off into the dark clouds. I pull my arms across my body as I fall apart inside. I stand in the landing area, waiting for the pain to dissipate. But it doesn't leave—it consumes me.

Everyone has left. Everyone I care about could soon be gone.

War is on the horizon. There's nothing but darkness now.

The next few hours go by in a blur. My appetite has disappeared. All I can do is pace the empty corridors, over and over again. Everyone is gone.

A heavy sadness pushes me under like a flood, further into the dark depths of my mind. I plod my way over to the makeshift stable area. Only Cashel remains. I wrap my arms around his neck for a moment before sliding down into the corner of the stall, like I used to back in Cintrenia—with Darwith.

Darwith.

I pull my knees to my chest, rocking back and forth as my body becomes colder and colder, freezing from the inside out. I shut my eyes, attempting to let go of everything.

"I thought I might find you here," a soft voice says.

I lift my head to see Moninne leaning against the stall door, her green eyes bright like spring grass.

"You know, your father told me all about you." She smiles as if remembering something wonderful. Something I wish I could remember. "He told me how brave you were—how compassionate. He told me someday you'd help change everything."

Change. What can *I* change?

"Even before he knew you were a Light Keeper," she continues, "he knew you were special. He believes in you. *I* believe in you." She drops her chin. "You have the power to change the world around you. You only need to believe that you can."

I exhale, wishing I could believe the words she's saying.

"You're a Light Keeper. So keep the light."

"Thank you," I say. "I'll try."

She offers me one last kind smile. "I have some important matters to attend to, so I'll be on my way."

I wait for her footsteps to disappear before pushing myself up in the stall. I rub Cashel's muzzle, feeling his warm breath on my palm. My mind is somehow calmer after seeing Moninne. And regardless of all the darkness coming my way, I know she's right.

I must keep the light.

FORTY-FOUR

Moninne's words give me some hope, but there's still a shadow looming over me—a dark cloud. My mind darts to thoughts of my father. To Thayer. To Gattacan and the others.

I need to get out of here. I can't sit around all day, waiting for something to happen. Maybe a flight will clear my head—help me think of solutions.

I saddle Cashel and lead him to the landing area. A cool wind blows in from outside of the opening. I breathe it, letting it coat my lungs, letting it wake me. The clouds are low and thick, draping over the steel giants like a heavy coat. There's a storm brewing.

No one is around when Cashel and I take off. We fly into the low-lying clouds, gliding between the buildings. I turn Cashel toward the ocean, its salty mist pelting my skin, luring me closer.

We pass a few more buildings on either side. Then waves. They crash against the smaller structures and onto the water-covered streets. I haven't seen the ocean this close since I was in Sceilaran as a child. The waves of the Teal Sea were much less intimidating, rolling gently onto the white sandy beaches. This ocean looks angry, almost violent. It's as if it's revolting against being confined to its shores, when it wishes to explore—to expand. This turbulent water has something to say—*something to prove*. This ocean would swallow someone whole if it had the chance.

A chill runs through me. I wind my fingers through Cashel's mane and bring him to a hover. The sounds of the waves clashing against one another echo in my ears. I imagine Kase with the relics he stole—seeing him, but not knowing what to say.

A pain hits my heart. I don't know my brother. And now I'm sure—I never did.

I fly out farther away from the city, over the water, trying to see what lies past the clouds. How far does the sea go? What's beyond the dark blue waves that stretch off into the distance?

When I was younger, I daydreamed about what existed outside of Eirelannia: the people, the creatures, the land. I yearned to explore, just like the waves beneath me now. But when my mother left, my fate was sealed, tethered to Cintrenia. I needed to stay home and make sure my father and brother were cared for. That they were happy and loved—loved like I'd never been by my mother.

I turn Cashel back toward Nammden, realizing my distance from the shore. We hover in place again, looking back at the dark city, cloaked in mystery by a dense mist. It's a whole new view. The buildings stand tall, with unwavering resilience, even as the waves beat against their bases repeatedly. It's a strong city—one that refuses to give up. The way I wish I felt.

I glance below. We're high enough that the water swirling beneath us looks as though it's nearly still. But I know it's moving, tearing its way through itself, over and over again. And for a moment, I imagine falling into it, like I fell into the Knarrno River, knowing there'd be no way out.

There's no one to save me but myself.

The sky turns bleaker as we fly back toward the city. The cold drizzle makes me shiver, my body longing for the heat of the fireplace. Still, I don't want to go back to the Gray residence. Not yet. Not without a plan.

As we near the shoreline, something catches my eye to my left.

Way off in the distance, along the row of tattered old buildings lining the coast, there's something reflecting. Something shining.

A light.

It glows for a moment. Then it's gone.

I wipe the rainwater from my eyes, squinting past the clouds at the saturated city. Did I see something? I wait, scanning back and forth.

Nothing. No light. Great, now I'm imagining things—I must really need some sleep.

I turn back toward the Grays' building, but out of the corner of my eye, I see it again. It *is* a light.

We fly through the clouds toward the faint glow. There's a low rumble of thunder off in the distance. I lean closer to Cashel's neck as we fly lower, faster.

From the looks of it, all the buildings on this part of the shoreline have been abandoned. There are no Scalers in sight. No way they could live in buildings with water ripping through them every few moments. But if those structures are unoccupied, the light has to be coming from something else.

We fly closer to the light. It's glowing steadily now. From this distance, I can see it's coming from the top floor of a smaller building, maybe five stories high. The lowest levels are fully submerged, and the ocean waves pound the sides of the building, cascading up and over the roof, and then back down onto the flooded streets beyond.

There's nowhere to land.

But there's something inside.

I bring Cashel to a low hover near a row of broken windows on the front side of the building. The light pulses white, in and out, like a silent song.

Wherever the light is coming from, we're close.

A flash of lightning strikes somewhere behind me. Thunder rumbles. The cold water splashes around us, and yet a warmth is reaching out to me. The light glows brighter as we hover even closer. My skin warms, despite the frigid storm pushing its way across the sky. I should be cold, but I no longer feel the chill sinking into my bones.

I can *feel* the warmth emanating from the light. And that's when I know.

It's a relic.

~

My mind races.

I don't get it—all the relics of light are supposed to be gone. It's not possible. Surely the Laithlanners would've noticed this relic, perched out next to the Dark Sea. Someone would've seen it. Unless… unless the relic wasn't shining because there weren't any Light Keepers around to notice.

My eyes dart to my saddle, spotting the rope that's still attached from the night I left Galghesworp. I lean over Cashel's neck, hoping he can hear me over the whipping wind. "Get me as close as you can," I say, and his ears twitch.

Waves burst against the sides of the building as Cashel flies closer and closer to the rooftop, flapping his wings against the wind, until we are hovering over it. I take the rope and tie it snugly around the saddle. I tug on it, checking that it's secure. I grab the rest of the rope and lean slightly to the side, allowing it to hold my weight—it will work. The top of the building is only a couple of body lengths below, but still high enough I can't jump without hurting myself. And there's no way I'll risk Cashel's safety by trying to land on that wave-ridden deck.

I spot an open stairwell leading off of the roof. Thank the stars—at least there's a way down on foot once I touch down.

I tie a loop on the loose end of the rope and place my left boot into it. I take a deep breath and slide out of the saddle, holding tight to the rope.

"Stay steady—I'll be right back," I say to Cashel, moving down behind his flapping wings. His feathers brush my face, like soft reminders to hold on tight. The rope burns against my hands as I slide down, just until it jerks up, looping tightly around my foot. Then I push, so I'm in a standing position.

"A little lower!" I shout up to Cashel.

His silver wings swoop above me as he lowers me to the roof. I pull myself up on the rope and unhook my foot, dropping the remaining few feet onto the wet concrete.

I turn to face the turbulent waters just as a large wave rushes at me. My body braces for impact as the wave hits the side of the building. The water splashes onto the roof, crashing over me in an instant. It slams me to the ground, pushing me toward the edge and the street below. I reach out and grab the side of the metal stairwell as the water rushes around me, attempting to drag me with it, like a liquid chain.

Don't let go.

The wave leaves the top of the building as fast as it arrived. As I struggle to my feet, I spot another on its way, ready to strike.

"Wait here!" I yell up to Cashel. He's still hovering, just high enough to avoid the ocean's wrath.

I rush down the wet stairwell, catching myself from slipping. A loud crack of thunder shakes me just as another wave hits the building above. Water rushes through the stairwell, soaking me again from head to toe. Maybe this wasn't such a good idea, after all.

Keep going.

The light glows stronger as I reach the next floor. I exit the stairwell and peer out at the angry ocean through the open window across the room. The waves continue to grow larger, bashing against the building, as if they'll tear it down. There's a hallway to my right— *that's where* the glow is coming from.

I run toward the light as it illuminates the water-worn building around me. It shines from a room on my left. The warmth is stronger than ever, pulling me to it as if there's an invisible string reeling me in.

I hurry inside, squinting as the light intensifies. I scan the edges of the room first. One intact window. That must be where I saw the light shining from. I wait for the next wave to hit, half expecting it will burst through the window, relief washing over me when it doesn't.

My eyes dart to the middle of the room. There, on a rusty old metal chair with wheels, sits a relic—a relic of light.

I edge closer. It's the same shape as the relic of light I found in the Gray Forest: a silver box, one hand-length high and half the width. But the design on the side is different—two wave crests etched in black. It's much like the design I saw on the relic of darkness that Gattacan and I found in the hidden room, the one I thought might belong to Laithlann. It glows intensely out of the open top, its warmth surrounding my cold, wet skin like a hot towel.

How is it open? My mind races back to when the Grays told me the story about how a relic of light opened for me as a child with my father. Perhaps they open on their own when a Light Keeper is near—like a whistle of light, calling out for its keeper.

I slide the top closed, and it clicks shut. The room goes dark, the warmth dissipating as the cold sinks back in through my skin. I pull the relic closer, attempting to absorb the little warmth still pulsing out to me.

Thunder cracks—*Cashel*.

I rush into the dark hallway with the relic clutched to my side. I peek my head out to the open area by the stairwell just as a wave comes barreling in. I duck behind the wall as it passes, then bolt straight for the stairs, moving as fast as I can without slipping. I need to get off this level before another wave hits.

When I reach the top of the stairs, I stop, holding on to the rail as the next wave crashes onto the building. The water rushes at my feet, but passes quickly, leaving me unharmed.

Time to go.

I run out, and my eyes lock on Cashel, still hovering above the waves. The wind is pushing him away from the roof of the building—away from *me*.

"Cashel!" I yell out.

He spots me, and his wings flap with sheer force, until he's directly over my head. He lowers until I feel the flapping of his large wings, the air rushing past me like gusts of wind. The rope I tied to the saddle sways in front of me.

I hold the relic to my chest with my left hand and reach for the dangling rope with the other. My eyes dart to my right as another wave charges at us. I slip one foot into the loop while grasping the rope with my free hand.

"Fly!" I yell.

Cashel's wings flap harder than ever as he lifts straight up into the air. I slip my other foot into the loop as the crest of the wave breaks against my legs. We clear the roof, and my grip tightens on the rope as I start to spin.

Lightning flashes nearby as we fly higher. The wind howls, and rain pelts across my skin like small pebbles. There's nowhere to land in the darkness. Nothing but storm. And my grip is weakening.

"Find a place to land!" I call out.

Cashel flies through the storm, back into the city. We fly away from the waves and into the thick cluster of buildings. The rope is spinning fast now. I attempt to pick a building to keep my eyes locked on, so each time I circle around everything's not a complete blur. If I don't fall soon, I'm definitely going to be sick.

I spot a wide rooftop. "There!" I yell out, thanking the stars when I realize he's spotted it, too.

Cashel lowers me to the roof. I kick my feet out of the loop and fall back onto my rear, still clutching the relic of light in my left hand.

A gust of wind ensnares Cashel's wings, blowing him aside.

"Land now!" I shout, hoping he can catch himself.

Cashel flies up and away from the building.

I stand and move to the side of the roof, making sure not to get too close to the edge. The wind is pushing me from every which way like a tornado.

Through the storm, I spot Cashel flying straight at me. His hooves hit the roof as his outstretched wings slow him before he reaches the other side.

I run over to him and open my saddlebag, securing the relic inside. I swing myself onto his back and give him a squeeze. He turns around and takes off into a gallop, flapping his strong wings as his hooves leave the rooftop once more. Lightning strikes again, this time hitting a building only a little taller than the one we just left. I pull myself closer to Cashel's neck, his mane whipping across my face.

We fly through the maze of steel giants, back to the Gray residence. The rain beats against us. This storm isn't letting up.

I can barely see the opening of the building as we draw near, but Cashel somehow flies us inside without a collision. His hooves touch down on the dry ground, and I exhale as the sound of the storm fades behind us like a bad memory.

We're safe.

Cashel stops in the landing area for me to dismount. I glance around, there's no one in sight. At least I won't have to explain my absence—not yet, anyway.

I lead Cashel to the makeshift stable area and take off his tack. He shakes out his wings, raindrops sprinkling the ground. I finish drying him as he takes a deep drink from his water trough.

"Thank you," I whisper, petting the dark blaze on his head.

I take the saddlebag under my arm and head back to the landing area. The warmth of the relic pushes through the fabric, and I squeeze it closer. The wind howls and the rain hammers the building even worse than before. I can only hope this storm doesn't affect the others, wherever they're flying now.

I hurry down the corridor toward my room, water dripping off me at a steady rate. If it weren't for the relic at my side, I'd be shivering to my core.

Once inside my room, I push the door closed behind me. The saddlebag stays with me all the way into the bathroom, where I lock the door.

My eyes are on the bag in my hands. I slowly open it. The silver box is still inside. *The relic.* So I *didn't* imagine it.

I have another relic of light. I'm not sure how, but I do.

This changes everything.

FORTY-FIVE

Evening slowly edges its way into the Grays' building. The storm has passed, though the wind still howls like a sad creature perched outside my window. Despite the chill in the air, my skin is warm and dry, thanks to a hot shower and the relic of light.

Despite my best efforts to stay in Nammden and tell someone about the relic, something inside of me is urging me to leave now. I can use this light to save my father—to protect what I love. If relics are what Prince Sutagus is after, I must let him have one, or at least let him *believe* he can have it. These wars will never stop unless those who cause them are gone.

It's all so clear now: the prince, the king, and the rest of the nobility in Uladmond have long suppressed every person they can, holding them down, kicking them around like dirt. Cintrenia and all of Ivernister could end up barren and broken like Laithlann if something doesn't change soon. Light, darkness—it all needs to be in its proper place.

Balance *must* be restored. And I can help do that now.

My mind made up, I sneak back toward the makeshift stable area.

As I approach, several voices echo out from the landing strip. I clutch the saddlebag to my side and wait in the shadows.

"Hurry!" someone shouts.

I peek my head out to see Xander, Cloveman, and Thayer sliding off their steeds.

Thayer. My heart jumps in my chest. He's back—he's safe.

I glance at the saddlebag before hurrying out to them. I can't tell them about the relic. Not yet.

"We must tell King Vikmal," Xander says.

"What happened?" I shout as I near them.

"Aluma!" Thayer rushes over, pulling me close as my free arm wraps around him. He's shivering with cold.

"They're frozen—they're all frozen," he says.

"What do you mean? Who's frozen?" I ask, stepping back.

Thayer's face is devoid of all color, white as fresh-fallen snow. "Everyone. There's no one moving in Cintrenia."

My eyes narrow. "You're not making any sense—"

"They're freezing, like statues. Like they're frozen in time." He leans in closer, his eyes wide and full of fear. "My family, they were like—like stones." His voice cracks.

Xander and Cloveman are standing behind Thayer. I dart a look at them; there's no way what Thayer's saying is true.

Cloveman runs his hand through his hair. "My mother. She was still as a rock. She wouldn't move an inch."

"Same with my father," Xander says.

"But how is that possible?" I ask, my confusion growing.

"There was a dark cloud hovering over the whole city," Xander says. "When we flew in, it was as if there was a force working against us. Our steeds' wings were weakened—we barely made it to the ground without crashing. It was freezing. It felt like our energy levels were depleting by the minute. Everything else was stopped, as if something froze everyone and everything in place."

The violent sky reaches in at us, and I shudder.

"Then it's happening again," a voice booms out from behind us.

I turn to see King Vikmal approaching, his face pained.

"They've released the darkness. It is all-consuming," he says. "It won't stop until there's nothing left. And with the coming destruction, the king and the prince will finally be able to force everyone—and everything—into submission. They'll take our land and our lives. No one will be able to stop them."

"Why would they do such a thing?" Cloveman asks.

King Vikmal exhales. "It was only a matter of time before the rest of the resistance in Cintrenia was going to band together and rise up. The Uladmondians first response has always been to quash any form of rebellion at its core."

"The old will soon be made anew..." I whisper.

"What's wrong with everyone?" Thayer asks. "Why couldn't they move?"

"You must have seen the aftereffects of multiple relics of darkness combined and used all at once," Vikmal says, grimacing. "This is the same thing that happened here, generations ago. If left unchecked, the darkness will continue to slow things down until they're frozen through—until everything withers away and dies."

Thayer swallows. "What are we going to do?"

"With the last relic of light gone—" Vikmal sighs. "There's nothing we *can* do. All we have left is darkness, which would only add to the problem."

"So what will happen to everyone?" Cloveman asks, his voice quivering. "To our families?"

"With no light to counteract the darkness, the Cintrenians will continue to fall into a deeper freeze," Vikmal says. "Everything will stay that way indefinitely—at least until the Uladmondians decide to destroy Cintrenia and its people forever. With the relics of darkness, they have the power to wipe out everyone and everything that stands in their path, giving them a clean slate. We'll be the only ones left to oppose them."

The warmth of the relic pulses against my side as I glance at Thayer.

Lightning strikes outside, illuminating a figure winging toward us. Thunder booms as a steed and rider blaze in through the opening.

It's Elro—and Gattacan. And there's another pair flying in behind him—Wolkenna, on Taima.

Vikmal hurries over to his children and the rest of us follow. Thayer reaches out to me, his hand taking mine.

"They're coming!" Gattacan shouts. "Sutagus—the Empyrean Cavalry is coming!"

The two siblings dismount and close the space between us. Cloveman immediately pulls Wolkenna into a hug. Gattacan's eyes are locked on me, as if he's relieved *and* pained to see me. Then his gaze falls to my hand, still holding Thayer's, and his jaw clenches. He looks away, as if I've just slapped him.

"The prince and the Empyrean Cavalry were flying near Cintrenia when we spotted them," Gattacan continues. "They appeared to be approaching the Green Hills, heading toward the Gray Forest."

Vikmal nods. "If—*when* they get here they will release more darkness. We must prepare."

My voice leaps out of me. *"Prepare?"* My eyes dart over to the steeds still standing in the landing area. "Prepare with what—more darkness? You said that would only add to the problem." I glance around at the others. "We must take to the skies. We must *fight* for the light. If they reach Nammden, there will be nothing left to save, and no one left to save it. We should confront them over the Gray Forest—outside the city."

Gattacan's eyes meet mine again, now tinged with a hint of fear. "They had at least twice as many Empyrean Riders," he says, his voice low. "And with the darkness…there's just no way. We'll be better off standing our ground here."

"How can you say that?" I ask incredulously. "We have power, too. And if we don't stand up and fight *now*, we'll never have the chance to stand up for anything again."

"She's right," Thayer says. "If the darkness is what they released in Cintrenia, there won't be anyone left to defend there, anyway." He nods at me. "I'm with you."

Xander steps forward. "I will also fight with you."

"Me too," Cloveman says.

Wolkenna nods at me.

"What *power* do you have?" Vikmal asks, his hands raised. "The only relic your brother didn't steal is no use to us against more darkness. We need to evacuate as many as we can, and the rest of us will stay here."

"I have my own light," I say, opening the saddlebag and lifting out the relic.

Vikmal's jaw drops, his eyes on the black etching of the two waves on the side. Everyone else gasps.

"That's our symbol," Vikmal says. "That's Laithlann's relic of light. We thought it was lost forever." He shakes his head. "Where did you get that?"

"I found it on the coast," I tell him. "And I'm going to use it to stop the prince from attacking any of us, ever again."

"You should let us take that," Gattacan says, sharing a glance with his father. But I know full well they don't have another Light Keeper to open it. And I don't have any intentions of giving this one up—their symbol or not.

"No." I stare into Gattacan's dark eyes. "I'm a Light Keeper. I'm going to keep the light. And I will use it to stop the darkness from destroying anything—or anyone else I love."

He takes a step back, his eyes still locked on mine.

A moment passes. Everyone is silent. The thunder claps and sends vibrations through the floor, jolting us back into the moment.

"Then *we* will fight, too," Vikmal says finally. "A king doesn't let others fight his battles for him." He gives me a deferential nod.

"Father." Gattacan's eyes widen. "You can't be serious."

"You will stay here, Gattacan." Vikmal's voice is firm. "If something happens, *you* will be king."

"No—you can't," Gattacan says, his voice pleading. "You don't have time to assemble the troops!"

"You said it, Son—they're close. There's no time. Order the evacuations, and get your mother and grandmother to the safe room." Vikmal places his hand on Gattacan's shoulder. "Aluma's right—we must fight back. And *you* must stay here to protect our home."

Gattacan's nostrils flare as he turns to me. He shakes his head slowly, his eyes locking with mine again, as if he's willing me to stay right where I am—*next to him*.

My body tenses as I steal myself away from his gaze. I'm grateful that he's staying here. I can only hope he'll be safer this way.

"We should leave now," I announce, stepping forward, trying to brush off the urge to listen to Gattacan.

We quickly saddle the rest of our steeds and meet back in the landing area to retrieve our weapons and armor. King Vikmal stands beside Elro, adjusting his bow and arrows, his sword by his side. Queen Delna runs to him from the corridor. Moninne follows behind, helping Delna's mother, Nadie.

"Vikmal!" Delna wraps her arms around him, and they embrace.

Thayer leads Yulla to me. He pulls me into a hug. "I believe in you," he whispers, his breath warm against my ear.

I pull away and look into his eyes. "I know you do—you always have." I lean in, pressing my lips to his in a quick, desperate kiss, hoping this isn't the last time I'll feel his warmth.

Thayer and I mount our steeds. Moninne hurries over to me as I double-check my saddlebag and weapons behind me.

"I'm proud of you," she says. "You've found your light."

I smile and nod, imagining that my father is standing right there next to her, saying the same thing.

As my gaze shifts away from Moninne to Vikmal, Xander, Cloveman, Thayer, and Wolkenna waiting atop of their steeds, it occurs to me—aside from my father, this is the family I never had, but always wanted. These are the people who have my back. And thank the stars they're all here now.

I glance over at Gattacan where he's standing to the side with his mother and grandmother. His eyes are trained on me—fear, pain, regret passing through them all at once. I want to go to him, to say goodbye...to feel the cool sensations that come from his touch. But I don't. There's no time for any of that now.

"Let's go," I call out to the others, giving Cashel a squeeze.

We take off toward the lightning-riddled sky. I savor each hoofbeat beneath us, realizing I may never experience takeoff again. My eyes shut as Cashel's wings flap harder—faster. My mind remains calm as his hooves leave the ground and the rain showers us with the tears of what's to come.

⌒

The rain stops as we reach the Gray Forest. The only sound left is our steeds' wings keeping us airborne above the trees. I turn over my shoulder to see the storm behind us, still lingering over Nammden, lightning flashing every few seconds.

The moonlight is clear from above, illuminating the dark treetops that stretch up like tall soldiers, standing guard between us and Cintrenia. Beyond the forest, there's another storm coming in—but one without lightning. A storm like I've never seen before.

The darkness.

A shiver runs through me as the cold air blows against my wet clothes.

In front of the dark cloud, I squint to make out the group of Empyrean Riders flying our way in a V formation, the same way we learned in training. Even from this distance, I can see Prince Sutagus leading them. Gattacan was right—we're outnumbered.

I turn to King Vikmal. He stares out at the Empyrean Riders flying closer and closer.

"We need to take this to the ground," I tell him, glancing at the trees below. "We can use the forest for protection. We're close to where Darwith brought me to retrieve the relic of light. I know the place. Prince Sutagus doesn't. We'll have an advantage if we know our surroundings. We can take them down before they even reach the ground."

King Vikmal watches the Gray Forest passing beneath us, considering my idea. Then his narrowed eyes meet mine, and he nods in agreement.

We have a plan.

"Back to where we found the relic," I say to Cashel, hoping he remembers the way to my father's hiding spot. His ears twitch in recognition as he veers off to the left. King Vikmal, Thayer, and the others follow as we all descend to the forest.

I spot a wide clearing that's open to the sky. The field is littered with dead logs; it's ideal for taking cover. Relief floods me as I realize: it *is* the same place Darwith brought me to before. And somewhere along the border of the space is where I know I'll find the tree passage—the covered tunnel that leads to the hedge maze.

It's perfect.

King Vikmal flies Elro beside me. "Jeklers," he warns, his eyes narrowing.

I nod. "I'm counting on it."

A small grin forms on his stern face.

We swoop closer to the opening. Prince Sutagus and the other Empyrean Riders redirect in our direction. It's working—they're following us.

Cashel flies into the clearing first. His hooves contact the wet ground, sending murky water onto my legs. King Vikmal, Thayer, Xander, Cloveman, and Wolkenna all land behind me.

I hop off Cashel, my eyes darting around the large clearing, searching for the opening to where I found the last known relic of light—*which wasn't the last one after all.*

Giant dead trees lie zigzagged across the open area. It's as long as the field in the Empyrean arena and half as wide. There's plenty of space for us to hide behind fallen logs, and catch their Riders off guard before they land. Thankfully we don't have to face them in the sky—we're too outnumbered. I squint past the nearby fallen trees to the border of the clearing.

The opening.

"Over here!" I call to the others.

Rotting leaves squish beneath our feet as we lead our steeds through the enclosed tree tunnel. I step out first at the end of the passage, halting at the top of the massive staircase that leads into the domed clearing. The tops of the trees are once again blocking anyone from escaping—*or entering*—from above. Nothing can get to us in here, unless it comes through the passage and down the stairs first.

The others step out from behind me. Thayer's jaw drops. Everyone else's eyes widen. It's just as impressive to them as it was to me the first time I saw it.

"This way." I lead Cashel down the root steps, and the others follow.

At the bottom of the stairs, I spot the decomposing jekler off to my left side. It's in the same place Darwith struck it down. And for a moment, a sadness passes over me for the creature that lost its life—beast or not.

I turn, everyone's faces a mix of fear and disgust as they stare at the jekler carcass. "If you see one, *run*," I say, gesturing to it.

Thayer and the others nod.

"We can leave the steeds here," I tell them, releasing Cashel's reins. "They'll be safer. And if it comes to it, we can defend ourselves from behind there." I point to the first row of hedges, hoping we'd all be able to clear the wall of thorns atop our steeds if needed, just as I did on Cashel before.

Vikmal steps forward. "You should stay here—protect the light, until you're ready to use it."

"No—I'm coming," I tell him, my hand finding the hilt of my sword. "I'm going to fight." I don't wait for his approval as I rush back over to Cashel, retrieving my saddlebag with the relic of light hidden inside, and carrying it toward the dead jekler. Vikmal and the others gather their weapons and follow me.

An overwhelming stench of rotting flesh wafts out as I near the jekler. Holding my breath, I draw my sword, reaching it out to lift one of the jekler's legs. I toss the saddlebag underneath and let the limb plop back over the top of it.

I turn around. The others look as if they've just seen—well, exactly what they've just seen.

"*No one* will look there," I say with a shrug, then dart back up the staircase. "Come on!"

Vikmal moves in front of me at the top of the stairs before the tree passage. "I'll go first."

I nod, following after him as we move stealthily through the dark tree tunnel.

The king draws his sword as we approach the open clearing where we landed. I swing my bow around and nock an arrow. The others ready their weapons behind me.

My heart thumps in my chest, pounding like a battle drum.

King Vikmal holds his free hand high, signaling us all to stop. We do. No one makes a sound.

After a moment, the king inches forward, his sword outstretched. He steps into the clearing, scanning it. He stops. Gestures for us to follow again.

As I exit the passage, I keep my sights set on the sky. But there's no one. Nothing but darkness and moonlight trickling in through the tops of the bordering trees.

Vikmal and I edge our way over to a large fallen tree near the opening to the passage, crouching behind it. Thayer kneels next to me. The others scurry behind another dead tree. All of us are silent, our weapons trained to the sky. The massive bordering trees behind us create a shield of sorts from anyone flying in—or shooting at our backs. The Cavalry can only come in from one direction, and that's straight out in front of us.

The sounds of wings flapping—*hovering*—nearby echo out in the night air. I search the sky, my eyes darting from side to side.

"There!" Xander points to where we first entered the clearing across the way.

An Empyrean steed and Rider fly in and downward, ready to land. More and more hovering Empyrean steeds come into view.

My body tenses. This is it. There's no turning back now.

"There are too many of them—shoot before they make it to the ground," King Vikmal orders as he sheaths his sword and swings his bow around, drawing an arrow in a flash.

I pull in a ragged breath and peer over as Cloveman releases an arrow straight at the Rider on the closest Empyrean steed. The Rider is struck, screaming out as he plummets to the ground. Another

Empyrean steed blazes toward us, and the moonlight illuminates the silver tip of an arrow as its Rider draws it.

"Watch out!" I shout at Thayer, pulling him down behind the log with me.

The arrow whizzes toward us, hitting something nearby. I glance to my right to see it sticking out of the dead tree Cloveman, Xander, and Wolkenna are hiding behind.

"Attack!" King Vikmal commands, a sharp reminder for us all.

He shoots an arrow at the Empyrean Rider circling above, but misses. An enemy arrow blazes back, and we all crouch down as it strikes the dead tree in front of us. Another Empyrean steed and Rider attempt to land in the clearing, sending an arrow whizzing by us. Cloveman shoots back at the Rider, who narrowly dodges the assault.

I stand halfway and draw an arrow.

"Aluma!" Thayer grabs me.

Another arrow hits close beside us from the Rider circling above. I turn to meet Thayer's eyes, wide and full of fear.

Two more Empyrean Riders land in the open clearing. The Rider Cloveman missed dismounts and hides behind a log across from us, shooting arrow after arrow in our direction.

I wait for a pause in the stream of arrows and shoot at the Rider behind the log. I miss, and another arrow speeds right back at us.

More Empyrean Riders land. They dismount and shield themselves behind the fallen trees. Arrows volley around us. We try to keep up, shooting back in quick succession. But the six of us just aren't enough.

One of our arrows takes a Rider out before he dismounts. Another Rider fires his weapon from the sky, then falls from his saddle after Cloveman sends an arrow straight into his chest. His steed flies off, and my gaze follows its path as it disappears into the empty, dark sky.

I shift my focus to the fight here on the ground. Three more Empyrean steeds are landing in the clearing, slowing their speed. A wave of arrows comes rushing at us, but we dodge and duck. After a moment, the barrage comes to a halt, and I risk a peek over the top of the log. The Empyrean steeds fold in their wings as the Riders dismount. I squint, attempting to make out their faces.

I recognize *all* of them.

Barston Frost and Zarshona Mund draw their swords as the Rider behind them dismounts—Prince Sutagus Molacus.

I duck behind the log again, peering over at Thayer and King Vikmal. "Sutagus. He's here."

Everything in the clearing goes silent. And for a split second, I foolishly believe that the battle might be over, that the killing has finally ceased. But then I realize it's only because everyone is out of arrows.

The sound of steel blades being drawn echoes throughout the clearing, and my sense of peace passes as quickly as it came. King Vikmal moves out from behind the protection of the log, his sword outstretched in front of him.

I rise from the ground, my weapon in hand.

Across the way, someone charges at Vikmal. The king yells out as the stranger's face comes into view—a Rider I don't recognize, maybe a little older than me. Vikmal barrels toward the young man, both their blades glistening in the moonlight. I glance into Thayer's fear-filled eyes once more. He stands with his sword in front of him, his hands trembling. Wolkenna, Xander, and Cloveman wait with their swords readied as well.

I take a deep breath and dash around the dead tree, gripping my sword, preparing myself to come face-to-face with our enemies.

 FORTY–SIX

The clanging of steel vibrates through my body as my sword meets the blade of an Empyrean Rider. Battle screams echo out as we all clash together, a tidal wave hitting land.

The young man across from me is swift, matching my every move. He grits his teeth as he swings his sword, his eyes wide with anger. I block each strike, one after the other.

I step back, and then I'm stumbling—tripping backward onto the waterlogged ground. My body freezes as he lifts his sword to strike me down.

It's over.

Then the young man goes still, bloodied steel emerging from his chest. The blade withdraws, and he crumbles to his knees, revealing Thayer standing behind him. Blood drips from Thayer's sword as he pulls it back to his side. He reaches out his free hand to me, expressionless and no longer trembling.

My hand takes his, and I'm on my feet again, sword readied.

I turn in a circle as the moonlight glints off clashing steel. Cloveman dodges Barston Frost's advance. Xander and Wolkenna strike at Frille and Nuser—Wolkenna's fellow recruits from Galghesworp.

365

Prince Sutagus and King Vikmal lock their swords like two silver bulls butting their horns together.

"Behind you!" Thayer shouts as he fights off a young man.

I twist around as another Empyrean Rider charges me. I brace, holding my sword out in place. He lifts his blade high to strike. I drop to my knees, slicing through the side of his abdomen as he passes. He crashes to the ground and doesn't move again, the swamp bloodying beneath him.

I catch my breath, slowing it as best I can. A feverish chill runs through me as I glance up to find a pair of piercing golden eyes staring straight at me.

Zarshona Mund.

My hands clench my sword as she twirls her blade around in perfect loops.

"Aluma Banks," she sneers. "Are you ready to die, *traitor*?"

I raise my sword again. "To stop the darkness, yes." My heart thumps in my chest as we circle each other.

Zarshona smirks. "You can't stop what's coming. No one can. Not you." She pauses, inching closer. "And not your father."

I step forward. "I'm still standing, aren't I?"

"You'd think good old Lermyn Githah would've seen this coming. It's a shame, really."

"And why is that?" I ask, my grip tightening.

She huffs. "What, he didn't tell you all about me? I'm disappointed."

I wait for her next words, my nostrils flaring.

"You must know by now that you're in good company," she says, arching an eyebrow. "You're not the *only* Light Keeper here." She gives me a wicked grin and strikes.

Her sword hits mine, reverberating through my body. I pull away, whipping my sword in an arc. She ducks, missing the sting of my blade by mere inches. She swings low at my legs. I jump, narrowly avoiding her strike, landing squarely out of her reach.

"You're no Light Keeper," I tell her, my eyes narrowing. "We're supposed to *protect* the light, not ally ourselves with darkness." I shift into a crouch, watching as she moves around me like a ring of fire.

"We all do what we have to." She charges again. I dodge. She turns, and our swords dance together to a sinister song of steel clangs. Our faces meet, separated only by our blades.

"You've gotten better," Zarshona says grudgingly. "But you still don't have what it takes to defeat me."

"I have to," I whisper through gritted teeth. *"I have no choice."*

She pushes off with her sword against mine. Her expression is stone-cold. No more smirks.

Xander runs toward us. Zarshona's eyes narrow as she turns on her heels, swinging her sword. Xander's blade meets hers. Zarshona twists back to strike me. I block her advance. Xander and I circle her as she twists and leans, striking our swords. But despite all my training, she's still too fast.

The sting of her blade slices across my left arm as I slash her thigh. She stumbles backward, gaping at the gash on her leg. I keep my hands firm on my sword and glance at my arm, relieved to see that the cut is shallow.

Zarshona lifts her chin. Her eyes are wild—on fire. She lifts her blade and charges me and Xander, her leg bleeding heavily as she does. She swings, striking Xander on his side. He tumbles to the ground.

She turns to me and attacks again. I lean as far as I can to my right, turning my head as her blade nearly grazes the left side of my face. I lose my balance and tumble to the ground, dropping my sword.

The muddy ground engulfs me, holding me down. Zarshona's blade meets my throat, pressing hard enough that I think I feel myself bleed. "Let's stop this charade," she says.

I glare at her, lifting my chin defiantly.

"It doesn't have to end this way," She keeps her eyes on mine. "You can join us."

"I won't," I challenge back, my voice cracking.

She shakes her head. "Silly girl. You could have it all. Darkness has its perks, you know."

Behind her, Xander is back on his feet. He's holding his sword, ready to strike Zarshona from behind.

I exhale. "Wait—you're right," I tell her. "I'll join you."

I give Xander a slight nod, my eyes willing him not to kill her, but render her useless. But he's already thinking the same way. We don't want to kill. We just want to survive. Zarshona's eyes narrow as she catches me cheating a glance at Xander—right before he brings the butt of his sword down on her head.

She falls to the ground, out cold.

I roll to my side and grab my sword, jumping to my feet. My hands shake as I nod to Xander. She'll be dealt with later.

"Father!" Wolkenna's scream echoes out in the clearing.

I turn to see King Vikmal with his back pinned against a fallen dead tree, his sword on the ground. Prince Sutagus stands in front of him, his blade outstretched. Sutagus smiles wickedly as King Vikmal looks daggers into his eyes.

Wolkenna slices Nuser's leg and pushes him out of the way as she takes off at full speed toward her father. I'm right behind her.

Prince Sutagus plunges his sword straight into the king's chest.

I stop in my tracks, falling to my knees, my eyes wide with horror.

"No!" Wolkenna yells, continuing to race toward her father.

The prince rips his blade out of King Vikmal. And the king slumps forward.

Prince Sutagus turns and surveys the area. Cloveman is on top of Barston Frost, his fist making contact with Barston's face. The prince leers in my direction, peering past me to see Zarshona's still body. His burning eyes meet mine, and then he's charging at me.

I'm motionless—*frozen*—everything moving outside of time. Every sound blurred. Every movement clear and slow.

Wolkenna reaches her father, taking his head into her hands as she yells out, but I can't hear what she says. Thayer reaches Wolkenna and King Vikmal, shock filling his face. Barston Frost pushes Cloveman off and slices him on the side, sending him down. Xander strikes Frille and slides behind Barston, his blade striking him across the back. Barston falls to the ground as Xander helps Cloveman to his feet.

My eyes refocus as the prince draws nearer to me, his eyes burning with rage. Thayer waves his arms in the distance. His mouth is moving—he's shouting.

"Run!" Thayer's shouts return to full speed and volume. *"Aluma—run!"*

I snap back, pushing myself up to my feet. The prince is almost within striking distance, running at full speed.

My legs carry me as fast as they can back into the tree passage, the sounds of my ragged breath and pounding heart echoing in my ears. I exit the tunnel of trees and run down the root staircase into the domed clearing, turning over my shoulder as the prince leaves the tunnel and enters the enclosed space at the top of the stairs.

The steeds stand together, stomping their hooves. I run at them, waving my hands in the air.

"Go!" I yell out.

They run up the wide stairs, briefly blocking Sutagus's path to me. But in a moment they're all gone—all but Cashel, who circles back around to my side.

The prince charges down the root staircase, then slows his prowl as he takes in his surroundings. I step away from him, moving closer to the dead jekler, my sword outstretched.

Sutagus stares at me, another wicked smile creeping across his demented face. "There's nowhere to run now."

A haunting howl echoes out through the woods. And another— and another.

Jeklers.

The prince scans the clearing, his eyes darting around wildly, attempting to find the source of the howls. He looks back at me, and then at the dead jekler by my feet. I glance down at the beast's body; my saddlebag with the relic of light hidden inside is visible from where I stand.

Prince Sutagus cocks his head to one side. "You *know* this place?"

My eyes stay on him as I step behind the rotting carcass, closer to the beast's legs.

Another chorus of howls rings out, closer than before. Cashel steps in place, nudging me with his muzzle.

"Why don't we have a talk?" Prince Sutagus suggests, lowering his sword as he moves closer. "I have so many questions for you."

"*Talk*—the same way you just did with King Vikmal?" I say through gritted teeth.

"You see, Aluma, I can't figure out why you're on *their* side." He comes to a standstill, wiping his blade clean of blood—King Vikmal's blood.

I stand my ground, watching as he admires his now spotless sword.

"Your father, your brother. Your *mother*." He smirks, and a knot twists in my stomach. "Your whole family. They're *all* in Uladmond, in Tarmensil, safe from what's to come," he says, edging closer again. "I can't figure out why you'd want to be on the losing side. A Light Keeper like you would be much better off in a place of protection. Don't you think?"

"I think *you*, King Breasal, and anyone else who releases darkness in this land are the *only* ones I need protection from."

He creeps closer, step after step. My eyes fall on the dead jekler in front of me. The warmth from the relic pulses out.

The prince raises an eyebrow. "*You didn't.*" He chuckles, giving me a dubious look. "You found a relic of light—and you brought it *here*?" He moves closer to the spine side of the jekler, studying it for a moment.

A low howl calls out from the tree passage. The prince's eyes widen.

"You're a clever girl," he says, peering back at me. "But you're sorely mistaken if you think you're leaving here with anyone but me. Please understand, I made a promise to your dear mother. She's been so eager to see you again, *little Lumi*."

My breath escapes me. There's my old nickname again. The prince knows my mother? She's alive, and she wants to see me?

It's a trick—*it must be.*

I stand straighter, pushing the thoughts of my mother away. My eyes narrow at the prince as the relic warms at my feet.

Sutagus's lips curl up on the sides. "Give me the relic, and we'll leave this poor excuse of a kingdom. Together."

My head shakes slowly. "You'll never take my light. You'll never take anyone's light again. So long as I can help it."

A series of low growls rips through the clearing. A set of glowing eyes, and another, and another appear at the top of the staircase, blocking our only way out.

Jeklers.

Finally.

Somehow, seeing them now, they're far less frightening than the man standing before me.

Prince Sutagus turns as two of the jeklers move down the stairs, their bodies covered in coarse, wired hair. Their bared yellow fangs, dripping with...

Blood.

A shiver of fear runs through me. The others—*Thayer.* They may not have made it out before the jeklers came.

Cashel snorts and stomps his hooves behind me. My eyes shift from the dead jekler to Sutagus. He holds his sword out with shaky hands as the two jeklers edge closer to him. *He's afraid.* And he should be.

In one quick movement, I bend and lift the dead jekler's rotting flesh with my sword, grabbing the saddlebag with my other hand. The relic radiates warmth. I sheathe my blade with as little noise as possible and swing myself onto Cashel with one arm, holding the saddlebag in the other. My legs squeeze Cashel, and we take off at full speed toward the hedges, away from the jeklers and Prince Sutagus.

"Aluma!" Sutagus yells, and I glance back. His eyes are fixed on the jeklers as they inch closer and closer to him, ready to attack. "You're going to regret this!"

Cashel's hooves leave the ground, his wings tucked in by his sides. The prince shouts again behind us, followed by the sound of a jekler whimpering.

We land on the other side of the first hedge and continue to the second.

The snarls get louder. And louder. The prince screams out in pain. And right then, I know there's no way I'll hear another sound from him, ever again.

I don't turn around.

We take the second jump and land without falter. Cashel continues to gallop toward the next hedge as I open the saddlebag to retrieve the relic of light.

I still don't hear Sutagus. He must be dead—he has to be.

I slide open the top of the relic. The light beams out toward the low tree cover, the same way it did the last time I was here.

The third jump is only a few strides away. The tree cover opens above us, spreading apart to release the light into the dark sky.

"Fly Cashel—" I yell out. *"Fly!"*

Cashel expands his wings, flapping them hard as we reach the third hedge. His hooves leave the ground as we fly over the jagged thorns—and up higher toward the now-open tree cover. Howl after howl rings out as we clear the tops of the trees. I slide the relic closed, and the light vanishes back inside. The branches beneath us re-form over the tree canopy again, mending together like thick threads of bark. My heart is thundering in my chest as I secure my saddlebag in place, the relic stowed safely within.

We fly over the group of trees that must make up the hidden passageway leading to the main clearing—to the *battlefield*. The moonlight reflects off the bloodied ground ahead. I avert my eyes, not wanting to see the devastation.

"Aluma!" a voice calls out. I turn to my right to see Thayer flying toward me on Yulla.

"Thayer!" I breathe a sigh of relief.

"Are you okay?" he asks, his voice hoarse.

"Yes—I'm so glad you're safe." I want to reach out to him. To feel his warmth. "Where is everyone else?" My eyes dart around, realizing he's flying alone in the sky.

"Flown back to Nammden...with King Vikmal's body," Thayer says, grief filling his eyes as he looks off in the direction of the city.

I exhale, dropping my head. *He didn't make it.*

"They found Uladmond's relic of darkness, too," he tells me. "King Vikmal must have taken it from the prince without him knowing, before he—"

I swallow hard, trying not to think about our loss. "Prince Sutagus is dead."

Thayer's eyes widen. "What do we do now?"

"Now we bring this light to the Green to try to stop the darkness. And I'm going to tell the king of Uladmond it's time to end this," I say, feeling the warmth of the relic calling out for me again. "Then we'll bring this relic back to Laithlann—where it belongs. Balance is almost restored."

Balance *must* be restored.

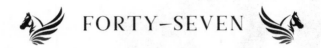

FORTY–SEVEN

As we fly toward the dark cloud looming over Cintrenia, the temperature drops. The darkness encircles our broken city, leaving it frozen in time. The relic of light in my saddlebag pulses warmer and warmer, as if it's trying to reach out to the darkness that lies ahead.

I glance over at Thayer. His shoulders are slumped forward, and he's barely watching where Yulla is flying. Cuts with splatters of dried blood cover his hands and face.

I know how he feels. I want this all to be over, too.

But it's not over. There's more left to be done. The prince is gone, but the king of Uladmond must still be reasoned with. The relics must be returned to their kingdoms, and I can only hope this relic of light will heal what's been done to Cintrenia.

We slow to a hover near the city. The darkness stretches out in front of us, a black roof capping the top of Cintrenia. Below, near the borders of the city, the cloud seems to be slowly circling, like a massive tornado, moving at a snail's pace.

I dart a glance at Thayer. "Do we just fly straight in?"

"That's what we did before," he says. "But it looks worse now… like it's growing."

I pretend not to be bothered by that statement—*it's growing*. My eyes narrow as if I'm concentrating on my plan. But I don't have much of a plan, other than to get in, release the light, and hope it works.

"If anything happens to me, protect the light and get out," I say.

Thayer turns to me. "You *are* the light. And we're getting out of this together."

My lips turn up, and despite the cold air from the ominous shadowy matter, a sense of calm falls over me. I nod and urge Cashel forward, Thayer and Yulla flying beside us as we head into the foreboding darkness.

It's freezing when we enter the black cloud. Almost like a switch has been turned off—as if a fire has just been extinguished. The frigid air travels through my nostrils and down into my lungs, coating them with a chill, making it difficult to inhale. I'm cold from the inside out, and I know instinctively that no one can survive these conditions for long—including me, even with the light. The darkness swirling around us isn't wind, but matter. It feels hollow. As if there's no density to the sky. As if there's no air for our steeds' wings to push away.

A void.

Cashel struggles to fly straight ahead, his wings flapping faster than ever before, as if he's swatting at nothing. The air *is* thin. He stretches his wings out, and we coast down toward the Empyrean arena, the only place visible through the dark clouds swirling around us.

As we near the arena, the streets come into view. They're completely empty, as if everyone thought a violent storm was approaching and ran inside just before the darkness hit. No one would have known—no one *could* have known what was about to happen.

Maybe it's better that way.

We swoop into the arena, gliding past the empty seats. The darkness is denser here—thick, like soot. I can barely see the ground when Cashel's hooves touch down. I reach back, placing my hand over the saddlebag, attempting to absorb some warmth from the relic of light.

"Thayer?" I call out. A moment passes, and I hear the *whoosh* of a steed's wings.

"I'm here," he says.

It's nearly silent. My breath. Thayer's breath. And our steeds' hooves against the ground. That's it.

I pull the relic of light out from the saddlebag and slide off Cashel.

Thayer dismounts Yulla, walking stiffly. "It's so cold," he says, rubbing his palms together as his breath forms in front of his face. "Do you feel it? The lag?"

"I do," I tell him, slowly lifting my foot from the ground, feeling as if I'm walking through mud. Everything feels heavy, like I could just lie down and fall asleep, and everything would be all right. But I know better.

We need to hurry.

Thayer glances at the relic in my grasp. His brows furrow. "How does this work?"

"I just have to open it," I say, warmth flowing from the relic to my fingers, through my arms, quelling the shiver erupting from my veins. "Feel it—it's warm."

Thayer touches the top of the relic. "Ow!" He jerks his hand away, shaking it out.

"What's wrong?" I ask, alarmed.

"It's burning! How are you touching that thing?"

My bare hands hold the relic, its warmth moving through me like a trickle of sunshine.

"Strange," I say. It's not hot to me. Not at all. Then I remember how King Vikmal wore gloves when he took the relic of light from me before. The gloves weren't to protect the relic, they were to protect himself. Others can't handle the relic of light like I can—they're not Light Keepers.

"I'm sorry. I didn't know," I say, watching as Thayer tends to his burn. "Are you okay?"

He grimaces, but nods. "It just stings."

"The pain will go away soon," I say, my fingers finding an edge on the top of the relic. "Shield your eyes."

Thayer lifts his forearm to his brow.

This better work.

I slide open the relic, and the light bursts out in a silent flash. White rays decorate the dark, swirling clouds, pushing through them until the light shoots out the other side. My whole body warms in an instant, and an energy dances inside of me.

The arena lights switch on in quick succession—*click, click, click*—adding to the glow emanating from the relic. I keep the top open for a few moments longer, until there's nothing but a bright white sheen coating everything around us—a blanket of light and warmth.

Finally, I slide it closed. The light continues to flow out until the top snaps shut beneath my fingers.

"You can open your eyes now," I say. There's no darkness left. Not even a sliver. The dark cyclone that was hovering over Cintrenia is gone, revealing the starry night sky above us.

"How in the...?" Thayer's eyes go wide, the cuts on his face healed. He looks at his just-burnt hand, then lifts the foot that was injured. "It's gone—the pain is gone," he says, studying his hand again, as if it were some kind of trick.

I smile gratefully. The relic healed Thayer. And it did even more than I'd hoped for the rest of Cintrenia.

Thank the stars.

"Did it work for everyone else?" Thayer scans the open arena.

I shrug, turning in a small circle. "There's only one way to find out."

I place the relic in my saddlebag, and we ride our steeds through the large arena tunnel, the same one they took my father out of in the medical karrier. We exit to the outside of the arena and curve around the road to the front of the structure, where all the twinkling city lights come into view. They're all back on.

"I think it worked..." Thayer whispers.

My eyes dart left to right as a few people emerge from the fronts of the shops, their gazes trained to the sky. It's as if they're searching for the darkness that had—unbeknownst to them—taken everyone here into a motionless slumber. One they would never have awoken from, if it weren't for the light. I reach back to the saddlebag, checking for the warmth of the relic. It pulses out, as if it has more to give.

Good. *More* light is what I need to save my father.

"I wonder if they know they were frozen," Thayer muses, glancing over at me.

"Let's hope not." There's no time to explain to a whole city something I can barely understand myself. It's bad enough the two of us are riding down the main street on steeds. At least it's nighttime, and most people will probably just sleep it off.

"My parents…" Thayer says as we near the Tarmen Bridge. "Do you think the light reached all the way to our farm?"

"Let's go take a look," I say, raising my eyebrows. He nods.

We continue over the bridge, picking up the pace when we reach the outskirts of Cintrenia. We pass Turtle Hill, and my home comes into view. For a moment, I want to turn Cashel down the road to our house. But I know there's no one there—it's an empty shell.

We reach the Pridfirth farm, agreeing that Thayer will ride ahead and check in through the windows. If his parents are all right and they spot him home, they'll have a cartload of questions to spring on him—questions we don't have time to answer. A few minutes later, Thayer returns on Yulla, a smile on his face, and I know in an instant the light reached his parents, too.

"Let's make sure nothing like this ever happens again," Thayer suggests.

I nod and smile, squeezing Cashel into a run. Maybe this is what it means to be a Light Keeper? It feels good to heal—to help. Cashel stretches out his wings, flapping them as he gallops. The dirt from the road crunches beneath us, and then it's silence, except for the whooshing of our steeds' wings. And we're back in the air, flying over the once-again sparkling city of Cintrenia.

∼

A blizzard of emotions fills me as we soar over the snowcapped Uladmond Mountains, following the Tarmen Canal toward Tarmensil. I'm exhausted mentally and physically, and I'm scared of what's to come.

But this time, I'm not afraid to be seen when I arrive at the capital—I *want* the king to find me. I want to settle this, once and for all.

As we pass the border of the mountains, the pale moonlight paints shadows over the open valley. The empty barn we hid in before comes into view. It's a small marker of where we've been, and a reminder of where we don't want to return: hidden, on the outside, fighting our way in to take back what's ours.

My father. Rinehart. The stolen relics.

This is the last time. I'll make sure of it.

"We're flying straight in?" Thayer asks, his voice tinged with fear, his cheeks flushed from the cold air.

"We are," I say, leaning closer to Cashel's neck as we speed up.

I glance down, noticing the part of the Tarmen Canal where Gattacan and I held hands and leapt into the icy water. A shiver runs through my body at the memory of swirling around in the strong current, and the pain that coursed through me when we failed to rescue my father from the palace. But there's no need to dwell on it—this time, I've got the light I need. And I'm not leaving until this is all sorted out.

We fly high over the wall, and the tunnel it obscures. From this distance, no Watchers will spot us, let alone shoot us down.

"What are you going to do?" Thayer asks over the sound of the wind.

I turn to see his nervous expression.

"I'm going to tell the king that the prince is dead. Then I will demand Cintrenia be released from Uladmondian rule."

He raises his eyebrows. "The king will never—"

"He'll have no choice. The rest of us are prepared to fight if he doesn't." All of us except for Vikmal. My head drops. King Vikmal. I can't imagine the pain Gattacan and Wolkenna, Queen Delna and Nadie are all feeling right now.

We follow the canal leading through the gleaming city, all the way to the ocean. Waves crash off in the distance, breaking against the rocky shore. Briny vapor coats my face as we fly overhead, the harbor below filled with giant water karriers—bigger than I've ever seen. And more in one place than I thought possible.

"Through there," I say, pointing my hand out past Cashel's head, toward the side of the palace. "There's an opening through that large gate—do you see it?"

Thayer squints. "I do—"

"The closer we get, the better."

There's not a person in sight as we fly toward the gate. No Watchers on the palace walls. No Uladmondians on a late-night stroll. No one. It *is* nighttime, but the lack of people still seems strange—particularly the lack of Watchers.

We swoop through the opening and down into the arena of sorts that fills the space between the stable and the palace. I land Cashel, Yulla touching down behind us. Thayer looks around at the darkened arena.

"I bet Darwith is in there," I whisper, gesturing toward the stable. I'm sure Kase brought him back to the prince—back to the same stable where I saw my mother's *stolen* horse, Blossom. Where Gattacan and I found the relics of darkness under the tack room.

"Wait here," I say, glancing at Thayer.

His eyes narrow, and he gives me a reluctant nod.

I leave my weapons attached to my saddle and take the relic with me. There are no lights on except for a few dim exterior lamps over the stable door. I walk through, glancing side to side at each stall along either side of the aisle, remembering where Blossom was—up on the left from this direction.

A whinny comes from ahead.

I freeze. I know that sound.

"Darwith," I whisper.

Another whinny. A hoof kicking a stall door.

My feet speed into action, propelling me to the end of the aisle. Darwith's black head peers out from the top of the stall as he whickers at me. I slide the door open, and he moves closer, rubbing his muzzle against my arm.

A slow clap echoes out in the stable. Bright lights flash on, one by one, leading back to the opening from which I came.

"Well done, little Lumi..." a slithery voice echoes out from a shadowed figure.

A sourness fills my stomach, bubbling up into my throat.

It can't be...

The final lights click on over the shadowed figure, and I feel like I'm going to be sick.

Prince Sutagus.

I shake my head in denial. "But you can't—"

The prince chuckles as he slinks closer. Darwith stomps his hoof in the dirt beside me. I twist around to the opposite end of the stable to find another Watcher stepping forward with an outstretched sword. The look in his eyes says *don't even think about running, you fool.*

There's no way out.

I turn back to find Sutagus even closer than before. I must be dreaming—this has to be a nightmare.

Wake up. Wake up.

"You know, I owe you my gratitude," Prince Sutagus says.

My eyes widen. Not a cut, bruise, or scrape on him. He's unscathed. He's *alive.*

"How did you..." I whisper, unable to finish my question.

"How did I *survive?*" The prince cocks his head. "Funny thing. When you use the light, it works on anything—or *anyone*—that's injured around you."

My jaw drops as I realize what I've done: *I saved the person I was attempting to destroy.*

"Oh, you didn't know? I assumed you'd know—unless no one told you how it all works. Perhaps your father should have told you who—*what* you are."

I move behind Darwith's neck, hoping he can somehow shield me from the reality that's threatening to sink its teeth into my bones.

The prince sighs. "That's how the light works—it can heal what's living, but it can't revive what's already dead." He raises his eyebrows. "You can't be selective with *whom* or what it heals. No, you'd have to learn to *control* the light for that—something you could learn here, if you were interested." He opens his hands out to his sides and grins.

I stand, dumbstruck.

"Not what you were hoping for, I see."

"You were dead…" I whisper. "I heard the jeklers."

He lifts a finger, wags it. "Ah—first free lesson: always check to make sure your opponent is actually dead." He smiles smugly, lowering his hand. "I wasn't dead. Despite your little plan of leaving me to be devoured by those beasts—quite clever, really."

Over Sutagus's shoulder, I see two Watchers shoving Thayer into the stable, their blades at his back. Thayer looks at me, an apologetic expression on his face.

"*Tsk tsk—so* many traitors these days," Prince Sutagus says, glancing at Thayer.

"Let him go," I demand.

"Or what?" the prince growls, peering back at me. "Or you'll use your light?" He snorts. "Apparently you've failed to notice *we* have the darkness. And as much as light can heal, the darkness can destroy." He scrunches his nose like a beast that's about to attack, then pulls out a smaller black box from his uniform jacket.

A relic of darkness. Ivernister's relic of darkness. Three tall lines upright. The last time I saw it was the day my father fell from the sky.

"It's amazing the destruction something so…*small* can unleash." He looks me over and smirks, placing the relic back in his jacket. "Especially when it can be *directed*—by someone like me."

I stare into his icy blue eyes, frigid like the darkness that was swirling over Cintrenia. "What do you want?"

"What do I want?" he echoes, giving me a vexed look. "What *I* want is for *you* to learn your place. Now, give us the light, and maybe we'll let you live." He peers at the relic in my hand, then shrugs, as if he's fine with either outcome—me living or dying.

I squeeze the relic tighter. "No—you've destroyed enough," I spit at him. "I've seen what the darkness does—how it destroys."

He smiles crookedly, like he's about to snarl at me.

"Hm, charming," he says, slapping his hands together. "Let's go see what the king thinks about this whole ordeal—shall we?" He snaps his fingers in the air, and the King's Watchers prod Thayer back to the opening of the stable.

I turn to see the other Watcher at my back approaching me and Darwith.

I push Darwith back into the stall. "I'm sorry," I whisper, shutting him inside. "I'll come back for you."

The Watcher stares at me, his gaze hardened like the steel of his blade. He edges closer with his sword, forcing me to move.

My body tenses as I follow Sutagus and the others toward the open stable door. I squeeze the relic to my side. There's a flicker of warmth, and I wonder—is he telling the truth? Can I not attack with light…in any way? I kick myself when I imagine how I could use a relic of darkness right about now. *Darkness has its perks*, Zarshona said. I don't want to destroy anything, but at least I'd have a weapon to fight back with.

Dawn is breaking as we step outside the stable, bathing the open arena in a soft morning glow. Thayer stands guarded by two Watchers, next to Cashel and Yulla, while Prince Sutagus waits for me to draw nearer to them.

A gate opens on the far end of the arena, and a line of King's Watchers march out, followed by the king—the person I'm here to speak with. They move closer to us, their boots crunching against the ground, like bones breaking underfoot.

Another person walks through the gate, and my stomach knots.

My brother. *Kase.*

He doesn't look my way, which is a smart move. Even from this distance, my eyes feel like they could freeze him under my glacial stare.

Moments pass, and another face emerges through the gate—a face I thought I'd forgotten, but one I recognize immediately. My heart clenches as an avalanche of emotions crumbles over me, stealing my breath away.

My mother.

FORTY-EIGHT

The prince grabs my shoulder and forces me closer to the king. My mother's bright green eyes gaze off into the distance, cold and empty, not noticing me. She wears a proper Uladmondian outfit, a dress fit for royalty. She looks like one of them—she *is* one of them. My chest expands sharply as anger sweeps over me, followed by a sense of betrayal.

All this time…she's been *here*. My hands grip the relic tighter as my mind races back to when I was a child, to when she left our family. I imagine her living a lavish life here in Tarmensil—with *Sutagus*, of all people. The most sinister person I've ever met. All those years my father tried to comfort me, telling me he didn't know where my mother was, and she was with *him*. The vile prince of Uladmond. I'm not so sure whether my father knew all along, or if he truly was in the dark about her whereabouts, too. I can only hope, for his sake, that it was the latter.

My hands clench into fists as my eyes trail to my mother's side. To my brother. He has a similar distant expression on his face—no remorse. None at all.

Traitor.

"What a wonderful family reunion," Sutagus says with a smile, gesturing to my mother, my brother, and me. "But wait—what would a family reunion be without the whole bunch?" He grins wickedly and waves his hand.

Four Watchers emerge through the gate, pushing a large, clear box. Inside of it, a swirling dark matter circulates around something—*someone*. It's a cage on wheels. As the Watchers push the clear cage closer, the swirl of darkness moves enough to reveal my father's blue eyes, motionless and full of sadness.

"No!" I lunge forward, and in an instant there's a pair of strong Watchers holding me back.

"Would you look at what we have here?" The prince ambles over to the glass cage. "Two Light Keepers, only one of them is not so *light* at the moment." He snorts.

My mother and my brother don't flinch. Their faces remain stony—just like their hearts. How can they be so cold?

"Why are you doing this?" I glare at the prince. The darkness continues to swirl around my father like an endless cyclone, keeping him frozen in time.

I glance at the relic warming in my hands. I could save him—right now.

"I wouldn't bother," Sutagus says, as if reading my mind, his eyes on the relic. "This here is a specially designed contraption. No light can penetrate it. You'd only be wasting precious resources."

"Aluma," King Breasal says, stepping forward.

I freeze at the sound of the king's voice.

"You have the light," the king says, nodding to the relic. "And I hear you're a special young lady." He looks to his left at my father and turns back to me. "But you seem to be a lot like your father—*stubborn*. And stubbornness won't resolve anything. Not here, not now."

I glance over at Thayer, now restrained by a Watcher. He shakes his head slowly. I huff as I stare at my feet, my body tensing, my fists tightening.

"You must choose your path," the king says. "You must decide who you want to fight for." He glances over his shoulder at my brother and my mother. "Not everyone gets this choice. But you're different, aren't you, Aluma?"

I don't move an inch. But I've already decided.

Prince Sutagus walks over to my mother and stands by her side. My nostrils flare as I turn away, ashamed. I'm ashamed *for her*. I don't even want to look at her face. My eyes move to my father, still stuck in time. It shouldn't be him in that cage.

"And if I give you the light…" I meet the king's gaze. "What will you do to my father?"

"Ah, negotiations." The king dips his chin in my direction. "That's progress."

"You have to let him go first." I won't give up the relic—it belongs to the Laithlanners. But the king doesn't have to know that yet.

"I would consider releasing your father…under *one* condition."

I nod, keeping my eyes on the king.

"*You* must stay here, to expand your abilities and train. You must fight for us."

The relic pulses, warm in my hands. And for a quick moment, I imagine opening it. Is Sutagus lying? Would the relic release my father, or would I be left with a drained, useless box?

I can't chance it—not now.

My decision is clear. I'll stay. I'll do what I have to in order to set my father free. I can deal with the repercussions later.

"Let him go now, and I'll stay here," I tell him.

The king stands motionless, considering my offer. Thayer is staring at me, his eyes full of pain as he drops his head.

The king nods to one of the Watchers beside him. He hands the Watcher a small vial, much like the one King Vikmal gave me to wake my father with. And I realize—both of them are wearing gloves.

The Watcher inserts the vial into a slot in the glass cage. A bright light pierces through the dark matter, and in an instant, the darkness surrounding my father dissipates. The box opens, and my father peers out at me, his eyes wide—*alert*.

"Aluma!" he shouts, stumbling out of the box. The Watcher grabs his arm and leads him over to me.

My heart quickens as I exhale. He's safe. He's healed.

I turn to the king, giving him an affirming nod. "And what of this relic? It belongs in Laithlann." My grip tightens. "The same goes for the relic of light that belongs to Ivernister—to Cintrenia. It must be returned. Balance must be restored." I dart a look in my brother's direction. He's the one who stole Ivernister's relic after I found it in the Gray Forest.

The king tilts his head to one side. He's considering it.

"Cintrenia belongs to *us*," Sutagus interjects from behind the king.

"Cintrenia belongs to its people—not *you*," I snap back, my words like daggers.

Sutagus chuckles, glancing at the king. "I told you about this one. She's got some nerve."

I glare up at the prince before turning back to the Watcher escorting my father to me. I hurry to my father's side, wrapping my arms around him. "Father..."

His blue eyes are glazed over with tears. "I'm here," he whispers before releasing me from his embrace.

The prince moves to stand beside the king. "You *will* hand the relic of light over to us," Sutagus says to me.

"Do *not* speak for me," the king says under his breath, glaring at his brother. "*I* am your king."

The prince's eyes are full of rage as he takes a few steps backward, standing closer to my mother. His skin reddens as he burns holes through the king's back.

"I have considered your proposal," the king says, turning to me and my father. "Your desire for balance is..." He pauses, as if he's looking for the right words. "Most admirable. And something I'm realizing our kingdom must now strive to attain." He pauses, almost turning to glance back at Sutagus, but instead keeping his gaze on me. "Something my younger brother would do well to learn."

A look of disdain crosses Sutagus's face at the king's words. He slides his hand into his uniform jacket. I adjust my grip on the relic of light, prepared to open it if the prince pulls out the relic of darkness.

But instead of the relic, a sliver of the morning sun catches the curved edge of a sharp dagger blade.

In a heartbeat, the prince plunges it through the king's back.

King Breasal's eyes widen in shock and pain.

Sutagus wedges the blade in deeper, straight into his brother's heart. He twists the knife, and the king drops to the ground, blood dripping from his mouth.

I choke back a scream of horror, and my father pulls me into his chest as the prince ends his own brother's life. The King's Watchers stand motionless, not even bothering to react. My mother and brother also remain calm, as if this was all expected—as if it was *planned*.

"I relieve you of your crown," Sutagus says as he tears his bloodied dagger out of his brother, a contemptuous smile crossing his face. *"I'm the king now."*

FORTY-NINE

Sutagus steps over the king's lifeless body. All of my muscles clench. Any ideas I may have had before are all useless now. I glance at my father, then back at the relic. My father shakes his head as slowly as possible, urging me not to act.

"I'm not as lenient as my big brother," the prince says, glancing at the king's corpse. "He was never meant to be king. He was merely born first. It's unfortunate I had to wait this long." He puffs his chest out and looks at me, his eyes aglow.

My father squeezes my shoulder as Sutagus inches closer to us.

"Now...*give. me. the. relic*," Sutagus growls.

"Never," I say through clenched teeth, clutching the relic with all my might.

The prince's expression turns cold. "Suit yourself." He pulls a pair of gloves from his uniform pocket, taking his time to slide each one on. Then he flicks a hand to the Watchers behind us, giving them a nod.

Two Watchers tap their blades against my father, forcing him to move forward, and away from me.

"Father!" I attempt to follow him as another Watcher draws his sword and holds it out, blocking my path.

The Watchers force my father past the prince, prodding him along with their blades. The prince looks over and waves his hand again, and the two Watchers leave my father to stand away from the rest of us. The Watchers step back with their swords held out as another of their number steps out from the group near the prince, a bow in hand.

"This is one of my finest archers," the prince says, his gaze on my father. "He *never* misses his mark." Sutagus raises an eyebrow, then steps over to me, opening his gloved hand. "I won't repeat myself again."

I pull the relic closer and meet my father's eyes trained on me from across the way.

"Don't give it to him, Aluma," my father says.

"*Shh*—she's a big girl. She can make her own decisions, no?" The prince holds his hand in the air, and the archer draws his arrow, aiming it straight at my father. Sutagus turns back to me. "Come on, little Lumi, I'm trying to give you a chance to make this right. You can still join us."

I shake my head in defeat, my eyes locked on my father, hoping he will forgive me. I have no choice but to let Sutagus take the relic if I want my father to live.

Sutagus steps closer, and out of the corner of my eye, I see him reaching for the relic in my hands. And then he's pulling on it, wrenching it from my grasp.

"No—" I say as the warmth leaves my fingertips.

My father's eyes widen and I mouth the words, *I'm sorry.*

"Now that wasn't so hard, was it?" Sutagus says, the sides of his mouth turning into an evil grin. He examines the relic in his gloved hands.

"Now, let my father go," I demand, my voice trembling.

Sutagus stares me in the eyes and nods to the Watchers. The archer lowers his bow, and the other two Watchers lower their swords. Thank the stars.

I sprint into my father's open arms. "I'm sorry," I whisper. "I had to—"

"Aluma," the prince calls out from behind me. "There's just one more thing."

I turn my head as the prince waves to the archer, and in an instant the archer lifts his bow and draws an arrow.

"On second thought," Sutagus says, his voice nonchalant, "we don't need any rebellious Light Keepers running around, now do we?"

Sutagus nods once, and the archer releases the arrow, straight at me.

"No!" my father yells out, twisting his body in front of me like a shield. He takes the hit—falling with his back to the ground.

"Father!" My heart pounds as I crouch beside him. An arrow sticks out of the middle of his chest. I glare at the prince, ready to charge him—*ready to kill.*

Sutagus sighs. "Well...that didn't go as planned."

"Don't," my father says, sensing my rage, his glossy eyes twinkling in the sunlight. He places his hand on top of mine, and a soothing warmth passes between us. "Revenge stems from darkness. It won't make you whole."

I hold my father's hand, squeezing it with all my might.

"You must get the light back..." He stares at me. "Take it far, far away from here—until it's safe to return."

I breathe in, but I'm not getting enough air.

"There's so much more...across the sea..." His voice grows fainter. "Fly from Nammden...north of the rising sun. You'll see..."

I hold on even tighter, grasping his fingers as his grip loosens. "No—don't leave me, Father—"

"I'm *so* proud of you. You're my shiny little girl..."

He tries to squeeze my hand once more, and I smile the best I can for him as his blue eyes tilt to the sky.

"Keep the light..." he whispers, and then his hand falls limp in mine.

My heart breaks, plunging me into a dark ocean of despair. I drop my head to his chest, as if I could will his heart to start beating again. Tears blur my vision—if only they had the power to wash everything away.

This can't be real.

But it *is*—he's gone.

My father is gone.

My head tilts to the sky. I want to scream. I want to wake up from this nightmare. Whizzing arrows fly past overhead, at everyone standing behind me, jolting me back to reality. At first I don't care where the arrows are coming from or where they're heading. I don't want to live.

I can't live now.

"Aluma!" Thayer yells from somewhere behind me.

I stand as the sounds of battle break out. But I'm in a daze—shocked. An Empyrean steed flies overhead, then another, and another. I turn as they swoop down toward the open arena, shooting arrow after arrow—at the Watchers, at Sutagus.

It's not the Cavalry.

A white Empyrean steed swoops closer, one that would stand out anywhere—Elro. Gattacan's black hair blows around his face as he peers down at me from the steed's back, his eyes dark as night. He aims another arrow and hits Sutagus in the chest.

Sutagus drops the relic of light as he falls to his knees. He looks around for a Watcher to protect him, to grab the relic—*the relic*—but they're all preoccupied with shooting back at the perpetrators in the sky, or fleeing.

This is my chance.

My whole body lurches forward as I sprint straight in Sutagus's direction. When I get close, I slide low on the ground, snatching the relic out of his reach. Then I pop up to my feet, running as fast as I can back toward my father's body.

Over my shoulder, the remaining Watchers create a human shield around Sutagus, carrying him to the gate as a steady stream of arrows continues to hit them, peeling away the prince's layers of protection. My mother and brother run through the gate just before the Watchers carry Sutagus in. The riders in the sky send arrow after arrow at the remaining Watchers while dodging their futile counterattacks.

I reach my father and crouch down beside him, the relic of light in my hands. My fingers find the top and I slide it open. There's a flash of light—I imagine it flowing straight to my father and nowhere else.

After a moment, I snap it shut, my eyes readjusting. My father is still lying there, the same as he was. Still gone.

Then I remember what Sutagus said: *It can heal what's living, but it can't revive what's already dead...*

I'm too late. It's over. He's not coming back.

I take a deep breath, lifting my father's hands to his heart, wishing I didn't have to leave him here—not like this. But then a Watcher is running straight at me, holding a sword outstretched.

"Goodbye," I whisper to my father, before turning and sprinting toward Cashel. Thayer is already on Yulla's back, ready to go. I look behind me as an arrow strikes the Watcher on my tail, sending him to the dirt.

When I near Thayer and the stable, I hear whinnies and snorts coming from inside.

Darwith.

I change my direction, making a beeline for the stable.

"Aluma!" Thayer calls out.

"I'm not leaving without Darwith!" I yell as I run through the open stable door. When I glance back, Gattacan, Wolkenna, and Xander are landing their steeds in the arena.

I race over to Darwith's stall and throw the door open. He canters out, exiting through the front. Outside, Gattacan is storming toward the gate to the palace courtyard—the same gate where Sutagus, my mother, and my brother retreated moments ago.

Darwith darts straight to my father, as if he could sense right where he was. My heart clenches as he pushes my father's lifeless hands with his muzzle.

"Darwith!" I call, running over to him.

Voices yell out from the gate as I reach Darwith and my father's body. More Watchers advance on us as Gattacan blazes forward, swinging his sword, striking one after another—a cyclone, tearing apart anything in its path.

"Aluma—hurry!" Thayer yells from behind me.

I look down at my father's body once more, knowing this is the last time I'll ever see him. He's utterly still, and somehow peaceful.

Blue eyes gazing at an endless sky. I imagine he's flying free among the stars now.

This is it. I take a shaky breath in and let it out as the warmth of the relic pulses between my hands. I clasp it tightly, remembering my father's last request.

I will keep the light.

Darwith bows low. My free hand grabs a large tuff of his mane and I pull myself onto his bare back, holding the relic to my side. I give him a squeeze, and we gallop over to Cashel, Thayer, and Yulla.

"Let's go! Come on, Cashel!" I yell out as we get closer.

Over my shoulder, Sutagus storms out from the gate opening—no arrow, no wound. Beside him, unmistakable golden eyes focus in on me—*Zarshona.* She must have used a relic of light on Sutagus. Or perhaps the one *I* just opened to try to save my father with healed the prince, yet again.

Darwith lifts us into the air, Thayer following on Yulla, and Cashel right behind them. Wolkenna and Xander take off after us. Gattacan retreats toward Elro as he continues to fight off a never-ending supply of Watchers—thank the stars they're only armed with swords.

Gattacan swings himself onto Elro, and they ascend into the air moments later, flying at a steep incline, straight at us.

We slow to a hover when we're high enough above the arena. Down below, Sutagus pulls out the small black relic of darkness from his jacket. He slides the top open, and a thick black line streams out like a snake, up toward Gattacan, as if he's willing it right at him—attacking him with its venom.

My eyes widen as Gattacan lifts another relic of darkness from his saddlebag. He opens the top and a similar stream of darkness slithers back down to Sutagus.

The two lines of darkness clash in the sky until they're one ensnared line of soot, pushing back and forth against one another like two entangled serpents. The line swells, bulging out as if the darkness might burst and spread all around them, threatening to consume us all.

"Go!" I yell out to Thayer, Wolkenna, and Xander. I squeeze Darwith, and he bolts back into flight. We fly away from the darkness that the two princes—now *kings*—are releasing on one another.

Kings of darkness.

Another snaky black line shoots high into the sky behind us. I glance down, far below—Zarshona holds a relic of darkness. Two relics of darkness against one. She wills the darkness straight at me and the others as Gattacan hovers below us, directing his darkness straight at Sutagus's.

"Higher!" I yell out to the others as Darwith ascends, the darkness moving toward us like a raging flood. The relic of light warms, beckoning me to open it—to fight back. But I don't know how to control it, how to weaponize it. Any attempt would likely be a waste of its power.

My father said to *keep* the light. So that's exactly what I'll do.

There's a loud boom—like a clap of thunder. I glance below as the darkness canopies out beneath us, a mushroom cap, slowly swirling, just like the darkness did over Cintrenia.

The rest of us slow our ascent, hovering in place above the cloud. Everyone tries to catch their breath in the thin air. My body shivers, and I pull the relic of light closer, absorbing some of its warmth.

Gattacan is still down there…

My fingers tremble over the top edge of the relic, ready to open it if I must.

And then, out of the dark cloud, Elro's white body emerges—Gattacan on his back, his face like a turbulent storm.

"To Nammden!" Gattacan yells as he circles once around all of us before flying straight toward the outskirts of the city.

I give Darwith a squeeze as we follow Gattacan and the others away from Tarmensil. Over my shoulder, a bright light erupts, piercing through the dark cloud over the palace. The darkness slowly dissolves, fading back into a blue sky.

"We don't have much time!" Gattacan shouts back to us.

The relic pulses against my side, though it's still sealed shut. They used their light—Zarshona did.

I'm *not* the only Light Keeper left. But I'm the only one here who doesn't know how to control the light. And I'm still disposable—even more so now that I'm their confirmed *enemy*.

 FIFTY

We all fly in silence, unable to process the events that just occurred. The pain in my chest is unbearable; it's as if someone is squeezing the life out of me. My father is gone. Gone for real—gone forever. My hand finds my heart, trying to detect if it's still beating.

Thump thump, thump thump.

Every pulse sends a new wave of sadness through me—a tsunami of grief.

I can't go on without him. I'll never be the same.

Cintrenia passes beneath us as I follow the others back toward Nammden. Little shapes form our farm—what was *once* our farm, anyway. I doubt I'll ever be able to return there, and certainly not today. Sutagus will follow us with the Cavalry, with Zarshona—ready to take the light, ready to take my life.

I have no home now.

The cold air bites at my skin—an icy predator. Autumn is shifting to winter. I hold the relic closer, absorbing its warmth, but I feel as if someone is still trying to steal it away from me, trying to destroy any light that's left in my heart.

I imagine my father's blue eyes as they tilted to the sky one last time. *Keep the light...*

And I *will* keep it—I must. I have to hide the relic. Not here. Not in Cintrenia. Not in Nammden. Anywhere I go in Eirelannia, they *will* find me. Anywhere I hide the relic, another Light Keeper could sense it and find it—the same way I found the light on the coast of Nammden.

Zarshona could find it.

My father's words echo in my mind: *Across the sea...Fly from Nammden...north of the rising sun.*

He was right—there's nothing left for me here now. No one left for me to save. My brother and mother seem to be just fine where they are. I'm the one who needs to leave.

The Gray Forest takes over after we fly northeast, away from Cintrenia, and over the Green Hills. The dark trees stand ragged—grasping for any fragments of light in the sky—skeletons hiding even more lost souls in the darkness below. I imagine where I found the relic of light, hidden behind the hedges of thorns. They said it was the last, but it wasn't. My mind races to the coast, and the relic of light I found there. Maybe there are more relics, across the sea—more relics of light. If I could find them...if I could bring back more light...I could *fight* the darkness.

I could defeat Sutagus. And maybe, I could return home.

The morning sun disappears behind a shroud of gloominess, leaving the Gray Forest cloaked in mystery. The final trees pass beneath us, the ground shifting to marsh. The water from the distant ocean pushes its way even closer to the forest. The ocean—the Dark Sea.

My future.

As we enter Nammden, the water surrounding the steel giants appears to have risen—higher than ever before. The city is silent as we weave through the maze of buildings, and there's not a Scaler in sight. It feels...abandoned. Broken.

Our steeds' hooves echo as we land in the Grays' building. I halt Darwith by everyone else, but no one says a word.

Thayer wraps his arms around me as soon as I dismount. I hold the relic of light out to the side, being careful not to burn him with it.

He holds me for a long moment in silence. As we pull apart, I meet his gaze. His eyes are full of sorrow. He takes my free hand and squeezes it. I know what he means to say, but he doesn't need to say it at all.

My father is gone, and no amount of tears will bring him back.

Wolkenna approaches me, her face pallid and her eyes tired. We hug, both of us grieving the loss of our fathers. Both of us falling apart.

"Where is everyone?" I ask, realizing there's nothing but the wind howling in from outside the opening.

"I'm not sure," Wolkenna says distractedly, peering at Gattacan as he dismounts Elro. She turns to me, and her bottom lip quivers. "My brother—something's wrong. The darkness…"

Gattacan approaches from behind her. I nod at her to let her know he's coming.

"Gattacan," Wolkenna says, turning to face her brother. His eyes appear almost black, as if some of the darkness he released from the relic still remains inside of him. He glances at me, and then at Thayer, standing by my side. The crease in his brow deepens, and he directs his attention back to Wolkenna.

"We must prepare for war," Gattacan announces, his voice low and hoarse. "They'll be coming for *that*." He nods at the relic in my hand, a look of disgust sweeping across his face.

Wolkenna shakes her head, placing her hand on his arm. "No, brother, we should leave Nammden. We can't fight all of them. Not now."

He shrugs off his sister's touch. "I'm going to kill Sutagus," he seethes through gritted teeth. "He *murdered* our father."

My jaw tightens. Both of our fathers are dead because of Sutagus. But revenge won't bring them back to life.

"Wolkenna is right," I tell him. "We should go."

"What do you know, *Light Keeper?*" Gattacan darts a bitter glare at me. "Look what the light has done—*nothing*. It didn't save my father, and it didn't save yours. And as we all saw, they have their own Light Keeper. What good are you?"

My nostrils flare in indignation. But it's true—I can't fix anything right now. All I can do is listen to what my father said. "We need to leave—"

"I'm not leaving here," Gattacan growls. "I'm the *king* of Laithlann. I will stand my ground. And I *will* kill Sutagus." He clenches his fists, looking daggers at all of us. "You should all go. I don't need any of you."

My stomach sinks. He's not the same Gattacan who rescued me from the Knarrno River. He's not the one who protected me before. He's a well of dark energy—of *hate.*

Thayer reaches for my hand. "Let's go."

I exhale. I want to say something to Gattacan, but no words come out. His body trembles as we walk past. Out of the corner of my eye, I see Wolkenna reach out to him once more, but Gattacan merely gives her an icy stare. With a sigh, she leaves him standing alone.

"I'm leaving Eirelannia." The words escape me involuntarily.

Everyone turns, watching me.

"Sutagus will come for this." I hold the relic. "I have to keep it safe. I have to find a place to hide it—across the sea."

"Then I'm coming with you," Thayer says from beside me.

"It's not safe," I protest. But when he looks into my eyes, unmoving, I know right then that he won't back down. He's coming with me— thank the stars. At least I won't have to figure out how to say goodbye to him, as well. Not again.

"I'm coming, too," Wolkenna says, glancing over my shoulder at her brother, and then back at me.

"Are you sure?" I ask her.

"I'm sure." She turns on her heels and starts off toward the corridor. "I'm going to find the others," she calls back, "and see if I can get my hands on a map."

"I am going back to Cintrenia," Xander announces. "I have to find my father and fight the darkness."

"I understand," I say. I can only hope he stays safe and that we will meet again soon.

Gattacan walks past us, and his eyes land on me for a moment. They're darker than ever. A sadness passes through me as I turn away from him, unable to hold his gaze. It hurts too much. I hurry back over to our steeds, busying myself with attaching another bag to Cashel's saddle.

"What about your parents?" I ask Thayer as he loads his own saddlebag with supplies.

"They'll be safer if I don't return," he says. "At least until this is all over. Plus, they've probably gone south by now."

A few moments later, Wolkenna hurries back over to us, Moninne and Cloveman in tow.

"Your mother and grandmother?" I ask Wolkenna.

Her shoulders slump as she exhales. "They're staying…but they gave me this." She lifts a rolled piece of paper. "It's probably outdated, but at least we'll know where to find land."

"Good," I tell her, thankful for any direction beyond my father's words. "What about you, Cloveman?" I ask, checking him over with some concern. His hand rests over a bandage wrapped around his abdomen—his wound from the battle in the Gray Forest.

"I'm going with you—with Wolkenna," Cloveman says. "My mother wouldn't want me to return to Cintrenia after all this, and she's probably already heading to Sceilaran to be with family. Plus, I've been across the sea—you may need me."

Wolkenna nods. "I'll go get his steed ready," she says before taking off.

Moninne watches me carefully. Her eyes are full of grief. I don't have to say it—she knows my father is gone. She holds me at arm's length, then pulls me into a hug. No words are necessary. She loved my father.

My sight blurs, as tears cloud my vision. "Come with us?" I ask her.

"I should stay. This is my home, and they'll need a medic here, now more than ever." Her voice is fragile, like cracked glass. My heart sinks. I don't want to leave her. "It will be okay," she tells me, gently holding my face in her warm hands. "Come back to us when it's safe."

"I will," I tell her as the tears fall.

Wolkenna and Cloveman hurry out with Cloveman's steed. On the opposite side of the opening, Gattacan storms in with a group of Laithlanner soldiers following behind him.

"They've entered Nammden," Gattacan snarls at all of us. "If you're planning on leaving, you best go now."

I hug Moninne one last time.

"Until we meet again," Xander says, nodding at each of us as he mounts his steed. "Be safe, my friends."

"You too," I say to Xander. His lips pull into a hard line as he gives his steed a kick. And in a moment, he's gone.

The rest of us mount our steeds. Gattacan mounts Elro and moves him to the landing area, off to the side.

"Let's go," I say, looking over at Thayer, Wolkenna, and Cloveman. Darwith stomps in place beside us. I squeeze Cashel, and we speed toward the opening of the building.

Gattacan watches me from atop Elro. He doesn't flinch—he only glances at me, an intense sadness flashing across his ever-darkening eyes.

My gaze stays on Gattacan until we pass him. No goodbyes. Nothing at all. If I weren't falling to pieces over my father, I might go to him. I might tell him I will miss him—because I will. I already do.

Cashel's hooves leave the ground as his silver wings take us out into the clouded sky. Darwith soars next to us. I turn Cashel, banking to the left as the others follow. The ocean beckons to me from beyond the buildings, as if it's calling out, asking: *How far would you fly for freedom?*

I'll fly as far as I can—as far as I have to. I'll keep this relic of light safe until we can return.

I draw in a deep breath as I direct Cashel northeast, toward the Dark Sea. Salt water clings to my skin as I take in the cold air. My hand drifts toward my saddlebag, and the warmth of the relic pulses out, a reminder of the good that still exists. A reminder of the future that *can* exist.

As we pass the rocky shoreline, I glance back at Nammden once more—a dark city, full of pain and ready for revenge.

My fingers wind through Cashel's mane as I turn to face the wide-open sea. My father's words linger in the air, my mind wandering to the lands beyond the vast expanse. *There's so much more...*

Up here in the sky, I am free. There are no watchful eyes—no constraints. My choices are my own. And I've made my choice.

I am a Light Keeper.

And I will keep the light.

ACKNOWLEDGMENTS

Writing this story was a learning process. What came after the drafting phase was a labor of love and many lessons in determination and patience, all fueled by a desire to share the world I'd experienced in my dreams (and write about flying horses, of course). Perhaps the most challenging part of it all was learning how to finish a book with revisions, edits, and proofs. And if it weren't for the many people who contributed to my journey, this book wouldn't be what it is today. I am so thankful to all of you.

To the first editor I ever worked with, Erin Young, thanks for loving and believing in Aluma's story from the get-go. Your eagerness to work on this book was an essential spark in my publishing journey. Thanks for your early guidance, your creative advice, and your solutions and input—and thanks for encouraging me to illustrate my words.

To Micaela Alcaino: thanks for sharing your talent by designing my first cover. All of your cover design options were beautiful, and I'm so happy with the final result. I also can't express how giddy I was when

403

I first saw your illustration for my map. It really brought my original drawings to life and somehow made this book feel even more real.

To Lauren Smulski: your edits on this book helped bring it to the next level. Thank you for taking the time to answer my questions with such patience and cheer, for your willingness to help guide me, and for our brainstorming sessions.

To Kara Aisenbrey, proofreader extraordinaire. You have such an amazing eye. Thank you for the detailed proofread, and for all your help. I'm so thankful you were able to do the final read of ALITS before it goes out into the world.

To the Damonza team, for the wonderful formatting and layout work you did for A Light in the Sky.

To Tasha Gorel, for capturing my author photos with such positive energy.

A big shout-out to the writing community and everyone who offered their knowledge on how to write a story or explained their insights into publishing. To Christine of Better Novel Project, for sharing your excellent research with the world. To Ashley R. Carlson, for your advice about publishing and for your words of encouragement. And many thanks to Karin Biggs, Jennifer Acres, Briana Morgan, Anna Hill, and Jon Coffey, for your encouragement, support, and insight.

To everyone involved in the making of the ALITS book trailer—thank you! To the amazing cast who brought Aluma, Thayer, and Gattacan to life: Lily Lequerica, Daniel Ferrell, and Michael Banks. To Jen Baxter, for sharing her beautiful Friesian, Princess D, with us. To C. Ernyey, I. Ernyey, and P. Limon—thank you for allowing us to film in your wonderful stable and for your hospitality. To Sheila Lequerica and the Lequerica family, for sharing Mike and your beautiful property with us. To Tango and Jeremy, for coming out to assist. To Julin and Chris, for their hard work and collaboration. To Maria Hartley, for being a powerhouse and doing so many things to help. And to Brian Baker for being a sound wizard in the studio and making my voiceover shine. Thank you all!

To Natalia, for sharing your amazing talent by creating beautiful original character art pieces.

To Jessica Shepherd, for the stunningly detailed coloring page.

To everyone who subscribes to my newsletter—thank you for following along on my author journey and for your interest in A Light in the Sky.

To the beautiful country of Ireland and my experiences there. Thanks for inspiring me with your green hills, your beautiful shores, and for the Rock of Cashel (one of my favorite places in the whole world).

To all the many horses I've met and loved: thanks for showing me how special the bond between horse and human can be. And for letting me feel what it's like to "fly" for those brief few moments while jumping through the air.

To those who inspired me long before I started writing this book:

First, to Virginia, thank you for your many years of kindness, your listening ear, and your thoughtful advice. The impact you've had on my life is immeasurable. I will always be grateful to know you.

To the late Merlyn: thank you for letting my family and I ride your horses. Those experiences have stayed with me and inspired me, and I will always cherish them.

To my sixth-grade English teacher, Mrs. Nichols: thank you for helping me write and share my first stories, and for awarding me a creativity award for "writing books." Teachers like you change lives. Thank you for changing mine, by showing me I could be an author.

To the many friends who supported my author journey, thank you. To my childhood friend Alissa—thank you for riding horses with me when we were kids. Thanks for letting me ride Strawberry and for the memories of collecting fresh eggs from the chicken coop for breakfast. To Guenther Goerg, thanks for your excitement about this book and all your kind emails.

To my in-laws: thanks to Joan for your early feedback on some of my very first ideas and writings for this book. To Delilah Marvelle, for your publishing insight and your kindness—thank you. And to the Bucci family, for your interest in my author journey, for your encouragement, and for making me feel like part of your family.

To Beth and Ben: thanks for your continued encouragement during this journey to my debut. For being excited to hear about updates on A Light in the Sky and my author journey. For giving me feedback on my covers. For embracing me as a daughter. Your love and support has meant the world. I'm so thankful to have you both in my life.

And to my immediate family, for believing in me from the beginning:

To my late maternal grandmother, Margaret. I may not have been able to read your work, but it always meant something to me to know that you were once a writer.

To my late paternal Granddad and my late Grandmother Stearns— you will always be a great source of inspiration. Thank you for loving me and making me feel like I belonged. I hope this book would've made you proud.

To my dad (Ken), thanks for brainstorming ideas for book trailers, for writing an ALITS song with me, and for your support. For inspiring me with your love of creativity and invention. And, most of all, for leading by example with your hard work ethic. I've always admired the success you've achieved while also pursuing your passion.

To my youngest sister, Ali, thanks for your love, support, and encouragement. Your bravery and strength never ceases to amaze me.

To my dad (Alan), thanks for sending me books on writing, for introducing me to some of my favorite reads, for building me a little barn for my toy horses as a kid, and for showing me what hard work looks like. And, of course, for letting me ride Fred in wide-open spaces.

To my mom, thank you for showing me the joy of horses at such an early age, and for letting me ride them (and train them) way back then, too. I'd need a whole other page to list the many horses you've introduced me to—the ones that still run across my memory, like horses galloping freely across an open field—but thanks for all of them. And thanks for the many books that stocked my shelves as a child, and for the books you still send. Your creativity and love of the written word inspire me. And my deepest thanks for helping me write (by hand) and design my first two books in grade school. You embraced my earliest endeavors as a writer and helped me tell my earliest stories. I love you.

To my sister, Jess, the second person to read a draft of this book and my go-to for all input. Thank you for all of your support and encouragement throughout this process. You've been there for me from the first draft (well before that, actually), and your early read was a game-changer. Thanks for the brainstorming session, and thanks for giving me your opinion at the drop of a hat—on everything. For your great creative eye. For your love of books. And for letting me read to you when you were a baby. And lastly, thank you for helping me find the perfect title for this book. <3 <3 (green)

To Toby and Tank, for years of cat cuddles and love—you were the best writing companions I could ever ask for. You both brought me many smiles and so much joy while I wrote and polished this book. Thank you for the frequent, welcomed distractions and calming moments you shared with me. Sadly, before I was able to publish A Light in the Sky, my sweet Toby passed away at the age of 19. His memory will live on, and every page of this book is a reminder of what he helped me create. I love you and I miss you, sweet Toby. You're forever in our hearts, until we meet again.

And most of all, to Ben: you are the light in my sky. My husband, my best friend, my love. Thank you for always having my back and for pushing me toward my dreams. This book wouldn't be here today if it weren't for you. Your love and support sets me free, and you inspire me in so many ways. Thank you for the hours you spent reading and critiquing my first drafts, for your clever ideas and solutions, and for the long and helpful conversations on our walks together. Thanks for encouraging me to publish independently. For your love of freedom and your deep thoughts. Thank you for building me an amazing wing for my book trailer, and for all you did to make that particular dream of mine come true—I couldn't have done it without you. You're always there to help me make my dreams a reality, and I am forever grateful to you for loving me and believing in me every step of the way. I love you, Bear.

Finally, thank you, dear reader, for taking the time to read this story. For going on this journey of my imagination. I may not know you personally, but thank you so much for choosing to spend a part of your life reading my book. It means the world to me and makes all the difference. Thank you—and, as always, keep shining.

SHINA REYNOLDS grew up in Nebraska, riding horses through wide-open fields. She wrote her first two books in her sixth-grade English class, the second of which went on to win an award at the Nebraska Young Author's Conference. She earned a Bachelor of Arts degree, graduating with honors in art history and with a minor in anthropology. Before writing her debut novel, *A Light in the Sky*, she worked in film, music, and modeling. Shina currently resides in Texas, where she spends the majority of the year trying to stay cool and imagining she lives in Ireland. When she's not writing, she can be found painting abstractly, exploring the outdoors with her husband, and entertaining her mostly cuddly cat.

She invites readers to receive updates, giveaways, and more by subscribing to her newsletter at:

ShinaReynolds.com/subscribe

Visit her on the web at:
ShinaReynolds.com
or follow her on Twitter and Instagram
(@ShinaReynolds)
and on Facebook at:
Facebook.com/AuthorShinaReynolds

CPSIA information can be obtained
at www.ICGtesting.com
Printed in the USA
LVHW090000221021
701122LV00004B/86